GRUMPILY *Ever After*

OTHER TITLES BY TEAGAN HUNTER

SEATTLE SERPENTS SERIES

Contemporary Sports Romantic Comedies

Body Check

Face Off

Delayed Penalty

Empty Net

Top Shelf

CAROLINA COMETS SERIES

Contemporary Sports Romantic Comedies

Puck Shy

Blind Pass

One-Timer

Sin Bin

Scoring Chance

Glove Save

"Game Changer"

Neutral Zone

TEXTING SERIES

Contemporary New Adult Romantic Comedies

Let's Get Textual

I Wanna Text You Up

Can't Text This

Text Me Baby One More Time

Textin' Up My Heart (novella)

SLICE SERIES

Contemporary Romantic Comedies

A Pizza My Heart

I Knead You Tonight

Doughn't Let Me Go

A Slice of Love (novella)

Cheesy on the Eyes

ROOMMATE ROMPS SERIES

Contemporary Romantic Comedies

Loathe Thy Neighbor

Love Thy Neighbor

Crave Thy Neighbor

Tempt Thy Neighbor

STARS SERIES

Contemporary Upper YA Emotional Romances

We Are the Stars

If You Say So

STAND-ALONES

Contemporary Romantic Comedies

The DM Diaries

Best Friends for Never

GRUMPILY *Ever After*

TEAGAN HUNTER

This is a work of fiction. Names, characters, organizations, places, events, and incidents are either products of the author's imagination or are used fictitiously. Otherwise, any resemblance to actual persons, living or dead, is purely coincidental.

Published by Montlake, Seattle

www.apub.com

EU product safety contact:
Amazon Media EU S. à r.l.
38, avenue John F. Kennedy, L-1855 Luxembourg
amazonpublishing-gpsr@amazon.com

ISBN-13: 9781662534058 (paperback)
ISBN-13: 9781662534041 (digital)

Cover design by Letitia Hasser
Cover image: © Wander Aguiar Photography; © Aaron Eakin / Getty

Printed in the United States of America

For anyone who has ever felt cursed with bad luck.
You're not cursed. Just a little unlucky.
Don't give up hope, and kick that "curse" right in the ass.

CHAPTER ONE

Noah

"No."

"Please?"

"Absolutely not."

"But—"

I hold up my hand, interrupting my younger sister's begging before it actually works. I've told her yes countless times in her twenty-six years on this earth, but I'm putting my foot down this time. For the sake of my sanity, I have to. "No, Izzy. My decision is final."

She narrows her eyes and crosses her arms over her chest. "But I don't understand *why* it's final."

"Because last I checked, Stick Taps is a cidery, not a wedding venue."

"It can be both!" She tosses her hands into the air. "Especially for *my* wedding. I'm your little sister, Noah. Don't you want to see me married somewhere beautiful, like all this gorgeous land you have, and not at the community center like literally everyone else in this town?"

"Not literally. The Middletons were married down by the pier last month, and it was a fine ceremony. Why not get married there?"

She turns her nose up. "Because it'll look like I copied them."

She can't be serious. There are only so many places to get married in a town of roughly twelve thousand people. It's not like whatever place she chooses will be wholly unique.

"Big whoop. There aren't that many venues in Port Harbor. Bound to be some repeats."

"Exactly! That's my point. But here you are, sitting on a gold mine . . ." I level her with a look, and she holds her hands up innocently. "I'm just saying. You could make a killing by renting this space. Why not use my wedding as an advertisement?"

"Which is it, Iz? Do you want to be unique by having your wedding here, or do you want everyone to copy you?"

"Whichever gets you to say yes." She blinks up at me with those damn brown eyes—the same ones my father and I have—that I've never been able to say no to and a grin that nearly has me saying yes.

Somehow I resist, shaking my head. "No. It's not happening."

She groans, tossing her head back dramatically as I reach for a rag and start wiping down the bar that isn't even remotely dirty.

While Stick Taps is usually packed, we're having a lull today, and I suspect it has to do with the 5k happening near the harbor. Izzy has been my only customer in hours, so I've cleaned this bar top at least fifty times since then.

Still, it keeps me occupied while my sister continues her attempt to get me to rent out my cidery to her.

If I'm being honest, I can see her point. There's a lot of space with the five acres of land, and being in Washington State, we have no shortage of beautiful scenery, especially not with the mountains in the backdrop.

The biggest issue would be *where*. Does she want a tent wedding? Or something in the open air? Would I have to construct something for her to get married under? Does she want the reception here too?

My mind drifts to the big barn we have sitting on the property. We haven't done anything with it since we bought the land except use it for extra storage and to house all our cardboard boxes. There's a giant tractor sitting in the middle that doesn't run, and the roof has more holes than it does good wood. I keep saying I'll refurbish it, but I haven't had the time. I've been too busy building the cidery to worry about the aesthetics of the farm.

This could finally be my chance, though. I could— *No.*

I shake away that thought, not wanting to go down that road.

A good excuse to finally do something with the barn aside, I don't want Stick Taps to be a wedding venue. I bought the farm to run a cidery, not host weddings. Besides, it would be a bit hypocritical of me to do so. After my marriage ended in a heated divorce, I don't exactly advocate for tying yourself to one person for a lifetime anymore.

It's not that I don't believe in love—I'm not entirely coldhearted—but legally binding yourself to someone? Been there, done that, got the receipts from lawyer fees to prove what a massive mistake it is.

"You don't understand, Noah," Izzy says, reaching over the bar and grabbing a bowl of mixed nuts. She sets them in front of her, then picks through them for the cashews I know she loves.

I want to yell at her for it, but it's clear she's having a rough day. Instead, I move to our small pantry, grab a can of fresh ones, pour them into a bowl, and swap that for the nut mixture she plundered.

"Thank you." She digs into them instantly.

"What don't I understand?"

"Huh?" she asks, still focusing on her snack.

"You said, 'You don't understand, Noah,' so I want to know what I don't understand."

"Oh." Her shoulders sag in defeat. "I just . . . I wanted to get married somewhere I love, and I love this place. It feels like home to me. I didn't want my wedding to be impersonal, you know?"

Well fuck if that doesn't hit me right in the chest.

When I married Chelsea, it was as impersonal as you could get. I was barely involved in the planning, though it wasn't for my lack of trying. Every suggestion I gave her was squashed in an instant. So I stopped trying.

Izzy isn't the same as me, though. She won't give up so easily, which is why she's still sitting here begging me to use the farm.

"Besides, the community center was already booked for a wedding that day."

Ah, and there it is—the real reason.

"You're telling me this town has two weddings on the same day? How will the citizens decide which one to invade?" I say sarcastically.

She tosses a cashew at me, immediately replacing it with another and popping it into her mouth. "We're getting married in *ten weeks* and don't have a venue. What the hell else are we going to do?"

"I have a very simple solution." I pick up the discarded cashew and toss it into the trash, then grab a rag and an already-clean glass, settling back against the counter. I polish it because I need something to do with my hands. "Change your wedding date. You're trying to cram planning a whole wedding into ten weeks for no reason."

"It's not for no reason. I want to get married on my anniversary and don't want to wait a whole year. I've already waited long enough, and it's more romantic to get married on your anniversary."

"Romance, schmomance."

She groans. "Ugh. Don't start with your anti-love stuff."

"I'm not anti-love. I'm anti-marriage. It always ends in disaster."

"Just because your marriage to Chelsea didn't work out doesn't mean all marriages won't. Our parents are still married."

Shit. She has me there.

I run the towel around the inside of the glass again. "They're the exception."

"Craig and I could be the exception too."

Maybe she's right. Perhaps they could be the exception. But I wasn't, and I don't want that same heartache for her.

"I'm just saying you can continue to date. You're already living together. It's not like being married will change things all that much. It will—"

She holds her hand up, stopping me. "Save it. I've heard your 'marriage is a terrible idea' speech enough times since your divorce. Just let me sulk."

That's precisely what I do. I let her sit there and eat my cashews while she goes on and on about all the things she still has to do but can't because they don't have a venue, because—shocking to no one—everywhere is booked already. Of course it is. She's rushing the wedding. She could have everything she wanted if she'd just give it time.

Her troubles make me feel slightly guilty for saying no, which I'm sure is her goal.

For as long as I can remember, Izzy has had me wrapped around her finger. We might have a twelve-year age difference, but it's never felt that way.

I'm sure part of that might have been because I was busy as hell trying to carve my way into the NHL, and I didn't have time to be annoyed by her, but still. I remember when she was just a little bundle of pink and how I'd hold her in my arms like she was the most fragile thing in the world. Now she's getting married. It's wild how fast time moves.

"You could rebuild the barn like you've been talking about *and* a new chicken coop to keep Tootsie from getting out. This could be your reason," she says, voicing my thoughts from earlier.

I hadn't even considered finally building a new coop for our chickens, but she's right. Our resident escape artist, Tootsie, knows exactly how to break out of our current enclosure, no matter how many times I rig it so she doesn't.

Still, I don't want this place overrun with overly opinionated in-laws, bridezillas, and whatever else comes with planning a wedding. It's too much in an already jam-packed calendar. We already host events—like weekly trivia and bingo—plus musical guests on weekends, not to mention the production schedule we have to keep up with.

Juggling weddings on top of that is too tall an order.

Besides, what if we suck at it? Isn't a wedding supposed to be the "happiest day of your life"? What if we don't live up to that? What if we can't deliver? What if *I* can't deliver?

There's too much damn pressure that comes with it, and I don't know if I'm the right person to make that happen.

But I don't voice that fear. Instead, I sweep my hand out toward the empty taproom. "Kind of running a business here, Iz."

"Which is why you have Ezra to help you."

"What am I helping with?"

The man in question appears at the end of the hallway leading to the back office. He's got his laptop tucked under one arm and a stack of papers in his hand. He grimaces as he takes a seat at the bar, and I know the height of the stool makes him uncomfortable. But he ignores it, pretending it doesn't hurt as he settles into a spot, situating his things.

I ignore it, too, knowing he hates it when anyone says something about his limp, a result of a hockey play gone wrong. It's the same play that knocked him out of the NHL after just eight years.

He got half the hockey career I did, and I'd be lying if I said I don't feel guilt over that sometimes. Not that his exit was my fault, but still. Hockey is like that. You might be opponents on the ice, but off it, you're family. Your heart always hurts for your family.

"Running Stick Taps while Noah rebuilds the barn and a new chicken coop so that Toots can't escape anymore."

Ezra grunts. "Nothing's going to hold that old bird down. New coop or not, she'll find a way to escape. She always does."

I point to my business partner. "For the record, I agree with him."

"Why are you rebuilding the barn and building a new coop? I mean, not that I'm complaining. That barn has been on your to-do list forever, and we both know we need a new way to contain Toots."

"For my wedding," Izzy proudly announces.

Ezra's brows lift, his dark-green eyes shooting my way. "She's getting married here?"

"No." I glare at Izzy, who looks unbothered as she pops another cashew into her mouth. "She's not. She asked, but I told her no."

"You did?"

Ezra sounds surprised by this, which is fair given my history of always telling Izzy yes, no matter how ludicrous her requests are. Like when I was roped into being her duet partner for the town's talent show at the last minute because her fiancé had food poisoning. Singing Sonny and Cher's "I Got You Babe" with your sister was just as awkward as one can imagine, but the town took such pity on us that we got first.

My trophy sits on top of the fireplace on the other side of the cidery.

"I did, and I am sticking to that. We aren't a wedding venue."

Ezra nods a few times, then says, "We could be."

Now it's *my* turn to look surprised. "What?"

He shrugs. "I mean, it would make sense, yeah? We certainly have the space. The east pasture isn't being used, but it would make a great photo op with the mountains and shit. Plus, you're handy." He taps the bar I custom made when we couldn't find what we were looking for as we built the taproom. "Fixing up the old barn should be a breeze. We could rent it out and make a killing. A new coop for Toots is an easy fix, too, and a win-win for us. We could turn this place into a one-stop destination—ceremony, reception, and booze. Rake in the cash so we can use it for future ventures. It's a solid business decision."

Future ventures.

I know exactly what he means by that. He's talking about our late-night planning sessions on opening an ice rink. Hockey gave us both a life we could have never imagined. We want to give back to it, even if it's just in our small Pacific Northwest town.

While that extra money would be nice, I still stare at him, mouth agape.

"You can't be serious." I toss the rag into the bin and set the now *extra*-clean glass back where it goes. I fold my arms over my chest and watch my partner closely.

But Ezra doesn't crack a smile—not that he does often anyway—or tell me he's kidding.

He means it.

I raise my brows. "How can *you*, of all people, want to open this place up as the ultimate *wedding* destination?"

There's no hiding the disgust in my voice, but if anyone shares my disdain for relationships, it's him. Ezra is just as anti-marriage as I am. It's why we work so well together and gravitated toward one another when we did.

I was fresh off a divorce and leaving the game I knew and loved my entire life, and he was fresh out of his long-term relationship with physical therapy. We were a match made in grumpy heaven.

"Money."

He says it so simply, and, fuck, I guess it *is* that simple.

I think back to the plans I made four years ago when I decided to start my own business. I was still playing hockey, but I knew my time in the league was winding down. As much as I loved playing, I was aging out and slowing down in every aspect of my game. It was just a matter of time before the offers stopped coming in. I wanted to be ready once they did. I didn't want to be that retired player who didn't have a clue how to navigate the world beyond hockey or spends his time at the rink shooting the shit and reminiscing on the good old days. I wanted to do *something.*

So I dreamed up Stick Taps.

One of my favorite things about being on the road so often was trying new beer and cider from all over North America. While most guys were chilling in fancy restaurants or hitting clubs, I was off in my own little world, hanging at local breweries and cideries and trying everything I could get my hands on. I found comfort in them. Found a peace and sense of belonging that I wasn't getting with hockey anymore, not with the younger crowd coming in and the game getting away from me.

Lucky for me, Ezra wanted the same thing and immediately jumped in on investing and taking over the numbers side of it all, having recently completed a degree in business management.

A dinner and a handshake later, Stick Taps was officially born.

That was three years ago, and while we're doing well and turning a damn good profit, I still want more.

I guess Ezra does too.

"See?" Izzy says. "This was a good idea! *And* you can kick off your new venture by hosting my wedding and show this town what they'd be getting by booking their next event here. Just say yes, big brother."

She bats her lashes at me again, and dammit, if that, paired with Ezra being on board, doesn't crack my walls.

The odds are stacked against me now, and I fear I don't have a choice.

I'm still not sure we're the right match for it, and I have no fucking clue if we can pull this off, but what else do we have to lose?

"Fuck," I mutter, scrubbing a hand over my face. "Fine. Fine. You can have the wedding here."

"Oh my gosh! I can't wait. We have so many ideas. We—"

"*But,*" I cut off my sister's celebration, "the *only* thing I'm doing is helping restore the old barn. That's it. I'm not moving anything inside the cidery, and we're not doing anything else to the land. The barn, and that's it."

"And the coop for Tootsie," Ezra says, his fingers flying over his keyboard, probably already calculating potential profits and whatever other shit he's always doing behind the scenes. Those are our roles, though—he handles the numbers and business side of things, like making sure we're on schedule with our products and that apple shipments are never behind. I handle the farm, taproom, and all the activities we host. "If we're going to have big crowds here, we can't have her running all over the place."

"And Toots. I'll figure out something for her."

"Are you sure?" Izzy asks, chewing on her bottom lip, picking up on my apprehension. "I don't want to force you to do something you don't want to, Noah."

Bullshit. We both know she would.

And fuck no, I'm not sure. I *still* don't want to do this. But if it makes Izzy happy . . .

"I'm sure," I tell her.

"Excellent." She gives me a saccharine smile, reaching for her phone with a joyful shoulder shake.

"What are you doing?"

"Calling Odette."

I try not to react to the name that sends a shiver down my spine. I try not to let it show that Odette is the last person I want my sister to call.

"How lucky am I that my best friend is a wedding planner?" Izzy says, bringing the phone to her ear.

Yeah, she's lucky, all right.

Me? Not so much.

Odette Chambers is the last person I want to see. Not because I don't like her, but maybe because I notice her a bit *too* much, and I really fucking shouldn't.

She and Izzy have been inseparable since high school, and I was already well into my hockey career then, so I've only truly gotten to know her since I moved back here. Sometimes I wish I hadn't at all.

She's twelve years younger than me and completely off-limits, but it's hard as fuck to ignore how gorgeous she is with her soft-looking midnight waves and curves that go on for days, and the way she pushes all my buttons.

I bet she's behind this. I'm willing to toss down a hundred bucks on them scheming this together, trying to get me to turn this place into a wedding venue. It has Odette written all over it, and not just because she's a wedding planner. She came to me last year asking me to host a wedding here, and I told her no.

She didn't ask again after telling me off—which is precisely what I expected from her since she's been full of sass for as long as I've known her.

But now that Izzy's getting married . . . I'm certain this is the opportunity she was waiting for, and now she's ready to pounce. And I played right into her hands.

"She's going to be so happy. There's so much to work with here."

I drop my head back and groan, wondering just what it is I've gotten myself into.

CHAPTER TWO

Odette

"He said yes!"

"Really?"

"Yes!" My best friend screeches into my ear so loudly that I have to pull my phone away for a moment. When I put it back, she's jabbering on. "Ezra's on board too. They said we could use the farm and cidery for the wedding."

I was hoping we'd get the farm, but I didn't think she'd be able to swing the cidery too. "Even inside the taproom?"

Please say yes. Please say yes.

It would be perfect to use for a cocktail hour after the ceremony. The booze is already there, so why not?

"Even inside." *Yes!* "Though we aren't allowed to change anything in here."

That news ruins my excitement just a little, but I catch a certain word that's important. "Here? Are you there now?"

"I am. Noah's glaring at me."

Of course her brother is being a big grump. He usually is. I have no idea why he and Ezra, his business partner who is even grumpier than he is, opened a cidery where customer service is pretty essential.

It makes no sense to me, but whatever. That's their business. Mine is wedding planning.

Which is why I know that changing the interior is necessary if we're going to use it for a cocktail hour.

I picture the layout of Stick Taps in my mind. As cozy as it is for its current purpose, it's not ideal for such a large gathering. We'd need to remove the couches and chairs and rearrange the tables at the very least. Don't even get me started on taking down the hockey memorabilia from the walls. Nobody wants that in their wedding photos. Plus, there are the neon signs and lighting behind the bar.

All simple fixes . . . if we can get Noah on board.

"Tell him he's being ridiculous."

"Odette thinks you're being ridiculous," she says to him, and I have no doubt his glare just deepened. "I don't think he liked that too much."

I laugh. "Will you be hanging out there for a while? I can be there in ten minutes." I push off my couch, the papers stacked on my lap falling to the floor. "Make that fifteen."

"Yep. Craig has meetings all day, and I had no plans other than to bother Noah, so I'll be here."

"Go home, Izzy," her cranky older brother tells her.

"Stop being mean, or I'm telling Mom."

"Not if I tell her first."

I roll my eyes at their antics. Izzy is twenty-six like me, and Noah is pushing forty, yet they act like children. I'm sure if I had a sibling, we would be relentlessly teasing one another and threatening to tell our parents about it like they do. But here I am still living vicariously through them as I have since I was a teen.

"See you in a few," I say to Izzy, though I'm not sure she hears me as she and Noah bicker back and forth.

As much as I love having a front-row seat to a good argument between them, I have a wedding to plan and not a lot of time to do so, thanks to Izzy's brilliant idea to get married in ten weeks. It doesn't help that my contacts list keeps shrinking by the day since the last fiasco I was part of.

It's not my fault the tent caught fire during the Jefferson ceremony and caused half the guests to flee in panic. That was all the catering company and those damn butane burners they insisted on using. I don't care what they claim otherwise.

Chambers Charming Ceremonies Wedding Planning is on its last leg. I am officially now known as the worst wedding planner in the tri-county area, and while I always wanted to make a name for myself, I didn't mean *that* kind of name.

It's crap that I got this label, especially since so much of it was out of my control, but I guess that's the risk you take when you put your name on something.

And I guess the risk you take when your family is cursed.

I know it sounds ridiculous, and people whisper about us behind our backs because they think we're fools for believing in it, but it's hard not to when you look at the facts.

My nonna—my grandmother—has been married four times, and each marriage has brought heartache. Her first husband died in a freak accident eight months after they got married. Her second ran off with her best friend after three months. The third was the longest, lasting four years, until he informed her he was gay. Needless to say, that ended quickly. And her fourth was a whopping ten-day marriage to some guy who turned out to be a con man and disappeared with a quarter-million dollars.

Nonna is just the tip of the iceberg. My mother has been married twice, secondly to my father, who decided he didn't want to be a dad. He left us when I was six. Walked out one day when my mother was at work, and we never heard from him again.

Add to this the fact that neither my aunts nor I have had successful relationships, and it's safe to say that the curse is *very* real.

I wish it weren't affecting my business, too, but that's what I get for making my living from true happiness—the one thing the curse hates.

There was never anything else for me, though. I fell in love with weddings when I was just a kid, ever since I watched my aunt Collette walk down the aisle. She was stunning in a big, puffy white gown and *so* happy. Everyone was. My grandmother was in love, my mother was married to my dad, and even all my aunts had someone. It was such a rare feat in the Chambers timeline that I wanted nothing more than to bottle up all that happiness and keep it forever.

Of course, all that eventually went to hell, as it always does—Collette never could resist a pirate—but that feeling never disappeared. I vowed that one day, I would find it again. That I would be the one to create that magic for people . . . and maybe even myself one day.

Then I grew up. I watched every woman I love get hurt. *I* got hurt. And I realized that marriage just wasn't in the cards, thanks to the curse. So I've resigned myself to the fact that I won't ever have a wedding. I'll just plan them.

I shake away the thoughts and bend to retrieve the scattered papers, stacking them together neatly. They are primarily contracts for a catering company that I guess hasn't yet gotten wind of my terrible luck, plus notes for Izzy's ceremony.

My hand pauses over the oldest piece of paper in the stack, the one that's crinkled and worn out with about ten different colors all over it. It's the same piece of paper I've tucked into the back of every notebook I've ever had—the culmination of fifteen years of ideas for *my* wedding, the one I'll never have now, thanks to the curse.

I shove the paper full of silly dreams back into the stack and drop it onto my coffee table to look at later tonight, maybe with a glass of wine.

Going to my bedroom, I trade my comfy sleep pants for a gray pencil skirt and my old worn shirt that I got from a concert ages ago for a crisp blush button-down. I might be meeting friends, but this has become a business matter. I need to look the part.

After giving my coal-black hair a quick spritz of dry shampoo and fluffing it up as best I can, I swipe on some mascara and lipstick and slip into my favorite pair of heels, which makes me feel like one of those in-charge New Yorkers you see in the movies.

"Bye, Beans!" I yell to my one-year-old cat, who is likely hiding beneath the couch like she always is. "I'll be back later."

I grin when I hear a soft *meow* in response, then close the front door of my apartment and make my way to my car.

I steer my little BMW, creeping on its last leg, down Cascade Lane toward the edge of town, where Stick Taps sprawls out over farmland.

The waterfront sidewalks are crowded with people as I drive through town—no surprise since the weather is incredible today and there was an event downtown this afternoon. I wave at several people, knowing practically everyone in this town.

That's just how it is here, though.

Sitting along the Puget Sound, Port Harbor is one of those towns that feel like a secret. It's small, but not so tiny that you get bored too easily. There's always something happening, always something to do. We're far enough from Seattle that this feels like its own little pocket of the world. Add in the quirky name because, apparently, the founders couldn't decide if they wanted to be a port or a harbor, and you have the perfect little town.

Even though I threw a fit about moving here after my father bailed and my mother wanted to move closer to Nonna, I'm glad we did. I can't imagine living anywhere else now. Moving back here after completing my bachelor's in hospitality management was a no-brainer, just like starting my business, even if I am struggling now.

Dust kicks up around my tires as I chug along the dirt road toward the taproom. My eyes immediately go to the barn, which looks like it has seen better days. Where some may see a lost cause, I see good bones. I see a bride and groom sharing their dance, a father crying over his baby girl growing up, and two people starting their lives together.

With a bit of time and a whole lot of love, it will be the perfect venue for a reception. This farm is too beautiful not to use for purposes other than a cidery. It deserves more, and selfishly, I think that *more* is weddings.

I park my car next to Izzy's swanky SUV, which costs more a month than my rent thanks to Craig's fancy tech job, and trudge into the cidery that's come to feel like a second home since it opened.

I'm greeted by the gorgeous view of the Cascades, a wall of windows taking up one side of the building. The hills of the farmland look like they go on for miles, then pull your eyes up, up, up to the view of the snow-covered mountains.

As good as the cider is here, I must admit that the view is my favorite part of Stick Taps. It looks like something ripped right off a postcard.

"Odette!"

I grin at my friend sitting at the bar. She has her arms slung wide for a hug like she hasn't seen me in years, never mind that I saw her for dinner just last night, when we demolished two bottles of wine and ate chicken Alfredo with breadsticks until we felt like we were going to burst.

I step into her embrace, then pull my jacket off and drape it over the stubby chairback of the stools at the counter before sitting next to her.

"You look like you're feeling better," I say.

She lifts her cider to her lips, grinning at me over the edge of her glass. "That's because I have a wedding venue."

"That you do."

All right, so we *might* have schemed last night over dinner to get Noah on board for hosting weddings here. Granted, we bet a lot of it on luck, because we had no idea Ezra would agree so easily, but man, am I glad he did. *He* was our biggest hurdle, not Noah. He never tells Izzy no, so we sent her in alone. I had the idea to turn this place into a wedding destination last year, but Noah shot me down. I've been biding my time ever since, waiting for the perfect moment to pounce.

This is it.

Just like this is the perfect venue. It's unique. Everyone else in Port Harbor gets married at the community center, the pier, or in their backyard. All the photos on my website are evidence.

But this . . . this could be a game changer. Maybe people will stop seeing me as the wedding planner who messed up and will start taking me seriously. Not just another victim of the Chambers curse—and certainly not a failure just because a few couples got divorced shortly after I completed their weddings.

I push away those thoughts that keep tickling the back of my mind, focusing on the fact that we finally secured a venue and can officially plan the wedding.

The wedding that will go off without a hitch and lead to a marriage that will last a lifetime.

"I see you wasted no time to swoop in."

Noah pulls me out of my head, setting a tray of freshly cleaned glasses on the counter. He grabs one, puts it under the spout for Stick Taps' bestselling cider, Neutral Zone, fills it to the brim, and slides it my way without spilling a drop.

"Thanks," I mutter, taking a pull from the semisweet apple-and-strawberry mixed cider. I set it down. "How are you, Noah?"

His lips press into a thin line. "You're not changing anything in here, Odie, so don't go getting any ideas in that head of yours."

"I don't know what you could possibly mean." I give him my sweetest smile, even though I want to flip him off for using the nickname I hate. He's been calling me that since I was a teen, and try as I might to get him to stop, he won't. It reminds me of the dog from *Garfield*. While it's annoying on its own, there's nothing worse than your former crush likening you to a cartoon dog with too-big eyes.

His eyes narrow. "I mean it. You're not moving anything."

"Of course I'm not, Noah." I bat my lashes, my smile widening. I have every intention of ignoring him and moving whatever I want. I *have* to if I want this wedding to succeed, not just for Izzy but also for my business.

"I'm serious," he says firmly.

"Sure you are."

He grunts, then heads back toward the bar, still looking as surly as ever.

I try not to laugh, but it's impossible not to.

Noah should know by now that I'm going to do whatever I want, despite what he says. It's just who I am.

"He's so going to regret saying yes to this," Izzy comments.

"I think he already does."

"He does." I turn to find Ezra sliding onto a stool. I hadn't even noticed his mess of paperwork and a laptop on the counter when I first came in. "But don't make me regret it too."

There's no playfulness behind his words. Even when Noah's glaring at me, I still know he's never truly being mean or serious.

But with Ezra? I can't read the guy at all, and believe me, I've tried. If I thought Noah was grumpy, boy, was I wrong. His business partner has him beat by a mile.

"Roger that," I tell him seriously, suddenly feeling nervous that this will not turn out as I hope it will.

Izzy grabs my arm and shakes me hard. "I'm . . . *gah*! I'm *so* excited! What are your plans? Tell me everything!"

Her excitement is palpable, washing my nerves away as we slip off our stools and walk around the taproom.

"I think we'll start here," I say, pointing to the two cozy couches facing each other. There's a coffee table between them, the bottom shelf lined with various board and card games. "We'll need to clear this area to allow room for mingling during the cocktail hour while you and Craig get your photos done."

"You're not moving anything," Noah reminds me.

I ignore him, then gesture to the two high-backed pleather chairs surrounding the fireplace and the small table between them. "Those will need to go too."

"Did you hear me? You're not moving a damn thing."

I wave my hand over the hockey memorabilia lining the walls. "And personally, I think this will need to go, but if you want to keep it, we can work around it with some dark lighting."

"Odie!" Noah snaps his towel against the bar, then rounds it, practically stomping over to where we are.

"Yes, Noah?" I ask innocently as Izzy barely holds it together beside me.

"I said you aren't moving anything. We have this place just the way we like it. If you want something different, then go somewhere different. I—"

"We can make those changes," Ezra says, drawing our collective attention. His back is to the bar now, his bulky arms crossed over his chest as he watches us with emotionless eyes.

"What?!" Noah barks out.

Ezra shrugs. "I can see their points. Besides, if we make this part of our business model going forward, we want to show how accommodating we are, no?"

"Business model . . . going forward . . . *hmph.*" Noah grumbles between each word, annoyed that he's being ganged up on. He looks at his sister. "Is this what you want, Iz?"

She nods. "It's what I want. Well, minus removing the hockey stuff on the walls. I like that part."

"You do?" I ask. I wrinkle my nose as I take it in. If this were my wedding, I wouldn't want that stuff in the photos. But that's not something I'll ever need to worry about.

"Yes. Hockey was as much a part of my life growing up as it was his. Remember when my mother used to take us on a girls' trip to see him play in Anaheim? He would always throw the pucks over the glass for us? Make sure we were spoiled with good seats? Those are some of my favorite memories, and I want to combine those with the best day of my life."

I remember what she's talking about, but I remember them for far different reasons.

Back then I was captivated by Noah. I distinctly remember sixteen-year-old me pressing my nose against the glass and practically salivating over twenty-eight-year-old Noah. His broad shoulders and brown eyes that are far too pretty for their own good. The scruff lining his face was not yet thick enough to cover his dimples. I thought for sure he'd be the man I married one day.

But thanks to Izzy, I got over the fantasy of marrying a professional hockey player and stopped crushing on my best friend's older brother.

I still remember the look of absolute horror on her face when I told her I had a crush on Noah. We were eighteen and just about to graduate from high school, so we snuck wine coolers from her mother's stash down to the harbor to celebrate. I apparently got a little too tipsy, because I was suddenly spilling my secrets, including my biggest one about her brother.

She wrinkled her nose and said, "Ew. Please. Stop. Never say that to me again."

So I didn't. We never uttered another word on the subject, but I heard her loud and clear—Noah was off-limits, and it was never going to happen with him.

She was right. It never *is* going to happen.

Yes, it's true that he's gotten only better looking with age, but I don't have those feelings toward Noah anymore. I can't have feelings for *anyone* anymore. I refuse to subject myself to the same heartbreak my maternal family has experienced so many times over—the Chambers curse.

I had hoped that I wouldn't be affected by it, that maybe it would skip a generation, or that my nonna was wrong. But I was wrong, and my heartbreak from my college boyfriend proved it. I just wish I had known that wouldn't be the only heartbreak I'd endure from the curse, and that my future wasn't on the line because of it either.

Noah's hardened face softens, and he drops his arms from his chest, settling his hands on his hips. He exhales heavily. "All right. Fine. You can move the furniture. Decorate however you want. Just don't . . . don't touch the hockey stuff, all right?"

"Wouldn't dream of it, Bubs."

His perpetual scowl deepens at Izzy's old nickname for him. "And especially don't touch the puck, all right? That's the puck I got when I—"

"Scored a hat trick in game seven of the Stanley Cup Final against Detroit to secure the Cup—a five-to-four double-overtime win," Izzy and I finish simultaneously, having heard this story countless times over the years as if we hadn't been there to watch it.

We exchange a grin; then I shoo him away.

He throws his hands up as he backs toward the bar. "Fine. I'll be over here if you need me."

"I could use another Face Off," Izzy tells him once he turns around.

He lifts his hand, signaling he heard her request for the green apple cider, then disappears behind the counter.

We plop onto the sofa, and I pull my phone from my pocket, scrolling through the list of ideas I have jotted down as Izzy rattles off her own.

"We don't have much time to turn this place around," I say when she finally takes a breath. "I guess it's a good thing your best friend is a miracle worker, huh?"

"Is that what you're calling yourself now? What was the last review you got? *Set my wedding on fire. Do not recommend.* Or something like that."

Even though he's right, Noah's words don't sting any less. I'm not a miracle worker, and my failed weddings prove that.

But you can be. You can turn it around. You can make it right with Izzy's wedding.

I tell myself that over and over as Noah sets fresh ciders in front of me and Izzy—a fresh cider I didn't ask for. He can act like a big grump all he wants, but he did that out of the kindness of his heart.

He pulls my jacket from his shoulder and sets it beside me with my purse. "Keep your shit together. You never know what weirdos are lurking around."

"But this is Port Harbor."

"Exactly," he says with a disbelieving huff before returning to his post behind the counter.

He's only semi-joking. Or at least I assume so. Port Harbor does have its fair share of weirdos. We might be a small and close-knit community, but a few people here are just . . . odd. They don't *mingle* well, to put it nicely.

Like Mr. Garrison, who has been yelling at kids to get off his lawn for the last sixty years even though the place is littered with trash and old cars. Dale down at the hardware store who used to be a clown and still occasionally shows up to work with his old red nose and makes balloon animals for customers.

And, of course, our strangest of all . . . Peaches.

She's our resident hippie, and while she's a hoot half the time, the last thing you can do is trust your bag around her. Not because she'll rob you—she would never—but you can expect her to dump a cat in there. She has a hoard of them and always tries to get residents to adopt one. She slipped one in my bag six months ago while I was working on the Stewart wedding, which is how I got Beans.

Peaches is lucky I've been lonely lately and can use Beans's company. I can't imagine my life without her now, even if she drives me up the wall half the time with her need to "make biscuits" on me at two in the morning when I'm dead asleep.

"He's right. I stopped at the coffee shop this morning and heard that Peaches managed to palm off two more cats just this week," Izzy says.

"Are we ever going to question this woman about where she's getting these cats? Because they can't all come from her."

"Who knows?" She takes a sip of her cider. "Anyway, what's on that list of yours?"

"I'm so glad you asked."

I launch into my ideas to make the property wedding-ready, including rehabbing the barn and creating a space for the wedding party to get set. I also have a contingency plan in case it rains—this is the Pacific Northwest, after all—and my proposal for what to do with the animals.

"While I think Tootsie would make an incredible wedding guest," I say, "I don't think the other attendees would agree."

"I don't see why not. She's so cute. I mean, look at her."

Izzy nods toward the windows, and I turn to find the Houdini-like chicken out of her enclosure and strutting up to the taproom. I can guarantee this isn't the first time she's done so this week. She always finds ways to escape, even when she definitely shouldn't.

"Noah!" Izzy calls. "Toots is loose!"

"Again?!" he yells from the back room.

He comes barreling out, slinging a keg up onto the counter like it weighs nothing, then marches to the double doors that lead out back.

"That fucking chicken. I swear," he mutters as he pushes outside, waving his arms at her.

And while it's funny to watch him chase the little escape artist off, I'm too busy focusing on how his forearms looked after he threw that keg up on the counter. He must have rolled up the sleeves of his black-and-white-checkered flannel while in the back room, because they were certainly on display. My gosh, were they defined. Not just from all his years of playing hockey—*thank you, stick handling exercises*—but also from his labor around the farm and cidery.

I look at the coffee table between the couches, admiring the woodwork that Noah put so much time into. It's going to be a pity storing it away for the wedding.

"I don't know why he even bothers. She's just going to escape again." Izzy shakes her head with a smile. "All right. What's next on the list, wedding planner?"

And just like that, I'm sucked right back into the planning and most definitely *not* thinking about how hot Noah looks today.

I grab my phone, turning back to Izzy. "So here's what I was thinking . . ."

CHAPTER THREE

Noah

"I don't understand why you can't listen to me."

I stare down at the little lady before me.

"Or why we must go over this again and again. Why you can't be a good girl and follow directions."

I set my hands on my hips and shake my head as she says nothing.

"What? Nothing to say to that?"

Finally, Tootsie clucks.

"Because I'm the boss. That's why."

Cluck.

"No, you're not getting extra treats. Those are only for good chickens who follow directions."

Cluck.

"I don't care how cute you are, Tootsie. It's not happening."

Cluck.

"Stop back talking and get in the damn coop already."

I pick her up, tucking her under my arm.

She clucks again, but I ignore her, carrying her into the coop full of all the other well-behaved chickens that don't escape every time I turn my back. She's always strutting off somewhere she shouldn't be.

One of these days she's going to regret it, and it'll be all her fault and my guilt to carry.

"There," I say, setting her on her favorite spot in the back. "Now stay put, dammit. I do not want to chase you back in here *again* today. Got it?"

Cluck cluck.

I'm 99 percent sure my chicken just told me to fuck off.

I get it. She wants to be a free-range bird, but that's impossible with all the people we have coming and going here. The last thing I need is her getting sassy and pecking someone. That sounds like a whole lot of paperwork I don't want to deal with.

"I'll let you out later when we're closed, got it?"

Cluck.

I roll my eyes, then check on the other chickens—who are all snug in their enclosure—before locking it back up. I go through my routine of setting boards and bricks in front of the door and covering any little spot Tootsie could climb through. When I'm satisfied she won't get out again, I take the time to check in on the other animals on the property.

When I envisioned owning a cidery, it didn't include a farm, but when this place came up for sale in my hometown, no less, I knew it was perfect, even if it came with a bunch of animals.

Thank fuck the old guy who sold me the land is just a phone call away. Without him and the internet, I'd never be able to run this place otherwise. I don't know the first thing about farming. I never pictured myself running a place with a bunch of animals or selling eggs alongside cider, but now I can't imagine anything else. It's hard work, but I enjoy it.

I stop by the pens and make sure the goats have what they need, then head to the pond to check on the ducks.

"Hey, Larry," I say as she comes swimming over. I have no idea why they named her Larry, but she answers to it, so I guess that's all that matters. "Are you behaving out here?"

She nuzzles against my hand.

"I'll take that as a yes. I'll bring some lettuce out for you later, okay?"

She nudges me once more before swimming back to the flock of ducks across the water.

I watch her leave, then I take my time heading back to the taproom. While I love being there, I need a moment to myself before it becomes chaotic and fills with nothing but love, hearts, and whatever other romantic nonsense they can dream up. The same kind of nonsense I swore I'd never let myself get wrapped up in again after my divorce.

I can't believe I agreed to this. I can't believe *Ezra* agreed to this.

But I did, and he did, so now here we are.

I meander my way to the old barn that hasn't been properly used in I don't even know how long. Right now, it houses an old tractor that doesn't run, leftover lumber from when I built the taproom coffee table and bar top, and some beat-to-shit stalls that used to house the horses the old owner took with him.

I won't lie—I was most looking forward to the horses out of all the animals I got in the deal, but now I'm glad he took them. I can hardly keep up with what we have now, never mind adding more to the mix.

The door creaks when I pull it open and step into the barn. Dust kicks up around me, and I fan it away as I look around, taking mental notes on everything I will need to do to get this ready for Izzy's wedding.

First, there's the obvious, like getting this damn tractor out of the way so I can really get down to business, like fixing several holes in the roof. It wouldn't surprise me if I had to replace the whole thing. I need to dismantle the stalls to open up the space, reinforce it in several areas, and repaint what I can.

Never mind the general cleaning I need to do, like getting rid of the extra supplies, old boxes, and all the hay left over from the horses.

It's a lot, and I have no idea how I'm going to complete it *and* the chicken coop in just ten weeks, all while running Stick Taps.

"Fuck," I mutter, running a hand over my face. "Fuck, fuck, fuck."

"You might be a few years removed from the rink, but you certainly still sound like you're on the ice."

I turn to find Odette leaning against the door I left propped open. One hand on her hip, legs crossed, and looking entirely too damn good with the light backing her. The light curls around her curves in the most delicious of ways.

I try to ignore that as she shoves off the door, her heels clacking against the concrete as she struts farther into the old building.

"Sorry," I say.

She shrugs. "Please. I've heard way worse while attending your games."

I wince. Shit. That's probably true. Given how close my family always sat to the benches, I'm sure she did hear a lot of what we were chirping at one another—and it wasn't family friendly.

"Where's Izzy?" I ask.

"She went back home to her lover boy. She was missing him or something. I have no idea," Odette says, sounding a bit like me whenever relationships are mentioned, and I have a feeling it has to do with all the curse rumors. "You okay?"

"Yeah." I nod. "Yeah, just trying to get a game plan together. Figure out what I need to get done. How much I'm going to let Izzy down when I don't."

I'm used to disappointing people, though. That's what I did when I let my team down in my final NHL game, letting a puck slip by my stick and giving the other team a breakaway, which led to the game-winning goal. And that's definitely what I did with my ex. I could never find a way to make her happy.

"Are you kidding? She worships you. You could never let her down." She jabs her finger into her chest. "Me, on the other hand, you could easily disappoint. *Especially* if this wedding turns out to be a disaster like my last one."

"And the one before that."

She cuts me a glare. "Did you really have to go and bring that up?"

"Hey, I'm not the one who ordered flowers that the bride is allergic to."

"I didn't either! That was the florist!"

I tuck my lips together, saying nothing because she will argue with me no matter what I say. That's how Odette has always been.

Maybe she ordered the right flowers and was sent the wrong ones. Or perhaps she screwed up and doesn't want to admit it. Either way, it doesn't change the fact that the bride—who happened to be the mayor's daughter—had a horrible reaction. One that puffed up her face so much that she couldn't open her eyes.

It's probably why Odette's business is in such a rough spot. I overheard Izzy talking about how she had three different couples pull out of their contracts after the mayor's daughter's wedding. I'm sure it doesn't help that Odette's *next* event also went awry or that two couples she planned weddings for got divorced within six months.

I'd be willing to bet she'd blame it all on the curse her family suffers from, and a part of me gets it. I'm a hockey player, so I understand superstitions better than most. Maybe it is a curse. Or perhaps she's just letting it get inside her head. Either way, she's in trouble.

"Whatever you say," I tell her. "I just know this wedding is going to be a lot of work." I tap the beam next to me, and the old wood creaks beneath the gentle touch like it's about to give way at any moment. Guess I'd better add that to my list of shit to fix. "Starting with this barn."

"I can help."

I look over, brows raised. "Excuse me?"

"You heard me, Noah Stevens. I said I can help. Hand me a hammer or something. Some nails. A ratchet. Twenty bucks. Whatever. We'll get this place fixed up in no time."

I can't help it—I laugh.

And Odette doesn't like my reaction one bit, if the pinched expression she has on her face says anything.

"What?" she barks at me. "Quit laughing."

"I'm sorry." I cough, beating on my chest. I can't remember the last time I laughed that hard. "It's just . . . I'm trying to picture you in overalls wielding a hammer."

She notches her chin higher. "I'm extremely handy, thank you very much."

"Yes, you look it with your Jimmy Choos and fresh manicure over there."

"These are Manolo Blahniks, for your information." She looks down at her long nails coated in a deep pink. "But you're right. That is going to mess up my nails." She shrugs. "Whatever. I can handle it."

I shake my head. "No, darlin', you can't."

"And why not? Because I'm a girl?"

I shoot her a look. "Please. The strongest woman in the world raised me. You know I don't think women are inferior to men in the least. If anything, I believe the exact opposite. Women should be running this world, not men. They're far smarter and stronger than we are, that's for damn sure."

She chews on that a minute, knowing I mean every damn word of it. Odette's seen firsthand the work my mother put into raising me and Izzy, my parents' "oops" baby, born twelve years after they thought they were done having kids. It wasn't easy having two children at different places in their lives, especially with one who played, lived, and breathed hockey and spent all his time at the rink. She knows the work my mother put in to make sure she was there for Izzy just as much as she was there for my hockey career while my dad worked long hours between his clinic in town and the hospital one town over.

There's no way I'd ever think I could be better than her just because I'm a man.

"Then what is it?" she asks.

"You want to know why I think you can't handle hard labor?"

"Isn't that what I just said?"

I rake my gaze over her, taking in her high heels that make her already long legs look even longer, her skintight skirt, and her pink blouse that matches the color of her lips whenever she's not wearing lipstick.

"I think you can't handle it because, for one, you don't do hard labor. *Ever.* And two, you don't do things that'll make you wet or dirty, both things you'll certainly get if you help with this project. Hell, I remember when you had a swim birthday party and didn't even get in the pool."

"Because it was freezing."

"It was the middle of August. It's because you were too damn scared to let those moronic teenage boys—who were way too old for you, by the way—see you with your hair wet, and you know it."

She opens her mouth to argue, then clamps it shut because she knows I'm right.

Just like I'm right about her inability to handle this kind of work. I appreciate the offer of help—especially since I'm going to need it if I want to complete this on time—but I'm going to have to do a bit better than Odette.

"I just want to help. I . . . I need this to go right, Noah," she says softly, her eyes falling to the floor, shoulders slinking inward. "For my business. I can't . . ." She sucks in a deep breath and looks up at me. "I just can't."

Fuck if her blue eyes and her wobbling lip she's trying so hard to conceal don't do me right in.

It's clear she's struggling. That she needs *something* to go right. This could be that something. I could help her make it that something. I understand that need to prove you're not a complete failure more than she realizes.

"Then we'll make this the best damn wedding Port Harbor has ever seen."

Her lips pull up at the corners, but only barely. "And I can help?"

Knowing I will spend more time fixing her mistakes than it'll take me to do this alone, I find myself nodding anyway. "You can help, Odie."

She huffs at my nickname for her. "I am *not* a dog."

"No, but you should still be a good little girl and run along." I pat her head because, although she's five foot eight, she's still short compared to my six-foot-four frame. "There are too many things in here you can get hurt on. At least let me finish looking it over. Need to make sure it's safe before we go any further."

She swats at my hand, smoothing her already perfect hair as she scowls at me. "Fine. But only because I don't want to get my Manolo Blahniks dirty."

And she thinks she can help rebuild a barn.

I return to my inspection, noting the exposed nails that need to be tamped down or taken out as she retreats to the bar, her heels clacking along the floor the whole way.

I squat to pick up a discarded saw blade. *Where the hell did that even come from?*

"Hey, Noah?"

I turn, my eyes trailing up to her, and I have to make sure I don't react to just how damn good her legs look from this angle.

"Thank you," she says, tucking a strand of hair behind her ear.

I tip my head to the side. "For what?"

"This." She gestures toward the barn. "The farm. Everything. Thanks for letting Izzy have her wedding here. You don't know what this means for her. For . . . me."

But I do know. I know what it's like to want to create something you're proud of, to have your name associated with something you've worked so hard for. And I know what it's like to fail. Hell, I did it plenty of times back in my playing days. I did it plenty of times in my marriage, according to Chelsea.

I nod. "Sure. It's no big deal."

The smile on her lips tells me it is a big deal.

I'm just unsure if it's a big deal for her, me, or both.

◆ ◆ ◆

Patching the roof isn't going to work. We're going to need a whole new one.

"How much?" Ezra asks from below. He's been standing beside the ladder, crunching numbers for the last two hours as I dig around and find problem after problem.

"Add another two grand to the roofing budget."

"Fuck," he mutters, but I hear him punch it into his calculator—the one that's never too far out of reach—anyway. "We're over."

He means the budget. He immediately set one aside for repairs for the wedding. A lot of it is stuff we've been meaning to do anyway, but now, at least, we have motivation and a timeline. A ridiculously short one, but still.

"I know," I tell him. We were over about thirty minutes into this big inspection of ours.

"We shouldn't have let them talk us into this."

No, shit. That's what I was saying from the beginning. But I bite my tongue, instead saying, "I know."

"We might be upside down on this."

"I know."

I sigh. There is no "might." We *will* be upside down on this. There's no doubt about it. And not just because we're giving Izzy a killer deal on the venue either.

"But," Ezra says, "it just means we're investing in ourselves. In our next venture. This is good. This is really good."

I'm unsure if he's trying to convince me or himself of this.

I climb down the ladder, the metal clanging until my feet hit the concrete that still needs to be swept. That's the least of my problems, though. Right now, my biggest issue is the roof, which will cost us about eight grand to replace, and that's just material costs. It doesn't include my time that'll be spent doing it.

"Are you sure you want to do this?" I ask for probably the hundredth time since we came out here.

He grunts. "Do we have a choice?"

"You're kidding. We had a choice hours ago when Izzy gave me puppy dog eyes. We could have said no then. Actually, I *did* say no. You're the one who convinced me to say otherwise."

"Please." He rolls his eyes. "We both know putting your foot down with your sister wouldn't last. It never has before. Why start now? For her wedding?"

"I was going to stand my ground."

He gives me a disbelieving look, and okay, fine. He *might* be right. There was a chance I'd cave for sure. But it was minimal, no matter what he says.

"Whatever. I guess we're in it now." I nod toward the calculator he's clutching like a lifeline. "What's the damage?"

Now it's his turn to sigh. "Twelve. But I think I can get it down to ten."

I run my hand through my hair. "That's a lot of cash for something we aren't sure will work."

"Yeah, but think of it this way: We spend the dough now, we get this place looking good, we let Odette make it all fancy and shit and photograph the hell out of it, and boom—we're raking in fistfuls. Think what we're putting in times five, possibly more."

"Five times? Fuck. That's a lot of money. You really think so?" I ask.

He nods. "I do. I mean, shit, what are the options all those lovesick losers have now? That church, the community center, the courthouse, and the docks? That's about it unless people want to travel farther out, which they don't. We could even attract business from neighboring towns and cater to those who don't want to travel far. Weddings are already expensive, even to attend. We'd be the better option if they could have them here in Port Harbor. So, yeah, I think we have a big opportunity here. Not to mention, the profits I'm projecting could set us up to buy the iceplex."

Having both played hockey, we know what it costs to get into the game, and it sure as hell isn't cheap. Ezra knows that better than I do, being raised by a single mom who worked two jobs to make ends meet.

Training centers like the one we're trying to create are what got him to the NHL.

We've spent a lot of late nights dreaming up the iceplex and have even found the perfect location—an old rink not too far from Port Harbor that's in desperate need of some love. We want to buy it, renovate it, and offer free ice time and training to low-income families. Maybe even run a special training camp out of it in the summer. Who knows what we could do with it?

But I do know that the extra money from the weddings would certainly come in handy with the sale. We could buy it now, but it would mean dipping into our personal funds in ways neither of us are prepared to do. The new stream of revenue would fix that issue.

And he's right about the neighboring towns too. We get a lot of business from them already. I've even met people who have driven from other states just to try our cider or get an autograph. We have something here, so I guess investing a bit up front will all be worth it, especially for Izzy.

And Odette too.

Fuck, her face earlier said it all.

She's desperate for this to work. For this to become what she's known for, instead of all those disastrous weddings she's had lately. She was right about her business tanking. I've heard the rumors. I know what they're saying about her wedding-planning abilities, and none of them are good. They claim she's a disaster. A wreck. *Cursed.*

That one always makes me laugh, given the Chamberses' family history with curses. I always thought it was a bunch of baloney that they were plagued with bad love, and I still do. They aren't cursed. Terrible shit happens to good people sometimes. Odette can get through it, and I'm going to help.

"Are you listening?"

"Hmm?" I drop the crowbar I took up the ladder into my toolbox. "What'd you say?"

"I said, we need to start soon. Like tomorrow soon, if you want to get this finished in time. That schedule . . ." He shakes his head. "Fuck, it's tight. Why can't Izzy get married next year? Or six months from now? Literally anything else other than in ten weeks."

"Because they want to get married on their anniversary or other romantic shit like that."

"Gross." Ezra shivers. "Well, whatever. We'll just have to work with the timeline we're given. Well, *you'll* have to work with it."

He grits his teeth together, knowing full well that most of these restorations will be done by me because he can't physically help with them. Not with his hip.

Guess it's a damn good thing I'm competent with a hammer. I have my dad to thank for that, always making me help him with house repairs when I was younger. This will be my biggest project by far and will test my skills, but do I really have a choice at this point?

"It's fine," I reassure him. "I'll just need some help in the bar. I know dealing with the public isn't your favorite, but . . ."

He waves off my words. "I got it. I'm going to bitch the whole time, but I can handle it."

I chuckle, knowing full well he's telling the truth. "All right." I bend and snap my toolbox closed. "I think we're done for the night." I push to my full height. "Want to grab some burgers in town?"

Ezra pats his stomach. "Fuck, man. You're reading my mind. Dickie's sounds perfect right about now. I could go for a mushroom Swiss."

"That sounds disgusting," I complain, unlocking the ladder and letting it slide down noisily back into place until it's a much more manageable height before kicking the legs together.

"Don't understand your mushroom hate, man."

"It's not that I don't like mushrooms. They don't like me. Allergic, remember?"

"Some things are just worth the risk, and Dickie's mushroom Swiss is one of those things."

“I’ll take your word for it.” I set the ladder against the wall near the door, my toolbox going right next to it for tomorrow. “Come on. I want to enjoy my last night of freedom before spending all my waking hours in this place.”

“It’s going to be worth it,” Ezra promises. “Wait and see.”

I wish I had the same confidence as him . . . and hope that he’s right.

CHAPTER FOUR

Odette

"Food. Need."

"Are we not doing full sentences today?"

I glower at the guy behind the counter of my favorite coffee shop. This may be my favorite coffee spot in Port Harbor, but it's too early in the morning for full sentences.

"Food," I say again.

He laughs. "Guess not. Your usual?"

"Please."

"Ah, there are those manners of yours I know and love." He punches buttons on the screen with a grin. "Twenty-ounce honey lavender oat milk latte and an Asiago bagel with cream cheese, lightly toasted. Anything else?"

I shake my head. "Total."

Kai reads me my total—which I should know by heart since I come here nearly every day—and I tap my card against the machine. I leave him a little extra on his tip since I know I'm not my usual chipper self today.

I stand at the end of the counter, where my stuff will come out, and lean against it, looking out the window toward Harborview Boulevard, which runs along the waterfront.

The sun is barely up, so things are still calm, but if I give it thirty minutes, the place will be buzzing. Port Harbor might be small, but it's mighty. The townsfolk are always out and about, supporting the local shops. We take pride in backing up our own.

That's why I'm up far too early. I'm headed to the Stick Taps property to start on all the renovations Noah has planned for the wedding.

When I insisted that I help him, I didn't anticipate him texting me last night with instructions to arrive at 5:30 a.m. I heard rumors that time existed in the morning, but I've never seen it before. Sleeping until nine or ten is a luxury I've afforded myself since starting my business, and I've taken advantage of that as often as I can.

Kai slides my coffee over to me first—bless him—and I immediately pull the latte to my lips, sipping the steaming-hot drink. I don't care that it burns. The caffeine fix is worth it.

The light inside Artfully Yours across the street flicks on, drawing my attention, and I can say with certainty that I had no idea the pottery shop opened this early. Actually, I had no idea the coffee shop did either. I just drove here on autopilot and was pleasantly surprised to find the doors unlocked.

"Kai?"

He pops his head out from around the corner. "Yes?"

"Do you always open this early?"

He chuckles. "Technically, we don't open until six, but you looked desperate, so I didn't say anything."

"What? You're not even open yet?!"

He shakes his head. "Not until six."

"Kai! I . . . wh-what . . ." I sputter. "Why did you let me in?"

He shrugs. "Told you. You looked in serious need of a coffee. And, honestly, a little scary. No offense."

"None taken." I'm sure I *do* look scary. I'm not even sure if I put on underwear. That's how tired I was when I rolled out of bed. "And thank you. You didn't have to let me in. You could have told me to get lost."

"Could have, but I have a soft spot for my favorites." He shoots me a wink. "Your bagel is almost done. I'll go grab the cream cheese from the back. To go, right?"

I nod, then pull my phone from my purse to check the time because the last thing I want is to be late, especially since I insisted on being included in this.

I ignore the email from my landlord—a reminder that rent is due, I'm sure—and go right to the waiting text message.

What psychopath is even up at this hour?

Oh, right. The one who set this date.

Noah: Are you on your way?

Noah: Because you'd better be on your way, Odie.

My fingers fly over the screen.

Me: you are SO damn bossy

Me: yes

Me: OMW

Me: coffee first

Noah: You stopped for coffee? Are you planning to break every law on the way here?

Noah: What does OMW mean?

I chuckle. Of course he doesn't know shorthand text. Sometimes I forget the large age gap between us and that we don't have what is basically a secret language like me and Izzy. We can text each other a single letter and know what the other means. It's weird.

Me: on my way

Me: && not all laws, just some

Noah: Just don't be late.

Me: yes, sir!

I shake my head, dropping my phone back into my purse.

Leave it to Noah to be so overbearing this early in the morning. He's always played the big brother role to a T.

If only he knew that I've had thoughts about him that certainly *aren't* brotherly at all.

I'll admit, I stood at the barn door for a little too long yesterday before making my presence known. I couldn't help it. He looked so good standing in the middle of it, his hands on his hips as he looked at every minor imperfection. I could tell it was overwhelming him, the thought of having to rebuild it, but he would do it anyway if it made his sister happy. That's just who he is. A stand-up kind of guy. Dependable. The type of guy you can lean on when the going gets tough.

That's why I know he'll make this wedding the best this town has ever seen and help me save my business.

That email about rent being due is just another reminder of how badly I need this. I have the money, thanks to the savings I padded back when I was actually getting clients, but it's dwindling fast. I shouldn't even be here buying coffee and breakfast, but it's a necessity to get through this day with Noah. That's an acceptable splurge, right?

Noah.

Pain-in-my-ass yet oh-so-amazing Noah, who is doing all this for me and his sister out of the kindness of his heart.

I know it's unfair to put the future of Chambers Charming Ceremonies on his shoulders, but I *need* this. I can't let another thing go awry. I can't be a failure at business. I'm already destined to fail at love. Isn't that enough?

"Here you go." Kai slides the bagged bagel my way.

"Thanks," I tell him, grabbing it off the counter. "Could I get one more thing?"

◆ ◆ ◆

I'm late.

Sure, I gave Noah a hard time and swore I wouldn't be a problem for him, but it's not my fault Mr. Taylor took all six of his dogs on a walk this morning and got tangled in the crosswalk, leaving me stuck at the stop sign while I waited for him to sort his life out.

I just hope this coffee in my hand works as a peace offering. It was going to be my *thank-you* for letting me help, but now it's an "I'm sorry I was late" gift.

I yank open the door of Stick Taps and come to a skidding halt right in front of a very grumpy—okay, so he always looks grumpy—Noah.

His big arms are crossed over his chest, and his lips are turned down into a frown. "You're late."

I hold out the to-go cup of coffee. "I got this for you. It's black?"

It comes out as a question, and I'm unsure why. Probably because I have no idea how Noah takes his coffee, but black seemed appropriate, given his usual demeanor. It matches his soul and all.

He stares at it skeptically for several moments before finally taking it from me and bringing it to his lips. I watch—admittedly far too closely—as he takes a sip.

His Adam's apple bobs when he swallows, making *me* swallow, too, even though there's no reason for it to be so attractive.

I avert my eyes, but not before seeing a soft *ahh* roll off his lips.

"Good?" I ask, looking at the floor.

He grunts in response, then turns on his heel and marches toward the bar.

My feet follow him before I realize I do. He nods toward an empty stool, and I slide onto it, clutching my own coffee between my hands as I watch him pop open a familiar-looking yellow box.

Sunnie's.

Also known as the *best* place around if you're looking to satisfy your sweet tooth.

I guess Noah was this morning.

He sets out two napkins, pulls a delicious-looking fritter from the box, and places it on one before sliding it my way. He grabs another from the box, takes the napkin and fritter, and leans against the back counter, one leg crossed over the other. He bites into the dough, which I know is light and fluffy and just sugary enough. A few pieces of the glaze cling to his lips, and I barely resist the urge to leap across the counter and lick them away.

I point to mine, my mouth watering despite downing my bagel on the drive here. "Chocolate banana?"

A brow lifts. "Would it be anything else?"

He doesn't have to say another word. I pounce, biting into the treat, not caring enough to be embarrassed by the moan that leaves me. It's completely warranted. These fritters are that damn good.

While I love all their flavors, the chocolate banana is my favorite. Noah knew it too.

"God, I love these things," I say through a mouthful. I meet Noah's eyes. "Don't you love these things?"

He doesn't say anything. He just watches me.

I chew, and he stares. I swallow, and he stares. I take a sip of my coffee, and he stares.

And all the while I'm growing hotter and hotter under his gaze.

It's probably just the heat. He has it cranked in here, which isn't surprising since it's so cold this morning.

"Noah?" I finally say.

It's like something in him snaps, and he realizes he's been watching me.

"Sorry," he mutters, then shoves his fritter into his mouth, his eyes now on the floor.

Huh. Weird.

I shrug it off, and we finish our breakfast in silence.

When we're done, Noah tosses our napkins in the trash bin, then puts the box from Sunnie's under the counter on the shelves I know are back there.

"Got more for later," he says as an explanation. He grabs his coffee off the bar top. "You ready?"

I sigh. "As I'll ever be."

"Nobody asked you to do this, you know."

"I know. I want to."

He gives me a disbelieving look but doesn't say another word. He just waltzes toward the front door, and I guess I'm supposed to follow him because he stands there with it open, looking back at me expectantly.

"I guess we're getting started now," I say under my breath as I slide off the stool.

He holds the door open as I slip by and moves himself out of the way, careful not to touch me.

I didn't realize I repulsed Noah so much, but I'm too tired to comment on it.

When I head toward my car, he grabs my elbow.

Guess he's not that grossed out after all.

"Leaving already?"

"Just got to grab some tools."

His brows crush together. "Tools?"

I don't answer him as I pull out of his grasp and open my trunk, then reach for the toolbox I stashed away last night.

I'm unsurprised when Noah bursts out laughing.

"You can't be serious."

I shove my shoulders back, determined to be unbothered by his laughter. "Oh, I'm very serious."

"No."

"Pardon?"

"You heard me, Odie. No. You're not bringing those."

"And why not? Because they're pink?"

I hold up the hot-pink box I bought when I got my first apartment. The last thing I wanted was to wait around for some maintenance guy who would just mansplain everything to me if something ever went wrong. So I went out, bought a toolbox, and learned to fix things myself. This thing has never let me down in all the years I've had it, so you bet I'm using it to help fix this barn too.

"Yes! It's ridiculous. Besides, I have tools you can use."

"I prefer mine." I slam my trunk closed, then march past him, toolbox in hand.

I glance over my shoulder when I realize he's not following me.

"Well, are you coming, Noah? I thought we had a barn to rebuild."

He rolls his eyes with a sigh, then shakes his head, muttering something as he takes three long strides to catch up with me.

I ignore him until we reach the barn. He pulls open the door, and I see that the state of it is far different from how I left it yesterday.

"What the . . ." I glare up at him. "Did you start without me?"

"Yes. I wanted to get the hard shit out of the way."

"Hard shit? So you mean stuff *you* deem hard for me?"

He huffs. "No, Odie, I mean stuff that was hard for even *me*. Ezra was out here helping me last night. We were inspecting things, and I was already up on that godforsaken rickety old ladder, so I figured why not do a few things that only I can reach anyway?"

When he puts it like that, it makes sense.

Still, he's trying to exclude me, and I *hate* being excluded. It makes me feel like a little kid all over again. Like that annoying little sister who is always trying to tag along and get everyone's attention. But I'm *not* his little sister. Not by a long shot. Noah said I could help, so he should let me help with *everything*, even if my tools are pink.

"Fine. I just . . . don't exclude me because I'm small compared to you, okay? That's not fair. I'll let you know if I feel like I can't handle something. And stop being an ass about my pink toolbox. This thing helped me redo the wiring in my bathroom a few weeks ago when the breaker kept popping every time I plugged my hair dryer in. I finally got sick of it and redid the whole thing."

"*You* redid the wiring? Can't you call maintenance for that?"

"Sure, but I'm a strong, independent woman who can figure it out for herself. One trip to the hardware store and a few YouTube videos later, I learned everything I needed and didn't have to wait around to let someone in. It was a win-win."

His jaw has slackened, eyes wide with surprise, and that's fair. I'm sure I don't exactly give off Ms. Fix-It vibes, considering I wear heels 99 percent of the time and am almost always dressed up. It's not that women in heels can't fix things, but still. I understand societal norms, and I don't fall into that category.

I reach up, pushing Noah's jaw shut with a single finger. "Better close that before you let a fly in."

My finger lingers longer than it needs, and Noah lets it, not moving away from my touch.

When I finally pull it away, the fight in him is gone, but the tension in the barn definitely isn't. If anything, it's higher than before, but there's something entirely different about it.

I shake it off and give him my back, needing a moment to gather myself without his prying eyes.

What the hell even was that? Why did I keep touching him for so long? And why didn't he move away?

I sit my toolbox on the ground and open it to retrieve my pink gloves. After slipping them on, I get to work moving the debris he has gathered.

Noah instructs me to make a pile near the door while he starts stripping more rotted panels off the wall.

We work together in silence for a long time. I have no idea how long it's been, but it's long enough that my stomach is growling, and the sun is blasting into the barn, making it warm enough to feel sweat beads rolling down my back.

"Break?" Noah asks.

I nod, looking at the pile with a frown. "Yeah, but just a short one. I still have a lot to do."

"Doesn't help that I keep adding to the pile. I'll take a break after lunch to help you get this moved. Good thing is the tow truck is coming tomorrow to get the tractor out of the way. We'll have more room to work afterward."

"Wait. You're getting rid of the tractor?"

"Uh, yeah." He scratches at his scruff, which, while it could use a trim, is still too good looking for its own good. "What else am I supposed to do with it?"

"Keep it."

"What the hell for? It's old, and it doesn't work."

"So? You could use it for photos. It gives the farm a nice rustic feel. People love that kind of thing."

He ponders that for a moment before nodding. "All right. I can see that. So where do I move it?"

"Could you put it next to the barn?"

"Yeah, I suppose that would work." Another scratch at his scruff, a move that's always signaled uncertainty for him. "You sure it won't look tacky out there? Like we're trying too hard with this whole farm-aspect thing? Because I'm not a farmer. I'm a hockey player. Or at least I was."

He says that last part quietly, like it's still something he's getting used to. I'm sure he is, considering the game was part of his life for so long. If I suddenly lost my business, I'd feel like I was missing a limb because I've been working on this for so long. I bet that's how he feels about the game he gave so much of his life to.

"Playing or not, you're still a hockey player. You'll always be the one who not only captained a team but also scored the game-winning goal in double overtime against Detroit to lift the Cup."

He grins just thinking about that career-defining moment. "Yeah, I guess you're right."

"I am. Just like I'm right about keeping the tractor and moving it to the side of the barn won't look tacky. And it won't make you look like you're trying to play Old MacDonald either. You're paying homage to the original purpose of the land, like you're paying homage to your love of the game by naming the cidery Stick Taps, giving hockey term names to all your ciders, and your decor—even if it is hideous for weddings." He narrows his eyes at the dig. "Besides, the kids will love it. You could even put a scarecrow or something behind the wheel. Dress it up to match the holidays. Oh! Like big, cute eyelashes and heart eyes for headlights for Valentine's Day."

"Absolutely no to the eyelashes and heart eyes."

Dammit. I knew I'd pushed it too far.

"But the rest?" I ask.

He grunts, but it's not a no. In fact, I can tell he actually likes the idea, since he doesn't argue further.

As he passes, he kicks at the pile of wood and old roof tiles and heads toward the door. "Come on. I'll make us lunch up at my place."

"You're cooking?!" The words come out a squeak, halting him in his tracks. My stomach revolts at the idea, remembering the last time he made food for his family—and me, since the Stevens clan can't shake me, being they're like my second family at this point. It was so bad that we ended up throwing it away and ordering pizza. Sometimes he'll help his dad at the grill, but that's under careful supervision.

He shoots me a look that says *watch it* loud and clear, and I hold my hands up.

"I'm not saying a thing," I promise as I follow him out of the barn, all the while thinking about what I have stashed away in my purse. I usually keep an emergency granola bar in there because I've been known to get hangry. And when it happens, it happens *fast.* It's best to be prepared.

"Shit," Noah mutters, coming to a sudden stop, and I nearly run right into him.

"What's wrong?"

"You mind driving? I forgot I told Ezra he could use my truck for . . . well, whatever it is he does."

"Oh. Uh, yeah. No problem. I'm over here."

I lead us to my BMW, which could use a wash, pulling my keys from my pocket and unlocking the car as we go. I cringe when we approach it. There's a mess of clothes in the back seat, a few purses, and I don't even know how many pairs of shoes from on-the-go outfit changes when rushing to meet clients and for when I have to get event-ready on a time crunch. Maybe, if I'm lucky, Noah won't notice them.

"Probably going to be a tight fit for you," I say as I climb inside, flipping the visor down and checking my hair. It's a mess after hours of hard labor. And no wonder Kai let me in this morning. I'm pretty sure I still have yesterday's mascara smeared under my eyes.

I wipe my face as I continue. "You're tall, and I'm pretty sure the seat is pushed back as far as it goes. At least, I assume. I have no idea. I've never actually sat over there before. I just—" I glance over to find Noah staring into the car but not getting in so we can go. "What are you doing? Get in. I'm starving."

"On second thought, I think I might walk."

"What? Why? Why are you . . ."

His eyes darting downward have my words fading away because right there—right in plain sight with no mistaking what it is—is a pair of panties.

My panties.

So much for him not seeing the clothes.

I snatch them off the seat and stuff them into my purse.

Not that it does any good. The damage has already been done. Noah has already seen my underwear.

"Sorry about that," I mumble, refusing to look at him as he slides into the passenger seat.

Just as I suspected, he barely fits. His knees are tucked against the dashboard, and his neck is slightly bent as his head brushes the roof. He looks ridiculous, but it's nothing compared to how I feel—absolutely mortified.

We're silent as I fire up the engine and drive us to his place just up the road.

For the entire ride, I pray a pit opens up and swallows us whole. Anything to escape the awkwardness because Noah Stevens just saw my underwear.

My best friend's older brother. The man I've been crushing on since I was a teenager.

And they were my favorite pair.

CHAPTER FIVE

Noah

Pale-pink lace. Red hearts. A matching bow.

It's the only thing going through my mind as Odette's little white BMW bumps along the gravel road to my place.

Another perk of buying this property was the house. I needed a place and wanted something secluded yet still close to town. Fortune favored me again with finding this place.

It did not, however, favor me when I opened Odette's car door to find her panties sitting in the front seat.

Pale-pink lace. Red hearts. A matching bow.

I squeeze my eyes shut, trying to rid myself of the image, but it's impossible.

They were so small, so delicate. So fucking sexy.

No, Noah. Not sexy. This is Odette we're talking about here. She's not sexy. She can't be.

I inhale deeply and exhale, peeling my eyes open slowly as my heart rate slows. I blink once, then twice, trying to get my bearings.

I'm good. I'm good. Totally good, I tell myself.

Then my traitorous eyes dart right to the purse sitting between us. Right to the material I can still see poking out.

Pale-pink lace. Red hearts. A matching bow.

Fucking hell!

I snap my attention back to the road as Odette pulls up to my two-story traditional farmhouse. She doesn't even have the chance to shut the engine off before I push open the door and stumble out of the too-small car.

I don't bother waiting for Odette. I can't. I need to put as much distance between us as possible.

She's just closing her door as I pound up the steps to my house, which have certainly seen better days. Between running the farm and the cidery, I haven't had as much time as I'd hoped to fix this place up. I could easily pay someone to get it up to date, but I decided when I bought it that I wouldn't do that. I wanted it to be something *I* built, not someone else. I'll get to it one day.

The old screen door creaks as I pull it open and push inside. Since it's just me out here, I don't bother locking it up much, especially not when I'm still going to be on the property. I've never been more thankful for that as I barrel through the door, rush through the living room, and go straight to the kitchen. I pull a glass from the cabinet and press it against the water dispenser on the fridge. Once the glass is full, I chug the entire thing in three swallows before filling it again.

I don't know why I'm so desperate for water, but I am.

Pale-pink lace. Red hearts. A matching bow.

Oh, right. That's why.

I close my eyes as I take another drink, slower this time, as Odette strolls into the kitchen. I should feel like a bad host for leaving her to fend for herself, but she's been here before with Izzy. She knows her way around plenty.

She proves it by setting her purse on the scratched-up kitchen table that came with the house. Then she makes her way to the pantry, pulling out the bread and chips. She sets them on the counter and moves to the fridge. I step out of her way, my eyes darting to her purse again.

Pale-pink lace. Red hearts. A matching bow.

On the counter she sets the fixings for sandwiches—mustard, mayo, turkey, lettuce, tomatoes, cheese—then shoos me out of her way as she rolls up her sleeves and moves to the sink.

Given my history in the kitchen, I don't argue.

I know my strengths and weaknesses, and doing anything in the kitchen definitely falls into the latter category. I tried cooking for Chelsea a few times over our six-year marriage, but it always ended poorly. I eventually gave up trying and never really got into it post-divorce either. I survive just fine on the few things I can make, so who cares?

I go around the other side of the island and stop at the fridge to refill my water. After setting it on the small two-person dining table, I grab another from the cabinet and shake it toward Odette in a silent question.

"Do you have any lemonade?"

I nod, not trusting myself to say anything, and fill her glass with lemonade before returning it to the fridge. I make sure to grab the pickles from the top shelf because I love them with my lunch.

Odette finishes our sandwiches just as I pull a bag of Doritos from the pantry, and we settle at the table together.

"Thanks," I say, focusing solely on the delicious-looking meal before me. I can't bring myself to look at her yet.

"No problem." She pops a chip into her mouth, her crunching filling the otherwise quiet room.

It's awkward between us now, and we both know exactly why.

Pale-pink lace. Red hearts. A matching bow.

I close my eyes against the image that won't leave my mind.

I don't get why I'm reacting like this. I've seen plenty of women's underwear before. It's not my first time by a long shot.

Yet, here I am, unable to shake that damn adorable pink thong from my thoughts. Unable to stop thinking about how soft it might be. How good Odette's ass would look in it.

My pants tighten—not for the first time—and I shuffle, trying to adjust myself inconspicuously.

Odette's so wrapped up in her lunch that she doesn't even notice, and thank fuck for that. The last thing I need is to be caught popping a boner.

Stop thinking about the damn underwear, Noah. Think about something else. Literally anything else. Your to-do list for the wedding. Your to-do list for your house. Your to-do list to get the business where you want it so you can use the profits for the iceplex. Count the damn scratches on the table—anything but Odette's pink panties.

"Something wrong?"

I snap my head up to find her indigo eyes on me. "What?"

She gestures toward my untouched lunch. "You're not eating. Did I make it wrong?"

"Oh." I shake my head. "Uh, no. Sorry, I just needed a minute to chill after all that work."

She nods, then takes another bite of her sandwich. A bit of mayo clings to the corner of her mouth.

My fingers twitch with the urge to lean over the table and wipe it off.

I repress the urge and pick up my sandwich, shoving half of it into my mouth. It's ridiculous, but I'll do whatever I can to avoid making a fool of myself. Again.

What kind of grown man reacts to underwear the way I did? It wasn't a big deal. Odette laughed it off. Why couldn't I? Instead, I acted like a teenager and ran away from her—literally.

That's why she's staring at me like she is—like I've lost my mind.

"Guess you were hungry, huh?"

"Hmm?" I ask, sandwich back in my mouth, my bite smaller this time. Not that there's much of the sandwich even left at this point. I've demolished nearly all of it in just two bites.

Maybe that's why she's looking at me like she is. Not because I'm visibly bothered by seeing a pair of panties, but because I'm eating this sandwich like I haven't had any sustenance in years.

Pale-pink lace. Red hearts. A matching bow.

I chew and swallow, then wipe my mouth with my napkin like I have some class and am not a total caveman. "Hungrier than I thought, apparently."

She nods. "Me too. Who knew all that work would make me so hungry? And that's even after two breakfasts."

"Two?"

"I had a bagel on the drive here." She takes a sip of her lemonade. "Kai always toasts it perfectly."

Kai.

She means that jackass who works at the coffee shop who is always flirting with any woman who walks through the doors.

Okay, fine. So maybe not every woman. He flirts with everyone. And he's not a jackass. He's actually really nice.

I'm just being irrational, and I don't know why. I'm flustered from the underwear still.

Yeah, that's it.

I take a big swig from my water glass, then another bite of my sandwich, this one smaller. I really should have savored it more because this thing is damn good. It's just a basic lunch, but everyone knows sandwiches are better when someone else makes them.

Just like they're always better with pickles.

I trade my sandwich for the jar of pickles, twist off the top, and pull out a spear. I hold the jar toward Odette, who crinkles her nose.

"Ew. No, thank you."

"You don't like pickles?"

"Unless they are battered and fried, no."

I shake my head, grabbing another from the jar before recapping it and setting it aside. "I knew something was wrong when Izzy brought you home."

"Hey! Rude!" She throws a chip at me, and I catch it effortlessly, popping it into my mouth along with the pickle. It's not the worst combination, but it's not a good one either.

Still, I eat it anyway, enjoying the shocked look on her face entirely too much.

"That was disgusting."

"Hush up and eat your lunch. We have more work to do, and we're losing daylight by the minute."

"Losing daylight? How late are you planning to work tonight, Farmer John?"

I ignore her jab. "Need to get it stripped down more. Need to see what I'm working with still."

"But it's already stripped pretty far down. We need to go deeper?"

Go deeper.

Pale-pink lace. Red hearts. A matching bow.

I take another swig of water. She didn't mean a damn thing by those words, but my head is still so twisted up that it doesn't matter.

I nod. "Yep. Redoing the roof completely. Don't want it coming down while everyone's doing the Electric Slide, do we?"

"Okay, first of all, we will *not* be doing the Electric Slide at all, because *ew*. There will be no group dances."

"I did group dances at my wedding."

"Yeah, and look how that turned out," she says, referring to my divorce.

I try not to laugh. There's no love lost between me and Chelsea, and if I were allowed to have been involved in the wedding planning, I wouldn't have had group dances either. "Fair enough."

"Secondly," she continues, "it didn't look that bad to me. Are you sure we need to strip it naked?"

Strip it naked.

Naked.

I take another drink, hoping she doesn't notice the shake of my hands. "Yep. I'm sure."

She shrugs. "All right. Then let's finish this up. Apparently we have work to do."

So that's what we do. We finish our lunch in silence. I clean up the kitchen while Odette runs to the restroom.

The second she's gone, I breathe a sigh of relief, and my shoulders drop from my ears.

I had no idea I was holding such tension until now. I knew I was keyed up, but damn. This seems a bit extra.

Get a grip, Noah, I tell myself as I rinse the crumbs off our plates. *She's Izzy's best friend. That's all she'll ever be.*

I inhale a long, calming breath, then exhale it just as slowly, trying to get myself back in the right headspace and definitely *not* thinking about Odette Chambers in ways I shouldn't.

I'm just about done loading the dishes into the dishwasher when I hear my name hollered from across the house.

I spring into action, dropping the plate I was holding and taking off toward where Odette is calling for me.

"Noah!"

"What? What's the matter?" I yell back, skidding to a stop in front of the closed bathroom door.

"There's a spider!"

Holy fuck. Is she serious?

"Seriously?" I say through the door. "That's why you're screaming like someone's trying to axe murder you?"

"No, I'm screaming like someone's trying to axe murder me because there's no toilet paper, so I can't even wipe and escape this beast before I get eaten alive!"

Shit. I completely forgot to restock the downstairs bathroom. Now she's stranded in there, panicking if the sound of her harsh breathing is any indication.

"Uh, can't you drip-dry or something? Then I can come to kill the spider?"

"Drip-dry? Drip-dry?! What the hell is wrong with you, Noah Stevens? And you are *not* killing the spider. You're going to trap it and release it back outside where it belongs."

I'm going to what?

I shake my head at her, even though she can't see me.

I grip the edge of the doorframe. "Just hurry up, will you? We have work to do."

"You hurry up! Get me some damn toilet paper!"

"But that's all the way upstairs."

"You're right. Upstairs *is* a long way to walk. I'll just use this old shirt lying on the floor, which I certainly have questions about, because why are you showering down here?"

She's right. I don't usually shower down here. I have a nice, newly renovated bathroom upstairs, which is the only spot in the house I've done something with. But I was so gross last night after working on the barn, and I felt like I was covered in dust and spiderwebs. I stripped as soon as I walked in the door and showered downstairs.

Now I regret it. She's about to use my favorite shirt as toilet paper.

"Wait, wait! I'll go grab some. Just . . . don't use my shirt, okay?"

"Then hurry! Before I become this spider's lunch!"

I bolt up the stairs to my bathroom, grab a fresh pack of toilet paper, and sprint back downstairs.

"Open the door, Odie," I call to her.

She doesn't respond right away, and for just a second the illogical part of me thinks that the spider may have actually eaten her.

Then she talks.

"It's unlocked," she says, sounding much less annoyed than earlier. "Just . . . just close your eyes and set it on the counter. I'll grab it."

Even though I want to roll them, I close my eyes instead. Why would I want to check her out right now? This is so not the situation for that.

Yeah, and neither was you nearly popping a boner earlier because you couldn't stop thinking about her damn underwear, yet that's precisely what happened.

I shove away my thoughts and push open the door.

"Stop peeking!"

I growl. "I'm not fucking peeking, Odie. Can't you see me bumbling around like a fool? I can't even find the counter."

"This is your house. How do you not know where the counter is?"

"I don't normally navigate it with my eyes closed."

"Whatever. Just hurry already. You should see the size of this damned spider, eyeing me like I'm a piece of fried chicken or something."

"Which is it—do you want me to keep my eyes closed or look at the spider?"

"Closed!"

My lips twitch as I reach into the room as I'm told. But the only thing I find is the door. I push it open farther and take a small step into the bathroom.

"What are you doing?!" Odette yells, and I realize then that my *small step* is rather large, especially given how tiny this bathroom is, because she's close.

Too close.

"I don't know!" I yell back, toss the packet of toilet paper I don't know where, and spin on my heel to get the hell out of the room as fast as the small room will allow. This is exactly why I prefer my bathroom upstairs. It's wide, where this one is just long and narrow.

Which means speed-walking out of the bathroom with my eyes shut is a terrible idea.

"Ow! Shit! Fuck!" I grab my face as pain shoots through it as I slam nose-first into the side of the door.

I've played hockey since I was four years old, so I know instantly that I'm going to be black and blue. And that there's a chance my nose is broken.

There's a scramble behind me, and I hear Odette getting off the toilet.

So much for not being able to move. And so much for being deathly afraid of the spider.

"Oh my god, Noah! Noah! Are you okay?" Her hand lands on my back. "Are you—"

"I'm fine!" I roar, shoving the door so hard it bounces off the wall and smacks into my side as I race out of the bathroom.

"But your face. I—"

"Just go to the damn bathroom, Odette," I say, grabbing the handle and slamming the door closed hard enough that it rattles the walls of the old farmhouse.

Odette doesn't say another word, and I don't blame her.

Well, I kind of do.

If she wasn't being so damn stubborn, I could have just set the toilet paper on the counter with no problem, and I wouldn't be walking around with a busted beak right about now.

I finally open my eyes, pressing my back against the wall and sucking in breath after breath, trying to get myself under control.

I can't believe that just happened. I can't believe my face hurts so damn bad. I can't believe I yelled at Odette like that.

I push off the wall and stomp through the house, going back upstairs to my bathroom, which has more than enough space, so I won't be running into doors anytime soon.

There's a nasty gash across the bridge of my nose, blood leaking down the sides of it and dripping over my chin onto my shirt. Other than that, it doesn't look too bad, though. For now, at least. I have no doubt I'm going to have a black eye—or two—tomorrow.

I press around it, feeling for any signs of it being broken, but I think I'm okay. I got lucky, that's for sure.

After cleaning the cut with my first aid kit I'm now really damn glad I brought, I change out of my bloodstained shirt, pop a few ibuprofens to combat the swelling, and head back downstairs.

Odette's sitting on the second-to-last step, her chin resting in her hand. Even from behind, she looks deflated. What does she have to be upset about? I'm the one who got hurt.

She flips around when she hears me coming, then scrambles to get out of my way.

When she looks up at me, there's no mistaking how her eyes widen as she takes in the damage she's caused.

"Noah, I . . . I didn't mean to—"

I hold my hand up, stopping her. "It's fine."

She nods, worry still covering each inch of her features. "Are you . . . is it broken?" she asks with a wince.

I shake my head. "No, I don't think so. Going to bruise, and it hurts like a son of a bitch, that's for damn sure, but not broken."

She breathes a sigh of relief. "Good. That's good."

Her fingers play with the edges of her shirt. She looks worried and even a little scared. She looks sorry.

"Listen, I think we should call it a day."

She snaps her blue eyes back to mine, tilting her head to the side. "But . . . the barn. I thought we were going to work on it for longer. Until dark?"

Damn going back to working on the barn.

I need to clean myself up more, heal, and get far, far away from Odette Chambers.

It's been a long enough day as it is, especially since I've been up since four, and I don't need it to be any longer with the way my nose and eyes are already starting to swell.

"We'll do it later," I say through clenched teeth, trying to ignore the pain radiating through my face. "Go home, Odie."

She frowns, her shoulders sloping down, her chin nearly meeting her chest.

I instantly feel bad for upsetting her. I don't like seeing her this way.

But I also don't like that I'm now going to lose a few days' worth of work because I went and busted up my nose trying to help her out.

"Okay," she says. "I . . . I'm sorry, Noah."

"It's no big deal," I tell her, even though we both know it is.

The people in this town are nosy, and I serve them booze every day. They're going to want to know what happened, which means I'm going to have to come up with a damn good story, because there is no way I'm telling them the truth.

She nods but doesn't say anything else.

I hold the door open for her as she climbs down the steps I need to get around to replacing one of these days, then gets into her tiny car.

Pale-pink lace. Red hearts. A matching bow.

I squeeze my eyes shut, shaking away the thought for I don't even know how many times today, and pain from my nose radiates through my face.

I've only been working with Odette for one day, and one thing is for sure—I'm already in way over my head.

CHAPTER SIX

Odette

I can't remember the last time I was so thoroughly embarrassed, and that includes the previous two disastrous weddings I planned.

First Noah got an up-close-and-personal look at my favorite pair of underwear.

Then he busted his nose because I needed toilet paper and threw me out of his house.

And that doesn't even include the wipe of shame I had to do in front of the spider that I'm pretty sure is still sitting in Noah's bathroom, waiting for its next victim.

I have half a mind to sacrifice myself.

Anything to escape the complete awkwardness of the Stevens family dinner.

This get-together happens every other Saturday or so, and it includes the Stevenses, me, and my mother, who has been best friends with Izzy's since they were kids. Any other night, I wouldn't be bothered to be here. I love our dinners. This place is like a second home to me.

But then again, normally, the events of two days ago don't ever happen either.

I slide my eyes over to Noah as subtly as I can. He's been wearing aviator sunglasses all evening, making it obvious he's trying to hide something. Even when he's gone inside, he's not taken them off, and I know that because I've been watching him far more than I care to admit.

It's probably a good thing he's wearing them. If his mother saw the state of his face, she'd have a conniption. I know only because of the texts he sent the morning after it happened.

I pull my phone from my purse, looking over the exchange again.

Noah: image

Noah: You did this to me.

Me: Me? I'm not the one who made you run into a door.

Noah: Yes, you are. You should have just drip-dried, and I wouldn't look like I went ten rounds with Tom Wilson.

Me: Who?

Me: You know what? I don't care. It's not my fault. And for the last time, I can't just "drip dry"! WHY ARE YOU LIKE THIS?!

Noah: Because you made me like this.

Me: 🖕

Noah: I don't know how you did that, but right back at you.

That's the last we spoke to each other, but I know he's still sporting that bruised look under his sunglasses. He has to be.

"So, Odette," Lydia Stevens says, pulling my attention.

I tuck my phone away and take a sip of Mr. Stevens's signature drink of the evening—a peach mango Bellini. He switches it up every week, and it's adorable how much effort he puts into making each one fun, little umbrellas included. "Yes?"

"Iz was telling me about your ideas for the venue. She said you and Noah were working on revamping the barn. How's that going so far?"

"Uh, good. We made good progress the last time I was out there. We haven't worked for the last few days since . . ." I drag my eyes to Noah, who, while he looks *very* invested in cooking the meat, is definitely eavesdropping. I don't know how I can tell, but I can.

"Oh, right. He said he got something in his eye. It's why he's walking around with those silly sunglasses on even though it's far too dark out for them." Lydia says that last part a little louder and pointedly to her son.

He lifts his head and looks right at me. Sure, I can't see it, but I can certainly *feel* his stare. It's hot, and not in the fun kind of way.

"Hazard of the job," he says, then takes a swig of his cider. It's Glove Save, a dry and slightly bitter cider he makes at Stick Taps.

I will myself not to react since I know exactly what "job" he was doing when it happened.

I haven't told anyone about the incident, and I guess Noah hasn't either.

"Poor kid," Lydia says, like Noah is still a young boy and not a thirty-eight-year-old man. "I wish he'd take those sunglasses off and let his father look at it as if the man hasn't been a doctor for over twenty-five years. He's not retired yet."

Brian Stevens has been the town doctor forever. He was my doctor as a teen and is still my doctor today, but at the end of the year, he's hanging up his stethoscope and enjoying retired life. Not having him working in Port Harbor will be weird, but I'm excited about what's coming for Izzy's parents. They've been talking about buying an RV and traveling the countryside for years. Now they can finally make it happen.

Not that she'd ever tell her parents, but it's a huge reason Izzy is hurrying to get married. She wants to be settled down before they go off on their adventures and not have to drag them back here for the wedding. She's doing it all for them.

I wish she'd do it for her, though. She always had plans after college to go to Europe and backpack and find herself, but then things got serious with Craig, so she never did. I wonder if she would have followed through with that plan if they had never gotten together.

"He's just being Tough Noah like always, Mom. You know how he is," Izzy chimes in.

She's right. He's downplayed his injuries for as long as I can remember, like when he battled through the playoffs with a broken ankle *and* a groin tear.

But that's hockey players for you. They're built differently from the rest of us.

Sometimes they are a little *too* different—like being too stubborn to take their sunglasses off even when it's getting too dark to wear—but they are different.

"We all know how stubborn Noah can be." He snorts at my comment, and I glare at him. "Something to say, Noah?"

He shakes his head once. "Not a damn word, Odie."

It's the most he's spoken to me since I got here. Usually we're picking fights all evening just because we can, but he's been quiet tonight, which means I've been right about what's going on—Noah is avoiding me.

I've tried to get him to let me come help with the farm over the last two days, but he's refused me at every turn. I wanted to drive out to the cidery yesterday when he told me no again, but I didn't get the chance thanks to my meeting with a new florist running late. Still, even after, I had half a mind to show up and . . . and . . . well, I don't know exactly what I would have done other than demand he talk to me. But at least it would have been something.

"Odie." My mother laughs, pulling my attention away from Noah, who looks far too good each time he takes a drink from his bottle. "You always hated that nickname."

"And I still do," I say loudly enough for Noah to hear.

He ignores me. Or maybe he's focused on what he's doing as he flips the burgers over the flame. I can't believe his dad is trusting him to do that.

"Why'd we start calling her that again?"

"That would be my brother's fault, Elaine," Izzy says. "He found a dog collar at Disneyland and bought it for her, remember? Then he bet her that if she threw up on the teacups, she had to wear it for her school photo."

My mother snaps her fingers. "That's right. And our poor girl puked all over the place."

Everyone laughs as I sink lower into a gray Adirondack chair, casting a sideways glance at Noah, who is smirking as he rotates the brats, listening in on us.

That was such a different life back then. He was my best friend's somewhat famous older brother I had a crush on.

He certainly wasn't the Noah I know now.

"To be fair, chokers were making a comeback then. It was cute," Izzy says, trying to stick up for me as our mothers continue giggling over it.

She shoots me a wink, and I grin, but deep inside, I still feel mortified over it, especially since Noah was around to witness that whole debacle.

I dare a glance at him again, though I don't know why. It's like I can't stop looking at him, and I know it's because of what happened the other day.

I need to talk to him. Need to make amends. And I want back in on fixing up the farm. This wedding means far too much for me to leave it in Noah's hands. I have to make sure it's being done right.

"I'm grabbing another drink," he announces. "Anyone want anything?"

"I'll take another Bellini, please," my mother requests.

"And grab that bowl of chips, dear," his mother says.

He nods, then heads inside.

I find myself pushing to my feet and following behind him, mumbling a quick "I'll go help him" before taking off.

He doesn't need help. I know that, and Noah knows that too. But still. I want to talk to him alone for a moment. I want to make sure we're genuinely okay and that he's going to allow me to set foot on the farm again.

I sneak through the sliding glass door, and it snicks closed behind me.

He's standing at the fridge, doors wide open as he reaches for the six-pack he brought along.

"Let me see it," I demand, knowing full well he knows what I'm talking about.

He glances over his shoulder, not the least bit fazed by my sudden appearance. "No."

"Dammit, Noah." I walk farther into the kitchen. "Just let me see how bad it is."

"Not a chance. Get lost, *Odie*," he says as he pulls the pitcher of booze from the fridge and sets it on the counter.

I ignore him and shove myself in front of him, reaching for the sunglasses sitting on top of his busted nose.

Being the skilled former hockey player he is, he easily dodges my advances.

"Stop being such a pain in the ass."

"You're the only pain in the ass in this room," he counters. "Or should I say pain in the nose?"

I glare at him, then reach for the glasses again.

Yet again, he dodges me.

"Noah . . ."

His name comes out as a threat, but all he does is grin.

"Odie," he counters.

I reach for the glasses again, and I don't know if he's just too damn cocky for his own good or what, but this time I get them. My fingers curl around the thin piece of metal, and I yank them toward me.

My victory is short-lived because Noah snatches them right back, and we're suddenly fighting over them like they're the last breadstick in the basket.

I pull on them. He pulls harder.

He gives another tug, and the unmistakable sound of plastic breaking echoes through the kitchen. He holds one half of the glasses while I hold the other.

I guess there's no hiding now.

My eyes go straight to his face, and I gasp.

"Holy shit, Noah . . ." I rush toward him, my hands cupping his face. He tries to pull away from my touch, but I don't let him. "Stop moving."

He does.

"I . . ." I wince as I take in the purple, black, and blue bruises under both of his eyes. "I can't believe it's that bad."

"Yeah? I guess that's what happens when you run nose-first into a door because *someone* was scared of a little spider that didn't even exist." His jaw tightens under my grasp.

I run my finger near the cut on the bridge, the one that's still fresh looking, and he flinches like it hurts. *Of course* it hurts. It looks terrible.

"I'm sorry, Noah," I say, tearing my gaze away from his wounds and looking into pools of brown. "So, so sorry."

He says nothing, only stares.

We're standing so close that his warm breath, which smells like apples, tickles my nose. So close that I feel each breath he takes, his chest brushing lightly against mine. So close that I realize just how gorgeous his brown eyes truly are.

No, not just brown. They're more than that. They're russet and cinnamon and chocolate and toffee. Swirls of various shades, darker on the edges and lighter toward the pupils, which are definitely dilated.

Then those same eyes drop lower, lower, lower . . . right to my lips.

I don't know why I do it—maybe just to see his reaction—but I roll my tongue along them, even though they aren't dry.

Noah tracks the movement with laser focus, like he's scared that if he looks away, he'll miss something.

So I do it again, and he watches me just as closely.

Then suddenly he's not just *watching* closely—he's *getting* closer.

I don't move. I don't know *how* to move. I don't even know what's happening.

Is Noah Stevens about to . . . *kiss me*? Am I about to *let him*?

Yes.

The thought filters through my mind effortlessly.

Yes, I would let Noah kiss me. Yes, I would kiss him back. Yes, it would probably completely rock my world. And yes, it would be a colossal mistake.

But I don't care. I've wanted Noah to kiss me since I was sixteen and I realized that my feelings for him were not so innocent. I may have given up the idea of him doing it years ago, but it doesn't mean I'm about to push him away now that it's happening.

"What the hell?"

We spring apart like we've been caught doing something wrong and find Izzy standing at the back door, her hand over her mouth as she takes in Noah's face.

"What happened to you? Did you get in a fight?"

Noah takes a few steps back, putting distance between us like we didn't just almost lock lips.

Me? I'm busy looking anywhere but at my best friend as she comes barreling into the kitchen, her hands going to her brother's face.

"What happened?" she asks again, worry lacing each word. "And don't give me that same load of crap you gave Mom. You didn't get something in your eye. This is way worse than that."

I peek up at Noah just as he slides his eyes over to me.

Izzy doesn't miss it.

"Wait . . . this happened when you worked on the barn, didn't it?" Izzy gasps. "Oh my god, did you punch him, Odette?"

Before I can answer her, she's hitting her brother, yelling, "What did you say to her? I swear I will beat your ass if you were being a jerk to my best friend!"

"I didn't—hey! Watch the nuts, Iz!" Noah blocks her assault, covering his junk.

I'm only slightly ashamed to admit that my eyes follow right along with the gesture.

"Is this why you two are acting so weird tonight? Because you were being an ass to Odette?"

She noticed we're acting weird? Shit. Did anyone else notice too?

I realize then that Izzy is still hitting him.

"Iz! Stop it!" I pull her off her brother, and she comes away kicking and screaming—literally. "Calm down."

She shakes me off, brushing her hair out of her face. "I will *not*. Not until you tell me what happened."

"First, I didn't punch your brother."

"Yes, because that's what's important and not the fact that I didn't say a damn thing."

I glower at Noah, who is still covering his nether regions. "You'd best keep that covered," I warn him before turning back to Izzy. "He's right, though. Noah's been a perfect gentleman. It was an . . . accident."

"An accident? That looks like a pretty brutal accident to me."

"It felt brutal too."

I wince, remembering the loud thud Noah's nose made when he hit the door. I was certain Noah's nose was broken, and I'd need to drive him to the hospital.

I still think he probably should have gone, but I assume he didn't want to have to explain that to anyone, let alone his father.

"So what happened then?" Izzy asks.

"It's a funny story really . . ."

Noah snorts at me. "*Funny* isn't exactly the word I'd use to describe it."

I ignore him, then tell his sister what happened in the bathroom—from the lack of toilet paper to the spider ready to eat me to Noah slamming into the door.

By the time I'm finished, Izzy is staring at me. Not even blinking. Just watching.

"Iz?" I say.

Finally, she blinks.

Once. Twice.

Then she's gone.

No, not *gone*. She's just doubled over, clutching her stomach and laughing loudly.

"See? I told you it was funny," I say to Noah, who shoots daggers at Izzy.

"It's not funny," he tells her, but it's useless. She's laughing too hard to hear him.

And Izzy's laughter makes *me* laugh, too, making Noah angrier.

His lips pinch together. Wrinkles bracket each narrowed eye. And I swear the few gray hairs at his temples double in numbers.

"If you don't stop laughing, I'm telling Mom it was *you* who scratched her Volvo and *not* a cart in the grocery store lot."

That sobers Izzy up instantly.

I remember that summer. Noah was here during a hockey break, and he brought Chelsea with him. She was driving Izzy bonkers with her nitpicking of everything Noah did, so Lydia let us take the Volvo to the market for some ice cream to get us out of the house. When we got home, there was a giant scratch down the side of the vehicle, and we swore up and down that it was like that when we came out of the store, a cart not too far away.

Not that I would ever tell anyone this, because best friends don't rat on each other, but it wasn't a cart.

Izzy tried squeezing into a parking spot she couldn't fit into, but she ran the car right alongside one of those yellow concrete poles, scraping the passenger door.

I guess Noah knew the truth all along.

She points at her brother. "You wouldn't dare."

"Try me," he counters, puffing his chest out.

It's all so ridiculous, and I feel like I'm in high school all over again, especially the part where I just let myself get swept up in a fantasy about Noah Stevens kissing me.

I must have been imagining it. I had to have. No way was that going to happen.

"Okay, okay." I step between them, holding my hands up. "You're both done. You're too old to run and tattle to your mother. Now let's figure out how we'll cover Noah's face, since he clearly doesn't want anyone asking questions, and his sunglasses broke."

"Fine," Izzy says, casting one last menacing look Noah's way. "I have some sunglasses in my purse you can borrow. Come on."

Noah follows Izzy out of the room, and I exhale heavily once they're gone.

Not just because I no longer have to keep them from killing each other, but because I'm glad to be rid of Noah.

I can't believe I actually thought he was going to kiss me. I can't believe I would have let him.

And I can't believe Izzy nearly caught us.

How terrible would that have been, especially when she made it clear she doesn't want me dating her brother?

I mean, not that kissing him would mean dating him, but still.

I shake the thoughts away, grab the pitcher of Bellinis, and head back out onto the patio.

"Oh, Odette! We were just talking about you," my mother says as I walk outside.

"You were?" I refill her glass, then Lydia's. I leave mine untouched as I set the pitcher on the table and settle back into my chair. "Anything good?"

"That's what we're wondering. Are you bringing a date to Izzy's wedding? If not, I think I have the perfect guy to set you up with. He's a nurse at the hospital in Belleflower."

It wouldn't be the first time Lydia has tried to set me up with someone from our neighboring town's hospital. And it wouldn't be the first time I've turned her down.

"Thanks, Lydia. I appreciate the thought, but I don't have time to date, what with planning the wedding *and* my maid of honor duties." *And avoiding the Chambers curse,* though I don't say that part out loud.

She nods like she understands, but it's not her I'm paying attention to.

It's the look in my mother's eye that she's always given me whenever I brush off dating.

Pity.

But she, twice divorced, understands better than anyone why I can't date. She's the same way I am. She's also given up on love.

"I suppose that makes sense. Maybe you can get together with him sometime afterward? I'll tell Brian to pass on your information."

"I'll do whatever she asks," he says from the grill, lifting his tongs into the air like a salute of sorts.

I grin. If anyone would make me want to be in love again, it would be those two, but I know just how mean the Chambers curse can be, so I don't. I don't want love. I just want to help others find their happily ever afters. I might not get my own, but damn, it feels good to be part of someone else's story . . . even if things don't always go the way I hope. It's still nice to bask in the happiness, if only for a short while.

A wave of worry hits me once again. Am I doing the right thing in helping Izzy with her wedding? The curse has already affected so many of my clients. Do I truly want to pass that bad juju on to my best friend?

Stop, Odette. It's not the curse. It's not you. Izzy will be fine.

I exhale a breath just as Izzy and Noah stumble back onto the deck, laughing like they weren't just about to maim each other inside.

"Nice glasses," Brian remarks to his son. He exchanges a glance with his wife. They say a lot without speaking a word, and again, I'm envious of them.

I push that feeling deep down, along with all the doubt clawing at me, sip on my Bellini, and spend the rest of the evening pretending that I didn't want Noah Stevens to kiss me.

CHAPTER SEVEN

Noah

I was going to kiss Odette.

My lips were a mere inch away from hers. All I had to do was lean in just a bit closer, and they would have collided. I would have finally learned if all that sass she gives off makes her taste sweet or salty.

My money is still on sweet, but I'll never get the chance to find out because my sister ruined the moment.

I'm as pissed as I am relieved, especially since I shouldn't want to kiss her at all.

Yet . . . I do.

I wish I could say running into a door and messing up my face because of her turned me off, but that'd be a lie. If anything, it's gotten worse. She's been on my mind more often than not these last two days, and not just because every time my face aches, I think of her.

It's more than that, but I can't seem to place my finger on what that *more* is.

Still, I won't be crossing our carefully placed lines, no matter how enticing they are.

"Pass me that plate, will you?"

My dad's words knock me out of my stupor, and I reach for the serving dish and hand it to him.

"Thanks, kid," he says as if I'm not a grown-ass man. "You doing okay?"

"Yeah, Pops. Why do you ask?"

He shrugs. "I don't know. Those silly damn sunglasses covering what I know is most definitely not a work accident, for one."

"Just don't want to worry Mom, you know?"

He nods. I'm sure he understands. She might be a little desensitized thanks to all the horror stories from his years as a doctor, but I'm her son. It's different.

"Probably smart. Just make sure your sister gets those shades back. I don't feel like hearing about how you stole them for the next . . . oh, gosh, how long has it been since you took her Taylor Swift CD? We still haven't heard the end of that."

"Because I did *not* take it."

All right. Fine. I took it. But it was for the team. We were on a hot streak, and for some reason—I still don't know why—"22" became our locker-room anthem. And because I had a superstition about needing to listen to my Walkman before puck drop, I stole Izzy's CD so I could get pumped for games.

I'd do it all over again too. We won the Cup that year, and it was—and still is—worth her bitching.

"Whatever you say, kid," Dad says with a knowing smirk.

I look away because if I don't, I'll laugh, and then he'll really know I'm guilty. My attention goes straight to Odette, just as it has all night.

She doesn't know, though. She's too busy regaling my mother, hers, and Izzy with a tale about how she got into the movies free with a no-cost upgrade on her popcorn two weeks ago by flirting with the ticket attendant.

I want to tell her I saw him give Ms. Barlowe—who is about fifteen years older than me—free tickets, popcorn, *and* a drink, but I don't bother. I let her have her moment.

Besides, she needs all the wins she can get lately, with how her business is nose-diving.

As much as I dislike weddings and all things lovey-dovey, I feel bad for Odette. She doesn't deserve it, and I know I shouldn't have ignored her these last two days.

I couldn't help it, though. It was easier to keep her away from the farm than to have her around, even if it was nice to have a helping hand.

She was a distraction, and I don't just mean because of her panties.

No, it was in the little things, like the soft grunts she made when she was lifting, the extra mayo she put on my sandwich because she knows that's how I like it, and how—even though it ended in disaster—I was the one she called for help.

It's silly that it delighted me as much as it did, but it's been a long time since I was anyone's hero.

Chelsea used to ask me to do all kinds of little things for her, like kill spiders or open jars. Then, one day, she stopped. Instead of asking me, she asked everyone else, then blamed me for always being gone.

She was right. I was gone a lot. But she knew that when she agreed to marry me. And instead of rolling with the punches and hectic life of a hockey player, she tried to change me and get me to quit the game I loved so much.

Worse? When I finally did retire—not for her, but for me—it still wasn't enough.

I wasn't enough.

No wonder we were divorced less than six months later.

So, yeah, even though I was the only option to help get rid of the spider, I was still an option, and I hate how much that meant to me.

"All right," my dad announces, holding up the tray of burgers and brats. "Dinner is served, ladies!"

They all clap, and he eats up the attention.

We move to the long table already set for dinner and pass around the food, filling our plates to the brim. Meat, potato salad, grilled corn on the cob, and green bean casserole go around and around.

We fall into easy conversation, which isn't surprising since we've been doing this for years. I missed many dinners when I was playing, but when I came back to Washington, it felt like I was never gone at all.

"I think you should do fairy lights all over the barn. Think of how pretty that will be at night."

Of course the conversation has turned to the wedding. That's how every dinner has gone since Izzy got engaged.

"Oh yes! I think it would be incredible. So romantic looking. What do you think, Odette?"

All eyes swing to her, and I can instantly tell she's nervous to be put on the spot. Her shoulders go rigid, her lips parting like she's lost her breath.

That's new. She's never been cagey about discussing weddings and details before. Part of me wonders if it's just nerves because of how her last few weddings have gone and her needing to save her business, or if it's because it's Izzy's wedding, and she wants it to be perfect.

I can't tell which.

"We can do whatever you want, Iz."

My sister claps excitedly, then deflates. "Ugh. I wish Craig were here so he could weigh in."

"Yes, where is my future son-in-law again tonight?" my mother asks.

"Work," Izzy answers. "He's trying to get ahead on his projects so we can go on our honeymoon unbothered, but it's really taking him away from the wedding planning. We're already short on time, so it's just stressful."

"Good thing you have the best wedding planner around." Elaine beams at her daughter, squeezing her arm.

Odette returns the smile, but there's a frailty at the edge that I'm not sure her mother catches.

Or maybe anyone else, for that matter.

Can't they see she's freaking out? Can't they see these bad reviews are crumbling her business? Don't they notice how she's barely holding on to her dream?

"Oh my god!" A loud gasp from my mother. "Your face!"

Izzy snorts a laugh. "He gets that reaction from all the ladies."

I flip my sister off and push my glasses—which have apparently slipped down my nose—back up as my mother rises from her chair and rounds the table to me.

I hold my hands up in an attempt to ward her off, but it's no use. She snatches the sunglasses off my face, her eyes widening as she lets out yet another gasp.

"Noah Brian Stevens! What on earth did you do to yourself? Got something in your eye, my ass."

She glowers down at me, and I can't help it—the young boy in me comes out instantly as I slink lower in my seat, my shoulders drooping with shame.

"Sorry. I just didn't want to worry you, is all."

"Now I'm *extra* worried. What did you have to lie about? What was so bad that I couldn't handle it?"

I force myself not to look at Odette. I *really* don't want to rehash this whole ordeal yet again. It was bad enough with Izzy earlier.

"Nothing was bad about it. I just . . . I got a little disoriented and ran into my bathroom door. That's all."

"Disoriented? Disoriented?! What's wrong? Are you sick?" She presses the back of her hand against my forehead. "You don't feel hot. Did you pass out? Were you dizzy?"

"Mom!" I yell, pulling away from her and pushing to my feet. Literally anything to get away. "Stop it. I'm fine. Totally fine. Not dizzy, not sick. Nothing. Maybe disoriented was the wrong word."

She puts her hands on her hips. "Don't you yell at your mother, Noah. You might be grown, but I'm still your parent."

I sigh, running my palm over my face. I wince when I hit my nose, which prompts my mother to launch at me again, but I ward her off.

"I'm sorry, okay? I didn't mean to yell. I'm just— Would you knock it off?" I say to Izzy, who has been cackling loudly this entire time.

She doesn't bother listening. She just laughs louder.

I roll my eyes at her antics. Of course she finds this hilarious. I'm sure I would, too, if this were anyone else, but it's not.

"I'm sorry, Mom," I tell her again. "But I'm okay. I promise. It's just a bump and some bruises. Nothing is broken. I've sustained worse injuries playing hockey."

She shakes her head, and I know I've successfully distracted her. "Tell me about it. I still can't get the sound of you colliding with that guy from the Carolina Comets out of my head."

I never told her this because I didn't want to worry her, but it took me a long time to stop thinking about it too. The hit came in my second-to-last year from Adrian Rhodes, a beast of a man and a player, and knocked the wind out of me so badly that I couldn't finish the game. It was clean, but it hurt like a son of a bitch. I ran into him and his wife at a charity thing a few months later, and we all had a good laugh about it.

"See? So, this?" I point at my face. "It's nothing. It'll be gone in a few days, and we can all joke about how dumb I am for forgetting I have a bathroom door."

She tips her head, considering me for a moment. Eventually, she nods. "All right. Fine. Just . . . don't lie to me next time, all right? I can handle it, no matter how gruesome or ridiculous it might be."

"I won't. I promise." I hold my hand out. "Can I have the sunglasses back? Elaine doesn't want to look at this ugly mug while she enjoys her dinner. Do you, Elaine?"

"Oh, me? Please. My first husband was a boxer. I've seen it all, honey."

Still, my mother hands me the sunglasses, but not without one last sad glance.

"Leave your brother alone, Izzy," I faintly hear my mother say as she resumes her spot at the table.

But I'm not paying them any attention. I'm looking at Odette, who is staring at me with the same amount of remorse she had in her gaze earlier.

I ignore it, sliding the glasses back into place.

Remarkably, we finish dinner without another incident, and as always, the kids clear the table while our parents chill on the patio.

"You got this, right?" Izzy says once we're inside the kitchen. "Come on, Odette."

"Wait, what?" Izzy pulls her toward the living room. "Where are we going? We have dishes to do."

"*We* do not. Noah's doing dishes tonight."

"He is?" She looks at me. "You are?"

I nod. "Yep. That was our deal. I got to borrow the sunglasses if I took over dish duty."

Her mouth drops open, taking in the mess before us. "Are you sure?"

I shrug. "It's no big deal."

She looks like she wants to stay and argue, but Izzy is dragging her from the kitchen before she can.

"Come on. Let's go talk wedding details," my sister says, having no problem leaving me behind to clean this mess up.

I sigh, then get to work, listening to them giggle in the other room. Guess Odette's shaken off whatever nerves she had earlier.

I push up the sleeves of my old hoodie and fill the sink with soapy water to wash the things that can't go in the dishwasher. After setting out the drying pad, I toss the dishes into the sink and start scrubbing.

My mind wanders to all the things I still need to do and all the time that is passing way too fast.

I need to finish tearing out the old wood in the barn and replace the roof, build a new chicken coop so Tootsie can *finally* stay put, and get that pasture mowed in the back so it doesn't look like we half-assed things. And, of course, run the bar. Ezra's been holding down the fort for the last few days while I recover, but I can't expect him to do it alone. We might have a robust staff, but we're partners for a reason. We live and breathe that cidery, and not a day goes by that at least one of us isn't there.

Thank fuck I got the tractor moved to the side of the barn already, knocking at least something off my to-do list. Ezra told me last night that kids were already playing on it and wanting pictures all day yesterday. I guess Odette was right about keeping it.

That's not all she was right about either.

As much as I don't want to use the cidery as a wedding venue, she may be onto something. Word is already spreading around town. Three people stopped me on my way to my parents' to ask about it. That tells me this thing will be much bigger than I anticipated.

"Want some help?"

The wooden spatula slips right out of my hand into the water, splashing it up onto my hoodie.

Odette smiles slyly, knowing full well that was her fault, then shrugs and settles beside me. She grabs a towel from the top drawer and begins drying the dishes already on the pad.

"What happened to Izzy?" I ask after several quiet moments.

"She went home to be with Craig. I swear she's lovesick over him." She rolls her eyes, and I agree with her sentiments. "I'm sorry again about the glasses. I didn't realize Izzy made the deal that you'd have to wash all these dishes by yourself. That's . . . that's . . ."

"Little sister behavior at its finest?"

Odette laughs. "Yeah, I guess it is."

I shrug. "It's fine. I kind of like washing dishes. I know it's not really good for the environment and whatnot—wasting all that water—but I find it soothing."

She tips her head at me. "That is . . . not something I expected from you."

"Why?"

"I don't know. You're a big tough hockey player. I didn't think you'd find something so gentle, so soothing."

"Would you believe it if I also said I like to crochet?"

Her eyes widen, and her mouth drops open. "No way."

I laugh. "You're right. I don't. I don't even know what crocheting really is."

"Fair enough. I'm not sure I could tell you the difference between knitting and crocheting, but my nonna could. She makes me a scarf every year for Christmas. They're always hideous, but I wear them anyway."

I know exactly the scarves she's referring to, and they are ugly.

Still, I like that she wears them for her grandmother. It's like what I used to do for my mother, who would buy me the most atrocious-looking tie every December. It didn't matter, though. I would still wear it to the game, even knowing I'd be photographed, because it made her smile.

"So," she says, wiping the towel inside my mom's favorite wooden bowl, "are you going to avoid me forever, or do I get to come back to the farm to help with the barn?"

I lift a brow. "You want to come back after what happened last time?"

She shrugs. "Sure, I do. It wasn't me who ran into the door."

"No, it was just your fault that *I* did."

She huffs like *I'm* the one who is wrong. "I don't want to get into it again. Can't we just say that we're *both* at fault and call it good so I can come back?"

I want to tell her no. I want to push the issue and tell her I don't need her. To piss her off so badly, she doesn't *want* to come back, because I can't afford the distraction.

But that's not what I say at all.

"You can come back."

"Really?!" She claps, far too excited about the idea of manual labor.

"Yes, *but*—and this is a big *but*—if you get in my way or injure me again, even accidentally, then you're out. We're on a tight schedule. I can't afford to lose any more days."

"I still think it wasn't my fault at all"—her lips twitch because *of course* she's arguing—"but all right. That sounds fair." She holds her hand out between us. "Shake on it?"

I pluck my hand from the water, sliding it against hers, not bothering to dry it.

We shake once, then twice, and I try not to pay attention to how soft her touch is beneath mine.

She's the first to pull away, flexing her hand at her side, like she can still feel my touch and is trying to shake it away.

Or maybe it's just the water still clinging to my hands, and I'm overthinking things.

You're the one with the problem, Noah. Not Odette.

"FYI, I won't be in tomorrow, boss," she says.

What the . . .

"But you just said you wanted to come help."

"I know, but tomorrow's Sunday." She shrugs like that explains everything and doesn't elaborate any further.

I don't bother asking questions either.

We work together silently to finish the rest of the dishes and clean up the kitchen, and I can't help but notice the space Odette keeps putting between us, like she's afraid to get close to me. I both hate it and love it.

Love it because I really shouldn't *want* to be so close to her. There's no reason to be.

But I hate it because, well . . . I *do* want to be close to her.

I try to push it out of my head while I put the last of the dishes away, then give the counters a good wipe down. It's overkill, but my parents have taken care of me my whole life. This is the least I can do to repay them.

By the time we're done, it's pushing eight, and I'm beat.

Apparently, so is Odette. She lets out a big yawn, which only makes *me* yawn.

"Knock it off," I tell her.

"Sorry," she says through a second one. "I didn't get much sleep last night. Beans thought it would be a good idea to dig her paws into my stomach at three in the morning. Then again at four. She's lucky she's cute."

"I hear you. Tootsie starts waking me up every morning around five to get her feed. She is not so cute. Just lucky I don't put chicken on the menu at the cidery."

"Noah! Stop threatening to eat your pets!"

"She's not a pet."

"She has a name. She's a pet."

I don't continue arguing with her, because it's no use.

I hitch my thumb toward the back door. "I'm telling the parents bye, then heading out. You staying?"

"No. I have to get up early tomorrow for breakfast, so I'll go with you. Just let me grab my"—she swallows thickly—"purse."

I almost forgot about her underwear. Almost completely let the whole incident from the other day slip from my mind.

But now . . . now it's back, right in the forefront.

Pale-pink lace. Red hearts. A matching bow.

Fuck. When am I going to stop thinking about that? When am I going to move on? It's been days at this point. There's no reason for me to still be hung up on them. To be hung up on *her*.

Odette comes back into the kitchen, purse tucked tightly under her arm, avoiding all eye contact with me.

Guess I'm not the only one still thinking about it.

"Let me guess," my mother says, pushing to her feet as we walk out onto the patio, "you're heading out?"

"Sorry, Mom. I have an early morning. The farm doesn't take care of itself."

"My baby boy, the farmer." She shakes her head with a smile. "Never thought I'd see it."

"Me either." I wrap my arms around her, giving her a quick hug, then kiss her cheek. "I'll see you next weekend."

"Boy, you'd better see me before that."

I chuckle at the warning in her tone. "Yes, ma'am."

I move on to Elaine, then my dad.

"Let me know if you want me to take a look at that nose," he says in my ear. "Be our little secret."

I nod. "Thanks, Pops."

"See you tomorrow, kiddo!" Elaine calls to Odette as we're walking out to our cars.

She sends her mother a wave as I push open the gate for her. She gives me an extra-wide berth, making sure not to brush against me.

Really? That's how it's going to be now?

Annoyed, I make sure to walk extra close to her between the houses, and she notices and steps to the side.

I follow.

She moves.

I chase.

"What the hell are you doing?" she asks after the third time.

"What am *I* doing? You're the one being weird."

"I am not."

"Are too."

"Are not!" She groans. "Ugh, you're making me sound like a child."

"Then stop acting like one. You keep moving away from me every chance you get."

"Because you're . . . you're . . . you're being a butthead!"

I roll my lips together. "A butthead?"

"Yes!"

She huffs, then speeds up, which only makes me laugh. I have at least seven inches on her. Catching up to her is a breeze.

She rolls her eyes when I do. "You're so annoying."

"So annoying, yet you still want to come work with me on the barn."

"I don't *want* to. I *have* to. Someone needs to supervise you."

I know she's just being stubborn, and she doesn't mean in the same way Chelsea used to think I needed supervision because I couldn't complete things to her liking, but it still sucks to hear.

"And you've volunteered for the job."

"What can I say? I like giving my time to charity." She shrugs. "I'm a Good Samaritan like that."

"Sure you are." I open the door to her BMW, which earns me another eye roll. "What? I'm being a Good Samaritan."

"Are we done here?" she asks, lips thinned into a straight line.

"We're done here."

"Thank god," she mutters, sliding into the driver's seat.

She grabs the door, trying to pull it closed, but I stop her.

She huffs. "What is it now, Noah?"

"I just . . . I wanted to tell you something."

Except I don't have anything to share. Not really. Truthfully, I'm delaying our good night because I don't want to say good night. I'm tired as hell and need to sleep before my early morning tomorrow, but I also want to banter with Odette more. I want to push her buttons. I want to see what makes her tick. Get her to sigh and roll her eyes and admit the reason she's acting weird is because she wanted me to kiss her.

But she won't do that. I know she won't.

"Well?" she prompts when I don't say anything. "Spit it out. I don't have all night, you know. I have things to do and weddings to plan. *You* to get away from."

I decide to go with the first part—pushing her buttons.

"Nice panties, Odie."

One. Two. Three.

That's how many seconds it takes for her cheeks to turn a deep red. For her eyes to widen. For her entire body to freeze as she stares up at me in complete shock.

"See you Monday," I say simply, like I didn't just knock her entire world off its axis.

I toss her a wink, close her car door, and head to my truck.

By the time I'm backing out of my driveway, Odette still hasn't moved.

I can't help but be satisfied that it's all because of me. It's her turn to stew.

I'm done thinking about Odette Chambers . . . and her pink panties.

CHAPTER EIGHT

Odette

As much as Saturdays are for dinners at the Stevenses', Sundays are for breakfasts with the Chambers women.

Every Sunday, we meet at the diner, take up two tables, and gab for hours until we're all talked out.

It's my favorite day of the week.

Not just because I love my family, but because these are the only other people who truly understand what I'm dealing with—the curse.

They all live it themselves, so they know how challenging it can be, and why it's because of the curse that my business is failing. Or at least that's what I choose to believe because there is no way I'm *that* bad of a wedding planner . . . right?

"He was bald! His profile picture showed a full head of hair, but I swear, that man could have been a cosplayer for Mr. Clean, especially since he wore all white." My aunt Krista shakes her head as she recounts the fiasco that was her latest date. I keep trying to tell her this is what happens on dating apps, but she won't listen. She's determined to find someone. She's one of the few of us who haven't given up on love completely.

"All white to a pizzeria? Is he a supervillain or something?" my mother says. "I'd have dropped sauce all over myself in the first five minutes. Everyone knows the pizza at I Heart Pizza Pie is extra saucy."

"That's what I thought. And honestly, I wouldn't have cared if he were bald. I think bald men are sexy. What I didn't like was being lied to about it. I should have seen it coming, though." She crosses her arms over her chest, sitting back in her seat. "All men do is lie."

Unfortunately for my aunt, her only "marriage" was to a man who was already married. He bled her bank account, then fled the country with his actual wife and two kids. It was a whole huge thing and shook our small community. There was even national media coverage.

Now, though, she's back on the dating scene, and it's going about as well as any of us expected—poorly.

That's the curse for you, though. It's been like that for all our lives, and it's clearly not going to change anytime soon. Some of us find moments of happiness, but it's never true. It's never lasting.

As much as I try to deny it, I want true. I want lasting.

"Someone else tell a story. Mine is making me sad," Krista says.

At once, everyone at the table looks to me.

"What?" I ask, blinking at them. "I'm not dating anyone right now."

"Or ever again," my cousin Lucille remarks.

She's right. I don't plan to ever date seriously again. One-night stands? Sure. I'll have those to scratch my itches. But full-on dating? No, thank you. I'll pass.

Besides, I have bigger fish to fry, like making sure my business doesn't go kaput and that I don't go completely broke in the meantime.

I shrug, not a bit bothered by it.

Or at least that's what I keep telling myself.

If I weren't bothered by it, I wouldn't have been disappointed yesterday when Noah didn't kiss me. It was silly to think he was going to. I know that. And it was even more foolish to let myself *want* it.

Ugh, Noah.

Just thinking about him has my cheeks heating.

"Nice panties, Odie."

His parting words stayed with me all night long and were the first thing I thought about this morning.

It wasn't just *what* he said. It was *how* he said it. Like he'd been looking at them, and I don't mean a passing glance. I mean *looking* looking.

And I'm still not sure how I feel about that.

I do know that I'm nervous about spending time with Noah, and that's never happened before.

What if . . . what if I wasn't imagining things in the kitchen? What if he truly was about to kiss me?

No, no. Stop it, Odette. Stop getting your hopes up. You aren't a sixteen-year-old girl with a crush anymore. You're an adult. He wasn't trying to kiss you.

Right. It was nothing. Absolutely nothing.

"You're still a secret romantic like the rest of us. You wouldn't be planning all these weddings if you weren't," Aunt Krista says.

They all nod, agreeing with her.

"Am not."

"Whatever you say, dear." She takes a sip of her drink and flags down our server. "Another round of mimosas, Uli!"

"Coming right up, Ms. Krista."

I swear she blushes.

Maybe she's right. Maybe I am a secret romantic. I wouldn't be so in love with weddings if I weren't, right?

"You're too young to swear off love, little one," Nonna says from across the table like she can read my mind.

Little one, her name for me because I'm the youngest child of her youngest daughter.

"I'm not swearing off love," I lie to her.

"Hmm."

There's so much disapproval in one sound that it has me sitting up straighter, raising my chin. "I'm just . . . I'm focusing on my business, that's all. Now I just need one of you to find love so I can plan more weddings and generate more buzz for Chambers Charming Ceremonies. So, chop-chop!"

"Isn't that what Izzy's wedding is for? How's that coming, by the way?" Lucille asks.

She's right. That is what Izzy's wedding is for, and—not to get ahead of myself—I think it might be working. I've already received four emails from potential clients just since last week. Sure, they've all put stipulations along the lines of "we'll see how Izzy's wedding goes," but it's still *something*. A step in the right direction.

I hope.

"Good. Great, actually. I think I've found a new caterer and florist to work with, and more importantly, we found a venue."

"Where?" This from my other cousin.

"Stick Taps."

They all gasp, and it's not even them being dramatic.

Every person in this town knows about Noah's relationship with his ex-wife. The divorce was tumultuous, at least on her end. He tried to settle things civilly, but she wasn't having it. She wanted everything from him and then some.

I don't know the particulars of how they settled it, but I do know that whatever it was, it made Noah the grumpy man he is today. He'd always been a bit quiet and surly, but nothing like he is now. He was never anti-love, that's for sure.

"Oh, that's going to be beautiful," Lucille's mom says, hand over her chest. "That farm is just darling. Tell me you're using the barn for the reception."

Aunt Collette has always loved weddings like me, so I'm not surprised that's instantly where her mind went.

I nod. "We are. They'll be exchanging vows in the field with the Cascades in the background, then guests can mill about the cidery for a cocktail hour while the newlyweds take photos. We'll finish the night with a party in the newly renovated barn. I'm helping Noah work on it."

"You?!"

I glare at my cousin. "I don't appreciate that tone, Margie, but yes. Me. Why do you sound so surprised?"

Every woman at the table exchanges a glance, but it's my nonna who speaks up.

"Because you're *you*, Odette. You wore heels to the movie theater last week."

I open my mouth to argue, but then I remember, yeah, I did do that. And I looked damn good in them too.

But I don't see why that matters.

"Well, heels or no heels, I'm still helping him. I'm heading back out there tomorrow, actually."

"So you're telling me you're spending all your days with Noah Stevens?"

I glance at my other cousin, who is practically foaming at the mouth at the idea. "Yeah . . ."

"Ugh." She tosses herself back in her chair. "You're so lucky. That man is . . . he makes my lady bits tingly, that's all I'm saying."

"Jody Ann!" Aunt Krista chastises her daughter.

She just shrugs. "What? I'm just saying. You know it's true."

"Well . . ." Krista wiggles around in her chair. "He did grow up to be a fine young man."

"Ew. He's, like, forty," Lucille says.

"He's thirty-eight," I correct. Several ladies of the group raise their brows at that. "Not that it matters," I add. "But I'm just saying. He's not forty yet."

My mother makes a noise that has my attention swinging her way. She sips on her mimosa, looking anywhere but at me. Still, I can tell she wants to say something, so I ask her.

"No, nothing to say, *Odie*."

My cheeks heat, and I wish I could say it wasn't because of that damn nickname, but it is.

And Noah. It always leads back to him.

Luckily for me, the conversation turns to something else—Jody Ann and her new professor boyfriend—and I'm able to escape without any further questions about Noah.

He doesn't escape my mind, though. No, he's still right at the front, the same place he's been for days now.

"Nice panties, Odie."

I swallow the lump that's settled into my throat, then reach for my mimosa, hoping nobody notices my shaky hand as I replay the words in my mind over and over.

His deep voice. That not-so-subtle cocky smirk of his. It was too much. I have no idea how long I stayed sitting in my car staring after the spot he vacated, but it was long enough that by the time I got home, Beans was pissed at me for serving her dinner late.

I couldn't move, though.

"Nice panties, Odie."

He said it so casually, as if that wasn't a top-five most embarrassing moment of my life. And though I'm sure I was imagining it—just like I was when I thought he was about to kiss me—there was a sparkle in his eye. A *flirty* kind of sparkle. The ones you see in the movies when the hero is looking at the heroine with all the charm in the world and it's working.

God, did it work.

"You coming, Odette?"

I snap my head up, surprised to find everyone standing, gathering their purses.

Oh. I guess breakfast is over.

I missed the last half of it, my mind out at the cidery.

"Yeah, sorry. Just finishing this drink."

I tilt my mimosa back, even though the glass is bone dry.

Jody Ann's brows wrinkle, but she doesn't say anything.

I shove to my feet and slip my bag over my head. I reach inside and toss a twenty down for a tip. We might sit here for hours and drink far too many mimosas, but we always leave the server a little extra for having to deal with us. I'm convinced it's why they let us keep coming back.

Nonna leads us out of the diner as usual, and we all line up for hugs.

I'm sure we look absurd, like we're in some sort of funeral line, but it's what we've always done.

When I get to her and she wraps her arms around me, smelling like fresh-baked sourdough—which she's sort of famous for around these parts—I lean into her embrace, needing it far more than I realized I did.

"Don't give up, little one," she says so only I can hear. "I know you think we're cursed, but we're not. Maybe a little unlucky, but not cursed. Besides, if we are, we all know a curse can be broken with true love's kiss. Maybe that's all we're waiting for."

It's not the first time she's said something like that. She believes that all we need to do is find true love. That it's the real reason we're all still cursed. We haven't found real love yet.

I love that even after all the heartache she's endured, she's still so positive. Still so certain that love is out there for us and each and every one of us will find it one day, even if we have to kiss a few frogs in the meantime.

I might still be young, but after watching my grandmother, my mom, and each of my aunts and cousins get their hearts broken over and over, I have no faith for me.

I could be wrong, but it's going to take a hell of a lot to prove it so.

Seven came far too early this morning, and when my alarm clock went off, the last thing I wanted to do was peel myself out of bed.

But I did it anyway . . . eventually. I crawled out of my blankets at seven thirty, threw on a pair of shorts, a ratty old Anaheim T-shirt I used to wear to Noah's games, and boots I haven't worn in years. My first stop was coffee and breakfast, where I then ran into Peaches, who tried *very* hard to convince me that Beans needs a brother.

I checked my purse three times before I left, just to make sure she hadn't snuck a cat in there. She hadn't, thank god, but the whole interaction made me late.

I speed into the parking lot of Stick Taps and throw my car into park, slinging open my door just as Noah comes barreling out of the taproom.

"Figures you're late," he calls over his shoulder, on his way to the barn as I struggle to keep up with him.

"I'm here, aren't I?"

"I said be here at eight." He stops, turning on his heel as he checks the watch on his wrist. "It's eight thirty."

"Right, and I *was* here at eight, then I realized I had forgotten my pretty pink hammer, so I had to run home and grab it. I honked. Didn't you hear me?"

Noah looks like he's about to blow a gasket.

I'm lying. He *knows* I'm lying.

But still, he doesn't call me on it. He just huffs, then takes off for the barn again. I trail after him, holding my pink hammer and gloves in one hand and fresh coffee in the other, a bag full of fritters tucked under my arm.

Maybe if he stops being a grump, I'll let him know I brought him one too. *Maybe.*

"We're going to finish the roof, then start tearing down the stalls in the back," Noah says as he leads us inside. "While I'm working on the stalls, you can tap down the nails. A lot are sticking out just waiting to be run into." He looks down at the hammer in my hand. "Guess it's a good thing you brought your *pink* tools after all."

I grin up at him. "See? It was a good reason to be late."

"Never mind that I have extra hammers here," he mutters.

"What was that?" I take a loud sip of my coffee. "Can't hear you over this refreshing caffeine."

He rolls his eyes. "You got all that? Understand what we're doing today?"

"I heard you loud and clear, Captain."

I salute him, and he doesn't look the least bit amused by me as he turns, setting the toolbox he's been carrying on the floor. He just digs through it without another word.

Jeez. He's grumpier than usual today.

Maybe now would be a good time to mention the fritter.

"I brought you breakfast."

He pauses, then slowly turns toward me. "You did?"

I nod. "Yep. A fritter."

"Chocolate banana?"

I arch a brow at him, just like he did last week when we did this same song and dance. "Would it be anything else?"

I hold the bag of goodies out to him, and he accepts it, pushing to his full height.

I tip my head back, following him up, up, up.

Sometimes I forget just how tall Noah really is. And I forget just how attractive I find that.

I watch him as he practically tears the bag open and pulls a pastry free. He holds it out to me, but I shake my head.

"I already ate one."

"Yeah, but if you don't eat another, I will. Take it."

I don't argue. I accept it, then sit cross-legged on the dirty floor.

Eventually, Noah follows along, and I have to stifle a laugh.

"What?" he asks through a mouth full of food. If his mother could see him, I know she'd have something to say about his manners, or more accurately, his lack of them.

"Nothing. It's just . . . you're tall even sitting down."

"That's usually what happens when you're my size, pip-squeak."

"Hey! I am well above the average height for women. I'm just not a giant like you."

He shrugs, taking another bite of his fritter.

He really does look ridiculous, sitting crisscross applesauce, eating a fritter he could easily down in one bite. His usual flannel is replaced by a simple gray long-sleeve shirt that's already rolled up, showing off his forearms, which are far too good looking, especially as they flex every time he takes a bite.

I look away, taking my own small nibble of the breakfast treat I brought, even though I'm not hungry. Anything to distract myself. Anything to not have Noah occupying my thoughts like he has been every waking moment.

"Nice panties, Odie."

I internally scold myself for the reminder, then take another bite.

Noah scarfs down his first fritter, then the second in no time flat.

I've managed only four bites of mine by the time he's finished his.

"Are you about done, or are you going to nibble that like a rabbit the rest of the morning?" he asks as he stands. He grabs a tool belt, securing it around his waist. I swallow, telling myself I don't suddenly find men with tool belts hot. "We have shit to do."

"You're cranky today," I accuse, following him up. I don't bother wiping the dust off my bottom. I'm sure I'll get even dirtier by the day's end. "Good thing I brought you a fritter to cheer you up."

"Yes, the fritter that made you late and put us behind schedule."

I narrow my eyes. "And yet you're not cranky, right?"

"No. I just want to get started. I have other things to do around the farm, you know."

"Is this because of the report on Chelsea that she's marrying that quarterback?"

He comes to a halt, slowly turning toward me. "What?"

Oh. He hasn't heard. That much is clear from the look on his face. The shock in his brown gaze. The hard set of his lips.

I tuck a stray hair behind my ear. "I, uh, I figured you were extra crabby because they announced their engagement today. I saw it on Instagram this morning while waiting for my coffee . . ." I trail off as one of his brows goes up. "I take it you didn't know?"

He shakes his head once, then turns, going back to work like I said nothing.

I sigh. I have a feeling this is going to be a long, long day.

And I'm right. It *is* a long day.

Noah's in a bad mood, not uttering a single word my way, just cussing out the wood as he breaks down the old stalls. At some point he silently handed me a pair of safety glasses—I guess so nothing flies out and accidentally hits me—then went right back to work like nothing happened.

He didn't even stop for lunch—which I can't really fault him for, given our history—so I decided to work through it, too, not wanting to piss him off any more than I already had by being late and delivering the blow his ex-wife has officially moved on.

I'm surprised he's so upset by it. I didn't think he was still hung up on her, but maybe I had it all wrong about their relationship. Maybe he cares more than he's let on.

When it finally hits five, Noah throws a crowbar down, then the other one he's been using to bash in the walls of the old stalls. It doesn't take much work to break them down since they were already falling apart, but I can tell it's cathartic for him, anyway.

"I'm done."

I look up to find him with his hands on his hips, breaths coming in harsh as sweat rolls down his face.

"Oh?"

He nods. "I'm fucking starving."

"Well, maybe if you hadn't made us work through lunch, you wouldn't be," I mutter, tucking my hammer into my back pocket and peeling off my matching gloves.

"I didn't make *you* work through lunch."

"I wasn't going to stop working if you weren't. We're a team, remember?"

He mumbles something I can't quite catch.

I shove my goggles atop my head. "What was that, Mr. Grumbles a Lot?"

"I said, a forced team because, for some unknown reason, you're determined to help with this."

Frustration courses through me, and I do my best to tamp it down as I calmly say, "Because it's my project, too, Noah. I'm the wedding planner, remember?"

"Ah, right. And you need to save your *business*."

The way he says that last part, like the brand I've spent years building doesn't mean shit, hits me hard and, frankly, pisses me right off.

I've played nice all day. I've let him be grumpy. Allowed him to stomp around and be a sourpuss. But I will *not* have him talk shit on my business.

"You know, Noah," I say, taking a few steps toward him until we're standing only a foot apart, "just because you're a bitter old man doesn't mean everyone is like that. Some people want to make their wedding the best day of their life. Some people want happiness."

His eyes darken. "And some people just want to be a pain in my ass and get in my way."

Is that what he thinks I'm doing? That I'm just out here sweating my ass off and ruining my nails I pay damn good money for to annoy him? Have I not been going behind him and removing the debris he's been slinging everywhere? Have I not been on my hands and knees tamping down nails? Have I not been helping tear down old boards?

"You want to know why I'm helping you out here?"

"I already know why. It's because you don't trust me to do it right. You want it your way or the highway. Because it's never enough, just like it was never enough for her."

"Her? Who are you—" I shake my head. "You know what? It doesn't matter, because you're wrong. I'm not here for you at all. I'm here because everyone has their eyes on this wedding. If I fail, I'll just be another name in the long line of Chambers women who couldn't make it work, be it love or business or whatever. If I fail, I'll have spent years building this all for nothing. If I fail, then there truly is no hope for me. If I fail, the curse wins."

He scoffs. "Enough with the fucking curse already. It's not real—it's total bullshit, and you know it."

"Yes, it is!" I toss my hands into the air because *of course* he doesn't get it. Nobody else ever does. "Don't you see that? It's real. I went to college. I invested thousands of dollars into branding, an office, and all the right outfits to impress clients. I offered my services for free. I built my business on trust. I did all the right things—all of them—and I am *still* failing. I am one bad wedding away from everything I've worked for being ripped out from underneath me. So, no, I am not out here to *get in your way*. I'm out here for me and me alone. To prove to *myself* that I can do this despite the curse. That it *won't* win. That I will *not* be another name people whisper about. It has nothing to do with you, Noah, and everything to do with me."

I suck in a long breath when I'm done, not realizing how badly I need it or the way my hands are shaking at my sides. *When did that even start?*

Whatever. It doesn't matter. All that matters is that Noah understands that I want to help because I *have* to. This wedding has to succeed, or that tiny shred of hope I've held on to all these years about the curse being nothing more than just a string of bad luck will snap, and I'll be left with the reality—it's real, and I am destined to be alone.

Noah towers over me, staring down at me with that damn brown gaze of his. But it's not hard like before. It's softened. He's not grumpy anymore.

No, it's worse than that.

Now, he feels bad for me, and I don't want that either.

"Odette, I—"

"Uh, hey, guys. Everything all right in here?"

I whirl around to find Izzy standing in the doorway to the barn. Her eyes dart between me and her brother, brows furrowed.

Shit. I forgot I had planned to meet her at the cidery tonight. We were planning to go over some more wedding details, but now all I want is to kick my feet up and unwind after this.

"Yep," I tell her, glancing back at Noah, who still has his hands on his hips and hasn't moved an inch. "We're done here."

CHAPTER NINE

Noah

I'm being a dick.

Worse? I *know* I'm being a dick, yet I can't seem to stop.

Odette thinks it's because I'm angry over Chelsea getting engaged, but it couldn't be further from the truth. No, I didn't know about my ex-wife's engagement, but I still don't care. It's not why I'm pissed off.

I'm angry because every time I've looked at Odette today, I had to talk my dick down.

I know that's a *me* problem and not a *her* problem, but it still pissed me off.

I should be able to control myself. Just because she's wearing impossibly short shorts that damn near show off her ass cheeks and a T-shirt that hugs every single curve doesn't mean I need to react to it. It doesn't mean I have to want to peel each article of clothing off her.

And it certainly doesn't mean that I have to take my frustration out on her.

I'll admit, I didn't expect things to get so heated with her out in the barn. I had no idea that was why she was so invested in this project. It makes sense, though. I know the curse weighs on her. She might be a little flippant about it and crack jokes, but I see how it affects her. She fully believes this thing controls her destiny.

I wish she could see that it's not some curse. Sometimes things happen for no reason. Sometimes relationships don't work out. And sometimes good people, like Odette and the rest of her family, get the short end of the stick no matter what they do.

My eyes drift to her as she sits across from Izzy on the couch. One leg is tucked under the other, a notebook sitting on her lap and the cap of a pen lodged between her teeth. My sister is going on about something and Odette's listening intently, scribbling something on her paper every so often.

I have no doubt they're talking about wedding stuff.

Just because I said Iz could have the wedding here, I didn't mean I wanted them to plan it here too.

But after today, I don't have the heart to kick them out.

I screwed up. I shouldn't have let Odette think I didn't appreciate her help. I do, even if she is the most distracting thing on the planet.

When I see she's low on cider, I fill a new glass with Neutral Zone for her and a Face Off for my sister, then drop the drinks off to them.

"Thanks, Bubs," Izzy says, but I'm not paying attention to her. I'm looking at Odette, who avoids eye contact with me.

Fuck. I *really* screwed up.

Whatever, though. It's for the best.

"It's no big deal," I mutter, then sulk back behind the bar.

Even though I was out in the barn all day and am tired as hell, I'm still behind the counter helping out where I can.

If I'm being honest, I don't want to be home alone. All I'll do is replay the conversation with Odette, just like I did when I ran home to shower after our fight.

I couldn't stop thinking about the hurt look on her face when I said the curse was bullshit. How betrayed she looked.

Worse? I didn't even mean it. Not really. Not when I understand why she believes she's cursed. I felt like I was a few times during my career, which is why I built so many rituals. My pregame meal was always the same. My warm-up routine never wavered. I taped my sticks just so. Hell, I even measured my laces, so they were cut to an exact length. They were my own superstitions to keep my game where I needed it. My own way of taking control so that if I failed, I could at least say I gave it my all.

I miss those days sometimes. The rigidity of the schedule. The certainty of what the day would hold. And I sure as fuck miss the feeling of being on the ice. The calmness it brought me. The peace. I could use that right now, especially after my fight with Odette.

"You okay?"

I turn to find Ezra standing at the end of the bar, arms crossed over his chest, eyes hard as he watches me watch Odette. I didn't even realize I was looking at her again until now.

I quickly grab a towel and start cleaning a glass that doesn't need it—anything to make myself look busy so I won't be caught fixating on Odette.

"Yup. All good. Why?" I ask casually.

"Probably because you're staring at your little sister's best friend like you want to clear this place out and throw her on the table, then have your way with her?"

The glass goes tumbling to the floor, splintering into tiny pieces.

This bar is way too busy for him to be saying shit like that.

Several people look our way at the ruckus—including Odette and Izzy—and Ezra laughs as he walks behind the bar, grabbing the broom we keep stashed in a tiny alcove.

"What the fuck?" I say to him, taking the broom from his outstretched hand. "Why the hell would you say that?"

"Uh, because it's true."

"It is not." I cast a quick glance at the bar, making sure nobody can hear him. The only person sitting nearby is Uli from the diner, but he looks so invested in his phone that I'm not too worried about him. "Now shut the fuck up before I fire you."

"We're fifty-fifty partners. You couldn't fire me even if you wanted to, which you don't. You just don't like that I'm right."

"Shut up."

It's a juvenile comeback, but it's all that I have.

He is right. It's exactly what I want to do to Odette, and I fucking hate myself for it.

I sweep up the glass, dump it into a bag, then thrust it at my business partner. "Take this shit out."

He laughs, shaking his head at me. "Someone's in trouble. Capital *T* and everything."

"Ezra . . ." I growl.

He doesn't look the least bit threatened, laughing the whole way out of the taproom.

I go back to polishing my already-clean glasses, anything to act natural and not think about what he said. I replay that exact scenario over and over again in my head.

What would Odette say if I marched over and kissed her? Would she kiss me back? Would she beg for more? Would she let me kick every damn patron out and have my way with her on the coffee table I built?

Fuck, I hope so, and I hate that I hope so.

"Noah! Noah!"

I lift my head to find Izzy waving me over.

"Come here!" she calls.

"No!" Odette smacks her arm down. "Stop it, Iz."

Of course, Izzy ignores her, and all it does is make me curious.

I drop the towel I was using to wipe down the counter and make my way over there.

"Uh, yeah?" I ask, darting my eyes between my sister and a *very* grumpy Odette.

Dirt and grime from our barn duties still cover her crossed arms. Her hair is a wreck, pieces sticking out every which way, and the safety goggles I forced upon her earlier are still sitting on top of her head. I wonder if she even realizes it or if exhaustion has set in that much.

"Noah, tell Odette she can't come solo to my wedding."

The woman in question huffs, blowing one of her errant hairs out of the way. When it falls again, she shoves it back up. She seems startled when she touches the goggles. She pulls them off her head with surprise.

I guess that answers my question.

"Why?" I say to Izzy. "I'm coming solo to your wedding too."

"What?!" she practically screeches. "You are not!"

"Uh, yeah, I am."

"No, you can't." She looks at Odette. "*You* can't either."

"I'm kind of busy planning the thing. I don't have time to find a date."

"Then go with Noah."

"What?!"

I'm not sure which one of us says it louder, Odette or me.

Either way, we're both looking at Izzy incredulously.

She is officially out of her mind.

Me? Go on a date with Odette? Yeah, fucking right.

Izzy laughs. "You two are acting like I'm asking *you* to get married. It's just a date. One night. I don't see the harm. Besides, you'll both be in the same pictures with me anyway. It just makes sense."

"The harm is that I don't want to date Odette."

Odette looks up at me like she's offended. "Oh, I'm sorry. I didn't realize I was *so* disgusting that you couldn't possibly fathom dating me."

That's not at all what I meant. If anything, the opposite.

But I can't tell her that. Not in general, but certainly not with Izzy sitting right here. She might think it's harmless for her brother and best friend to go on a date for an evening, but it's not as meaningless as she thinks, especially not with my growing attraction to Odette.

So, no, I don't correct her. I let her continue believing that's the exact reason I won't be her date.

It's safer that way. Smarter. No risk.

"First of all, Odette is a babe, and you're an ass."

Odette makes a disgruntled noise. "You can say that again. He's been one all day."

Izzy gasps. "Is this because of your ex-wife? I saw she's marrying that football guy. He's hot." She waggles her brows suggestively at Odette.

I hate that Odette seems to agree, and I don't know why. I shouldn't care who Odette thinks is attractive at all.

"Why does everyone keep bringing that up?"

"Uh, because it's sort of a big deal. Chelsea has moved on, but you haven't."

I grit my teeth together at Izzy's comments. "Because there's nothing to 'move on' from. I was over the relationship long before we even got divorced. You know that."

"Then why haven't you been on a date since? And why won't you go on a date with Odette?"

"Yeah, Noah," Odette says, smirking up at me. "Why won't you go on a date with me?"

"So you want to go on a date with me?" I toss back at her, enjoying far too much the way her face falls with shock.

She never expected me to turn that back around and put her in the hot seat for a change.

"That's sweet. I'm touched. No, *flattered.*" I put my hand over my chest, returning that same cocky smirk she gave me. "But I don't think of you that way, darlin'. You're like a sister to me."

Her mouth drops open, and I can't help myself.

I reach out, tuck one finger under her chin, and push her mouth closed. "Better close that before you let a fly in."

Ezra's smirking at me when I walk back to the bar.

"What?" I bark at him, that same crankiness returning tenfold.

"Nothing." He shakes his head, still fucking smirking. "Nothing at all."

I wish I could say the rest of the night was a breeze, but everything that could go wrong did, and when I finally crawl into bed at nearly eleven, sleep eludes me.

And it's because of what I said to Odette and what a total crock of shit it was.

◆ ◆ ◆

"I'm up, I'm up," I grumble as I push back the heavy black comforter that I *really* don't want to crawl out from under.

But I have no choice—I'm being summoned.

Though small, Tootsie makes a hell of a ruckus if she doesn't get her feed by 6:00 a.m.

I check the clock on the bedside table.

5:55 a.m.

Yep, right on schedule.

I sit on the edge of my king-size bed, trying to coax myself to actually get up. I'm used to running on a shitty sleep schedule, thanks to all my years of traveling for hockey, but I thought I'd be done with that when I retired.

Clearly, I was wrong.

Tootsie clucks loudly again, and I finally push myself out of bed. I do my business in the bathroom, get dressed in my new uniform—jeans and a simple T-shirt—then head downstairs to start the coffeepot.

The hen might be in a hurry, but I am not leaving this house without some caffeine.

While it's brewing, I comb through the cabinets for something to eat. The only thing I can find is a protein bar. I have no idea how old it is, but I scarf it down anyway. I guess I'll be hitting the grocery store this morning before opening the cidery.

After the coffee is ready, I pour it into my favorite to-go cup and head outside.

Tootsie is at my feet in an instant, pecking at the tops of my boots.

"I know. You're starving." I crouch down to pet her. "Come on, then. Let's get you some food."

She darts off the porch and down my long driveway toward the farm. I trail behind her, chuckling at how fast she's moving. Nothing motivates her more than the promise of food, which is how she makes it all the way to my house every morning to make sure I'm up to feed her.

Truthfully, I don't mind it. The morning walk is nice, and it helps me start my day with a clear mind. There's always something so calming about walking between the big evergreens that line the road. It's not like the farm is far from town, but it feels hours away when I'm out here like this in the early morning, the fog rolling over the hills and through the trees. It's peaceful.

Something I can use more of lately since Odette started working at the farm.

We've been working together for a week and a half now with no incidents to report. No almost kisses, no running into doors, no black eyes or busted noses.

Nada.

I wish I could say we've found a good rhythm working together, but all it consists of is grunts—that's me—and sighs—that's all her. We barely talk. We certainly don't banter. We don't even share breakfast anymore. We just work, argue over silly shit, then go our separate ways.

I know it's because of what I said to her, that she's like a sister to me.

God, I wish I could take it back. Every damn fabricated word of it.

But I have to keep telling myself that until I believe it, especially since the days are getting warmer and her shorts are getting shorter.

I try to shake the thoughts from my head as Tootsie leads us into her coop.

I spread some food and collect the fresh eggs they've laid to add them to our egg stand before stopping by the pond to check out the goats. After, I head into the barn to get a list of supplies I'll need. If I'm going into town this early, I may as well stop by the hardware store. I grab the gas cans from the shed for the mower since I'll need to mow that pasture before it gets too out of hand. The last thing I need to add to my to-do list is cleaning up piles of grass before the wedding.

I've been doing that enough by tearing apart the barn. Every time I take something down, another issue pops up. I have no clue how this thing hasn't completely blown over in one of our windstorms. But I just know I'm going to build it back stronger than ever. I'm going to make this the best damn wedding this town has ever seen, and not just for Izzy.

Much like Odette wants to do this to show the town she's not a failure, maybe I want to prove I'm not one either. I may have failed at marriage and being the husband and man Chelsea wanted me to be, but I'm not going to fail at this too.

I don't have to believe in marriage, but it doesn't mean I can't make this place a damn good venue. Ezra was right that this could turn into something big for weddings.

When I finally make it back to my place, it's seven.

That's good. Everything will be open by the time I get into town, and I can get this all done before Odette shows up here in an hour.

I shoot Ezra a quick text as I'm heading out the door.

Me: Running into town. Need anything?

Ezra: 🖕

Ezra: For you not to text me before 8.

Ezra: And also, napkins. Our supplier isn't dropping them off until tomorrow, and we're low. Just enough to get us through today.

I shoot him back a quick "got it," then make my way into town in my truck, which was my parting gift to myself when I left the NHL. I figured if I would be working on a farm, I would need a big vehicle to haul stuff around in. I was right. This baby has saved us more times than I can count.

Ezra would never admit it, but it's way more useful than the swanky sports car he drives around. It makes him stick out like a sore thumb, but he doesn't seem to care. That's Ezra for you. He's never really given a shit about what people think of him.

I hit the hardware store and load up my truck with new boards, nails, screws, and shingles. I'm determined to get that damn roof done this weekend. Thankfully, it's summer, so we're in the drier months here in the Pacific Northwest. We haven't really had to worry about the rain too much, but I want to be prepared just in case. Besides, we're now down to just eight weeks to make this place perfect. I need to make some major progress—and soon.

I make sure to grab a few bags of feed for the chickens and goats too. The last thing I need is Tootsie getting pissed at me and running amuck all over the farm. Well, more than she already does.

Once I have all the lumber supplies I'll need, I pull into the gas station and grab the cans from the bed of my truck.

I'm just about done when I hear my name being called.

I turn to find Peaches . . . and a cat in her arms.

Oh shit.

The older woman is wearing a pair of wide-legged pants that look about three sizes too big on her, a flower-print shirt that could double as a dress, and her trusty gardening hat. Her long, nearly white hair flows behind her as she speed-walks my way, a pair of threadbare flip-flops making that obnoxious *thwack, thwack, thwack* with every step.

"Noah! Noah!" she hollers.

I yank the gas nozzle from the can, not caring about the fact that it's not yet full, and race to screw on the cap.

But I'm not fast enough.

"Hey," Peaches says, holding a tiny tuxedo-colored cat out to me. "Pork, meet your new dad, Noah."

I don't know if it's because I'm completely mystified by the name she's given it, or if it's just out of pure instinct, but I take the cat from her outstretched hands.

And dammit if the thing doesn't start to purr instantly, so small it fits perfectly into my palm.

"Aw, see? He likes you." Peaches scratches under the kitten's chin. "He's going to like living with you just fine."

"What? Living with me? New dad?" I hold the cat back out to the old woman. "Peaches, no. I can't take this cat."

"But you already did." She grins up at me, taking a step back. "And look how happy Pork is. I've never seen him so pleased before."

"Yeah, well, that doesn't mean much. He's had a short life." The little guy lets out a big yawn, as if he's as tired of Peaches's bullshit as I am. I thrust the cat at her again. "I can't take him."

"But you have to. He chose you." She takes another step back. "That's how this works. The cats come to me and ask me to give them a home, and I do." She points across the street in the direction she came from. "I was just over there, and Pork saw you and started meowing his head off. He knew you were his person."

"Peaches, that's absurd. Where are you getting all these damn cats?"

"Cats have sex, Noah, and from the sex comes new cats. That's how the animal kingdom works."

I can say with certainty that I didn't have talking about cat sex and the animal kingdom on my bingo card when I decided to come into town today, especially not before 8:00 a.m.

Yet here I am anyway.

"I understand that, but how are *you* always finding them?"

"Because they come to me." She tips her head to the side. "I'm not understanding what you're not understanding here."

"I—" I shake my head. "You know what? Never mind. I still can't take this cat."

I hold the kitten out, and once again Peaches takes a step away.

"I can't take them back. That's not how it works."

"Not how it works? I—"

"He's weaned. He's ready for the big boy food. All he needs is care and love. Good luck."

"Good luck? Peaches! Peaches!"

But my protests are fruitless. She spins on her barely there flip-flops and runs. Literally *runs* away.

And she's quick too. She's already across the gas station parking lot before I even fully realize what's happening—she's seriously leaving this kitten with me.

I stare after her, trying to figure out what the hell just happened and what exactly I'm going to do with this cat. I don't have the time or patience for a kitten, especially not now.

I look down at the little fella tucked into the crook of my arm, and he peers up at me with green eyes that are far too intense for such a young age.

"I guess you're coming home with me." *Meow.* "But don't get used to it," I warn him. "You're not staying."

Meow.

I huff, then toss the gas can back into the truck bed. With the cat curled up on the passenger seat, I steer toward the cidery, praying I don't get stopped along the way and get saddled with *another* cat.

To my surprise, Odette is already at the property when I pull up.

She's leaning against her old BMW, her hand curled around a to-go cup of coffee, a fritter clutched in the other. I already know she doesn't have one for me. She hasn't brought me one since the morning we fought.

It makes me regret what I said to her even more. Not because I want a delicious breakfast treat, too, but because it means she's being standoffish toward me.

The worst part is that I don't entirely blame her. I would be, too, after the way I embarrassed her like that.

I hop out of the truck, then reach inside and scoop up the little ball of black and white. He fell asleep about five minutes into the drive, and not that I'd ever admit it out loud, but it was very hard to keep my eyes on the road and not on him. He just looked so sweet curled up.

"What the . . ." Odette pushes off her car when she sees the kitten. "Peaches got you, too, didn't she?"

"I certainly didn't get him of my own accord," I grouse, trying not to be too charmed when the little thing nuzzles against me. "He's going back tomorrow, so don't get attached to him."

"Of course he is." But she grins. She grins, and I know exactly what kind of grin it is.

She doesn't believe me.

"He is," I insist.

"Uh-huh. Whatever you say, Noah." That fucking smile widens. "Can I hold him?"

"Be my guest. I have work to do."

She crams the rest of her fritter in her mouth, then takes the kitten with her free hand, snuggling him against her chest. "Hi, little baby," she coos at him. "Hi there. It's so nice to meet you."

I look away, focusing on getting the supplies out of the truck and not at all on how fucking adorable she looks holding him.

"He's so cute," she says softly, like she's trying not to disturb him. "What's his name?"

"Pork," I say through a grunt, pulling a heavy piece of lumber out of the pile. "Peaches said his name is Pork."

"Pork." She smiles down at him. "Well, it's nice to meet you, Pork. We're going to become very good friends."

And I'm going to be spending the entire day acting like I'm not jealous of a cat getting all of Odette's attention.

The worst part? It's nobody's fault but my own.

CHAPTER TEN

Odette

I've been cranky, and it has everything to do with Noah announcing to all of Stick Taps that I'm like a sister to him.

But I think Pork is healing me.

The cute kitten lets out a big yawn as he sleeps on his back in my lap. Beans will be so mad when I come home smelling like another cat, but I don't care. The scene before me is worth it.

"How can you not love this adorable little fella?" I run a finger down his tummy, and he shudders like it tickles.

"Because I have a heart of stone, and there's no use getting attached to it, because I'm not keeping it."

I gasp. "What do you mean you're not keeping Pork?"

"I mean, I'm not keeping him. End of discussion." He sighs. "Are you going to help me at all today or sit there and play with the damn cat that is most definitely finding a new home as soon as possible?"

I haven't been playing with the cat *all* day. Just most of the day. Since lunch, at least, and that was a few hours ago at this point. I likely could have left a long time ago, especially since I have a few vendors I need to call, but I didn't want Pork to be alone. And honestly, I didn't want to be alone either. Even though it's a Friday, I don't have much else going on at the moment except planning Izzy's wedding, and we're meeting to work on that more tomorrow.

"I'll take the second option, please."

"Then leave. You're in the way."

"Yes, I'm *so* in the way, just sitting here on a stool and minding my own business."

"You're right, you are."

I ignore him, then go back to rubbing Pork's belly. I giggle at that.

"What?" Noah asks with a grunt, pulling his hammer back in a way that shouldn't be even remotely hot, yet *definitely* is.

Noah's comment about his sibling-like feelings toward me were like a bucket of cold water, extinguishing any flame I held for him. It doesn't mean my body doesn't react to seeing him work. Watching him sling lumber around all day or swing heavy hammers like they weigh nothing.

Just like he is now.

I roll my tongue over my lips as he takes another whack at the board, the muscles in his biceps flexing with the movement.

"Odette?"

I snap my eyes to him, hoping he didn't just notice what a trance he had me in. "What?"

"That's what I want to know. You just giggled. What's so funny?"

"Oh. Um . . ." *Shit. What was I just thinking about other than Noah's incredibly sculpted body?* "Pork belly!"

He pulls a face. "What?"

"I was running my finger over Pork's belly, and it reminded me of pork belly. Do you think Peaches names all her kittens after food? Is that like a thing because *she's* named after food?"

Noah just raises his eyebrows in response.

I throw my hands into the air. "I don't know. I thought it was funny, and I'm bored."

"Again, you're free to go home."

"Really? You don't need any more help today?"

"Actually, he does."

We both turn to find Ezra strolling into the barn. His gait is stuttered as he strides toward us.

He didn't grow up here like Noah did, but everyone's embraced him as one of our own, which means we all know about the injury that knocked him out of hockey and left him with a slight limp. But I haven't seen him walking this stiffly in some time.

"Sophie's grandma fell and is in the hospital. I let her go to deal with that," he says, wincing in pain as he comes to a stop before us. "But our bartender needing to leave isn't the problem. We have a storm rolling in."

"We do?" I look to Noah. "We do?"

"I heard rumblings, but I hoped they would die out by now."

"Sorry to deliver the bad news, but it's getting worse, not clearing up. They're calling for high winds with gusts over sixty miles an hour. Heavy rain too. Not this pissing rain shit we're used to."

"Fuck," Noah says. "Shit. All right. Fine. Well, you can handle the taproom while I—"

"Can't," Ezra interjects. He points to his hip. "Got that doctor's appointment over in Seattle, remember? I can't miss it. I'd call up one of the production guys to take over while I'm out, but they're—"

"Not here. It's the last Friday of the month. Shit."

"What's the last Friday of the month?" I ask.

"We give the production team the day off because they have to pull Saturday shifts sometimes to meet demands," Ezra explains. "It's our way of rewarding them for all their hard work."

That's nice of them. Unfortunate for situations like this, but still nice.

The guys exchange a look of understanding.

Noah nods. "All right. Then I guess it is what it is, and I'll assess the damage after the storm. This might all be for nothing"—he taps the new piece of wood he just installed—"but oh well."

"What? No." I shake my head. "We aren't losing all our hard work."

"Then what do you suggest?"

"Me."

"You?" He laughs. "Uh, no."

I tip my chin up. "Why not?"

"For starters, you've never worked in a taproom before."

"No, but is it really that hard? People order; I pour. I take their money. How difficult can that be?"

He rolls his lips into a flat line, looking every bit like he wants to argue.

I'm surprised when he says, "Yeah, I guess it's not that hard."

"Good. It's settled, then. Odette, you're officially in charge," Ezra says.

"You hear that, Noah? *I'm* in charge."

He pinches the bridge of his nose—the same one still bearing a mark from his bathroom door—like he's utterly exhausted by me. "Just go inside, Odie."

"Be nice. She's doing us a favor. A favor *we* appreciate, Odette," he says pointedly to Noah.

Ezra's kindness shocks me. Not that he's ever been outright mean before, but he's even grumpier than his business partner most days. I'm not used to this side of him.

"Of course. Besides, it's not like I'm doing much just sitting here, anyway."

Carefully I lift Pork, loving the beautiful green as he peers up at me with tired eyes. "I'm sorry, little buddy," I say to him. "Hang out in this box while I go to work, okay? I'll check on you later, but it's work time now."

I drop him into a giant cardboard box—something left over from an earlier delivery—that I've turned into his room for the day. Inside is a towel for him to curl up on and some food I had in my car. I've been meaning to take it inside for Beans, but thank gosh for my chaotic brain, huh?

"You know where to find me if you need anything," I say, then head for the cidery.

From behind me, I hear the guys still talking.

"Where the hell did that cat come from?" Ezra gasps. "Oh shit. You've been Peached, haven't you?"

"Shut the fuck up, Ezra," Noah grumbles.

I laugh the rest of the way to the taproom.

The taproom is dead.

And by *dead*, I mean we've had all of two customers the entire time I've been in here. While this place is usually hopping unless something big is happening in the harbor, I'm not surprised with the incoming storm.

I've tried distracting myself with rearranging the taproom—moving a few tables here and fussing with some decor there—but I'm still bored. Which means I've been spending far too much time paying attention to Noah as he moves around the farm, trying to get everything ready for the storm that's about to hit at any time.

When the clock strikes five, and I haven't seen a single soul for forty-five minutes, I decide to call it a day and venture outside in search of him.

I find him at the pond, hands on his hips and looking entirely too damn good from behind.

His strong shoulders stretch his plain black shirt impossibly tight, and the wind whips his hair around like a model on a book cover.

"Listen here, Larry, you will get your little ass out of the pond, or I'm going in after you. Those are your choices. Either way, you're coming inside."

What the . . .

I walk closer and am surprised to find he's not talking to himself—he's talking to a duck.

Quack.

"I am being serious, Larry." Noah grabs the hem of his shirt as if to pull it over his head.

Quack.

"I mean it." He drags it up, exposing tanned skin that looks soft and hard all at the same time.

All I can do is stand there and think, *Don't listen to him, Larry. Make him go after you.*

Quack.

"I swear, I'll come in after you."

Do it, do it, do it, I chant in my head.

Quack.

But a dip in the pond isn't necessary, because Larry comes waddling out and goes straight to Noah.

He bends, running a hand over the back of the duck. "Fucking hell, Larry. You're a stubborn woman, you know that?"

Woman? I did not see that coming.

"But that's okay. My life is full of stubborn women, so I know how to handle them." He looks up and out at the dark clouds rolling in. "Even that obstinate . . . gorgeous Odette."

Gorgeous.

He just called me gorgeous.

Sure, he said I was obstinate first, but still. Noah Stevens thinks I'm gorgeous.

The teenager inside me likes that far too much. But the full-grown woman version of me? Oh, who am I kidding? She likes it too.

I clear my throat, and Noah whirls around. The second he realizes it's me, his brows pull low as he shoves to his feet.

"What are you doing out here? Who's in the taproom?"

I shrug. "Nobody."

"What the hell? You can't just leave the customers in there to go wild. You can't—"

"I mean literally *nobody*," I cut off his ranting. "Not a single soul has been in for over an hour, so I made an executive decision and shut down shop."

"You can only make executive decisions if you're actually in charge. Which you aren't, in case you were wondering."

"I believe Ezra's exact words to me were *You're officially in charge.* So that made me the boss, and, as the boss, I called it a day." I point at the sky, which I swear has grown darker in the last minute. "I think everyone's prepping for the storm, not worried about getting cider."

"You don't know that. People usually come to fill their growlers. Something to do when we inevitably lose power."

"*If* we lose power. We don't know that we will."

He gives me an unconvinced look, which I don't blame him for one bit. We've lost power for less, that's for sure. With the way these winds are already whipping and the fact that the worst of it hasn't even come through yet, I'd say we'll definitely be kicking it old school with candles and firelight tonight. Especially if that low thunder I hear actually turns into something. Thunderstorms are rare here—we lack sufficient humidity—but when they happen, they cause significant damage because people are unprepared.

"Were you really just fighting with a duck?" I ask, nodding toward Larry, who is staring up at us like she's watching Mom and Dad argue.

"Yes. She was being a brat."

I don't even bother trying to hide my smile. "Whatever you say."

He narrows his eyes. "Come on. I could use your help with the goats."

He leads us to their pen, Larry trailing behind us the entire way.

We work together to lock goats into their pen, then secure anything loose and keep the animals calm as the sky gets darker and darker, fighting the wind the whole time.

"Think this is going to hold?" I ask over a big gust.

The coop—which Noah planned to redo anyway—is struggling against the windstorm already. It'll be a miracle if it makes it through the night.

"It's all we can do on such short notice," he yells back. "Come on. Let's head inside. I felt a raindrop."

The second we step through Stick Taps' doors, the sky opens, and water pours from the clouds.

It's heavy and relentless, with more rain than we've seen in some time. Despite what most people think about the Pacific Northwest, the summer tends to be sunny and dry. We haven't been hit like this in a while.

"Jesus." I stare out the door as the sky brightens with lightning. "I really don't want to drive in this," I mumble.

"Good, because you're not going to." He stomps toward the bar, and I'm stunned by the finality in his words, almost like he would physically stop me from leaving if he had to.

"What are you doing?" I ask as he grabs a glass and sticks it under the Neutral Zone tap.

"Cartwheels. What the hell does it look like I'm doing? Getting us drinks."

I don't argue. Instead, I move to the bar, slipping onto a stool as he slides the cider toward me.

He pours himself a pint of Glove Save, then crosses one leg over the other and rests his back against the counter.

Just as I take a sip, the power goes out, and we're bathed in darkness.

I let out an involuntary squeak, and Noah laughs.

"Give it a sec," he says. "The generator will kick on."

As promised, the lights come back on within a few seconds.

I breathe a sigh of relief, and he doesn't miss it.

"You okay?"

I nod. "Yeah, just always feels so weird when the power goes out, you know? Eerily quiet."

"I know what you mean. I can't sleep for shit when it happens. Need some sort of sound. I used to bring a mini fan on the road for games. The noise always helped me sleep in those unfamiliar hotel beds."

"I don't know how you did that for so long. My bed is my best friend. I could never give it up so willingly."

"It's the only thing I hated about being on the road. I loved everything else. Exploring new cities and trying new food and drinks. Finding those little pockets of what made the city the city, ya know?"

He talks about it like he misses it.

"That sounds nice," I say. "I haven't been to very many places outside of Washington. Even when we didn't live in Port Harbor, we were still in the state. Anaheim is really the only place I've been for . . ." I trail off. He knows why I went to Anaheim.

For him.

"Do you miss it?"

"Miss what?" he asks.

"Hockey. Do you miss it?"

He takes a long, slow drink of cider before answering, almost like he needs liquid courage.

Finally, he looks at me, his brown eyes sadder than I've ever seen. "Every fucking day."

It comes out a whisper as if he's afraid to say it too loudly.

"I'm sorry, Noah."

I don't know what else to say besides that. I can't imagine giving up something I love so much. It's why I'm working so damn hard to save my business.

He shrugs. "It's fine. I mean, I had to hang my skates up at some point, yeah?" He shrugs like it's no big deal, but we both know it was. *Is.* "Besides, I've got plans to keep the game in my life."

Oh? I haven't heard him talk about that before.

"What kind of plans?" I ask.

"Ezra and I want to help train the next generation. We've, uh, we've been looking at building a rink. Somewhere safe to skate.

Somewhere they can learn without having to drive into the city like I always had to. We both know how expensive hockey is to play, so we want to offer something for kids who are interested in playing but whose families can't afford it. We potentially found a place, but nothing final yet."

It's not what I expected from him *or* Ezra. They're both so . . . closed off. Some might even say cantankerous. I never thought they'd care so much to help the kids like that.

I smile, imagining Noah and Ezra out on the ice with little kids, trying not to curse or get frustrated by their parents.

"What?"

"Nothing." I shake my head. "Just picturing it."

"Me playing hockey? You've seen it plenty of times before."

"No. I mean, you bossing the little kiddos around."

"I'm a great boss."

I snort out a laugh. "You're something."

"Hey, I was captain of an entire team for ten years. I know how to command a room."

"Sure you do, *boss*."

His eyes darken at the name, and I swear he's about to yell at me, but another loud clap of thunder has the bar shaking.

I jump.

I look at Noah, expecting him to have a comment or two about me being scared, but he doesn't. All I see is understanding.

"I hate storms," he says, and I wonder briefly if he's just saying it to make me feel better. Even if he is, I don't care. It's exactly what I need. "Especially at night when I'm . . ."

Alone.

He doesn't have to finish that. I understand it all too well.

Silence falls between us. It's not exactly comfortable, but it's not uncomfortable either. Still, I feel the need to fill it.

"Wonder how long the power will be out," I comment.

"Last I checked, the storm was expected to last until eleven at least. I'm sure we'll be low on the priority list for restoration. Why? In a hurry to get out of here?"

"No," I say honestly. Much like Noah, the last thing I want to do is go home and sit in my apartment alone while the storm rages on around me. I like the comfort of having someone else around too much. "I just need to text Izzy, make sure she can check on Beans while— Oh my god!"

"What? What's wrong? What happened?" Noah shoves off the counter, on full alert, as I hop off my stool and race toward the door.

"Pork!" I yell behind me. "We forgot Pork!"

Then I push through the front doors of Stick Taps and step into the storm.

Wind and rain pelt me, and I'm instantly soaked. I don't care, though. I care only about getting to the barn to grab the kitten, who is probably scared, uncertain, and desperate for warmth. It's freezing out here.

I can't believe we forgot about him. I can't believe we abandoned him.

My feet feel heavy as I sprint to the barn, and I know it's because the ground is waterlogged, and the parking lot already is one big mud pit.

When I finally reach the barn, I skid to a halt, my feet slipping in the wetness, and I fall to one knee.

It doesn't matter, though. I pull myself up and wrench open the door. I hear the kitten as soon as I step through.

I run to the box I left him in earlier, and tears spring to my eyes at the sight.

He's wrapped in the towel, his little face wet from falling into his food, probably. He looks so sad and so helpless. My heart hurts.

I scoop him up, holding him to my chest as he shakes in my arms.

"Oh, little guy. I am so, so sorry. We didn't mean to forget you. We just got distracted by everything else going on. But I'm here now. I'm not going anywhere."

I run my finger over his head, rocking him like a baby, praying he'll forgive me for leaving him out here all by himself.

"Odette! Odette!"

I hear Noah before I see him.

The doors are slung open, and he comes pounding into the barn, rain falling off every inch of him. His brows are pulled in tight as he scans the space, and they drop even lower when his eyes land on me.

"What the fuck, Odette?" he roars at me, stomping my way.

"The cat. We forgot about the cat."

His features soften as he takes it in. "Shit. We did, huh?"

"Yeah," I say softly, passing the kitten off to him. "I feel so bad."

He runs his finger over its head, and it's the most affection I've seen him give the creature. "Poor fella."

He holds it for a few moments, being softer and gentler than I've ever witnessed, before setting the little guy back into the box.

Then he doesn't look soft and gentle at all.

No. He's scowling at me.

He's mad. *Really* mad.

"What the fuck were you thinking?" he says through clenched teeth, taking a step toward me.

"The cat. I—"

"I don't fucking care. You don't just run out like that in the middle of a storm. It's raining its balls off. There's lightning. It's dark as hell out here. You could have gotten hurt." His eyes trail down to the mud covering one of my legs. "You *did*."

"I'm fine," I insist, even though I can feel a scrape hidden under the mud. I'm sure if I were to wipe it away, I'd find blood. "I was worried about the cat."

"Yeah?" He takes another step closer. So close I have to tip my head back to even look at him. "Well, I'm worried about *you*."

"What? Why?" Then it hits me. "Oh, right. Because I'm like a *sister* to you."

"That's not— I—" He squeezes his eyes shut, shaking his head once before opening them again, his gaze piercing right through me. "Odette, I— I didn't—"

"Mean it? Of course you did. Why wouldn't you? You see me as a little kid still and nothing more. You—"

"Lied!" he shouts. "I fucking lied, okay?"

His words stun me. They completely take me by surprise.

He . . . lied? He doesn't view me as a sister? Then what does he see me as? A friend? Or . . . more?

Does that mean . . . was he really going to kiss me in his parents' kitchen?

"I lied, Odette," he says softer this time. "I lied, and I'm tired of lying. I'm tired of pretending. I'm just . . ."

But he doesn't finish his sentence. He just lets the words hang between us. Words I have no idea what to do with.

The storm rages around us, the wind lashing against the old barn, thunder shaking the fragile building, and the sky brightening with each lightning strike.

My heart beats wildly right along with it.

Thump thump. Thump thump. Thump thump.

Noah looks like he's wrestling with something. What, I don't know. But his oak eyes are troubled, his breaths coming faster and faster by the second.

"What?" I ask. "You're just what?"

He runs his tongue over his bottom lip. "I'm . . ."

"Yes?"

Then he steps closer, and any distance between us is gone as he slips his hand behind my neck. His touch is warm, softer than I expected from him.

He stares at my lips.

"Noah . . . what are you doing?" My words are a mere whisper. Barely even audible.

Slowly, he drags his eyes to mine and says, "I'm saying fuck it."

Then Noah Stevens kisses me.

CHAPTER ELEVEN

Noah

She's sweet.

It's the only thing I'm thinking as our mouths move together as if they've met before instead of for the first time.

She tastes so fucking sweet, and not just because of the cider she was drinking in the bar. No, it's her. It's Odette.

Holy fuck, I'm kissing Odette.

Her lips are silky and pliable as I grab her waist, tugging her even closer. She melts against me, and I let her. Hell, I welcome it. She feels good. Too damn good. Like nothing I've ever felt before.

I slide my tongue over her lips, testing the waters, and she opens for me.

I waste no time slipping into her mouth, and she wastes no time rolling her tongue against mine. It's like all the barriers we were hiding behind have been broken, and we can't get enough of each other.

I can't get enough of *her*. Of how she smells like rain and that familiar floral perfume she always wears. How she tastes like apples and strawberries and something else so damn sweet I don't think I'll ever be able to name it.

How she feels pressed so tightly against me.

There's no way she doesn't notice how rock hard my cock is. No way she doesn't know just what she's doing to me.

Odette fists my shirt like she's afraid I'll disappear, and I slip my fingers under hers, desperate to touch her. I'm unsurprised that her skin is just as velvety as it always looks.

She shudders, her whole body vibrating in my arms at the simple touch.

I go higher and grin when she softly grunts as I press my thigh between her legs. She rocks her hips against me as our mouths continue to move together, so in sync that I can hardly believe it.

I've never kissed anyone like this before. I've never *felt* anything like this before. Not even with my ex, and I *married* her, for fuck's sake.

It was never like this. Never so good. It never made me feel like the earth was spinning, yet everything once askew was righted all at once.

I inch my touch upward, needing to feel more of her, and I relish the way goose bumps break out across her skin. How her fingers dig into me even harder. How she's pressing even tighter against me until I can't tell where either of us begins.

Somewhere in the back of my mind, I know I should stop this. This is Odette. A woman who is twelve years younger than me. A woman who is so off-limits, it's not even funny. Someone who drives me absolutely wild.

I *should* stop.

But I don't.

If anything, it makes me want her more. It makes me want to lay her down on one of these old hay bales and see if she tastes sweet everywhere else too. See if I can make her moan. Make her beg for more. See if I can undo her just as she's undone me.

When my fingers touch the edge of her bra, she wrenches her mouth from mine, and the cold that hits me is so sharp it knocks my breath from my lungs.

Or maybe that was Odette too.

"Wait," she says on a gasp. "Wait, wait, wait."

I stop, not moving another inch as I rest my forehead against hers.

"I just . . ."

But she doesn't say anything else, and I don't say anything either.

I don't know what *to* say, even if I could talk, which I don't think I can. I can hardly breathe, let alone string together a full sentence.

I'm not sure how long we stand like that, but it's long enough that I realize she's shaking.

No, *trembling.*

I wish I could say it's all from the rain and the cold, but it's not. I know it's not. Because I'm shaking, too, and it's with nothing but absolute need.

"Are you . . ." I slide my tongue over my lips. They taste like her. "Are you okay?"

She bobs her head up and down at first, then it slowly shifts left and right.

Fuck.

I've pushed her too far. I've taken advantage of her. I shouldn't have kissed her. Shouldn't have touched her. And I really shouldn't want to do it all over again.

"Listen, I'm—"

"No," she says, pulling back and putting distance between us—too much distance.

She's backing away. Farther and farther, still shaking her head.

I take a step toward her. "Odette?"

"I'm sorry."

It's all she says before turning on her heel and doing the last thing I expect.

She runs.

I didn't sleep for shit last night. I tossed and turned, waking up every half hour or so until I finally just got out of bed.

I was up so early that I was already sitting on the porch with coffee in my hand when Tootsie waddled down the driveway, looking for food.

I have no idea how she escaped the shed I put her in last night, but of course she did. They should have named her Houdini instead.

"Ha. Beat you to it today," I say as she comes and pecks at my boots.

Cluck.

"Yeah, I know. I'm surprised I'm up first too."

Cluck.

"Why so early? I slept like shit."

Cluck cluck.

"What'd I do? Something foolish."

Cluck.

"I kissed Odette Chambers."

It's the first time I've said it out loud, but certainly not the first time I've thought about it.

I replayed our kiss all night. Over and over, trying to figure out what made it so different. All I could come up with? *Her.*

Cluck.

I look back at Tootsie, who is staring up at me.

"Where is she? She ran away."

Every part of me wanted to chase after her last night, but I didn't. I knew she didn't want me to follow her.

Instead, I stared after her for far too long. It wasn't until Pork meowed that I realized I was still standing in the middle of the barn, wet and cold and in desperate need of a drink.

So I bundled the kitten in the towel, trudged through the rain to my truck, and drove home.

The kitten, who has been by my side since, pushes to his feet and looks down at Tootsie.

I expect his hair to rise or for the hen to react poorly, but none of that happens.

No, the little cat jumps off the porch swing I've been sitting on since before sunrise and walks right up to the chicken like they're best friends.

Tootsie is apprehensive as Pork sniffs at her, trying to figure out exactly what she's looking at. But the chicken doesn't react. She just lets the cat explore and sort it out for himself.

After a few minutes of uncertainty, Pork sits beside Toots and meows. The chicken clucks in response, and that's what they do. They sit side by side as I sip on my coffee, the early-morning sun showering the land in light, chasing away the fog that flits between the evergreens.

I wish I could have slept better last night. Based on the limbs and debris in my yard, I can't imagine how rough it looks up by the cidery, which means it will be a long day of cleaning.

Maybe it's what I need, though—something to distract me from the thoughts that won't seem to leave my mind.

I pick up my phone to check for a response to the last text I sent Odette, but there isn't one.

I read through the messages from last night instead.

Me: At least tell me you made it home safely.

Me: Come on, Odette.

Me: If you don't answer me within five minutes, I'm driving to your apartment.

Her response came swiftly after that threat, though I wish it hadn't come at all.

Odie: Home. Don't send the cavalry. Need time.

And that was it.

I texted her again this morning to ask if she was okay, but all I've gotten so far is silence, which I'm sure I'll continue to get.

Fuck. I messed up. I messed up so damn bad, and now I don't know what to do.

If this were anyone else, I wouldn't care. It was just one kiss—big deal.

But it's not just anyone. It's Odette.

What the hell was I thinking?

Oh, right. I was thinking that she ran out of the bar into the storm with panic in her gorgeous blue eyes, and all I wanted to do was make sure she was safe. I was thinking that she did it to save a cat because of that big heart of hers, and it's the kind of selfless thing I like about her. I was thinking that she looked fucking beautiful, even soaking wet. I was thinking that I've been wanting to kiss her for far too long, and there was no time like the present.

I was thinking that, for the first time in my life, I didn't *want* to think. I just wanted to act.

I wanted to kiss Odette.

And I did.

Now it's clear she's not talking to me, and I have to live with that.

Once my mug is empty, I head inside with Pork trotting along behind me, trying to push all thoughts of her aside as I get ready for the day.

It works until I make it down to the cidery and my eyes go straight to the barn where I kissed the hell out of her.

Then, the only thing running through my mind was how soft she felt under my touch and the soft sounds she made as I kissed her. How she melted against me, how she pulled me closer.

And the look on her face when she realized what we'd just done and ran.

I tear my gaze away, focusing instead on all the damage.

As expected, there are limbs and debris all over the place, and a tree fell by the pond, making me glad I herded the ducks toward shelter.

The chicken coop is wrecked, and I've never been more thankful for the shed than now, sparing the poor hens from the carnage.

The goats are fine, their pen holding steady. I'm not surprised since it's newer than the coop and definitely newer than the barn.

I look back at the building again and decide to rip the Band-Aid off. I'll need to go inside and inspect the damage eventually. Might as well be now.

The second I step inside, my attention shifts right to the spot where I kissed Odette, and just like that, she's back at the front of my mind. Not that she ever really left.

I check my phone again just to torture myself, but there's nothing.

I pocket it and continue my inspection.

Miraculously, the damage is minimal. A few panels are missing from the sides—older ones I hadn't gotten around to replacing yet—and some water leaked in, but that's it. It's actually in damn good shape, all things considered.

Thank fuck, too, because I was worried we'd just spent all that time working for nothing and we'd have to start over, which would inevitably put us behind, which would mean I'd be disappointing my sister.

I can't do that. And I can't disappoint Odette, either, even if she isn't talking to me right now.

A low whistle has me turning on my heel.

Ezra stands just inside the door, his arms crossed over his chest. "Damn. This held up better than I expected."

"Yeah, me too. Guess they really don't make them like they used to."

He huffs out a laugh, something he doesn't do often. "There is a big tree down on the drive up, though. You can squeeze around it with some finesse, but we'll need to figure out what to do with it."

I sigh. "All right. I'll add it to the list." I flick my chin his way. "What are you doing here so early anyway?"

"Same thing as you: inspecting the damage." He takes a step, then winces. "And I couldn't sleep with this fucking hip."

He says that last part through gritted teeth.

My initial reaction is to feel bad for him, but Ezra doesn't want my pity. Drastic weather changes tend to irritate his joints, making his hip hurt worse. I'm not surprised he wasn't able to sleep either.

"Since we're both up, we might as well take advantage of it. I'll get started on the debris, and you do something with the tree?"

"Are you sure?" I ask him, not missing the pinch to his lips as he takes another step.

He shoots me a look, and I hold my hands up.

"Yeah, sorry," I say. "You're sure."

"Damn right I am. Besides, moving is good for me. Sitting still just makes it worse. It'll work itself out eventually."

It'll work itself out eventually.

Maybe that's what I need to tell myself regarding Odette.

She'll text eventually. Or stop by. Either way, the situation will sort itself out.

Besides, it's not like she can avoid me forever, right? We're working on the farm together. She wants to be here to save her business. She'd never abandon her dream.

Ezra and I spend the morning working on cleanup. By the time we open the cidery, it's not perfect, but it's a hell of a lot better. Plus, using the chain saw to break up the tree was fairly therapeutic, and I've barely thought about last night all day.

People come and go all morning, some even stopping to help with the cleanup because that's just how Port Harbor is, and we have roughly twenty customers in the taproom by two o'clock when Izzy waltzes through the doors. I'm surprised to find Craig trailing behind her. I know he's been working a lot lately and we haven't seen him around much.

"Noah!" he calls with a grin. "Good to see you, brother."

Brother.

He's taken to calling me that since they got engaged. I can't say I'm a fan of it, but it always makes Izzy giggle, so I allow it.

"Hey, Craig," I say, setting aside the plans I'm drawing up for the new coop. If I'm going to have to rebuild the thing, I'm doing it right, and I'm giving the girls a bit more space. With any hope, I can make it Tootsie-proof too. "How you been?"

"Busy." He sighs, slinging himself onto a barstool. "Working long hours a lot lately."

Izzy looks surprised by this. "I thought you were going to the gym after work?"

"Yeah, babe. That's what I mean. The gym is work, too, you know. How else do you think I get these muscles?" He kisses her cheek, and she giggles. She's always doing that with him.

As anti-marriage as I am, I'm glad my sister is happy. Nobody deserves it like she does.

"I hear you on the long hours."

"I'm sure you do with working so hard on the farm," Craig says. "It looks great. We really appreciate everything you're doing for the wedding."

I shrug. "It's no big deal."

I mean, yeah, I'm busting my ass making this place everything my sister could ever want, all while trying to run a business, a farm, possibly buy an ice rink, *and* have some semblance of a personal life, but whatever.

It'll all be worth it to see my sister smiling.

And for Odette too.

I swallow just thinking of her, then try to push her out of my mind just as quickly as she's entered it. The last thing I need to be doing is thinking of her in front of my sister. I worry she'll be able to read my thoughts, and they certainly won't be PG.

I'm not ready to divulge what happened between me and her best friend just yet, especially since I don't even know what it meant. Or if it meant anything at all.

"Can I get you guys something to drink?" I ask.

That's right, Noah. Work. Something to distract yourself.

"Oh, surprise me," Craig says. "I'm not picky."

It's one of my least favorite things customers do. I don't want to surprise them, because what if what they like isn't what I give them?

But I don't push it.

"Anything for you, little sister?"

"Water, please."

"She's my designated driver." Craig grins at her. "That was the deal if I came to this thing."

"What thing?" I ask as I turn around, grabbing a pint of Neutral Zone since it's our best seller, then a bottle of water for Izzy.

"Wedding planning."

Wedding planning? Does that mean *she'll* be here too?

Fuck, fuck, fuck.

I can't have her here. Not today. Not after last night.

I—

"Hey, you're here already!"

The glass I'm holding slips right from my grasp. I scramble to catch it, the other pints on the counter clinking together in the chaos.

"You okay, Bubs?" Izzy asks, not missing the commotion.

"Mm-hmm," I say over my shoulder.

I'm not ready to turn around. I know when I do, I'm going to see *her*. The woman who I know is so fucking sweet. The one I can still taste on my lips.

Odette.

"Bubs." Craig laughs. "Still not used to hearing *the* Noah Stevens being called *bubs*."

"Better than being nicknamed after a dog."

I turn around for the first time, and the blue in her eyes nearly knocks me on my ass.

And so does how nonchalant she appears. How unaffected she looks.

Where are the dark circles under her eyes? Or the apprehension in her gaze? Why does she look so goddamn beautiful when I'm a fucking wreck?

"Ready to get started?" she asks Craig and Izzy.

My sister claps excitedly. Craig, not so much.

He taps the bar twice. "Wish me luck, brother."

"Good luck," I tell him, but I can't help but think back to my own wedding and the lack of involvement I had in planning it. I wish I could have helped more, but Chelsea wanted to take control.

That should have been a sure sign of what would come, but I ignored it.

They make their way through the taproom, and I pretend like I'm not watching Odette's hips sway the whole way there.

She looks gorgeous today, but that's no surprise. Her dark hair is curled expertly, hanging loose around her shoulders. She's wearing a tight-as-hell black skirt. Add in the hot-pink heels she's rocking, and fuck, she's doing things to me she really shouldn't be.

It takes everything I have to drag my eyes away from her as she and Izzy put their heads together, looking over the gigantic binder she's pulled out of her bag.

They're at one of the longer tables near the back, the same one I walked in on Odette moving last week. She'd disappeared to use the bathroom, and when she was gone way longer than necessary, I went searching for her to find her messing around in here. She claimed she had to rearrange things for "aesthetics." We argued for five minutes on that until I eventually walked away and let her do whatever she wanted. I hate admitting it, but I do like the new layout. In fact, I've liked everything she's done in the taproom so far, from moving the tables and chairs around to redoing the decor on the walls to replacing our old board games without my permission. It's small stuff, but it's already making a difference with our customers.

"Worked the numbers again." Ezra walks into the bar from the back office with his laptop, setting it down in front of me. "Don't know what you're doing, but we're actually under budget on the barn."

"I'm not done with it yet."

"I know, but keep that up, and we might stay that way."

He closes the laptop, rests his back against the bar.

"They working on the wedding?"

"Yep," I say, still not looking away from Odette. Even though I should, I can't seem to make myself do so.

Or want to.

As if she can feel my stare, she looks over at me, and our eyes connect.

I lose my breath. It's like someone has reached right into my chest and has wrapped their fist around my lungs, squeezing so damn tight that I can't breathe even if I tried.

And damn, do I try. Yet nothing happens until Odette looks away, her attention falling back to Izzy.

I release the trapped breath shakily, and beside me, Ezra grunts.

"What?"

He shakes his head. "Nothing, man."

But the smirk on his lips doesn't say *nothing*. It says a lot.

And I don't know why I do it, but I find myself inching closer to him and saying, "We kissed."

Ezra doesn't react. Not a brow quirk or slackened jaw. Not even a twitch.

Did he hear me?

"We kissed," I whisper again, my eyes darting around to make sure nobody is paying attention. They aren't. Everyone is lost in their own conversations. "As in me and Odette. Last night."

"I heard you the first time," he says. "I'm just trying to wrap my head around why the fuck you thought that was a good idea."

I exhale heavily, running a hand through my hair that I did absolutely nothing with this morning. "Fuck, I don't know. I have no clue. I just . . . I did it."

"I know."

"What?"

"I know why."

"Yeah?" I huff. "Then tell me, oh wise one, why I fucking kissed my little sister's best friend?"

"Because you wanted to."

He says it so simply, like it's the only possible answer.

And he's right. I *did* do it because I wanted to, but I shouldn't want it. I shouldn't want her.

"I'm taking it Izzy doesn't know?"

"Not a clue." And I plan to keep it that way until I can figure out just what it meant.

He nods. "And Odette?"

"What about her?"

"How's she feeling about it?"

I don't know why, but I didn't expect Ezra to care about how Odette feels about it. He's not usually that kind of guy. Not that he's a dick—I would never partner with someone who truly is—but he's also not invested in personal matters. He doesn't like to talk about his life outside of work, which I appreciate about him.

"I don't know. She won't talk to me."

"Have you tried?"

"I texted her last night. She said she needed time."

"Then give it to her."

"I know. I know I need to. I'm just . . . fuck, man. I feel like I'm stuck on an endless merry-go-round. Like I'm being peeled out of my skin or some other weird sci-fi shit like that. I'm just . . . I don't know. I don't usually want to talk about my feelings and shit, but I need to know what she's thinking. She's not just some random person. She's . . . she's . . . *Odette.*"

He tips his head at me, watching me closely. *Too* closely. So much that it makes me feel like I'm naked, standing on a stage, and everyone is watching.

"What?"

"Nothing, man."

Except this time, when he says it, I don't give him any more ammo than he already has.

I keep my mouth closed and my head down. And I definitely don't try to talk to Odette, no matter how badly I want to.

She wanted space, and I'm going to give it to her.

Even if it does kill me in the process.

CHAPTER TWELVE

Odette

When Izzy suggested meeting here to get the preliminary seating chart in order so we could start mapping out the layout for the reception, it took everything I had not to scream into the phone.

Instead, I calmly agreed so as not to let on that there was a reason I couldn't be here today.

Now that I'm here and Noah stands a mere hundred feet away, I have major regrets.

I should have told her no and insisted we meet somewhere else, maybe at the diner. I take it over with my family every Sunday; why can't I do it again?

My eyes drift toward him, and I wish I could say it's the first time, but it's not. Far from it. Actually, I have no idea how Izzy hasn't said anything. How she hasn't noticed I'm watching her brother like a damn hawk and am barely paying any attention to what we're doing.

I know it's not fair to her. I should be more invested in this wedding than I've been in any other since I'm her best friend and maid of honor, but I'm not. I'm too damn distracted by the fact that I kissed her brother.

I kissed Noah Stevens.

I kissed my best friend's older brother.

And I really, really want to do it again.

It's all I thought of all night. He consumed my thoughts every time I closed my eyes. The way he looked at me like he was hungry and had never had a satisfying meal in his life. How he slid his knee between my legs, and I swear I'd never felt anything so damn good before. How he held me so tight, like now that he had me in his grasp, he was never letting me go.

I didn't want to let him go, either, but I did because the second his fingers grazed against my bra, I panicked.

Until that point, I was lost in a haze of lust. I was lost in *him*. I was lost in the fact that the man I'd been crushing on for over a decade was finally noticing me. It felt like a dream, and I never wanted to wake up . . . at least not until he was about to cross a line that we couldn't come back from.

Kissing is one thing, but going any further? We shouldn't.

No, Odette. Not shouldn't. Can't. *You can't afford to get your heart broken again. You can't get distracted by a crush that will go nowhere. Focus on your business. The curse is already destroying that. Don't let it destroy you too.*

I zero back in on the wedding planning and drag my eyes away from Noah, who looks entirely too good as he moves around the bar doing even the most mundane things.

"What if we put the deejay over here and move the gift table there?" Izzy points to two spots on the roughly drawn barn layout I sketched. "Then that would leave us more space for the dance floor on this side."

I think about the barn and its current layout, envisioning how it'll look once it's all done. "Yeah." I nod. "I think that will work nicely. Then we can do the cake table here."

"Yes," Izzy says, extending the word and kicking her feet excitedly as I label each table on the drawing.

I'm excited too. It's all coming together. Major progress is being made on the barn. And when I'm not rearranging the taproom, I've been booking new vendors, as many have reached out since they heard about the renovation. My bank account is no longer screaming at me, so it's definitely all looking up right now.

As long as I can get Izzy and Craig to nail down their seating chart, we'll be in perfect shape.

"Craig, any objections?"

When he doesn't answer, I look at him.

His nose is completely buried in his phone. He wasn't even paying attention.

"Craig?"

Izzy's voice knocks him out of his stupor, and he nearly drops his phone, barely recovering before it hits the table.

"Yeah, yeah. Sorry," he says, tucking his phone back into his pocket. "That was a work thing."

"On a Saturday?"

He smirks at her. "You're marrying a busy man, babe." Then he winks, and I swear my best friend melts in her seat.

I resist rolling my eyes at them and shove the sketch between them. "Well, Mr. Busy Man, any objections to the layout?"

He frowns. "We're having a deejay? I thought we were doing a live band."

"A live band?" Izzy sounds like this is the first she's hearing of it. "I thought we'd do a deejay. They're cheaper."

"Yeah, but are we paying for it?"

It's not the first time I've heard a groom say something along those lines, and it always annoys the crap out of me, but this time? It really bugs me. I know Brian and Lydia. I don't like hearing them talked about like that.

"You know what?" I push to my feet. "Why don't I let you two discuss this in private? I need to use the restroom anyway."

I don't wait for any objections—and may not get any since they're already locked in a heated argument—and make my way past the bar and down the hall to the bathrooms.

Truthfully, I needed more than a break from Craig and Izzy. I needed a break from Noah too.

I can't seem to stop myself from looking over at the bar with every noise he makes. Every time he laughs at something Ezra says, or every time he scowls. My attention keeps being drawn to him, and it needs to stop. I need to put our kiss out of my mind.

It will never happen again, so why bother obsessing over it?

I finish up in the restroom and pull open the door to find a dark figure leaning against the wall.

My heart leaps right into my throat, but not because I'm scared.

It's because of who it is.

Noah.

I look down the hall to make sure nobody is coming or paying any attention, but I really don't need to. It's dark down here. We're safely hidden.

"Hey, Odie." His voice is thick and quiet, and I swear it goes right between my legs, right to that spot he was pressed up against last night.

"Noah. What are you . . ." I swallow around the lump that's sitting in my throat. "What are you doing back here?"

"We need to talk."

It's the last thing I want to do with Izzy sitting in the taproom. She could walk back here and find us, and I really don't have it in me to try to explain to her what happened between me and Noah last night.

I shake my head. "No, we don't."

He scoffs. "The fuck we don't."

He shoves off the wall, stalking toward me.

If I were smart, I would flee. I could push right back through the bathroom doors and hide from him.

But I don't.

Instead, I stand frozen as he inches so close that all I can smell is pine and apple, and it's overwhelming, yet not enough.

"We kissed, Odette," he says like I wasn't there too. Like my lips don't feel permanently branded. "We fucking kissed, and you ran. What happened?"

"Nothing." I shake my head. "Nothing happened. I just . . ."

What am I supposed to tell him? That kissing him was a literal dream come true and also my worst nightmare, because how am I supposed to go back after that? Should I tell him that I've been crushing on him for years, and just when I felt I finally got him out of my system, he notices me? That I'm so damn scared to let anyone in, and it's all because of my family's drama that goes back decades?

I can't tell him any of that, so I don't.

"It was nothing, Noah."

He looks completely stricken, like I've just slapped him across the face.

He shakes his head. "No. No. That wasn't nothing, Odette. That was something. I was there. I know."

Then Noah Stevens kisses me. *Again.*

And I let him. *Again.*

He runs his tongue along my lips, and I open for him, loving the way he takes complete charge. He slips his hand into my hair, tugging me closer, and I go willingly. As if I could resist him at this point anyway.

"Fuck, Odette," he mutters against my lips. "You taste so good."

I taste good? He tastes good. Like cider and toothpaste, and I don't even know what else, but damn, it's addicting.

Then his lips are on me again, and his tongue is in my mouth, and I'm lost. So damn lost that all worries of us getting caught slip from my mind, and I allow myself to enjoy this. I allow myself to enjoy *him.*

Noah's other hand curls around my waist, and I love how it fits there like it's right where it belongs. His scuff scratches against my face, and I don't care that it'll likely leave a red mark. It's worth it for this feeling.

This wonderful, incredible, amazing feeling.

With one throat clear, it's shattered.

We spring apart like we've been doing something wrong, and we were. Something very, very wrong that felt so, so right.

I wipe my mouth—as if doing so will somehow erase what just happened—and find Ezra standing a few feet away.

"Just letting you know that they're beginning to wonder where you are," he says quietly. "So now might be a good time to break up whatever this is if you don't want Izzy—or anyone else in this town, for that matter—to know about it."

Oh god. How could I forget there's a bar full of people out there? That Izzy is out there? How could I have let myself get so wrapped up in Noah?

I dare a look at him, but he's staring straight ahead, posture stiff. His lips—the ones that were just telling me how good I taste—are pulled into a thin line. The red tinge on his cheeks is the only thing that gives away what happened.

"I'll be in the basement."

It's all he says before he walks away, leaving me alone with Ezra and staring after him.

His business partner sighs, shaking his head.

"What a moron."

That's what we both are.

"You okay?" Ezra asks.

I nod, even though I feel anything but okay. "Yeah. I'm good."

He points to his lip. "You might want to fix that."

Right. My lipstick. There's no way it's not smeared at this point.

"Thanks," I mutter, then duck back into the bathroom.

I stare at myself in the mirror, taking in the red splotches on my cheeks and little marks around my mouth from Noah's scruff. His hands messed up my hair, and his touch wrinkled my clothes.

I *look* just like I've been kissed thoroughly.

I don't know how long I stay in the bathroom, but when I finally make my way back to the taproom, Izzy and Craig are laughing and cuddling up next to each other, and a pang of jealousy courses through me.

I want something like that. I want someone to laugh with. Someone to cuddle. Someone to kiss, not just in the dark of night or in hallways.

I just want *someone*.

And even though I shouldn't, I want that someone to be Noah.

"Hey, there you are!" Izzy grins up at me.

"Here I am." I force a smile, then resume my spot. "So, did we decide?"

"Yep. We're doing a band."

I don't know why her answer disappoints me, but it does. She was so adamant about a deejay before. But whatever. It's not my wedding. It's hers. As long as she's happy, right?

The rest of the planning session feels like a complete blur, and Noah stays hidden in the basement, doing I don't even know what.

We finalize a few other key things, and I get a mile-long to-do list. I welcome it, needing the distraction because he's still all I'm thinking about even when I leave.

That's how it stays too. Throughout my appointment to get sized for my maid of honor dress, the phone call with the vendor for chairs, and the evening when I finally make it home and pop a cup of noodles into the microwave. Even when I crawl into bed.

Noah, Noah, Noah.

Noah and the way he kissed me.

Noah and how he uttered my name with his deep, husky voice.

Noah and how he hid in the basement, even after *he* was the one who said we needed to talk.

He's every one of my thoughts, which is why I crawl back out of bed—in my ridiculous pajamas with kissing dinosaurs on them and all—and slide behind the wheel of my car and drive straight to his house at ten thirty at night.

I shut my car off, but don't move to get out. Instead, I stare at the old farmhouse that could use a fresh coat of paint, trying to talk myself into getting out and going to the door.

I don't exactly know what I'm going to say or do. I just know this is where I want to be, and I can't sort out why, especially since it's the last place I should be.

After a while, the porch light flips on, and my heart rate picks up.

He knows I'm here.

A few minutes later, the door slowly opens.

Noah stands in the doorway, his silhouette illuminated by his foyer light. He crosses his arms over his chest, and even from here, I can see the hard set of his lips.

I don't know how long I sit staring at him before finally pushing out of my car and trudging up to the porch.

I take a deep breath, then ascend the stairs.

I only stop when I'm a foot away.

"Can I come in?"

He moves aside wordlessly, and I walk over the threshold and into his house.

The door clicks shut behind me, and I jump, the sound harsh in the quiet of the night.

He steps up to me, tugging at the jacket draped over my shoulders, and I allow him to take it. He hangs it on the hook beside the door as I go deeper into the house, toward the kitchen. My mouth suddenly feels dry, and I need something to drink. Or really anything to distract me from the fact that I'm at Noah's house.

I grab a glass from the cabinet, then fill it with lemonade from the fridge. I settle back against the counter and sip on it slowly.

The whole time, Noah watches me carefully, not saying a word.

I get it. I don't know what to say, either, but I do know two things.

One, I want to be here.

And two, I want to kiss him again. Or *again* again.

"What are you doing here, Odette?" he asks after a while.

I shrug. "I wanted to see you."

He nods like that's enough of a reason for him.

He stands in the doorway, his shoulder pressed against it and his hands in his pockets. He has no business looking so damn good in nothing but a gray T-shirt and black sweatpants. The moonlight filters in through the sheer curtains hanging over the kitchen sink, painting shadows over him in all the right places. All it does is make him look even more perfect, even with his dark brown hair a mess, almost as if he's been running his hands through it all day.

Is he more affected by our kisses than he let on earlier? Is this eating away at him too? Does he . . . does he want to kiss me again as badly as I want to kiss him?

A soft *meow* pulls my attention, and I'm surprised to see Pork trotting into the kitchen as if he's lived here all his life.

He kept the cat.

Mr. I'm Not Keeping the Cat kept the cat.

It makes me want to kiss him even more.

So I push off the counter and go to him.

He meets me halfway, his hands tangling in my hair, lips finding mine in the dark.

Although this is only our third kiss, it feels oddly like coming home.

I sigh against him as he slips his hands under my ass, lifting me off the floor with ease. On instinct, I wrap my legs around his waist, and I don't know where he's taking me, but it doesn't matter. I'd follow him anywhere at this point.

The coolness of the countertop stings, but all is made better as he fits himself between my legs. He kisses down my chin and over my neck. His touch is light, leaving behind the sweetest burning sensation with each feathery-soft kiss.

"Odette . . ." He says my name like it's a curse all on its own. "What are you doing to me?"

"Kissing you."

"Goddammit," he mutters, and it's the last thing he says before his mouth is on mine again.

He kisses me hard, and I kiss him back with just as much fervor. Sure, I've kissed him twice before, but it wasn't enough.

I'm unsure if it ever will be.

That thought terrifies me. The curse has already ensured that no matter how badly I wanted Noah, I could never have him. Not really.

Yet here I am, giving myself to him anyway because I can't help it. Because I want to.

Because damn the curse.

Damn the curse and all the heartbreak it's brought. Why can't this be different? Why can't Noah be different? Why can't I be happy too?

His hands find the hem of my nightshirt, and I nod against him, wanting him to remove it just as badly as he wants to.

He breaks our kiss to slide the material over my head and lets out a low hum of approval as he pulls back to look at me.

"Fuck," he whispers, and I laugh.

"Is that a good fuck or bad fuck?"

He drags his gaze away from my simple black bra and up to my eyes. "A good fuck. A *very* good fuck."

My smile is covered by his lips in an instant, his tongue finding mine again as his hands roam over me. It's almost like he's mapping out every inch of my skin, and I swear I could sit here and do this for hours.

But another time. Not tonight.

Tonight, I want more. I want *him*.

"Noah," I say when he kisses from my lips to my ear, grazing my earlobe with his teeth.

"Hmm?"

"Take me upstairs."

He pulls back, and there's no mistaking the apprehension in his gaze. "Are you sure?"

I nod. "More than sure."

I don't have to tell him twice. He drags me off the counter, and I groan when I rub against him in all the right places.

"You okay?"

"No," I whine. "I'm not okay. I'm not okay because I'm *dying*."

He laughs, then carries me up the stairs as if he does this daily. In the back of my mind, I know I should be worried we'll topple over, but I'm not. I feel safe with Noah. I always have.

He doesn't stop until we reach his room, pausing right at the threshold.

"This is your last chance, Odette. If we walk into my bedroom, there's no going back. I'm going to fuck you. I'm going to *take you*. I'm going to make sure you know I was inside you for days to come. So I'll ask again: Are you sure you want to do this?"

Am I sure I want to sleep with my best friend's older brother and possibly change the course of our relationship forever? No.

But am I sure I want to sleep with Noah, even though I know he's the same person? Yes. Yes, I am.

I lean forward, my lips ghosting over his as I say, "I am absolutely positive that I want you to fuck me, Noah Stevens."

A low groan rumbles from his chest, and he races into the room, dropping me onto the bed so quickly that I bounce back at him.

He flicks his chin toward me. "Off."

I know he's talking about my pants, and I waste no time pushing them off my legs and flinging them across the room. They land on his dresser, toppling something over, and I laugh.

And then I'm not laughing at all.

Noah pulls his shirt over his head, and it's the first glimpse I've gotten of adult Noah without a shirt on.

If anyone thought he might ditch his exercise routine after leaving hockey behind, they were wrong. He's still completely in shape, looking like he could lace up his skates and hit the ice like no time has passed.

He has his curtains and window pushed open to let the summer air in, and the moonlight streaming in is doing wonders for this moment, allowing me to see all of him. His broad shoulders, which I've spent far too many workdays staring at, seem even bigger, and his stomach is full of ripples. I can't even keep track of the number of abs he has.

When I reach his face, he's smirking, enjoying me checking him out far too much.

"See something you like, darlin'?"

It's cheesy—*so* damn cheesy—but I don't care. I'm in Noah's bedroom, sprawled out on his bed, and he's looking at me like he's about to devour me.

And I've never wanted anything more.

He places one knee on the bed, looming over me, and I'm captivated. Absolutely enthralled by all things Noah.

I couldn't move even if I wanted to, and I don't.

He sets his other knee on the mattress, then, slowly, he works his way up, trailing his fingers over my skin so lightly that goose bumps form in their wake. He doesn't stop until he's fit right between my legs, settling his hips against mine so he can capture my lips with his once more.

He kisses me softly this time. Less urgent than when we were down in the kitchen. Almost like he's savoring it. Savoring *me*.

Nobody has ever done that before. All my past experiences have been over quickly. We just get right down to business. No build up.

I want to be savored.

When he's had his fill, he kisses over my chin, down my throat, and right to the tops of my breasts, still encased in my bra.

Just when I think he's going to stop and kiss me there, he doesn't. He keeps going. Lower and lower and lower, tracing his tongue around my belly button and right to the top of my underwear—the same pair that started all this two weeks ago.

He pauses, looking up at me with hooded eyes.

"I'm trying to be patient, Odette. I really am, but I can't be anymore. I need to taste you. May I?"

Need to taste you. May I?

He sounds so polite, but there's nothing polite about his stare. About the absolute hunger in his eyes.

About the *need* in his voice.

I'm not about to deny him.

I let my legs fall open, a silent invitation.

"Thank fuck," he mutters, and it's the last thing he says before he disappears between my thighs.

CHAPTER THIRTEEN

Noah

I can't remember the last time I had such a desire to taste someone before. This overwhelming need to lick and kiss every inch. To commit someone's body to memory.

I nuzzle my nose against her pale-pink lacy underwear, the ones with the red hearts and matching bow—the same ones that have haunted me for weeks.

Sweet. That's how she smells, and I shouldn't be surprised. Odette always smells sweet. And if her lips taste it, too, then I bet her pussy will as well.

Patience, I remind myself. *Savor this. It might be your only shot.*

And it *should* be my only shot. I shouldn't pursue this. Hell, I shouldn't even be doing this now. I know that Odette is all hearts and flowers and love. She believes in it, even if she says otherwise. Helps orchestrate it even. And I don't want any part in forever with someone anymore. We want different things.

But none of that stops me. I don't think anything could at this point.

I take my time teasing her, kissing her everywhere but where she really wants me. The inside of each thigh, her smooth mound, even trailing down to her knees, and back up.

I do it until she's squirming against me, tilting her hips toward me in a silent plea.

"You're being a tease, Noah Stevens," she says, pushing up to her elbows and looking down at me.

"I am not, Odette Chambers. I'm taking my time."

She groans. "Can't you do that next time?"

I arch an eyebrow. "Next time? There's going to be a next time?"

She shrugs. "Depends on how well you do this time."

"Oh, a challenge, huh?" I smirk. "I love a good challenge."

Then I slip two fingers inside her panties, pushing them to the side, and I get my first look at her.

Fuck, she's beautiful. So pink and so pretty. So *wet*. She wants this just as badly as I do. Unable to stop myself, I lean forward and drag my tongue across her slit.

Fucking hell. I was right. She's sweet as sin, and I want more.

She groans, dropping back against the bed as I pull her underwear all the way off, then resume my spot between her legs.

I stop torturing us both and give in completely, losing myself in her pussy and loving every damn second of it. I suck her clit into my mouth, flitting my tongue over the sensitive bud, soaking up every little noise she makes.

God, she tastes so fucking good. Like nothing I've ever had before. I could spend a lifetime here and it still wouldn't be enough.

Her hands find their way into my hair, holding me closer as I eat her until I'm literally rutting against the bed, anything to relieve the ache in my cock. I don't recall the last time I was this hard. Maybe it's never happened before, but it's painful, and I want to come so fucking bad that I can't stand it.

But her first.

"Come on, darlin'," I say against her. "Give me what I want."

"And what do you want?" she asks through her panting, unable to stop being a smart-ass even when she's completely at my mercy.

It makes me want to watch her come undone even more.

"For you to come all over my face. Make a mess. Tell me who's making you feel so damn good."

"It's youuuuu . . ." The last word is dragged out as I suck her clit even harder, and she comes off the bed, nothing but harsh breaths and soft cries.

I smile around her, then flick my tongue, earning me another shaky exhale.

Sensing she's close, I slide a single finger inside her.

"Yes," she hisses.

I add another, hooking them toward me, and her pants grow louder and louder as I work her over with my tongue and my fingers.

"Noah," she says, uttering my name on a moan.

"That's right, Odette. Tell me who's in charge of this pussy."

"Noah, Noah, Noah."

She accentuates each word with a thrust upward, practically riding my face and tongue at this point, and I'm not mad about it. It's what I wanted, for her to make a mess all over me.

When I pull her swollen clit into my mouth this time, she's a goner, careening over that edge she's been so carefully teetering on.

I continue to lap at her as she comes down from her high, then kiss my way back up to her lips.

If she cares that I taste like her, she doesn't show it. In fact, she kisses me back hurriedly, like she's already aching for me again.

I'm aching for her too.

"Please, Noah," she begs in my ear as I bury my face into her neck. "Please fuck me."

I couldn't tell her no if I tried.

I slip out of bed and go to the bathroom for the condoms I bought almost a year ago when I thought I might give dating a shot again. That thought had quickly disappeared once I joined a few apps and immediately felt overwhelmed. The box has remained unopened since.

When I return, I take a moment to appreciate how she looks sprawled out on my bed. Her coal hair is a mess from writhing on the pillows, and her chest is red and splotchy, leftover evidence of her orgasm. Lips swollen from my kisses. Eyes glassy from lust.

She's a wet dream come to life, and I never want to wake up.

She smiles up at me, and if I didn't know any better, I'd say she's feeling a bit bashful under my stare. "What?"

"You're gorgeous, Odette. Absolutely fucking radiant."

Then I push my sweatpants down, taking my boxer briefs along with them.

I'm standing before her bare, and while I shouldn't be affected by this, having been in countless locker rooms in my day, I am.

Because nobody has ever looked at me like she is—like she can't get enough.

She swallows, her eyes on my cock that's sticking straight out. "I could say the same thing about you."

Fuck if that doesn't make my chest swell with some macho-pride bullshit.

"I want to taste you," she says, but I shake my head.

"No. If you do, I'm going to come right down your throat, and while that sounds like pure heaven, it's your cunt I want tonight."

She swallows, then nods, lying back down as I climb onto the bed, tossing the condom beside us as I fall between her legs.

I take my time revving her back up, kissing her until she's breathless before moving lower. I tug the strap of her bra down, tracing a line right to the cup and pulling her tit free.

Pink.

The same pink as her pretty little pussy.

I suck the hardened tip into my mouth, rolling my tongue over it as she squirms beneath me, searching for just an ounce of friction.

She's rewarded when my cock slips against her wet center, and we both groan.

"Son of a . . ." I try to catch my breath, choking on the rest of the words.

She feels so fucking good like this, and I want nothing more than to take her bare. To have nothing between us and to mark her.

But I resist, pulling away and grabbing the condom before I do something I can't undo. I rip it open with my teeth, then roll it over my cock, squeezing myself to stave off some of the pressure. If I don't, there's no way I'll last nearly as long as I want to.

I press the tip of my covered cock against her, my forehead resting on her own, and take a deep breath.

"Please," she begs when I don't move right away, and it's my undoing.

Slowly, I push into her, and the quiet gasp that leaves her might be my new favorite sound.

I give her a moment to adjust to me, then slide in more.

I do this over and over until I'm fully seated, and then it's *me* who needs time to adjust. Her pussy squeezes me so damn tight that it almost hurts, but it still feels so fucking good. *Too* good.

"This might be quick, Odette. I'm not sure how long I can last."

"That might disappoint some women, but I consider it a compliment." She kisses the tip of my nose. "Now fuck me, Noah, and make me feel you for days to come."

And I do.

I pull back out until just the tip of me is inside her, and I slam back home so hard that the headboard smacks against the wall.

We groan in unison, and then we're nothing but sharp breaths and groans as I pound into her over and over.

Her hands are lost in my hair, and I'm lost in her. So completely gone as I thrust into her. I've never felt so at peace before, and I'm not sure I ever will again.

"You're incredible," I say as I drop to my elbows, capturing her lips in mine, slowing my thrusts.

She nods against me like she agrees, trailing her hands from my hair down my back, her nails dragging against me. I love it. It feels like she's marking me.

I want to mark her too.

I kiss my way down her neck, sinking my teeth into her soft skin.

She hums appreciatively, and all it does is spur me on.

I suck on her harder as I drive into her with abandon. It's unsteady and hectic, but neither of us seems to care.

My orgasm builds, and I'm moments away from exploding. But I want her to come again. I want to feel her pussy squeeze me. I want her to milk me dry.

"What do you need?" I ask through heavy breaths.

She shakes her head. "Don't worry about me."

"Are you kidding? You're all I'm worried about right now."

I slip my hand between us, pressing my thumb to her clit, and she moans approvingly the second I do.

"This what you need, darlin'? You need my hands on you? You need me to touch this sweet cunt of yours?"

"Oh god," she mutters in my ear. "I'm so close. I'm—"

The rest of her words come out a garbled mess as her pussy squeezes me impossibly hard yet so fucking perfectly as she falls apart around me.

"That's it," I say as I rub her through her orgasm. "Come for me like the good little girl I know you are."

She moans and pants and begs for more, and I give it to her, not stopping until I'm spilling into the condom, and we're both completely spent.

I collapse beside her, trying desperately to catch my breath.

I can't move. Or at least I don't want to move. This spot seems as good as any to die.

"That was . . ." She laughs. "Wow."

"Yeah," I agree. "Wow."

That's all I can manage.

I just had sex with Odette Chambers.

I wait for the panic to set in, but it never comes, and I'm not sure how to feel about that either.

Maybe I'm just so blissed out that I don't care, and it'll hit me in the morning. Or maybe I just don't care anymore. I don't know, but that's a problem for Future Noah.

Odette slips from the bed, and I watch her go, loving how unashamed she is to waltz through the room stark naked. The moonlight glints off her curves, and I instantly want to drag her back to bed and fuck her all over again.

She comes back out a few minutes later, and I trade places with her. I get rid of the condom, then wash my hands before trudging back out to the bedroom.

She's curled up on her side, her eyes half closed and a small smile on her lips. I slide in behind her, tugging her close.

"Never took you for the cuddling kind," she says.

I'm usually not, but I don't tell her that. She already has enough ammunition to use against me for a lifetime.

She rolls over and then lays her head on my chest.

The room falls quiet, and her breaths start to even out as exhaustion sets in.

I'm nearly asleep when a thought hits me.

"You awake still?" She makes a noise, telling me she is. "Were those dinosaurs kissing on your pajamas?"

I feel her smile against me. "They were."

I chuckle, then kiss the top of her head. "Good night, Odie."

"Good night, Noah."

And I fall into the most peaceful sleep I've had in ages.

I'm unsure what I expected after sleeping with Odette, but an empty bed in the morning certainly wasn't it.

I run my hand over the spot next to me.

Cold.

She's been gone a while. I didn't even feel her move. The last thing I remember is falling asleep with her in my arms.

I want to go back to that. I want to go back to having her beside me.

I sit up, dragging a hand over my face as I look around the room. The picture of my teammates with the Stanley Cup is knocked over, my pants are hanging off the windowsill, and my T-shirt is over by my adjoining bathroom.

The place is a mess, a giant reminder of what happened and the fact that I'm alone in the harsh light of day.

I look for any sign of a note or indication of where she ran off to, but there's nothing, even as I listen closely, hoping to hear her moving around downstairs. The only thing to be heard is the sound of the kitten wreaking havoc.

I had every intention of giving Pork back to Peaches. I truly did. Then I stared into his green eyes just a little too long, and he nuzzled up to me just a little too closely, and I knew—he was mine.

I check the clock to see it's after seven, and I'm shocked that Tootsie isn't down there causing a ruckus too. I'd better get moving before she comes looking for me.

Muscles I forgot about ache as I crawl from the warmth of my bed and head for the shower. The idea of washing the smell of Odette off me sounds terrible, but I need to go into the town for a few things, and I don't need to go there reeking of sex.

Odette.

Everything about last night was unexpected, that's for damn sure. I was sitting up in bed reading when I heard a car on the gravel. I looked out, and all I could see were dimly lit headlights, but I knew. I knew it was her.

She turned off her car, and I stepped back out of view, just watching her for a while. I didn't expect to see her again, not after I left her in the hallway and hid in the basement until she left the cidery, but there she was.

So I made my way downstairs and let her know I was up. Let her know she was welcome inside. It took a while, but eventually she came to me like I'd hoped, and the rest . . . well, the rest was easily the best night of my life.

It was also easily the dumbest thing I've ever done, but I can't seem to want to take it back.

I can't. Not when I feel like I do. It reminds me of that high I used to get while playing hockey. I've missed that feeling, and last night was the closest I've come to it in quite some time.

I want it again.

I shake it from my mind before it consumes me and make quick work of getting ready, not bothering with coffee at home today before heading out.

With Pork sitting in the passenger seat, I drive down to the cidery to check on the chickens and am surprised to find they've already been fed.

"What the . . ." I stare at the food in the feeder, knowing full well I didn't do that last night before going home.

Maybe it was Ezra, but I don't see his fancy sports car anywhere, and Stick Taps doesn't open until noon today.

Was it Odette?

That thought makes me smile. I can picture her out here trying to feed the chickens in her dinosaur pajamas, all to let me sleep in later.

And that's how I stay the entire drive into town—smiling like a damn loon.

I wipe it from my face as soon as I park my truck along the street near the library, and Mr. Taylor looks at me like I've suddenly sprouted elf ears or something.

The last thing I need is everyone talking about how chipper I look. That will lead to nothing but questions from everyone, and I don't have any answers.

I grab Pork, not wanting to leave the little guy in the truck alone, and head toward the diner.

I don't come here very often because I usually just grab something at the coffee shop or Sunnie's, but I'm fucking famished this morning.

Laughter hits my ears as soon as I walk inside. It's loud, and I instantly remember why I hardly ever come here.

But I'm willing to suffer, especially if it means I can get a fat stack of pancakes drenched in syrup. And bacon. A fuck load of bacon.

"Hey, just you today?" a server asks. I nod, and they point at a booth. "Take that one. I know they're loud, but they should be gone soon."

I inwardly groan but scoot into the booth anyway. I'm too hungry to argue for a better table.

Pork shuffles around in the pocket I've stuffed him in, poking his little head out the top.

"What's up, buddy?" I say to him. "Loud, huh? Just settle back in there. We'll go home soon."

I flip through the menu even though I know exactly what I want. When the server still hasn't stopped by, I look out the window and count the number of people who walk past. Anything to distract me from the table—or should I say *tables*—next to me. They're laughing raucously, like they're the only people in here.

"That's a cat!" one of them screeches. "Oh my gosh, Lucille, look! A cat!"

I glance up and I know immediately *who* this loud group of women is—the Chamberses.

Fuck. Is it Sunday already? I completely forgot they meet here and take over the place.

Which means . . .

They all part as if on cue, and sitting at the end of the table is Odette.

And she's looking right at me.

CHAPTER FOURTEEN

Odette

I can still feel him.

He promised I'd be able to, and boy, he delivered.

I can't recall the last time I was so sore in so many good places.

It's made it really hard to focus on what's happening around me. The last time I tuned in, Aunt Collette was telling everyone about how Dale from the hardware store asked her out and how she was unsure if she should say yes.

So far, it's a tie.

They continue their debate, and I tune them out again.

I have more important things to worry about than a date with the town clown, like the fact that I slept with my best friend's brother . . . and that I want to do it again.

I knew it wouldn't be enough the second I kissed Noah in the kitchen and that I'd need more. Then he touched me and told me how beautiful I was and slid inside me, and I knew—I would never be the same.

Leaving his bed this morning was a chore. I hated to do it, though I knew that if I was late for breakfast, I'd be subjected to not just my mother's questioning, but also my aunts' and Nonna's.

I am not prepared for that, especially since I'm still trying to wrap my head around what happened last night.

I mean, I *know* what happened. I could never forget it.

But what does it mean? Where do we go from here? Do we talk about it? Do we forget it happened? Will it happen again? I implied it would, but it was in the heat of the moment.

And the most important question of all—do I tell Izzy I slept with her brother?

My stomach sours at the thought of having that conversation with her. She told me once a long time ago that she thought the idea of us together was gross, but was that just her being a typical teenager? Did she mean it? How would adult Izzy react? Would she be mad? Would she care at all? I don't know. I just know that I don't have answers, and even if I did, I'm not sure I'm ready to deal with them.

So instead I let myself slip into my mind and block out what's happening around me and go right back to last night and the look on Noah's face as he pushed his cock inside me.

It was euphoric. That's the only way to describe being with him. It was like everything and nothing I imagined. And I imagined it *a lot* over the years.

Now that it's finally happened, I can't believe my life ever existed without sex like that. Without feeling so connected and attuned to someone. He knew exactly what I needed and when I needed it. It was perfect. *He* was perfect.

"That's a cat!" Collette yells. "Oh my gosh, Lucille, look! A cat!"

Everyone turns to see what she's pointing at, and I look right at the last person I expect to see.

"Noah?"

In a very rare look for him, his cheeks redden, and he dips his head.

Is that because of me? Is that because of last night?

"Uh, hey, ladies," he says.

Everyone but me bursts into laughter.

I can't laugh. I'm too busy aching for him again.

How did he get so under my skin already?

"What are you doing all the way over there? Come sit with us."

My aunts and cousins scoot their chairs over as my mother gets up and grabs him a chair from a nearby table.

I sit there and stare, unable to move.

Apparently Noah is not as afflicted as I am because he slides out of the booth and onto the chair.

The one my mother had set right next to me.

I'm overwhelmed with the scent of something woodsy and warm. It's the same scent that surrounded me last night as I fell asleep with a smile on my lips.

I'm scared to look at him, but also scared to *not* look at him.

So I suck it up, and I do.

My breath catches in my throat when I find he's already staring down at me, his cocoa powder eyes boring into me.

"Odie," he says, and it's a damn good thing I'm already sitting down, because if I weren't, I'd fall right over.

I've always hated that nickname, but now? Now I just might love it.

"Noah."

"Aww," Aunt Rita says, placing her hand over her heart. "You two look so good together. Don't they look so good together, Elaine?"

"Oh, hush," my mother says. "Leave them be. We didn't invite him over to make the kids uncomfortable." She points at his chest. "We want to know what's up with the kitten."

Only then do I notice what the women were going wild about.

Pork pokes his head out of Noah's pocket as if on cue, looks right at me, and meows.

I laugh, then run my finger over his head. "Hey there, buddy. You miss me?"

"Wait, you know him already?" Lucille asks.

I just saw him two hours ago, I want to say, but I don't. Instead, I nod, still petting him. "Yeah, we got acquainted on Friday after Noah here got Peached."

"Oh no." My mother giggles. "You poor thing. That woman is always sneaking those cats around. I have no idea where she gets them."

"I said the same thing, and she said to me, *Cats have sex, Noah, and from the sex comes new cats. That's how the animal kingdom works.*" He shakes his head with a laugh, and I want to laugh, too, but I don't.

I'm too caught up on the word *sex*.

Sex, sex, sex.

It's what I had with Noah last night.

Good sex. *Incredible* sex.

My eyes flit to his, and once again he's already looking my way.

He gives me a soft, secretive smile. I return it with one of my own.

Relief washes over me.

It's not awkward. It's normal. *We're* normal. Sure, we've seen each other naked, and he gave me multiple orgasms, but everything is fine.

I squeeze my thighs together just thinking of those orgasms.

"Go on. Tell us about the little cutie, then," my mother instructs, pulling me from my naughty thoughts.

All my aunts and cousins rest their chins on their hands, leaning in close and fawning over Pork and Noah as he tells the story of getting the cat.

It's ridiculous, but I don't blame them. Very little in this world is sweeter than watching a grumpy, hard man melt for a baby animal.

I watch in amusement as he holds the kitten carefully, lifting him in the air like this is *The Lion King*, and he's showing off his cub to his pride.

He looks uncomfortable under the attention, which is funny, considering he used to sell out arenas.

My fingers itch to reach over and comfort him, but I don't do it. I settle for petting Pork under the guise of grazing my finger against the tuft of chest hair that pokes out of Noah's unbuttoned Henley T-shirt.

"What the . . ." The server looks around for Noah, then spots him at our table. He sighs. "Sir, you can't have animals in here."

Noah's eyes narrow. "Don't call me *sir*, Uli. I've known you since you were in diapers."

Uli is smart enough to look scared.

"And I'll be taking my breakfast to go."

"Aww, to go? Boo, hiss," Aunt Krista says, and I know it's because she's eager to hold the kitten. I always have to pry Beans from her hands whenever she stops by my apartment.

Uli sighs, holding his order pad in his hand with as much attitude as he can muster. "Fine. What'll it be?"

Noah orders pancakes with syrup on the side and *a lot* of bacon with a coffee.

As soon as Uli's gone, everyone goes back to cooing at Pork and discussing Peaches and how many cats she's passed out at this point. Nobody knows the exact number, but we're guessing it's somewhere around fifty, if not more.

We'd be more concerned if all the cats didn't find such good homes and Peaches wasn't such a sweetheart. A bit weird, but still kind all the same.

"Hang on. You have a cat named Pork." Jody Ann points to Noah, then to me. "And you have one named Beans. How adorable is that? They go together!"

"*They* go together too," Aunt Rita says, meaning me and Noah, and I swear, all the women start talking at once.

Half of them are trying to get Aunt Rita to hush up, and the other half agree. I think one of them has already started scheming to get us together.

Oh, if they knew just how "together" we've already been.

"On that note . . ." I rise from my chair, and they all boo. I laugh. "It's been fun, ladies, but I need to head out. I have wedding things to do."

"And I"—Noah stands next just as the server brings his to-go bag of food—"have some pancakes to enjoy."

Everyone groans collectively, and I laugh at their ridiculousness as I grab my jacket. Noah takes it from my hands and helps me into it, which earns another round of *ooh*s and *aww*s from the ladies.

I try to pretend as if I'm not *ooh*ing and *aww*ing on the inside too.

My mother pushes to her feet and wraps me in a hug.

"I know they can be overwhelming sometimes, but they mean well." She squeezes me tightly, then releases me. "But in all fairness, you two do look really good together."

"Mother!" I chide, casting a look at Noah, who, thankfully, isn't paying us any attention. He's too busy settling his check with Uli.

"What?" She shrugs. "I'm just saying. He's cute, and he seems to like you."

"He's Izzy's brother," I say, and I don't know if I'm trying to remind her, myself, or both.

"So what? Izzy loves you, and she wants you to be happy, even if it is with her brother. Maybe even especially." She winks.

I force a smile. I know Izzy loves me, but there's no telling how she'd react to Noah and me being together, especially given her past comments on the subject. I mean, sure, she was pushing us to be dates for her wedding, but that's completely different from us *actually* being together.

If we even *are* together. I have no idea.

Nonna hugs me next, and I inhale the familiar scent of sourdough. "These other old birds might not be smart enough to catch on, but I've been around a long, long time, Odette. I know when two people have seen each other naked."

I pull back with wide eyes, and she laughs.

"Don't worry." She taps the end of my nose. "Your secret is safe with me, little one."

I have no doubt that my cheeks are as red as they feel.

This is so not how I envisioned this breakfast going.

We wave goodbye to everyone else, and Noah follows me from the diner.

We both breathe a sigh of relief once we're free from all the scrutiny.

"Here you go," he says, holding a to-go cup out to me.

I didn't even notice he'd grabbed two.

"For me? Thank you."

"It's no big deal." He shrugs, sipping on his drink. "Want to take a walk?"

He . . . wants to hang out? I don't know why that surprised me, but it does.

"Sure," I agree. "Let's walk."

We keep a respectable distance between us as we walk to the town park.

There are kids scattered all over the place, parents watching them all intently. Walkers and joggers every hundred feet or so, and even a few cyclists are taking up the lanes.

I don't miss how Noah picks the least populated one, leading us toward the back of the park that butts up to the woods.

I don't mind, though. This has always been my favorite section. I like to think of a beautiful garden back here as a hidden treasure.

Once we're far enough away from prying eyes and ears and all the commotion, we settle onto a bench.

I sip on my coffee as Noah opens his to-go bag.

"Can cats have pancakes?"

I laugh when I see that Pork has popped his head out of Noah's jacket pocket again. "I'm pretty sure that's a no. Here, let me take him."

I reach into the pocket, and the kitten comes to me easily. Pork settles on my lap, flicking his tail back and forth as he takes in the outside world while Noah works on eating his breakfast.

Kids scream with delight in the distance, rounds of laughter echo off the trees, and birds chirp nearby.

It's a beautiful morning, and it would be even prettier if I knew what the hell it is we're doing.

"Is this weird?" I ask after several quiet moments, because I can't stand the silence any longer.

He tips his head left, then right, like he's weighing his answer before saying it out loud.

Finally, he says, "No. Is that bad?"

"I don't know. I haven't decided yet."

He shovels another bite of pancake into his mouth, a bit of syrup clinging to his lips.

Before I can even think about it, I reach over and wipe it off with my thumb, then suck the digit right between my lips.

Noah watches my every move, his nostrils flaring, eyes darkening.

Then he's kissing me.

I have no idea where it comes from or why it comes, but it's happening, and I'm kissing him back. In public. With all my aunts and grandmother and mother just a few blocks away. Where anyone can catch us.

Just as quickly as it begins, it's over, and Noah's back to eating his breakfast like nothing happened. Like I don't now taste like sticky-sweet syrup and vanilla pancakes, just like he does.

I touch my lips, trying to relieve the tingle I feel. "What was that for?"

He lifts a shoulder. "Wanted to."

And that's all he says.

We sit in silence as he finishes his breakfast. When he returns from tossing it in the trash, he plops down next to me, taking Pork from my hands.

The kitten snuggles against his chest, and I have to squeeze my legs together for the second time today.

"What happened last night?" The words burst out of me, almost like they've been begging to come out all morning.

"We had sex."

I huff out a laugh. "Yes, I am *well* aware of that, Noah."

He swallows hard, and I wonder if he's recalling his words from last night.

I'm going to make sure you know I was inside you for days to come.

I'm going to know, that's for sure.

"I guess I meant, where do we go from here?"

"I don't know." He drags a hand through hair that felt so good between my fingers last night and squints up at the sun. "I won't lie and say I never want it to happen again."

His honesty is refreshing, and something I didn't quite expect.

"It shouldn't."

Another honest statement.

"But I really fucking want it to." He looks at me. "I'm not a forever kind of guy, though. I've been married before and don't want to do that again."

"I'm not looking for marriage either."

He lifts his brows. "That's a bold statement for a woman who plans weddings."

I shrug. "I gave up on that dream a long time ago."

"Let me guess—the curse?"

"The curse," I confirm.

He looks like he wants to tell me it's bullshit again, but he doesn't, and maybe that's because it works in his favor. Maybe because he's hiding behind it, too, because he wants this as badly as I do, and this is the only way to protect ourselves.

"We can't tell Izzy."

That knot that's been sitting in my stomach all morning grows just at the mention of her, and I find myself nodding. "I know."

"Then okay."

"Okay?"

"Yeah." He nods, then gives me a devilishly handsome grin, one that says he's definitely up to no good. "Want to come over again tonight?"

I can't help but laugh at his eagerness.

"I think I can swing that."

Me: do u like wine??

Noah: I own a cidery.

Me: so????

Me: i'm trying to woo you with booze!

Noah: I really just want you naked in my bed. No wooing needed.

I swallow thickly, then type a quick response.

Me: understood

I pocket my phone and grab a bottle of my favorite wine, just in case.

I'm heading over to Noah's, and for some reason I don't want to show up empty-handed, so I've been walking around the grocery store with a basket full of snacks for the last fifteen minutes, trying to talk myself into checking out.

I'm sure the guy behind the counter thinks I'm lost or something, but I don't care. I'm nervous. It's silly considering we've already done this before, but that was unplanned. That was a heat-of-the-moment kind of thing. This is definitely planned.

I'm having sex with Noah again, and I can't fucking wait.

It's terrible of me, especially since I spent the day planning his sister's wedding, the very sister I'm hiding this from, but still. I've been looking forward to this since he walked me back to my car this morning, leaving me with a hand squeeze and a look in his eyes that told me he was just as excited about it as I am.

Gosh, I've really gotten myself into it, haven't I?

"Odette!"

The bottle of Riesling I'm holding slips right out of my hands.

I'm lucky enough to catch it just before it crashes to the floor.

"Phew. That was close," Lydia Stevens says with a laugh. "What are you doing out this late, dear?"

I brush my hair out of my face, tucking the bottle into the basket before I do something truly embarrassing like drop it again, and will myself not to turn red.

"You know how it is with us ladies. Once a month, we just feel like eating all the junk food and drinking the entire wine aisle."

I toss her a wink, and she laughs.

"Oh, boy. Don't I know it? Brian's grabbing us some ice cream, then we'll go home, pop open a bottle of wine ourselves, and likely fall asleep on the couch while the movie we've spent twenty minutes picking out plays in the background. When you've been married as long as we have, that's what your date nights look like."

It sounds like a great night to me. Like the kind of night I would want to have if I were married.

That same feeling I always get when I think about marriage runs through me. It's a mix of sadness and acceptance and I don't even know what else. Longing maybe? I can't decide.

I wasn't lying to Noah earlier when I said I gave up on my dream of marriage. I have. But sometimes . . . very seldomly . . . I dream of it.

I guess now is one of those times.

"Listen, I won't keep you, dear. I just wanted to say hello and tell you I love all the work you've been doing at the cidery with Noah. He needs someone in his life like you."

"Like me?"

"Yeah, someone cheery. Someone hopeful. I like Ezra, but that boy is all grump and numbers, and that's it. Noah needs someone in his life, especially after the divorce. I worry about him being alone for too long, you know?"

Oh, if she only knew how alone he wasn't.

She shakes her head. "Anyway. I'll let you get back to your night and go find Brian before he buys the entire ice cream aisle."

She gives me a quick hug, then hurries away to find her husband.

He catches her at the end of the lane, swooping her into his arms. She giggles loudly as he nuzzles his face into her neck.

They look like teenagers, so happy and carefree. So in love.

That same ache as before hits me, but I push it aside.

No time for aching now. I have somewhere to be.

CHAPTER FIFTEEN

Noah

I should feel bad for hiding things from my sister, but I can't find it in me to give a shit when I'm faced with the sight before me.

Odette lounges on a blanket in the back of the barn where I'm working, a bowl of grapes next to her. She's popping them into her mouth one by one, and it looks like something straight out of a fantasy.

The best part is that she's not even trying to be sexy. She just is.

She spent the night at my house again last night, except this time when I woke up, she was still there. That's the way it's been for the last week plus. She shows up at my place, we fuck until we can barely move, then we sleep and do it all again the next day. I can't remember a time I've been so exhausted yet relaxed at the same time.

Right now, though, I'm feeling anything but relaxed, and it has everything to do with Odette, who is pushing my buttons to the max in more ways than one.

"What's the purpose of these again?" I've been building two rooms for the last few days, and all they've done is cause me grief. She insists they're a necessary evil and even has Ezra on board. I don't know how she wrapped us both around her finger, but she has.

"They're make-out rooms."

I raise an eyebrow. "Is that so?"

"Yep. Want to test them out?" She waggles her brows at me.

"You're messing with me, aren't you?"

"Wouldn't you like to know?"

"Yes. Yes, I would."

I drop the hammer I'm holding, then pounce on her.

Her laughter carries through the barn as I fit myself between her legs and pepper kisses over her face.

"Shh," I say into her ear. "You're being too loud. Don't want any passersby to know we're in here, do you?"

She arches a rebellious brow at me. "Make me shut up then."

So I do.

I take her lips in mine, kissing her hard, and she opens for me instantly, letting my tongue in to caress hers.

My cock hardens in record time as she rubs against me, and my hands find their way under her shirt, that damn Anaheim she's worn too many times to count now. I swear she wears it because she knows what it does to me—it drives me absolutely fucking wild.

So damn wild that if I don't get my cock inside her, I might explode.

"Wanna fuck you so bad," I murmur against her lips.

"Here?"

"Yes. We're in the back. The doors are mostly closed. We're hidden." I pull away and look at her. "Can I?"

Her eyes are so glassy as she nods. "Yes."

"Are you a good girl? Can you be quiet?"

Another head bob as she rubs herself against my thigh.

"Say it."

She sinks her teeth into her bottom lip. "I'll be a good girl and stay quiet while you fuck me, Noah."

An animalistic growl leaves me, and I don't have time to analyze that.

"On your hands and knees."

She flips around, looking at me over her shoulder with nothing but pure desire as I unzip my jeans.

I yank her shorts and underwear down, and groan at the sight before me.

Fuck, she looks so good like this. Her bare ass in the air, her breaths coming in sharp.

She presses back, searching for my touch, and I can't help myself. I pull my arm back and lay a hard smack across her exposed cheek.

She lets out a low groan. "Fuuuuck. Do that again."

I oblige, loving the redness my palm leaves behind. If I had more time and I wasn't worried about someone catching us, I'd spend as much time spanking her as she'd like, but I'm too damn eager to be inside her.

I slip two fingers into her, loving the sound they make in her wetness.

"Oh god," she cries, and I remove my digits.

"You're supposed to be quiet. Good girls are quiet. Are you a good girl?"

She clamps her mouth closed, nodding fervently.

"Then hush while I play with this pretty pussy of yours." I slip my fingers back in, and she groans.

I want to be mean and tease her by removing them again, but I want to feel her squeezing me even more.

I reach into my back pocket for my wallet and grab the condom I tucked in there the other day, just in case. I rip open the packet with my teeth, then roll it over my cock while she fucks herself on my digits.

When I'm finally covered, I replace my fingers with my cock in one swift motion, and my good little girl lets out a loud sigh.

"Fuck," I say through gritted teeth as I slide out and back in. "Your pussy fits me so well, darlin'. Like a fucking glove."

She nods in agreement.

"This"—I press my thumb against the hole I keep getting glimpses of—"this looks fucking gorgeous."

This time she groans, and it's clear she's frustrated that she can't say anything.

I coax her forward with my free hand until her cheek is pressed against the blanket and her asshole is on full display. I spit onto it and press harder against the tight ring.

"This okay?"

She nods, but I want more confirmation than that.

"Say it, Odette. Tell me it's okay to play with your ass."

She whines, her legs shaking as I continue to rut into her, my thumb slipping into her even more. "It's okay. Play with my ass, Noah. *Please.*"

I grin, then slam into her harder, my thumb slipping deeper, and she goes off. Her cunt squeezes me tightly as she comes, her whole body shaking as I continue to fuck her hard and fast. I remove my digit and grip her hips, pounding into her until I'm spilling into the condom in a sudden burst.

I slow my movements as my orgasm winds down, then I slip out of her and fall straight to my back beside her.

She turns her head toward me, and I can't help but grin at the lazy, satisfied smile on her face.

"What?" she asks, the single word a little slurred.

"You look *very* pleased."

"Oh, I am." She laughs, then groans as she turns, joining me on her back beside me. "That was fucking hot."

"Indeed, it was."

We didn't even take our clothes off fully. Hell, the only thing exposed on me is my cock. I reach down and tug off the condom, tying it off and tossing it aside, making a mental note to grab it before we leave.

We lie there, trying to catch our breath after that. I have no idea what came over me. It's reckless, considering it's the middle of the day and anyone could be outside, but I couldn't help myself. I had to have her.

The craziest part? After all that, I want her again.

I try not to think too much of that, especially since we've been spending all our nights together lately. I know we probably shouldn't, since this is supposed to be casual, but I can't seem to get enough of her.

Tonight, I tell myself. *Tonight, we'll take a break.*

"So, what are these rooms really for again?" I ask, distracting myself from how badly I don't want to do that.

She laughs. "The bridal party. They'll need a place to get ready."

I sigh. "This is going to cost me more money, isn't it?"

"If I say no, does that mean you'll kiss me again?"

"Yes."

"Then no."

I ghost my lips over hers. "Liar."

Then I shove away, pushing to my feet, tucking my still half-hard cock back into my jeans and zipping myself up.

"Hey, no fair!" She pouts. "I said no."

"And you didn't mean it."

"I'm going to remember that later."

"Oh, darlin'. I'm counting on it."

"I'll do a Gorgonzola-and-avocado burger for here. Fries for my side, please. And I'll grab a drink from the cooler."

The worker behind the counter of Dickie's Gourmet Burgers nods and punches my order into the screen, then reads me my total.

I pay, then head to the refrigerator full of bottled sodas. I grab my favorite root beer and twist the top off, then scan the restaurant for a place to sit.

Taken, taken, taken.

Guess tonight wasn't the best night to decide to take a break from Odette and head back out into the real world.

Admittedly, it was hard as hell to walk away from her earlier and not invite her up to my house later like I have every other night, but I did it.

Now, staring down this packed restaurant and suddenly feeling very alone, I'm regretting it.

I resume my scan. Every table in this place is occupied by a couple or a family. I can't say I blame them all for cramming in here. Dickie's has the best burgers around.

Taken, taken, take—

Cobalt. A sweet-yet-sassy smile. Red-painted lips.

Odette.

She sends me a small wave, and I can't help but grin.

Of course I run into her the one night I'm trying to stay away from her.

I make my way over to the small two-person table she's nabbed in the corner.

"Waiting for someone, Odie?"

"I didn't think I was, but maybe so." She gestures to the empty chair. "Want to join me?"

I slip into the chair, taking a long drink from my root beer.

She wrinkles her nose. "Ew. You're a root beer guy?"

"You kidding? It's the only soda I drink."

"But that's what they give little kids to keep them off the caffeine. And it's so . . . spicy." She shudders like she hates the idea of drinking it.

"You're telling me you don't like root beer floats?"

"Of course I do."

"How does that work?"

"Easy. I have them with orange cream soda and call them orange cream floats." She grins, taking a drink of her orange cream soda.

My lips twitch at her smart-ass comment.

"So," she says, wrapping her hands around her drink and peeling back the label on the bottle, "is this what the old folks do on a Wednesday night? Get burgers and drink root beer out of bottles like the good old days?"

"Old folks?" I lean across the table, and Odette does the same, coming so close that I'm no longer overwhelmed by the scent of grease and burgers but instead by her. "You didn't think I was old in the barn earlier when I had my cock in your cunt and thumb in your ass."

Her eyes widen at my words as I casually sit back in my chair like I said nothing at all.

She takes another slow, steady drink, shifting in her chair as she sits back. "Touché."

But her words still bother me. Does she really think that I'm old? I'm not, but I have lived a whole life bigger than she ever has. I've had an entire career already, and she's just now finding her footing, or at least trying to. I was married, for fuck's sake.

"Does it weird you out? The age difference?"

She shakes her head before I even finish asking the question. "Not at all. You?"

I scratch at my chin, thinking about it. I'm sure it should, since I've technically known her since she was a teen, but I definitely wasn't thinking about an underage Odette in any sort of way other than sisterly back then. I barely even knew her, having only met her a handful of times in the summers.

It's a different story now, though. I don't think of her as sisterly at all. Far from it.

"No."

"Good." She nods. "Besides, if you did, I would just tell you all about how my nonna's third marriage was to a guy fifteen years her senior, so twelve years is nothing."

"And gay, if I recall correctly."

She laughs. "Yeah, that too. Maybe not the best example, huh?"

"Not really." I slide my bottle back and forth between my hands. "So, come here often?"

She rolls her eyes. "Please, you have better lines than that, I'm sure."

"Eh, you'd be surprised. I've been out of the casual hookup culture for a long time."

"Ah, right. The marriage."

The word doesn't sound as unpleasant to my ears as it once did, but I'm sure that's just because I've been tortured with wedding talk for the last few weeks.

The server sets our baskets in front of us, each overflowing with fries and a giant burger. We dive into our dinner, a comfortable silence falling between us.

When we're halfway through, Odette's the one to speak first.

"Can I ask you something?"

I nod. "Sure."

"Why'd you get divorced?"

I swallow roughly, and I tell myself it's because of the giant bite of food in my mouth.

But it's not that. Not at all.

It's the truth that's tripping me up.

"I, uh, I'm not sure, really."

She arches a brow at me. "You have to know. You didn't just undo a marriage for funsies."

No, I didn't.

I sigh, then set my burger back in the basket. I pull in a steadying breath. I don't talk about my ex-wife often, because it hurts. Not because I'm still hung up on the relationship or still have feelings for her, but because the reason we got divorced nearly four years ago isn't an easy pill to swallow—me.

"Chelsea and I were . . . we wanted different things. She wanted me to be someone I wasn't, and I couldn't make that happen for her. I tried. Fuck, did I try, but it wasn't enough. I . . . *I* wasn't enough for her. She told me this all the time. Sometimes in a subtle way and sometimes really fucking direct, but that was the issue. I wasn't good enough. I wasn't winning enough. I wasn't making enough. I wasn't attending parties enough. I wasn't around enough. I didn't want a family enough. I didn't try enough. I didn't love her enough. It just . . ." I exhale heavily. "I wasn't what she wanted. The life we carved out together wasn't what she planned for. So I ended it."

"*You* ended it?"

I nod. "Yeah, and she was not happy about it, which is why the divorce took so long to settle. She kept dragging her feet and wanted more and more money. I got tired of it, paid her what she wanted, walked away, and never looked back."

"I guess it's safe to say you really weren't upset about the engagement announcement then?"

"No." I laugh lightly. "I'm happy for her, you know? Things between us might not have worked out, but I still want her to be happy. That's all I ever wanted for her, actually. I hope she gets that."

Odette gives me a sad smile, and if she were anyone else, it might piss me off. But it's her, and I find myself not minding it as much.

"I'm sorry," she says. "Though I've clearly never been married, I have seen my fair share of people go through divorce, and I know it's never easy. So I'm sorry things didn't work out with Chelsea."

"Thanks."

"But for what it's worth, you deserve your happiness too. And I don't think you need to change anything about yourself. You are enough, and I like you just fine, Noah."

I'm sure that's easy for her to say. We're just having sex and having fun. We aren't in a real relationship. I might not be enough for her, just like I wasn't enough for Chelsea. I'm afraid what I'm doing for the barn won't be enough for Izzy's wedding either. That it won't be enough to bring in more revenue so we can make the iceplex happen. That no matter how hard I work, I am still not enough.

Still, I give her a soft smile, then hide all my doubts behind a bite of food.

But I really want to tell her *I like you just fine, too, Odette.*

And I'm not quite sure how to feel about that.

We finish our dinner with much lighter topics than my divorce, then head to the ice cream shop up the street.

I hadn't planned to spend my evening with her, but I'm glad I am. I was just going to go back to my place and read in bed until I fell asleep with my book on my face, but this is much better than that.

"Now you're getting the worst kind of ice cream too?" she complains as we leave the shop, each holding a cone.

"How is vanilla the worst?"

"Because it's *boring*. It's what people who can't make up their minds get. Or old people."

That's the second time tonight she's called me old, and the second time I feel like I need to prove to her I am far from it.

I grab her hand, tug her into a nearby alleyway, and press her up against the wall, pushing my knee between her legs.

She grins up at me, then brings her ice cream cone to her lips and licks it slowly. "Well, hi."

I growl, then kiss her, not caring that she tastes like cotton candy ice cream or that my own cone is leaking down my hand, making a mess.

I have to kiss her. I can't wait for another second.

I told myself I would leave her be tonight, yet here I am anyway, making out with her in an alleyway because I just can't seem to get enough. It's reckless. Anyone could walk by at any second, but I can't seem to find it in me to care. Not with the pleased noises she's making or the way she rocks against my thigh. How she's pulling me closer and begging with her body for more.

Not when she's got me completely under her spell.

"Noah," she groans. "What are you doing to me?"

"Kissing you." I echo her words from the night she showed up at my house, then take her mouth again.

Our ice cream is definitely a melted mess on this warm July night, but so what? It's worth it to feel her body that's so damn soft under me.

Her knee-length blue skirt that matches her eyes is bunched up high, and I can't help myself as I snake my hand between us and cup her pussy through her panties.

She's wet.

No, not just wet. She's drenched, and it's all for me.

I want to taste her. I want to hike her skirt up and see how she compares to this sweet dessert dripping down my hand, but I can't.

Not here.

I pull my hand away, and at the same time I wrench my mouth from hers, and she gasps for air.

"Ugh. You're such a tease," she complains through labored breaths.

I laugh darkly, running my nose over her cheek, capturing her earlobe between my teeth with a light nibble. "How about I take you back to my place and remind you just how old I'm not?"

"I think that sounds like a very, very good idea, Mr. Stevens."

I groan, dropping my head to her shoulder. "That's it. Boner ruined."

She laughs loudly, and I can't help but kiss her again.

This time it's quick, because if I don't get her back to my place soon, I might just fuck her right here against this wall.

And wouldn't that get the town talking?

I lead her to the truck that I parked back over by Dickie's, ditch my melted cone in the trash, then help her into the passenger seat.

"Do you have a napkin in here, by chance?" she asks once I'm behind the wheel. We're both a total mess, ice cream all over my shirt and hers still running over her hand.

"I doubt it, but check the center console just in case," I tell her, putting the vehicle into drive and steering out onto Harborview Boulevard.

She searches the console, then the glove box, but comes up empty.

"Oh well." She shrugs, then licks along the line of ice cream that's trailed over to her wrist.

"Fucking hell." I press down on a cock that's still heavy between my legs. "You keep doing that, and I'm not sure I'm going to make it all the way back to my house."

"Doing what?" She grins innocently, although we both know she's anything but. "I'm just eating my ice cream cone that's melting because of *someone*."

She drags her tongue over her index finger, then her middle, and it takes everything I have to keep my eyes on the road and not on her, especially as she begins to lick the ice cream like she would my cock.

Fuck, what I would give to feel her mouth wrapped around me.

"Take it out."

I dare a glance over at her just as we pass through the end of the downtown waterfront.

"What?"

"Your cock, Noah. Take your cock out. I want to see it."

It might be irresponsible and easily one of the most impulsive things I've ever done, but I do it anyway.

With one hand on the wheel, I undo my pants and pull my throbbing cock free. Her eyes widen as she takes me in.

"Touch it."

I do. I wrap my fist around myself, flicking my wrist upward lazily, and Odette runs her tongue over her lips as she watches me.

"God, that's hot," she whispers, and I realize then that she's got her free hand between her legs, that skirt that has no business being so fucking sexy pushed up high. I can't see her touching herself, but I know she is, and I'm not sure if that makes it better or worse.

I pull onto the dirt road that leads to the cidery and press on the gas, definitely going well above the speed limit, but I don't care. If I don't get inside her soon, I might lose it.

"Do it again, Noah," she begs.

I do, and she licks the ice cream at the same time.

I groan, imagining it's me she has her tongue wrapped around. Fuck, this is torture. It is delicious torture, but torture all the same.

I stroke myself harder and faster, and she licks on her ice cream as her fingers move under her skirt, and I'm dying.

I am going straight to hell for this, but I don't care.

We speed past the cidery, then hit the road for my place.

Her pants are growing harsher, my cock is growing harder, and we're both seconds away from making a complete mess in my truck.

I hit the brakes as I pull into my designated parking spot, jerk off my seat belt, then reach over the console for her.

She comes to me willingly, her mouth fusing with mine, her ice cream cone long forgotten and now a mess on my floorboards. I don't care. I'll clean it out later. I have more important things to take care of now.

She settles on my lap, my cock sliding against her wetness, and it's so fucking hot. I want to fuck her. I want to feel her tight little pussy around me.

"Odette," I say against her. "Get the condom out of my wallet."

She reaches behind me to grab the rubber I'm damn glad I thought to replace before leaving the house as I move my lips to her throat, sucking and nipping at her. She pulls it free, opens the wrapper, then slides the condom over my dick.

She follows it with her wet cunt, pushing her panties to the side as she sinks down on me with a long, low groan.

Yeah, so much for avoiding her tonight, indeed.

There's no slow buildup. There's nothing romantic. She just holds on to my shoulders and fucks herself on me, head thrown back as she finds a rhythm that works for her.

I let her, loving how she looks as the orange-and-pink sunset casts colors over her skin. As sweat forms along her brow and the windows steam up. As her lips part when she finds that spot that feels just right. And as she falls apart around me, taking my own orgasm right along with her.

She slumps against me, satiated and with a small smile on her lips.

I love this look for her—contented and sleepy.

I kiss her temple, trying to get my heart out of my throat.

"We should probably go inside," I say after several long minutes.

She pushes off me, looking up at me with pinkened skin and sleepy blue eyes. "Already ready for round two? I didn't realize old men could go again that quickly."

"Odette," I warn, and she laughs.

She pulls off me with a groan, then pushes open the door and hops out of the truck.

"Last one in owes the other an orgasm!"

Then she takes off toward the house, peering back over her shoulder with a laugh.

After tucking myself away, I chase behind her with a grin of my own and realize that if she asks, I might just follow her anywhere.

The thought isn't as scary as it should be.

CHAPTER SIXTEEN

Odette

Avoiding your best friend is a true art form, especially when you're the one planning her wedding.

I guess I'm a Picasso because I've avoided Izzy like it's my job.

Some of it hasn't been entirely my fault. She's been wrapped up in Craig and hasn't had time to meet me either. But there have been chances, and I've successfully dodged every one of them.

Why?

Because I'm too busy with her brother.

I told myself the other night that I'd take a break because maybe sleeping together in the barn in the middle of the day was a little too reckless and, while fun, a sure sign we needed to cool off a bit.

Imagine my surprise when he walked into Dickie's, and we ended up falling into bed together anyway.

I wish I could say I'm surprised, but I'm not. Noah is addicting. There's no other way to explain it. No matter how hard I try, I can't get enough of him. While I want to say I'm looking for a cure, I'm not. I'm just digging myself deeper into this obsession.

If I thought I had it bad for Noah when I was sixteen, that's nothing compared to how badly I'm crushing on him now.

I'm playing a dangerous game. I know that. Not just with my feelings but with the curse, too, as it always rears its ugly head. Like that time I thought I might have put the worst of it behind me, then my date turned out to be a thief and literally got arrested just before dessert.

It's a risky gamble, yet I can't stop myself.

And a part of me doesn't want to, curse be damned.

It's the first time I've wanted to openly defy it, and I'm not sure how to handle that, so I don't.

I park along the street near the coffee shop, where I'm meeting with Izzy and Andrea, the florist who reached out because she heard about the farm wedding and thought her vibe might fit with ours. Then we're on to For Goodness Cake for the cake tasting.

We're behind schedule on a lot of planning thanks to our shortened timeline, so it's going to be a long day of getting caught up, and I have no idea how I'm going to handle sitting next to Izzy, all while pretending I haven't seen her brother naked.

"You're here, you're here, you're here!" She bounces on her heels excitedly as I trudge up the hill toward the coffee shop, my trusty tote bag full of notebooks and binders slung over my shoulder.

Guilt flutters in my stomach when she wraps me in her arms.

Play it cool, Odette. She doesn't have a clue.

"I feel like I haven't seen you in forever. I was starting to worry you were ignoring me." She laughs. "I got over that quickly because I know you'd never."

Ugh. This is going to be harder than I thought.

I hug her back, then give her my best *I am definitely not hiding anything from you* smile. "I missed you too. Are you ready to get started? Andrea should be here any minute."

"Yes, please! I'm so ready to be over the planning stage and get to the wedding part. I don't know how people enjoy this. The anticipation of getting to the big day is just too much." She squeezes my arm. "Present company excluded, of course."

"I'm sure it's different when it's your big day."

She sighs contentedly. "*Big day.* Can you believe I'm having a *big day*?"

"Uh, yes. You and Craig have been together forever and you're ridiculously in love with each other. That man worships you. It was inevitable."

She smiles. "I'm sure you'll find your *inevitable* for you one day too."

It's sweet of her to think so, but it's not happening.

You deserve your happiness too.

I don't know why, but the words I said to Noah the other night flit through my mind. I had no problem telling him he deserved happiness, but I don't believe the same when it comes to myself. Why is that?

Oh, right. The curse.

I force away those darker thoughts and pull open the door to the coffee shop.

"Odette!" Kai calls out as I walk in.

I wave to him as we move to find a table big enough for the three of us and all the binders I brought along. I have a lot of flower ideas for this wedding, and I hope Andrea doesn't regret agreeing to work with me after this.

"Ooh. What about Kai? You could date him."

"What? Izzy!" I whisper-shout at her. "Stop it this instant."

"What?" She shrugs. "He's cute, that's for damn sure. And why not date him? He seems like he likes you."

"He literally just said my name. How does that equal him liking me?"

"Uh, because he didn't say *my* name, and I walked in right next to you."

"Your usual, too, Izzy?" Kai calls over to us as if on cue.

She gives him a thumbs-up, and I arch my brow at her as we set our stuff down. "You were saying?"

She huffs as we make our way to the front counter. "Whatever. I still think you should give him a shot. I mean, I see no reason not to. It's not like you're seeing anyone, right?"

I stumble. Trip right over absolutely nothing. And it's all thanks to Izzy's words.

"Shit. You okay?" she asks, grabbing me from behind to help steady me.

"Yeah, sorry. I'm just a klutz and tripped over a chair leg." I right myself, then keep going, refusing to look back and make eye contact with my best friend as I lie to her. "And right. I'm not seeing anyone, but I'm swamped trying to save my business, you know? So let's table the dating discussion for later, yeah?"

She sighs. "Yeah, you're right. Business first, sexy times with the hot barista later."

I shoot her a look as Kai emerges from the back room, my favorite bagel in hand.

I look him over. Izzy's right—he is cute. He clearly spends a good deal of time at the gym, and his dirty-blond hair and green eyes give him a very boy-next-door sort of look.

But he doesn't do anything for me in the ways he should. He's missing scruff along his jawline, graying hair at his temples, and creases at the corners of eyes that should be brown.

Simply put, he's not Noah.

And that thought is scarier than I care to admit.

We take our coffees and breakfast, then settle in at the table just as our florist comes through the doors.

She's wonderful. Absolutely everything I remember from our first meeting, and it's no wonder that one went on too long. She's so easy to talk to and perfectly understands what I envision for this wedding.

We end the meeting with everything finalized—soft blues and whites with pops of peach, calla lilies, lisianthus, roses, and sunflowers. A little simple, a dash of elegance, and some wild mixed in for the barn-and-farm theme.

Izzy's so excited when we leave that she skips—literally—the entire way to For Goodness Cake.

"Oh my gosh. I am starving," she says as we pull open the door, the sugary waft of air hitting us as we step inside the bakery. "I am *so* ready for all the cake. I just wish Craig could have been here for this."

"It is a bit of a bummer. Did he at least give you a list of what he likes?"

"No chocolate he says, but it sucks because I—"

"Love chocolate, I know." I tap my finger on my chin. "Maybe we can find a compromise that works for both of you. We'll see what Sybill can make happen."

The small old woman who has been making cakes in this town since day one, it seems, walks out from the back and wraps us both in hugs. She's one of the few contacts that hasn't abandoned me after the wedding disasters. I told her I would understand if she didn't want her business associated with mine anymore, but she just laughed at me, boxed up my favorite cotton candy cupcake, and sent me on my way.

We gather at her designated cake-tasting table—an old thing that's been sitting in the corner of her shop since forever—and Sybill loads up the table with different combinations, from customer favorites, big hits from previous events, and a few of her more original creations.

About fifteen different combinations later, we think we have it nailed down, but it would really help to have Craig here to make the final decision.

"Ugh, I can't decide. This is impossible." Izzy juts her bottom lip out as she stares down at the cakes.

"I know it's hard, but we really do need to get this sorted today."

"What would you pick if you were in my shoes?"

It's the same thing she asked me when meeting with Andrea, and I'm ready to give her the exact same answer when she points at me sternly.

"And don't give me that crap about you never being in my shoes. I know about your wedding wish list, remember? I know you've dreamed about it even if you want to deny it."

I clamp my mouth shut. To be fair, she's right. I have dreamed about my own wedding forever. Of course I have my cake picked out.

I have *everything* picked out. A few times over, even.

"Well, for a summer wedding"—mine wouldn't be, I'd get married in the fall—"I would do something fruity but not overwhelmingly so. Something light and airy yet yummy."

"What do you have on your list?"

My eyes go to my bag, where the list is tucked safely into the back of the notebook I have inside it.

"Lemon raspberry with a Swiss buttercream," I tell her, looking back her way.

"And for a nonsummer wedding?" she asks with a glint in her eye, like she's trying to prove a point.

"Apricot spice with cream cheese."

She grins. "That sounds lovely. And for your flowers?"

Dahlias, gerbera daisies, roses, hops, and celosia in mauves, burnt oranges, and terra-cotta.

But I don't tell her that. Instead, I say, "This isn't my wedding, Iz. It's yours, so *you* need to decide what *you* want."

She huffs. "But it's so damn hard."

The little bell over the door to the bakery chimes, and I know who walks through the door before I even look over.

I don't know how I know it, but I do. I can feel it in every cell of my body.

Which is why I'm not surprised when Izzy's face lights up.

"Noah!" she calls to him. "What are you doing here?"

His eyes widen when they land on me, and I pray Izzy doesn't notice.

It's the first time we've been together with her since we started . . . well, being *together*. It's strange, yet not, and I'm not sure if I should be unsettled by that.

While I know I should tell my best friend what's going on with her brother, it won't last, so what's the point? No point in bringing it up and freaking her out, especially not when she already has so much on her plate with the wedding.

"I'm, uh, grabbing some cupcakes," he answers, shoving his hands into his pockets and dragging his eyes away from me and to his sister.

"You are? Since when did you develop a sweet tooth?" Izzy asks.

I shift in my chair, remembering the other night in his truck. The ice cream I licked off myself. The words he uttered later, when he told me how cotton candy might be his new favorite flavor as he bent me over his couch, unable to make it to his bedroom.

He crosses his arms over his chest. "Can't a guy buy a damn cupcake without getting asked a million questions?"

Izzy holds her hands up. "Sorry, sorry. But now that you're here . . ." She kicks out the third chair that Sybill abandoned a while ago while we make final decisions. "Can you help us decide which one to choose? We can't pick between the triple-chocolate cherry and the vanilla with orange mousse."

Our eyes meet, and I know he's remembering our discussion about my feelings on vanilla.

I expect him to argue or make up an excuse as to why he can't join us, but to my surprise, he drops into the chair next to me, his thick, strong thigh settling alongside mine.

I could move. I could give him more space to stretch out.

I don't, and I have a feeling he wouldn't want me to anyway.

"Here. Try this one," Izzy says, giving him a forkful—*my* fork—of the triple-chocolate cherry cake.

He closes his mouth around the same piece of metal I just had my lips wrapped around, and I have to hold back my groan.

God, seriously? A groan over that? What is wrong with me?

He chews, then swallows. "Damn, that's good. Like really good."

"Yeah?" Izzy's eyes light up. "Okay, now try this one."

She loads the fork up with the vanilla one, and as soon as he takes a bite, I know that's the one he loves the most.

"Holy fuck." He moans, and the sound does things to me that it really shouldn't be doing in public. With his sister right here. "That's delicious. That's the one."

"Really? But the chocolate is *so* good."

"It is, but that orange is fantastic. It just screams summer wedding to me."

"Oh, so now you're a wedding expert, huh?"

He rolls his head my way, one brow lifted high, and he looks so cute right now that I could kiss him. I refrain.

"Am I wrong, Odie?"

He's not. It's the perfect cake and will satisfy the most people.

"Oh no." Izzy deflates. "You agree with him, don't you?"

I nod. "As much as I love the chocolate—and I do—Noah is right. But we could always do different flavors for different layers."

"Or cupcakes," Noah offers.

"Ah yes. I forgot your new cupcake obsession." Izzy narrows her eyes at him like he's up to something. "But the different layers don't sound so bad."

"Or a smaller, separate cake just for you."

"Do you think Sybill will hate me for making her do that? That's a lot of cake to make."

"I think Sybill has known you since you were a baby and would do anything for you. And plus, you're paying her." I wink at Izzy.

"All right. We'll do the main cake with the orange and a smaller chocolate one just for me."

"Good. Glad that's settled. Can I go now?"

Izzy shoos her brother away. "Yes, leave us be. We're busy."

"Yes, because I invited myself to this gathering," he says sarcastically, pushing from the table with another look in my direction.

I admit that for a second, I'm sad about it. I hate that he's essentially ignoring me, but I get it too. We said we wanted to keep this from Izzy, and he's just upholding that.

Still, I keep my eye on him as he heads to the counter, only half listening to Izzy as she waffles back and forth about whether she wants to get Craig his own groom's cake as well.

"Noah, my boy! How are you, sweetheart?"

"Hey, Sybill. How are you?"

"Oh, you know. I can't complain. Especially not when you're here." I grin at her flirting with him. "What brings you in today? Been a minute since I've seen you."

"Thought cupcakes sounded good."

"That so? What can I get you then?" she asks, grabbing the paper to-go box that's stamped with her logo.

"Can I get three vanilla and three cotton candy?"

"See?" Izzy points at her brother, and I honestly had no idea she was paying attention to him. "That's weird. He doesn't even *like* cotton candy." She huffs. "Sounds like something you'd get."

It *is* something I'd get.

What she doesn't know is that Noah's buying cupcakes for me.

And damn if that doesn't make me smile.

"Do you want another lemonade?"

"No!" I yell to Noah, who's in his kitchen. "But I need chocolate!"

"What kind?"

"Surprise me!"

I listen as he moves around, talking to Pork, who keeps meowing at him.

"You already had dinner." *Meow.* "You did too." *Meow.* "You're not getting more." *Meow.* "Do you want a treat?" *Meow. Meow.* "Yeah, that's what I thought."

I laugh at their interaction. For someone who claimed they weren't going to be a cat dad, he sure has taken to his new friend over the last three weeks. I can't count the number of times I've heard people talking about them in town, especially since Noah takes the little guy just about everywhere with him.

It's cute and does nothing to make me like him less.

Just like him leaving a cupcake I found sitting on the hood of my car last week didn't help.

There was a simple note tucked under the treat that said *See you tonight.*

He did see me that night. And the next one too.

Beans hasn't been happy with me leaving her so often, but I promised her I'd make Noah come to my place soon, mostly because I can't remember the last time I slept in my own bed for more than two nights in a row.

Actually, I haven't spent much time at my apartment in general. From working on the barn with Noah to planning the wedding—which I've taken to working on at Stick Taps for . . . *reasons*—to always running around town so I can meet with vendors, I haven't had much time to spend at my place. And that's solely because I'd rather spend my nights here.

Luckily, the TV flicks back to what we were watching before I can analyze that too much.

"It's on, it's on, it's on! Hurry!" I call.

I grin when Noah's footsteps pick up, and he skids into the living room. "What'd I miss?"

"They just walked into the exam room."

Noah settles onto the couch next to me, his eyes on the episode of *The X-Files* on his TV with a gigantic bowl of popcorn in his hands. He kicks his other arm up over the back of the couch, and I resume my spot attached to his side.

We found an app that lets you watch live TV, and we've been in the middle of a Mulder-and-Scully marathon for days now. The only rules? We can't pause anything. We have to use the bathroom and get snacks during the commercials, like you used to have to do before the days of TiVo and streaming. It was all Noah's idea, and while at first I didn't get it, I can see the appeal now. There's a certain rush from getting all the things done before the show comes back on. We've even perfectly timed how long it takes to make a new bowl of popcorn during the breaks.

"This is some trippy shit," he says, shoving a handful of our snacks into his mouth. Half of it falls back into the bowl, but I don't care.

I'm having too much of a good time, and all we're doing is snuggling on the couch.

"Did you grab the peanut butter M&M's?"

He leans over, pulls the already half-gone bag from his pocket, and hands it to me. "We should probably go to the store soon. We're running low on supplies."

We.

It sounds so . . . domestic.

And honestly, what we're doing *is* domestic. It reminds me of the date night that Lydia Stevens described to me. That same kind of night I longed for.

I don't want to think about that too much. I *can't.* These last three weeks with Noah have been going so well, and the wedding planning is right on track even with us having just shy of four weeks until the couple says *I do.* The last thing I need is to get too happy and let the curse break my spirit like it's done over and over again.

I scoot off him, giving him a bit of space and giving *myself* a bit of space.

My heart hammers in my chest, and I have to take deep breaths to try to get it under control.

I'm panicking, and I don't know why I'm panicking.

No, that's a lie. I do know, but I don't want to think about it.

I like Noah. Like like *him, actually. Too damn much.*

"You okay?"

"Huh?" I turn to Noah, startled a little. "Oh, yeah, I'm fine. Why?"

He looks like he doesn't believe me, but he lets it go. "Just making sure." He gives me a gentle, reassuring smile, and it instantly chases away the fear running through me. He nods toward the half-eaten dessert on the coffee table. "You like your cupcakes?"

"Like them? I *love* them." I smile up at him as I open the bag of candy. "Thank you. You really didn't have to get them, but I appreciate it."

He shrugs. "It's no big deal."

"You say that a lot."

His eyebrows inch together. "Say what?"

"*It's no big deal.* You say it a lot, even when it *is* a big deal. You went out of your way to buy me cupcakes. Took time out of your day and drove into town so I could have something sweet."

"It's just a cupcake."

Maybe to him it is, but to me, it's more than that. He thought about me. He wanted me to be happy. He *cared.*

I'm not sure I've ever had anyone care like that before.

I lean up, pressing my lips to his. It's a slow kiss, a soft one. Even as he slips his hand into my hair and tugs me closer. There's nothing hurried or hard. We're just kissing without it needing to lead to more.

When we part, he has a dopey grin that makes him look about ten years younger than he is.

"What was that for?"

I shrug. "Wanted to."

His grin grows, and so does mine, and we tune back in to the show.

While Noah's watching it, I'm not. I can't.

Because I'm starting to realize that this thing between us? It might not be so casual after all.

CHAPTER SEVENTEEN

Noah

Odie: garlic? not nuff

Me: I'm assuming that's you asking me to bring some garlic with me because you don't have enough?

Odie: LOL yessss

Odie: srry used to shorthand texts with Iz

Odie: forgot u were an old man

Me: I know shorthand text. I just don't understand fragmented sentences.

Me: And how many times do I have to tell you I'm not old? Do you need more convincing?

Odie: that a promise??

Me: It can be.

Odie: k you're done i'm trying to cook && don't need to be horny

Me: No, no. You're going to tell me more about how horny you are.

Odie: just come

Me: Oh, I plan to.

I chuckle to myself as I slide my phone back into my pocket.

"Hey, man. I'm taking off." I pull the rag from my shoulder and toss it onto the counter. "You need anything else before I go?"

"Just the name of the store where you got your balls of steel."

My jaw slackens as I stare at Ezra. "I'm sorry. My what?"

"Balls of steel. You must have them if you're sneaking around with your sister's best friend still."

"I'm not . . ." I can't even get the full lie out.

We both know I am, so there's no point.

I cross my arms over my chest. "Why does that require balls of steel?"

"Because I'm pretty sure your sister is going to rip them off when you inevitably break Odette's heart."

I glance around the bar, but it's pointless. We're about an hour away from closing, so the only other people in here are the other bartender, who is downstairs working on closing tasks; Dale from the hardware store, who is on his phone; and a couple sitting in the corner, busy picking up their kid's Cheerios off the floor. Nobody is paying us any attention.

"I'm not going to break anyone's heart."

"Right." He snorts. "The guy who doesn't believe in marriage and the girl who plans them aren't headed for a brutal demise."

"It's not like that. We're kee—"

"I swear to fuck, if you finish that sentence with *keeping things casual*, I will jump over this counter and beat the shit out of you. Fucked-up hip and all."

I flatten my lips. "Why? What's so wrong with that?"

"For starters, it's a line. Total fucking bullshit. There's no such thing as 'keeping things casual,' and the people who say that are usually the most delusional of the bunch. Someone *always* gets hurt in those situations, and I have a feeling it'll be Odette."

I gnash my teeth together. "I'm not going to hurt her."

"Do you believe in marriage?"

"No."

"And is Odette still a wedding planner?"

"Yes, but she doesn't plan to get married either."

He laughs—like full-on laughs, which is a very rare feat with him—and shakes his head. "You're an even bigger dumbass than I thought if you're buying that shit."

"No, I'm serious. She has this whole thing with her family. A curse is what they call it. Odette believes it's going to be her downfall. She doesn't want to get married because of it."

"I've heard about that. I've also heard that all the women in her family don't care and keep getting married anyway."

"Not all of them. Not her."

I'm not sure why I'm defending this so much, especially since I don't fully believe in the curse either. Nobody's life is dictated by something like that unless they let it be, and that's what I think the Chambers women are doing. They're letting the curse run their lives instead of living.

But here I am anyway, using the curse as an excuse so I don't have to admit that the thing I'm doing with Odette is likely going to end badly if we keep going the way we are.

I shouldn't be hanging out with her like I am. This was supposed to be just sex. Something fun. Casual. It wasn't supposed to be late nights on the couch, cupcakes just because, or her cooking dinner for me.

We're going way beyond what we agreed to, and it's all because I can't get enough of her.

"That may be the case," Ezra says, pulling me back to our conversation, "but it doesn't mean it's a good idea. What happens if Izzy finds out?"

"She won't."

"But what if she does? You're going to explain to her that you're sleeping with her best friend, but it's not serious? And that it's not going to affect their friendship at all when you stop bumping uglies with each other? That it won't make those combined family dinners weird? Is that really the kind of stress you want to put on her before her wedding? The wedding said best friend is planning?"

"No, which is exactly why Izzy isn't going to find out."

He holds his hands up at my not-so-subtle threat. "I'm not saying shit to her. But I am saying that *you* should, especially if you're going to be hanging out with Odette every night and letting this 'casual' thing turn serious."

"It's not turning serious."

He chuckles again, shaking his head. "Whatever you say, man. I think you're in over your head with no way out, but whatever. This is your shit show. I'm just here to watch."

He packs up his laptop and the stack of papers he always seems to be carrying around, then heads toward the back office.

Ezra is wrong. This isn't getting serious with Odette. Yeah, I'm spending a lot of time with her lately, but so what? It's still casual. We've just become friends, is all. This is a good thing, even. We're both stressed about the wedding. I want to get it right for my sister, and Odette wants to get it right to save her business. Us sleeping together is just a good way to blow off steam. It's no big deal.

I keep telling myself that as I gather my things and head out to my truck. I repeat it as I stop by my house for a quick shower and to grab Pork, who is finally getting to meet Beans tonight.

I keep it right at the forefront of my mind as I stop off at the grocery store, grabbing some fresh garlic, a bottle of the wine I know Odette likes, and a dozen cookies with peanut butter M&M's. Just before I reach the counter, I grab a six-pack of Stick Taps cider just so it doesn't look like I'm only showing up with stuff for her.

I park my truck in the back of her apartment complex just in case, then climb the two floors to her door.

When it swings open and she smiles at me, I'm not thinking about Ezra's words or how guilty I feel for hiding this from my sister.

All I'm thinking about is her.

"Noah." She reaches out, grabs me by my shirt, and tugs me into her apartment. She presses to her tiptoes, then plants her lips against mine. "Hi."

"Hi yourself." I kiss her again. "It smells good in here."

"I hope so. I spent an hour making the sauce for it." She holds her hands out for Pork, who happily goes to her. "And how's my sweet little baby?"

"Sweet?" I snort. "That thing's a demon. He woke me up eight minutes before my alarm went off this morning. He's as bad as Tootsie is when it comes to wanting breakfast by six."

"Aww. He's just a hungry, growing boy. Right, baby?" She rubs her nose against his. "You're just like Beans, whom I know you're going to love. If I can find her, that is."

"She's missing?"

"No." Odette shakes her head. "She just loves to hide, is all. She's probably under the couch. That's her favorite spot. She waits for me to walk by, then scratches at my ankles."

"I was wondering what those marks were from."

"And you never thought to ask?" She laughs. "Well, come in. You don't have to stand in the door all night."

In the time I've known Odette, I've been to her apartment once before and never made it farther than I have now.

So when I take a step, then another, they're heavy, and it feels like it has everything to do with my conversation with Ezra.

I push it out of my mind as I follow Odette into her apartment, closer to the heavenly smell wafting from her kitchen. She stops at the large pot, then stirs whatever's inside before nodding toward the bag I've set on the counter.

"Whatcha got there?"

"Stuff," I tease, opening the paper bag, loving the excitement that sparks in her eyes. She's like a little kid at their birthday party, one eye on the presents table at all times.

I pull out the garlic, and she grins.

"You're a lifesaver. I need that for the bread."

"You're making garlic bread?" My mouth waters at that thought. "I fucking love garlic bread."

"Then you're in luck, because I make the best around. Learned the recipe from my nonna."

"With all due respect, I'm a little hard, and it only sort of has to do with your nonna, but it's completely because of her cooking. I swear."

"Well, that's a relief." She rolls her eyes with a laugh. "What else is in there?"

I fish my hand back into the bag, then pull out the wine.

"Ugh. I could kiss you."

I close my eyes and pucker my lips, but instead of Odette, I feel Pork pressed against them, and he proceeds to lick me.

"What the . . ." I wipe my mouth. "Not cool."

"What?" She shrugs. "I said I *could* kiss you, not that I was going to. Anything else?" She pushes to the balls of her feet, trying to peer into the bag.

I pull out the cider next, and she boos.

"Watch it. I worked hard to brew that cider."

"Yeah, yeah, and we're all so impressed, which is why nearly every business in Port Harbor and within a fifty-mile radius sells it, including the coffee shops. Weird you bought it and didn't just grab it from the cidery, by the way."

"What can I say? I'm our biggest cheerleader."

She ignores that. "What else, what else?"

She's practically bouncing now. Ever since I left that cupcake on her car, it's sort of become our thing for me to bring her treats, so I know she's expecting one now.

Finally, I reveal the peanut butter M&M's cookies, and she squeals. She thrusts Pork into the air, running around the kitchen island like she's doing a victory lap. It's so damn ridiculous and adorable, and I can't seem to wipe the silly grin off my face as I watch her.

I catch her on the next lap, tugging her against me and kissing her long and hard until Pork is wiggling between us, trying to get free.

"Well, I'm certainly going to let you buy me cookies more often if it means I get kissed like that." She clears her throat, then steps back, thrusting the cat my way. "Okay, you take Pork. Sit on the couch with him and Beans will come out swinging—literally. I'm going to finish up in here and get the garlic bread in the oven. Then we can eat. I can't have you in here because I'm about two seconds away from ripping my shirt over my head and throwing myself at you like some sex-crazed lunatic."

"And if I don't take the cat?"

"Noah . . ." She groans, and I laugh, taking the kitten anyway.

She's right. We don't need to get carried away, not when dinner smells so damn good.

Odette ushers me away, and I head into the living room.

It's a small space, but it's nice. Far more modern than what I have, that's for sure.

The walls are light gray instead of my deep tan ones. The furniture is crisp and new versus my dated styles, which stopped being cool when my parents were born. And unlike mine, there isn't a single scratch along the dark hardwood floor.

It's everything I wish I had the time to make my house. We're three weeks out from the wedding and the barn might be done, but now I have to focus on the coop, all the mowing that needs to be done again, and putting a few finishing touches on everything so Odette can set up for the guests. After that, the goal is to start on the iceplex we're getting close to closing the deal on.

Maybe one day I'll find time to remodel my house and turn it into something that will make Odette feel more at home when she's over there.

I settle onto the fluffy black couch with Pork and wait. It takes a few minutes, but I feel it—Beans.

She paws at my ankle. It's gentle at first, then it turns violent.

"Ouch!" I scramble to get out of the way.

"What?" Odette calls from the kitchen.

"Nothing!"

I bend in time to see the calico cat slide back under the couch.

"Why, you little . . ."

She pokes her head back out, and I swear she narrows her eyes at me.

Go ahead and say it, the look says. *Call me a name. I dare you.*

I don't dare.

Instead, I scoop her up before she can run away again, ignoring the claws she digs into my hand.

"Be nice," I tell her, and she calms down a little, looking up at me in wonder. "Be gentle."

She stops fighting me as I settle her onto the couch, her long tail thwacking against the cushion as she sits and stares up at me like she's confused by this stranger in her home.

That's when she notices Pork.

I hold my breath and wait. They size each other up, uncertain if they'll be friends or foes.

Beans takes the first step, inching closer. Pork looks back at me in a silent *Can we trust her?*

"Go on," I encourage.

Slowly, they make their way toward each other, and after a few minutes, they're batting at each other playfully and wrestling like they're old friends.

Now that I know they aren't going to fight, I push off the couch and walk around, taking in the little details of Odette's place. Trinkets sit along the mantel over the fireplace, from a jewelry box with a ballerina mid-spin to a plastic ring that looks like it came from one of those quarter machines at the grocery store. Succulents that are lush and lively and pictures—including ones of my sister—line the floating shelves. And there's even a small shelf full of Blu-ray, mostly romantic comedies and TV show box sets. I grin when I see she has most of *The X-Files* in her collection.

A laptop sits closed on the coffee table, a stack of papers beside it. They look like legal documents of some sort. Likely contracts for her business.

Sitting near the bottom of the pile is a piece of paper that looks like it's been crumpled up and flattened about fifty times over. Curious, I tug it free.

Every inch of it is covered in writing. Different colors. A few doodles. It's a mess to try to decipher, but I give it a go anyway.

Dress—White with a deep V. That's marked out and replaced with *Mermaid*. That has a scribble through it with *Suit???* beside it.

What is all this?

I keep scanning the page. Among the items crossed out I recognize a few song titles, foods, countries, and . . . are those themes?

~~Cream puffs~~

~~Lemon tarts~~

~~Mini donuts~~

~~Pizza bar~~ TACOS??

~~Medieval~~

~~Princess~~

Rustic romantic

There are so many different types of flowers listed, color combinations, and random words scattered in the margins that make no sense.

Paper cranes

~~Fairy lights~~ something more rustic

Fall

Apricot and ~~buttercream~~ CREAM CHEESE!!!!

It almost reminds me of . . .

"It's a wedding wish list."

I look up from the page to find Odette leaning against the wall, watching me. A simple blue apron covers her black leggings and Taylor Swift T-shirt. It makes me think of my sister's CD I "borrowed" all over again.

"It's like a Pinterest board come to life."

She laughs. "Yeah, I guess that's one way to describe it."

"It's yours? For your wedding?"

She nods, padding farther into the living room. "Yep. I've had it since I was twelve years old and first fell in love with weddings. I mean, of course, I gave up on that dream a long time ago when I realized just how cruel the Chambers curse truly is, but I can't bring myself to throw it away. It was a lot of work for younger me."

Since she was *twelve*?

Hell, I hadn't even had some of my hockey equipment that long. Some guys play in the same pair of socks or use the same pads throughout their careers because they're too superstitious to break in new ones. Carrying around the same sheet of paper for that long seems about the same as that. It's some serious dedication.

Was Ezra right? Am I a dumbass for believing that Odette—a fucking wedding planner—doesn't want to get married? She might say she doesn't want to, but how could she not if she's still carrying this old thing around?

Does that mean . . . does this thing between us mean more to her than she's letting on? Is she playing some sort of long game, hoping I'll change my mind about where I stand on marriage?

And why doesn't the thought of that terrify me as much as it should?

She grabs the paper out of my hand, her eyes scanning the page. I'm not sure if she notices the sad smile playing on her lips, but I sure do.

"You know what? It's time. I'm getting rid of this once and for all."

She wads it up, then tosses it. For the life of me, I can't understand why I hold my breath as it soars through the air, dropping right between the cats, who immediately start batting at it like it's a yarn ball.

"Oh, goodie. A new toy!" She scratches behind Beans's ears, then Pork's. "You two seem to be getting along."

I clear my throat. "Yep. Sure are. Beans got me on the back of the leg, but I handled her real quick."

"I'm sorry. She can be rotten sometimes."

I lift a shoulder. "It's no big deal."

Odette gives me a look at my favorite saying, a coy smile on her lips. "Come on. Dinner's ready."

I grab her outstretched hand, letting her pull me toward the kitchen.

But just as I round the corner, I can't help but look back at the crumpled-up piece of paper . . . or think about how badly I want to pick it up.

◆ ◆ ◆

"This might be the greatest meal I've ever had, and I am fucking sad that I can't eat another bite."

Odette smiles, clearly quite proud of herself. She should be. I've never had spaghetti this good before. And her garlic bread? Fuck, I could eat that with every meal.

"I'm glad you think so. Next time, I'll make Italian sausage affogato. It's my favorite."

"Next time," I echo, already dreaming of it.

She sips her wine, then spins her glass between her fingers.

Pork and Beans run around the kitchen floor like they've been doing since we sat down. We tried to get them to separate and chill, but it's like they were meant to be together, not wanting to let the other out of their sight.

"Do you know what I just realized?" Odette says. "You get up at what—five thirty every morning?"

"Around there. Why?"

"Then why'd you have me show up so early that first morning we worked on the farm together?" She gasps. "Oh my gosh. You didn't think I was going to show up."

"Nope." I pop a piece of bread into my mouth even though I swore I couldn't eat another bite. It's just too damn good. "And you almost didn't, so I was almost right."

"Almost doesn't mean crap and you know it. You *hoped* I wouldn't show up, didn't you?"

"Well, you are kind of distracting."

She raises her brows. "Oh?"

I roll my eyes. "Please. Don't act like you didn't know what you were doing. Showing up to the barn every day with those tiny shorts. Which I get. It's hot as hell out. But, fuck, it was brutal as hell watching you and not being able to touch you."

She smiles. "You had a crush on me."

"I did not," I refute, though it's pointless. My red cheeks give me away. "I'm a grown man. I don't have crushes."

"Except for on your younger sister's *hot* best friend."

Just like that, all the lightheartedness is sucked from the room.

It was the one reminder we didn't need tonight—that we're hiding this from Izzy.

Odette slings back the rest of her wine, and I take a long pull from my cider, wiping my mouth with the back of my hand.

"You know—"

"Ezra said—"

We start talking and stop at the same time.

We both laugh lightly. Politely. *Awkwardly.*

I don't like awkward, not with her.

She motions for me to go first.

I sigh. "Uh, Ezra thinks we should tell Izzy."

Her eyes widen. "Ezra knows?"

"Did you forget he caught us making out in the hallway?"

"Oh." She casts her eyes down. "I, uh, yeah, I suppose I did."

"Oh, I didn't, darlin'."

Her blues find me again, and this time there's no shame, only heat as she remembers that kiss.

I shift in my chair, ignoring my cock stiffening in my jeans. "Anyway, he thinks we should tell her. Do you?"

"I mean . . ." She exhales shakily. "I don't know. We're just having fun, right?"

Right. Fun. That's all this is.

"Yeah." I nod. "That is what we said, right?"

"Right."

"Right."

She laughs, then slumps forward, banging her head off the table once, twice before sitting up. "I hate lying to her, though. Don't you?"

"I never have before."

She nods. "Me either. So maybe . . . maybe we tell her?"

"And maybe she won't care?"

She winces. "She once said that the idea of us was gross, so maybe she might."

"What? She did? When?"

"When we were sixteen and I told her I had a crush on you."

I can't help but grin. "You had a crush on me."

"I did not. I'm a grown woman. I don't have crushes."

"But you did. When you were a teen."

She narrows her eyes. "Like you didn't know."

I shake my head. "I didn't. Truly."

She looks surprised by this, then shrugs. "Well, whatever. Yeah, I had a crush on you and yes, I told your sister about it. She didn't like the idea, so I doubt she'd like it very much now, either, especially with her wedding three weeks away. She has enough on her plate, so let's not say a word, okay?"

It's the same thing I told myself earlier. There's no reason for Izzy to know about this now. Or ever maybe.

"Okay."

"Besides," Odette says, "once the wedding is over, I won't be hanging out at the farm every day, so there's really no reason to keep doing this."

Of course I've thought about this ending. How could I not with the potential fallout with my sister?

But I guess I never really thought about giving it a definite date. I knew this would come to an end eventually. I just never thought about when.

After the wedding makes the most sense, though. She'll move on to another wedding at another venue, and with any luck, I'll have my hands full with the iceplex. We won't have time to keep seeing each other.

I rub at my chest, a dull ache forming.

Huh. I'm sure it's probably from all the overhead hammering I was doing this morning before my shift in the taproom. We're still juggling things a bartender short with Sophie still being out to help her grandmother recover from her fall.

That has to be what it is.

"After the wedding, then," I say, tipping back the rest of my cider.

"Good. Now that that's settled . . ." She rises from her chair, grabbing her plate. "Stevens family dinner rules? You wash, I'll rinse?"

"Deal."

We clean up the kitchen, put away the leftovers—not that there are many—and make quick work of the dishes.

Odette sets a bowl out for Pork slightly away from where Beans has hers, and the cats go to town on the wet food.

"They work well together," she says, resting her head on my chest as she watches them.

"They do. Wonder if they have the same mama cat. Maybe that's why they've bonded?"

"Maybe. Or who knows—it could be true love or something."

"True love? That sounds awfully optimistic for someone cursed with failing love."

She snorts a laugh. "Yeah, I guess it does." She peers back up at me. "Race you to the couch?"

"Last one in owes the other an orgasm?"

We take off at the same time, but there's no keeping up with someone who played professional hockey. I beat her by a long shot, and she pouts as she settles beside me, breathless.

"No fair."

"Sorry. Rules are rules." I kiss the side of her head, and she curls her legs up under her, snuggling against me in her favorite spot. "But don't worry, I'll collect later. I'll let you get your Mulder fix first."

"He is hot . . . for an old guy," she teases.

I don't get jealous of her words, mostly because it's me she's holding on to and not him.

I don't collect on my winnings either. We spend the night watching TV. No sex, no fooling around. Just us.

And it's not until I'm falling asleep in her bed that I realize that's just as good, if not better, and that nights like these are quickly becoming a favorite of mine.

Ezra was right.

I am in over my head, and I'm not so sure I want a way out.

CHAPTER EIGHTEEN

Odette

"There's our girl!"

I wave to my mother and Nonna as I walk up my grandmother's driveway. Though I've always been told I look just like my mother, who has been told she looks just like *her* mother, it always surprises me when I see them together and realize just how true that statement is.

We all have dark hair—though Nonna's is more on the gray side these days—and our blue eyes are all the same shade. We even have the same small noses and dimpled chins. It's a little eerie sometimes.

I trudge up the stairs, knocking my boots against the last step and dropping my hood from my head. Aside from the storm that rolled through and trashed the cidery, it's been nice all summer. Nature must have decided it would make up for the lack of rain we've had.

Of course, my mom and grandmother are sitting out here enjoying every bit of it. It seems like two types of people live in the Pacific Northwest—the people who thrive even in the rain and the people who complain about it but don't want to move away because they still love it here.

These two are definitely the former. I think they sit outside during the rain more than they do when it's sunny, so it's no surprise they're on the porch with blankets and a pitcher of lemonade sitting between them.

"Oh, can I have some?" I ask.

"You go right ahead, little one. I made it for you."

I press a kiss to Nonna's cheek, then pour myself a glass of lemonade before pulling the spare chair over by them as they swing back and forth.

"So, how are my two favorite gals doing today?"

They exchange a look.

"Uh-oh." I wag my finger between them. "You two are up to something. Spill."

"Well," my mother says, dragging the word out. "I was at Sunnie's the other day getting a fritter. Did you know they have a peach cobbler one now? Gosh, it's so good. I don't know how they come up with these flavors, but I think I could marry that man."

She's talking about Ken, the guy who owns the joint. The bakery was named after his wife, who passed away about ten years ago. The whole town loved her, and we all miss Sunnie dearly. She might not be around anymore, but we're still treated to her amazing fritter recipes.

"I didn't know that, but what does the new fritter flavor have to do with whatever you're up to?"

"Oh, I'm getting to it. I'm getting to it." She huffs, and I hide my smile behind a sip of lemonade. "*Anyway*, I was at Sunnie's, and I overheard Darla—you know Darla, don't you? She's a receptionist at the high school?"

I know Darla. She ratted Izzy and me out when we skipped school. We were suspended for two days *and* grounded for a week.

"Anyway," my mother continues, "her daughter is getting married. Just got engaged last week, and they're already overwhelmed trying to plan. Of course I gave them your name, and they've heard of you, all right."

My mother frowns, and I can only imagine exactly what it is they've heard. Is it about the fire? Or the allergic reaction my bride had that was so bad she had to leave her own wedding for the emergency room? Or was it the tall tale of raccoons being set loose during a reception? It wasn't *raccoons*, it was *a* raccoon—only one, and it was domesticated. It belonged to a guest. I think.

"But all bad reviews aside, they've heard you're partnering with Stick Taps for Izzy's wedding and are *very* interested in meeting with you." My mother beams, clearly excited. "Especially since the bride wants to do a country chic wedding. She thinks the barn would be perfect."

It *would* be perfect.

Hope fills my chest, and not for the first time. My email has been lighting up over the last few weeks from hopeful future brides looking for someone to help plan their weddings . . . after they know Izzy's is a success.

It's a lot of pressure and why I haven't let myself get too excited about the sudden surge in potential clients. Every time that hope starts to balloon, I reach out with a metaphorical pin and pop it. I can't get ahead of myself. That's what the curse wants. It wants me to get comfortable so it can swoop in and shoot me down yet again.

"That's great."

My mother's smile falls. "*That's great?* That's all you have to say about that?"

"Well, yeah. It would be amazing, and I appreciate you putting it out there, but I don't want to get too invested in it. You know, just in case it doesn't . . . work out."

Nonna tsks. "Oh, little one, you're worried about the curse, aren't you?"

"Of course I'm worried about the curse. I'm always worried about the curse. That's what it does. It feeds on our happiness. I can't let myself get too excited because we all know what will inevitably happen—I'm going to get my heart broken and lose everything."

"That's no way to live your life. You can't let something as silly as this curse hold you back."

"Says the woman who hasn't been on a date in at least five years," I say to my mother.

"Five years?!" Nonna gasps. "Please tell me that isn't so."

"Well . . ." my mother hedges.

She feels the same way I do about the curse. She's just not willing to admit it out loud.

Nonna sighs. "Good heavens. I didn't realize the talk of the curse had affected your lives so much. Do I believe our family has some unfortunate luck when it comes to dating and relationships? Well, yes, I mean look at my own past. It's . . ." She laughs quietly. "*Tumultuous* would be putting it lightly, huh?"

We all laugh.

"However," she continues. "I don't want this hanging over your heads and keeping you from being happy like you deserve. I never let it stop me."

"No, you didn't, but you've had your heart broken how many times?" my mother points out to her.

"Too many to count. But so what? Heartbreak is part of life. You can't avoid it forever. If you do, you'll forget to live in the meantime, and what's the fun in that? We get one shot at this. We need to make the most of it, even if we get hurt in the process. If we get hurt, well, we can always pick ourselves back up, dust off our asses, and get back out there and try again."

Nonna doesn't use bad words very often, an indication she means business.

Truthfully, I can understand where she's coming from. If I had a friend going through this, I would probably tell them the same thing my nonna is, but I don't have that friend. I *am* that friend. *I* am the one whose life has been touched by this. *I'm* the one who's going to get hurt, and dammit, I don't want to.

I remember my mother's pain when my father left us. I remember the nights she used to cry alone in her room when she thought I was asleep. I remember that sad look in her eyes and how she didn't smile for months. How she couldn't watch anything with romance. And how she would sneer at couples who walked by.

Then she got better. She put herself back out there just like Nonna says to do, and the same thing happened. She lost her spark. She lost herself. She was heartbroken and devastated.

I'm scared that I'm doomed to repeat her life, and I don't want to.

"And," Nonna says, reaching forward and grabbing my chin between her thumb and finger, "that includes in business. I know you're scared of failure. I know you're afraid it won't work out because the curse is preventing you from being truly happy, but I believe in you, little one. You need to start believing in yourself as much as you believe in this curse. Cancel the other out."

Cancel the other out.

She makes it sound so easy, but it's not. It's when so much has been stacked against you for so long and you haven't been happy in years.

No, that's not entirely true. I've been happy lately, and there's only one reason for that.

Noah.

The only part of hanging out with him I don't like is lying to Izzy. Everything else is . . . well, it's really damn good. And I don't just mean because of the orgasms, which there have been quite a few, sometimes multiple in one night. Okay, always more than one in a night.

Sex aside, it's actually been fun. He makes me laugh, and he makes me feel safe, even when we are just curled up on the couch, watching TV together. I was worried things with him might be awkward, but they haven't been. I keep waiting for it to happen, for us to wake up one day and realize what we're doing is totally foolish, but it hasn't. If anything, the more time we spend together, the more comfortable I get with him. The more it feels like it was meant to happen.

Like *we* were meant to happen.

Could I . . . could I have dodged it? Could I have beaten the curse? Could Noah and I . . . could we work out?

Whoa, whoa. Slow down. You're being optimistic again, Odette. Don't let the curse know you're too happy. It'll take away everything that brings you joy.

"I hear you, Nonna. I really do. I'll . . . I'll try."

My grandmother nods, seeming satisfied with my answer. "Good. That's all I want. And that goes for both of you." She gives my mother a stern glare. "Try. Get back out there. Find love again. Find happiness again, even if it is only with yourself. Though I have a suspicion neither of you will end up alone."

She smiles like she knows something neither of us does, but I don't question it. I let her keep secrets.

It's only fair since I'm keeping one too.

And I can't wait to see him tonight.

I have no idea why, but I'm nervous.

Noah texted me this morning with the simple instructions: *Be ready at nine. Wear something warm.*

Considering it's the middle of summer, I am very curious about the "wear something warm" part. I have no idea where he's taking me so late, but I'm excited to go anyway.

At exactly 8:59, knuckles rap against my front door.

I race toward it, stopping myself at the last second so I don't seem too eager. I exhale a long breath, then brush my sweaty hands off on the front of my thermal leggings and open the door.

Noah is already smiling.

Before all this started with him, I would've been concerned, because Noah's smiles were few and far between.

But now? Now all it does is make *me* smile.

"Hi," he says, that deep voice of his doing something to me it shouldn't be. He told me we were on a strict schedule tonight, and there would be no room for tomfoolery.

But now that he's standing in front of me in a pair of jeans that hug his thick thighs and a simple dark-green sweater that makes his already gorgeous brown eyes ten times prettier, I *really* want to fool around with him. Especially when I spy Pork at his feet. Why is Cat Dad Noah so damn hot?

"Hi yourself," I say back, then point to the cat. "I take it he's staying here?"

"Do you mind? I had no intentions of bringing him, but I was halfway through town when I realized he was curled up in the back seat. I think he's been taking lessons from Tootsie on how to escape. I found him in the taproom yesterday. He was playing with the puck."

I instantly know he's talking about the one he has up on the fireplace mantel.

I mock gasp. "Not *the* puck!"

"Laugh all you want, but when I'm dead and buried, that puck will be worth something one day."

"And then I'll finally be rich."

He rolls his eyes, lips twitching. He doesn't want to find me amusing, but he definitely does. "Are you ready?"

I nod. "Yep, just need to find my purse."

I leave the door open for him and Pork to enter. The cat wastes no time trotting across my apartment, straight to the couch, where Beans is hidden underneath.

Pork wiggles his way under there, and I hear them meow at one another as if they're saying hello.

I make a quick stop in the kitchen to put some food in the spare bowl I have for Pork, then grab my purse from the coffee table.

"So, what's this mystery destination you're taking me to? And why do I need to dress warm in the middle of summer?"

"You'll see," Noah says coyly, and I want to be annoyed he's not giving anything away, but I can't find it in me to be.

His hand settles on my lower back as he leads me out the door, hitting the lock button on the keypad behind us. I relish his touch the whole way down the stairs and get entirely too giddy inside when he pulls open my door for me.

I've never been with someone who does that, and I don't think I'll ever get used to it.

Noah settles into the driver's seat, then leads us out of town. Music—an old eighties rock station that seems to play nothing but love ballads—plays in the background as we drive into the sunset.

"For being such a rainy day, it sure has turned into a gorgeous evening," I comment.

"Yes, yes, it has."

But when I look over at Noah, he's not looking out at the beautiful yellow and pink and orange hues that tint the sky.

He's looking at me.

His big hand falls to my thigh, and that's where it stays the rest of the ride, burning my skin beneath his touch.

We drive for twenty minutes before he finally pulls off into an empty parking lot. A big building sits in front of us, looking like it's seen better days.

I know I've driven past it several times on my way to Seattle, but I can't recall what this place is.

"I don't know what you had in mind, but it looks like this place is closed."

He ignores me as he pulls into a spot right up front and puts the truck in park.

"Uh, Noah?" I say when he pushes open his door. "Did you hear me? This place is closed."

"Do you trust me?"

"Says the murderer."

He chuckles. "If I were going to kill you, I would have done it all those weeks ago when you blackened my eye."

I roll my eyes. "I thought you were over that."

He points to the tiny red mark that still sits on the bridge of his nose. "No, I am not over it and I will never be over it. It will be with me forever, just like this scar I'm going to inevitably have."

I grimace. "Did I ever tell you how sorry I am about that?"

"Only about a hundred times." He nods toward the building. "Now come on. Let's head inside. We only have this place for so long."

"Because the cops are definitely going to bust us for breaking into this abandoned building, right?"

He sighs. "Has anyone ever told you you're exhausting, Odie?"

"Only after sex."

I wink at him, then climb out of his oversize truck, meeting him at the back.

He pulls a giant bag from the bed.

"Not going to murder me, my ass," I mutter as I follow behind him.

"Quit tempting me."

I grin as he pulls a key chain from his pocket and unlocks the door.

"Oh, good. You have a key. So we're not going to jail, but we are definitely getting tetanus."

He shakes his head at me, but I don't miss his grin as he grabs my hand and leads me inside the dark, creepy building.

Then suddenly it's not as dark and creepy when he flips the lights on. It takes my eyes a moment to adjust, but as soon as they do, I realize that this place isn't quite abandoned. It's just . . . well, not in great shape, that's for sure.

The tile on the floor looks like it could be replaced, the paint on the walls is peeling in multiple spots, and I'm pretty sure that was a mouse that just scurried across the floor.

Noah doesn't seem bothered by any of it as he leads us down the hall and pushes through double doors.

This room isn't dark at all. If anything, it's too bright.

But I know instantly where we are.

"Noah, this is . . ." I say as I look around, taking in the bleachers that have seen better days, the scoreboard that looks like it's barely hanging on, and two hundred feet of ice before us.

"A bit of a wreck?"

"Well, yes." I laugh. "But it's amazing too. What is this place?"

"An ice rink?"

I shoot him a look, and he chuckles.

"All right, so you've surmised that much, I can tell."

"Yes, I'm aware of what an ice rink is. I guess what I mean is, why are we here?"

"To skate."

"We're skating on this?"

"Yep." He drops the bag he brought inside with us onto the floor, then falls to one knee and unzips it. "You wear a size nine, don't you?"

"Okay, one, it's creepy that you know that, and yes, I'm a size nine. Why?"

"Uh, for your skates, obviously." He pulls out a pair of ice skates that look brand new. "I got a few different sizes because skates are funny sometimes and don't always align with your shoe size. Try the sevens first and see how those do."

He holds them out to me, and I take them, inspecting them. I have no idea how I'm going to fit into these, since they're two sizes smaller than I normally wear.

But that's not the real issue here.

"Noah, these are really nice and all, but I . . . I don't know how to ice-skate."

He grins up at me as he pulls out another pair of skates for himself, this style different from mine, and I know right away they're the skates he used to wear when he played. "I guess it's a good thing you came here with a retired hockey player, isn't it?"

"We're really doing this? You're really teaching me how to ice-skate?"

He shrugs, pushing to his feet. "If you want, yeah. But if you don't feel comfortable, then no. We can just sit here and take it all in."

"I want! I want!"

He laughs at my excitement, then points to a bench. "Take a seat. I'll get you laced up."

I do as he says and only slightly panic when the bench nearly gives way.

He winces, helping to steady me.

I watch in awe as he rolls his sleeves, effortlessly laces my skates, then settles beside me and pulls his own on.

"How do those feel?" he asks, nodding toward my skates, and I pretend I wasn't just admiring how hot he looks right now.

"Good."

"Not too loose?"

"Nope."

"Good." He hops to his feet, then holds his hand out to me. "You ready?"

I let him pull me up, then shrug. "I guess."

He senses the apprehension in my voice. "I'll hold on to you the whole time. I promise I won't let go until you tell me to. *If* you tell me to."

I nod, letting him lead me out onto the ice.

As expected, it's slippery, but not as much as I thought it'd be.

Still, Noah holds on to me as we keep moving. He lets me clutch onto the wall and him, not irritated at all over the fact that I'm going too slow, especially when he was a literal pro at this.

"Ah, whoa!" I yell as I almost go down.

To my surprise, he doesn't even laugh at me. He just tightens his grip and helps steady me.

"You're doing great," he says, watching my form.

"I'm not, but you talking helps. Tell me something else to distract me. Like what the hell it is we're doing at this derelict place."

He laughs. "I told you, we're skating."

"Noah . . ."

"Fine." He uses his free hand to squeeze the back of his neck. "You showed me your wedding wish list, so I wanted to show you something too." He blows out a breath, and it's shaky, almost like he's nervous to say the next part.

"You can tell me anything," I encourage him.

He nods. "I know. It's just . . . I'm scared, you know? I don't want to jinx it because it's not final yet." Another heavy exhale. "If things go our way, this is the future home of the Stick Taps Community Iceplex."

"The training camp you want to start?"

He nods. "Yeah. This is it. The current owner is looking to retire and doesn't have the funds to fix it up to sell it. Ezra and I have been eyeing it for a while now, biding our time until the old man was ready. It looks like he is now, so we put an offer in. Nothing is official yet, but it's looking like it's ours."

"Noah!"

I launch myself at him, wrapping my arms around his neck. He squeezes me tightly, almost as if he's afraid he'll lose me if he lets go. To be fair, he might, since I am definitely *not* a natural-born skater.

"That's incredible. I'm so happy for you."

"Thanks," he says into my hair. "I've been itching to find a way to give back to the game that gave me so much, and I think this is just the way to do it."

"You're going to be incredible at it. I mean, look how patient you are with me. You haven't laughed once."

"I have on the inside."

I pinch him, and he chuckles.

Then he's not laughing at all. He's kissing me.

His hands thread through my hair as his lips coax mine open. His tongue slips into my mouth, brushing against my own in slow, lazy strokes.

I wrap my leg around his, trying to climb him because I want more, and he laughs, pulling away.

"Easy there, Odie. You're wearing knife boots, and I'm not wearing protective gear."

"Boo."

He kisses the tip of my nose. "And you were worried *I'd* try to murder *you*."

"I still am." He tugs on me, pulling me away from the wall. "And clearly I have good reason to be. I am not skilled enough for open ice."

"Do you trust me?"

It's what he asked me in the parking lot too. And though I gave him a smart-ass answer then, it was only because I was too scared to tell him the truth.

I do trust him. More than he knows. More than I probably should.

I trust him with my heart . . . and that's the scariest part of all.

CHAPTER NINETEEN

Noah

"There she is!"

I look up from the grill as if I haven't been checking the door every five minutes.

This time, what I've been waiting for is here. Or I guess I should say *who* I've been waiting for.

Odette.

Her raven hair is tied up into a messy bun that sits right on the crown of her head, and I have the strongest urge to walk over and tug it free, then run my fingers through it like I have a hundred times before.

She's wearing a yellow sundress that barely kisses her knees, and it's just as gorgeous as the leggings and plain sweater she had on the other night when we went ice-skating.

She's fucking beautiful, and I want to kiss her so damn badly that I can't stand it.

Instead, I put my bottle of Glove Save to my lips and take a long pull—anything to curb the desire.

"Bestie!" my sister shouts, launching herself into Odette's arms, hugging her like she hasn't seen her in years.

It might feel that way, too, considering she's been spending all her free time with me.

I guess I should feel bad about that, but I can't be bothered. Not when I've been enjoying myself so damn much.

"Hey," Odette says, squeezing her back, but looking right at me.

To anyone else, I look indifferent to her presence, but I'm far from it. If anything, I'm *too* excited with my racing heart and tingling fingertips.

"How are you?" my sister barrels on before Odette can even speak. "Please tell me we can have dinner at your place soon? Maybe one last hurrah before I'm an old married woman? Oh, and you can make spaghetti. I love your spaghetti, especially with your garlic bread."

Once again, Odette's eyes find mine, and I'm sure she's remembering that the last time she made it, it was for me.

"Yes," she says to Izzy. "It's a date."

"Oh, Odette!" Her mother comes out onto the deck, a fruity-looking cocktail in her hand. "You made it!"

"Of course I did." Odette points to the drink. "What's this?"

"Sex on the Beach!"

"I did not authorize this!" my dad yells from inside.

Unfortunately, I had to have this exact same conversation twenty minutes ago. Apparently my dad lost a bet with my mother, and she got to choose the signature drink this week.

She wanted to pick something embarrassing for him to have to say he was making, so Sex on the Beach it is.

I'm just glad she didn't go with Porn Star or Slippery Nipples or even Blow Jobs. I'm pretty sure I'd swear off all family functions after that.

"Would you like one?" Elaine asks her daughter with a giggle, and I'd wager she's going to need a ride home tonight. "They're delicious."

Odette flicks her eyes my way, and while I've tried my best not to react up until this point, I can't help but grin, especially with how red her cheeks are. "Oh, um, that's okay. I think I'll settle for a water tonight."

Her mother shrugs. "Suit yourself. More for me and Lydia."

"Watch out! Sex on the Beach coming through!" my mother yells, waltzing outside with a tray full of drinks.

It's going to be a long evening.

The girls take their usual spot, settling into their Adirondack chairs around the low coffee table, while Dad joins me behind the grill.

"If I've got to deal with your mom knocking back those cocktails all night, then I need the good meat." He sets a plate of steaks on the table near the grill.

"What's the bet you lost again?" I ask.

"If you can believe it, it was how many marshmallows I could fit in my mouth. I told her it was at least twelve. I tapped out at four. She cheated, buying those new, ginormous marshmallows instead of the normal-size ones, but a bet's a bet."

I pat him on the back. "Better luck next time, Pops."

He sighs, a bit disgruntled, but I know he would make that bet over and over again. That's what I've always loved about my parents. They've never lost their spark over the years. They're still as playful with each other as they were when I was a kid.

They love each other, and I don't just mean a little. It's a soul-deep sort of love. The kind of love that comes around only once in a lifetime. *True* love.

I remember one time my father had to go out of town for a doctor's conference, and my mother slept on the couch the whole week he was gone. When I asked her about it, she said it didn't feel right sleeping in their bed without him. If I had been in that situation and Chelsea had left, I think I would've slept just fine.

That should have been my first sign she wasn't the one for me. That something was missing in our relationship. That spark. That longing. *Yearning.*

I've never yearned for anything until . . .

My attention slips to Odette, who has her head thrown back mid-laugh. I have no idea what the ladies are talking about, but whatever it is, she's clearly enjoying herself.

Seeing *her* smile makes *me* smile, and my father doesn't miss it.

"Anything on your mind, son?"

"Hmm?"

He nods toward where I can't seem to peel my eyes away from. "You seem a little distracted, is all."

I shake my head. "Nope."

He chuckles like he doesn't believe me, and I get it. I wouldn't believe me either. Not since my eyes have already drifted back toward Odette.

"I'm here if you want to talk. No matter what it is, even if it's about something that you don't think you should be doing but already are."

I swallow roughly.

Fuck. He knows. I don't know how he does—probably because I'm not being very subtle—but he knows.

I take a step closer to him to keep this conversation private. "Okay, so maybe there is a little something going on."

He lifts both brows comically high. "You don't say?"

"Please never quit your day job, Pops. Being a funny guy doesn't suit you."

"And sneaking around doesn't suit you either. If you're trying to be subtle, you're doing a damn bad job at it."

He's right. I am. Hell, I think I've *been* doing a bad job this entire time, and maybe that's for a reason. Maybe it's because what I'm doing with Odette doesn't feel like something I should be hiding. Something that feels so good can't be bad, can it?

Don't even get me started on how natural it feels to have her here either. I was worried it would be awkward, but it's not. It feels like any other Saturday, any other Stevens family dinner. It's like she's always belonged here with us, and I guess, in a way, she kind of has with being Izzy's friend. Now, though, it feels like more than that.

Or maybe I'm reading too much into things. Who knows?

"For what it's worth, I don't think what you're doing is wrong."

Now *that* surprises me. I figured he'd have a lecture about sneaking around with a younger woman locked and loaded. Or at least one about sneaking around with your sister's best friend.

He doesn't. He just gives me an understanding look.

"You don't?"

He shakes his head. "No. Sometimes the people in our lives become something bigger, something more, and it's okay to explore those feelings, even if you're worried about the outcome."

"She's Izzy's best friend."

"So what? That's not all she is. She's a person too. If Izzy can't see that, then that's her fault."

Tension claws at the back of my neck. It's that same tension I've had since Odette and I started this thing.

I reach back and squeeze it, trying to ease it as best as I can. "It can get messy, though. What if . . . what if someone gets hurt?"

What if I *get hurt?*

I've thought about it before, but I haven't *really* thought about it. Is that what I'm really afraid of? Trying and it not working out again? I think that might scare me more than I've ever let on.

"Do you have any intentions of hurting her?"

"What? No. Of course not. I like her. I . . . I don't want to hurt her."

"Then what's the problem?"

"For starters, she's a wedding planner, and I don't believe in marriage."

He laughs. "I'm pretty sure that's what every divorced person says. It's like getting drunk for the first time—you swear you're never going to do it again, but there's a ninety-five percent chance you're full of shit."

Fine. Maybe he has a point. I know a lot of divorced people who swore they would never remarry, and now they have. Is that what's going to happen to me too?

Do I even *want* that to happen?

Before all of this started, my answer would have been an automatic no. I would have adamantly said I don't ever want another serious relationship. I don't ever want to be tied down to another person again. I don't ever want to not be enough for someone.

But now . . . fuck, I already feel like I'm enough, and I know it's because of Odette.

I'm not saying I'm ready to walk down the aisle or anything, but now I'm not *not* saying it couldn't be a possibility in the future either.

That might be a little much, and I might be getting ahead of myself, especially since I don't even know what this thing is between us. But maybe I'm not as closed off to the idea as I thought.

And I know she's the reason why.

My eyes drift toward her yet again, and all I see is a person who makes me laugh. A person I like to spend my time with. A person I *want* to spend my time with. Someone I could miss. Someone I could sleep on the couch for.

Someone I could . . .

No.

I push away that thought before I can even finish it. This is just fun. This isn't serious.

That same ache I've been getting in my chest for a week or so now comes back, and I rub it, trying to relieve the twinge.

My dad pats me on the back. "Just remember, son, if you ever need to talk, I'm here."

I nod, then sling back the rest of my cider.

Dad and I work on the steaks, shooting the shit about mundane things, his feelings about his upcoming retirement, and how I am doing with renovating the barn. We don't talk about what might or might not be happening between me and Odette again.

Eventually, we all gather around the table, perfectly grilled steaks and plenty of sides laid out for everyone, and the conversation turns to the wedding yet again.

I don't get as annoyed over that as I did before. It just makes sense at this point, especially with the wedding being a week and a half away.

"So, Odette, do you have a date to the wedding?"

My ears perk at my mother's questioning, and I glance up just in time for Odette to flit her eyes my way briefly.

I'm sure she's remembering Izzy insisting we go together too. If only my sister knew what was happening between us now . . .

Odette shakes her head, patting her lips with her napkin. "I don't, no."

"What? Even your mother does."

She looks surprised by this development, raising her brows at her mother. "You do? Since when?"

"Well, my dear," she says, "since yesterday."

"Yesterday? But I just saw you on Thursday. What happened since then?"

"I took your nonna's advice."

Advice? What advice?

But Odette doesn't seem as confused by this as I am. Instead, her eyes light with happiness. "Oh, Mom, that's wonderful. Who is this mystery date of yours?"

"Ken."

"Ken? Ken from Sunnie's?!" Izzy explodes. "But he's like a serial nondater."

Elaine shrugs, a soft smile on her lips. "I guess he's breaking his own rule."

She looks happy, smitten even, and it's a good look on her.

Smitten? God, I sound like such a fucking sap. If Ezra could hear me, he would probably punch me in the balls on principle.

I kind of want to punch myself too.

My mother reaches over, squeezing Elaine's hand. "I'm happy for you, honey. I truly am. Ken is a wonderful man."

Elaine nods, agreeing.

Then Odette reaches for her mother next. "That's amazing, Mom," she says. "I . . . I hope it works out for you. I truly do."

They exchange a look, and I know instantly what it means—the curse.

They're both thinking that at any time the curse could strike, and all the happiness Elaine feels could be gone in a flash.

"You know, Odette," my mother says, "you could always go with Noah. He doesn't have a date either."

"That's what I said!" Izzy exclaims. "Can you imagine them sharing a dance together?" She snorts out a laugh.

"Yeah, I couldn't possibly imagine that." My dad chuckles beside me, and I shoot him a dirty look.

"Mom, Dad thinks you cheated at your marshmallow game," I rat him out.

"I won that bet fair and square, Brian Stevens, and you know it!"

My dad gives me a look that tells me I'm going to regret that later, but I don't care. For now it's gotten the attention off me and Odette, and that's all that matters.

When I look at her, I'm surprised to find she's not already looking back. She's still staring up at her mother, and there's no mistaking the worry in her eyes.

She's still nervous about the curse, and I wish there were something I could do to help her see she doesn't have anything to worry about.

Especially not when I might be falling for her.

◆ ◆ ◆

"I'm bored."

"Then go home."

Odette throws a cashew at me, and it brings me back to the day when Izzy sat here doing the same thing. That was when she tried convincing me to use my cidery for her wedding. Even though it was only two months ago, it feels like a lifetime somehow.

I laugh, pick the nut up off the floor, then fling it back at her.

The usual crowd left shortly after the trivia wound down for the night, so the cidery has been quiet for about thirty minutes now. We still have forty-five minutes to go until close. With the place being empty and Ezra being in Seattle for another doctor's appointment, I considered closing it down early, but I don't want Ezra yelling at me for missing out on revenue opportunities.

Odette showed up here ten minutes ago, and now she won't leave me alone. Not that I'm truly complaining. I like having her around. Probably a little too much even.

"You know, I kind of missed you being mean to me. It was hot when you were all grumpy and growly."

I look up from the inventory I'm doing. "You think I'm hot?"

"No. I'm just having sex with you because I'm bored." She rolls her eyes. "Of course I think you're hot, Noah. Look at you."

Look at me? Look at *her*. She rolled in here in the shortest pair of shorts I've seen her in yet and that damn Anaheim shirt she knows drives me wild.

I'm glad she wasn't around to help me finish the chicken coop earlier today. I'm not sure I would've gotten it done with her distracting me.

We are officially one week and one day away from the wedding, and the farm makeover is complete. Not to toot my own horn or anything, but it looks damn good.

Now it's Odette's turn to do her magic and really make this place wow the guests.

"You're bored now. Are you saying we should be having sex?"

"Is that all I am to you? A piece of ass?"

She's teasing. I know she is.

But I still can't let her think that's the case.

I drop my pen and push off the counter, then stand right in front of her. Stooping low enough so I can look right into those blue eyes I adore so much.

"No, Odette. You are not just a piece of ass. You're funny, and you're smart. You're an incredible problem solver. Every animal you meet falls in love with you. You're kind, and you don't think you're better than anyone. You always make time to talk with people, even if they are just trying to sneak another cat into your purse. And, yeah, you're drop-dead gorgeous, and you make my cock hard in the most inappropriate of situations, but you're not just a piece of ass. I wish you could see beyond the curse. Wish you could see what an incredible woman you truly are. You are so much more than every bad thought you've ever had about yourself, and I wish you could see you the way that I see you."

She blinks up at me, her perfectly pouty lips parted.

I've done the impossible and stunned Odette Chambers completely silent.

"Got it?"

"Got it," she whispers, tears brimming in her eyes.

Then she grabs me. Right by the collar.

She pulls me down to her lips in a hard kiss. It takes me by such surprise that I don't kiss her back right away, but once I realize what's happening, it's me who takes control.

I grab her face, holding her as I explore her mouth, and before I know it, we're both a panting mess.

She whimpers when I pull my mouth away.

"What? Noah, why?"

"Doors. Unlocked. Bar."

She laughs, just as out of breath as I am. "What?"

"I'm closing the cidery and locking the door. Get on the bar."

Her eyes widen, then she scrambles to follow my directions.

I flip the open sign to closed, bolt the door, and when I turn around, she's sitting on the counter, leaning back on her hands and looking like the fucking goddess she is.

I dim the lights, then practically sprint to her because I *need* to touch her again.

I don't stop until I'm fitted between her thighs.

"You know," I say, slipping my hands into her hair. She arches toward me, giving me access to run my lips over her neck. "I know I just gave a big speech about how you're more than just a piece of ass, and I meant every word of that, but I'm going to fuck you on this bar now, Odette."

I feel her swallow, then replace my lips with my hand, squeezing her throat gently as I look down into her eyes.

"Is that okay with you?"

She nods. "Yes, please."

I laugh at her politeness, especially when the last thing I want to be is polite.

I want to rip these shorts down her legs and bury my cock inside her until she screams my name.

But first I want to taste her. I might have just had her last night, but I already want more.

I'll always want more.

I release her throat, then drop my hands to flick open the button on her shorts. She lifts, letting me pull them and her panties away.

I follow the garments to the floor, dropping to my knees before her as I yank her to the edge of the countertop.

Somewhere in the back of my mind, I know we shouldn't be doing this right here. It's not technically closing time yet. Anyone could pull up at any moment. But I don't care about that or the security footage I'm certainly going to have to erase later. I'm too focused on the way Odette's watching me with anticipation.

"I might be here a while. Is that what you want?"

She nods, her chest already heaving, and I haven't even touched her pussy yet.

"Say it. I want to hear you say it. I want to hear you say you want to come all over my tongue."

"Lick me, Noah. Lick me until we're both sweaty and messy and completely a wreck."

"Oh, Odette." I grin up at her. "I'm already a wreck for you."

CHAPTER TWENTY

Odette

I want to believe that this is wrong. That I shouldn't be letting Noah eat me out on top of the bar where we're out in the open.

But I can't find it in me to believe that. Not when his tongue feels so damn good sliding over me.

"Noah," I moan.

He grins against me, and I slide my fingers through his silky hair that I love so much. It's getting long and he's definitely due for a cut, but I almost don't want him to. I like holding on to him, especially during times like these.

He drags his tongue over me, tasting every inch before sucking on my clit, and I should be embarrassed by the sounds that leave me, but I'm not. I'm so damn close to having the best orgasm of my life, and that's saying something considering all the ones I've had lately.

Noah eats at me, and I roll my hips against his face, practically fucking myself on his tongue.

He lets me, enjoying it just as much as I am, if the sounds of his belt clicking undone are any indication.

I wish I could see him stroking himself, but I'll have to settle for the sounds.

"Fuck, you taste good," he says against me. "I could spend all day here."

I wouldn't complain.

He laughs. "I bet you wouldn't."

Oh shit. I guess I said that part out loud.

"Maybe another time, though," he says, diving back in.

"I'm free tomorrow."

The vibrations from his laughter race up my spine as he closes his lips over my clit once again.

Before I even realize it's happening, I'm coming. My whole body lifts off the counter as I shake, and I don't know if I'll ever be the same again. I don't know if I want to be either.

But Noah doesn't stop there. No, he continues to lick me. Soft and slow. Lazily, almost like he's getting a head start on that whole "spending the day between my legs" thing.

His tongue trails lower and lower until it slides over my hole, and I groan.

Then he's gone before I know it, rising to his feet.

As I suspected, his cock is out and in his hand.

"Fuck, darlin'." He looks down at me as he strokes himself. "You should see yourself right now. I wish you could see how pretty this cunt is, dripping wet all over my bar top."

I blush at his words and how he's staring down at me like I'm a meal he could eat daily.

I reach forward, dragging him to me by his shirt, kissing him hard.

His cock brushes against my slick center, and if I moved just the right way, he'd slip right into me.

I want that, and if the growl that rumbles through his chest is any indication, he wants it too.

"I want to take you like this so damn badly," he says after he pulls his mouth away, forehead pressed against mine. "I want to feel you. *All* of you."

"Yes."

He pulls back, looking down at me. "Are you saying . . ."

"I want you to fuck me bare, Noah. I want to feel your cock inside, and I want to feel you filling me up with your cum. I have an IUD, and I haven't been with anyone else in a long time. So, if you're serious and want to do this, I'm okay with that."

He gulps. "I haven't been with anyone since my ex-wife, and I got tested after the divorce, just in case. Not that we had ever . . ."

That surprises me. "Never?"

He shakes his head. "No. She didn't want kids because she didn't want to 'ruin her body,' and I didn't want them because she wasn't . . . she wasn't the one."

There are a lot of unsaid implications behind his words. Implications that should terrify me, but they don't.

Instead, they have me saying, "Then what are you waiting for? Fuck me, Noah. Take me in a way no one ever has before."

His nostrils flare, and his eyes grow two sizes, filling with heat. "Oh, Odette . . ."

It's all the warning I have before he grabs me, spinning me around and placing me just how he wants me. I'm on my tiptoes with one leg up on a stool, and Noah's behind me, cock pressing against me.

"I can't promise this is going to last long. I fear once I'm inside you, I'm going to bust."

"That's okay. We can just do it again." I wiggle back on him.

Another growl, and I find I quite like that sound.

I push back farther, and he grunts.

"You're killing me," he complains.

"Then fuck me already because, at this rate, *I'm* not going to last long. I'm going to—"

The rest of the words die on my tongue as Noah slips inside me.

It's just the head of him, but it feels like so much more.

"Holy shit." I breathe harshly. "Oh god."

"I know," he agrees as he slips in more. "I fucking know."

He works his way into me inch by grueling inch until he can't anymore.

"Goddamnmotherfuckingshit," he mutters as he rests his head on the back of mine. "I think I've died."

Same. That's exactly how I feel, too, as his cock stretches me wide. I don't want to be dead. I want to feel more of him.

"You have to move, Noah."

"Can't."

"You have to," I beg.

He must hear the desperation in my words, because he does. It's slow, almost so much so that it's painful, but fuck does it feel so good.

He continues to rock into me softly, each time pulling out just a little more until barely just the tip is inside me, then he slams home.

I see stars. Bright, white shooting stars.

I cry out in pleasure as he does it again and again, his balls slapping against me with each painful thrust.

It almost feels punishing, but in the best way possible.

"It's better than I ever imagined," he says through his rough breaths, not slowing his movements. "And I've imagined taking this sweet pussy bare quite a lot."

I have too. Not this exact scenario, but still. This is incredible. *He's* incredible. I feel so many things that I can hardly describe them. Full. Admired.

Happy.

That last one sends a zing of fear through me, but it's quickly chased away by the orgasm that races through me without warning.

"Fuck, fuck, fuck," Noah chants as my pussy contracts around him, then he follows me right over the edge, filling me with his cum just as I asked for.

He grabs my knee, pulling my leg off the stool and dropping it to the floor before slumping against me.

I lie there, face pressed against the counter, my breaths so sharp they're fogging the laminated wood. Noah rests against me, struggling to find his own air.

"I don't know if I'll recover from you," he says when he finally does.

I don't know that I will either.

And that's the most terrifying part of this.

◆ ◆ ◆

"Oh my goodness. I missed you so, so very much, my sweet little baby."

I laugh as Izzy rubs her nose against Beans's head. My cat purrs loudly, loving the attention.

It's funny how she hides from me more often than not, but anytime someone comes over, she has no problems coming out from under the couch and begging for attention.

Which is precisely what happened the moment Izzy walked through the door.

She barely had time to kick off her boots and remove her jacket before Beans was on her.

I clear my throat.

"And I missed you, too, Odette."

I laugh and stir the dinner I've been working on for forty minutes.

Izzy is getting married in one week, so this is our last hurrah together before she's officially a married woman.

Not that I think our girls' nights will end, but I'm sure she's going to be so swept up in her new husband that they might be few and far between.

I can relate, as I've been just as swept up in her brother lately.

But tonight is not a night to think about Noah. Tonight is about us. It's about celebrating this new chapter in Izzy's life.

"A fresh bottle of wine is in the fridge," I tell her. "Help yourself."

"I always do."

She moves through my apartment, grabbing the bottle from the fridge and unscrewing the top. She pours us each a healthy glass, then hands mine to me.

"To you," I say, holding my cup out. "And your last week of freedom."

She grins, a small, excited giggle escaping her as she clinks her glass against mine. "I'll drink to that."

We both take a drink, then Izzy jumps up to sit on the counter, which has always been her favorite spot when she comes over. She's about as skilled in the kitchen as her brother, so I always cook and she supervises—a.k.a. she keeps my wineglass full.

"So, how are you really feeling?" I ask. "Nervous at all?"

"Not in the least. I knew I wanted to marry Craig after our first date, and nothing has changed over the years. I love him more than I've ever loved anything in my entire life, and I can't wait to be his wife."

Each word is filled with pure love, and I am so happy for my best friend.

But I can't help but feel a little sad too.

While I made peace with the fact that I won't ever get married, in this moment, I'm a little jealous.

I want that. I want my person. I want somebody who makes me smile when I just think about them. I want forever with someone who makes me giggle like a little girl. Someone who treats me well. Who takes care of me. Who knows me better than anyone.

Someone like . . .

I gulp, knowing *his* name sits on the tip of my tongue.

I don't dare think it, though. I can't. I can't let the curse know how happy he makes me. It'll rip him away without a second thought. It's what it's done so many times before.

"Hey," Izzy says, grabbing my elbow. "You'll get that too. I know you will. You just have to give it time. Or . . . you know, open yourself up to it."

Izzy knows better than anyone how I feel about the curse. She knows I've closed myself off to the possibility of forever with anyone. She was there in college when I tried to ignore the curse and gave my heart away, only to have it handed back in pieces.

I may have believed it was possible to find love years ago when I was younger and naive, but now I know better. It's why I never put a label on anything and stick to fun. To protect myself.

Kind of like what I'm doing with Noah now.

Except with him? With him, everything feels so . . . different.

It wasn't supposed to. It wasn't supposed to be like this at all, actually. I was supposed to live out my fantasy of being with the hot hockey player, and we were supposed to go our separate ways.

But this is starting to feel like *Brokeback Mountain* more and more every day, except we aren't gay cowboys.

I just can't quit him.

My thoughts drift back to the bar last night, and I don't just mean the mind-blowing sex we had.

No, it was when he said *I'm already a wreck for you.*

And dammit if I'm not already a wreck for him too.

I don't know when it happened exactly. Was it the night we first kissed in the barn? Was it when I saw he kept the cat? Or was it when he sat down at breakfast with my mom, Nonna, and all my aunts and cousins and waded through their parade of questions like it was nothing?

I have no idea. I just know that for the first time since I started planning this wedding, I'm not looking forward to it, because it means this thing between us will end.

And I really don't want it to.

"Odette?"

"Hmm?" I shake my head. "Yeah, no, sorry. I'm fine. I . . . I hear you, I do. Nonna said something similar recently too."

"Ahh." She nods. "I take it that's what led your mother to finally ask Ken out?"

"Yep, that's the reason why."

My mother has had a not-so-subtle crush on the baker/widower for years now, and she's never done anything about it. Not just because Ken has always had a look of sadness in his eyes, but because my mother is just as fearful of the curse as I am.

I guess what Nonna said the other day really got through to her, though.

It got through to me, too, but it doesn't mean I'm not still scared. I am. I am absolutely terrified of giving in to something real. Something lasting.

Besides, I'm not completely out of the woods yet with my business or this wedding. We still have to get through next week, and then maybe I'll reevaluate where my love life is at.

"Okay, please tell me my sweet little baby isn't so spoiled that she has to have a separate bowl for her breakfast, dinner, and water."

My eyes go to where she points at Beans's feeding mat.

Shit. I forgot to pick up the extra bowl I had set out for Pork.

I don't want to lie to her. I'm tired of lying to her. But Noah and I agreed to wait until after the wedding to say anything, if we even have to say anything at all.

"Oh, that's Pork's."

"Pork? As in my brother's kitten Pork?"

"Yep. I, uh, I watched him the other day for Noah."

It's not a complete lie. I did watch him while Noah was in the shower after we'd just gotten done with yet another sex marathon.

But that's beside the point. He was here, and I watched him. I'm leaving it at that.

"Oh. I didn't realize you were 'watching each other's pets' kind of close."

I shrug. "It's no big deal."

Crap. I even sound like Noah now.

Izzy purses her lips but doesn't push the issue any further, and I'm thankful for that because I don't know how much longer I can hold this secret inside.

If I had a sibling and they were seeing Izzy behind my back, I would be devastated by that. Not over the fact that they were seeing each other—I think that would be great—but because she felt like she couldn't come to me about it.

Then again, Noah and I aren't really seeing each other. It's just fun.

I hate that I have to keep reminding myself of that, and it really should be an indication that this thing has gotten way more out of hand than we ever intended it to, but I really don't have the time to evaluate that.

"How's Craig doing?" I ask, trying to divert her attention.

For the first time tonight, Izzy looks unsure.

"Is everything okay?"

She nods. "Oh, yeah. Everything is great. It's just . . . we haven't really talked about it a lot. Is that weird?"

I shake my head. "No, I don't think that's weird. I mean, you know you're getting married still . . . right?"

She doesn't answer right away, and my stomach sinks.

Oh no, please, please, please don't let anything be wrong. Please let them go through with this wedding. I need this so badly.

I met with Darla's daughter, whom my mother gave my contact information to, yesterday, and we hit it off immediately. Our visions lined up perfectly, but just like so many other brides, she wants to wait a few weeks to make her decision. I like to think it's just her doing her due diligence, but I know it's because she's waiting to see how Izzy's wedding goes.

It's just another reason I need this wedding to go off without a hitch.

"Right!" Izzy says cheerfully, shaking away . . . I don't even know what. Doubts? Worries? "Of course, it's still happening. I love Craig, and Craig loves me. We're getting married next week. Don't you worry about a thing."

I breathe a sigh of relief, but I can't help but notice that the tension in Izzy's shoulders isn't completely gone, and I really wonder if this whole them not talking about a thing is bothering her more than she's letting on.

"Anyway, enough about me. We've been talking about my wedding for weeks, and now I want to discuss the fact that you still don't have a date for it."

"That's still talking about your wedding."

"Shit. I guess you're right." She laughs. "Okay, let's pretend it's not *my* wedding. Let's just pretend it's *a* wedding. I still think you'd have much more fun if you came with a date."

I sigh. "Iz, seriously. I love you for being worried about me. I am not going to have time to entertain a date. I'm going to be worried about making sure everything goes perfectly for your big day."

"And while I love *you* for that, I trust you implicitly with this. The wedding is going to be incredible. There will be no hitches. There will be no problems. It is going to be flawless. It is going to save your reputation. I have complete faith in you, and you just need to have a little faith in you, too, and let loose for a change."

If only she knew how loose I've been letting myself get with her brother.

"I'm telling you, just go with Noah."

The spatula I'm using to stir the sauce falls right into the pan, completely coating it with marinara.

"Crap," I mutter, fishing it out and tossing it into the sink.

All the while, Izzy laughs beside me, and I shoot her a dirty look.

"What? Sorry. It's just so funny how you still get flustered anytime I bring him up. I swear you'd think you were still crushing on the guy with a reaction like that."

"I'm not," I rush out quickly as I rinse off the spoon. "I am absolutely not crushing on your brother, Izzy."

She holds her hands up. "Okay, okay. I get it. You're not crushing on Noah. Understood. But it's also why I think he makes a great date for the wedding. There's no obligation to go home with him at the end of the night, you don't have to kiss him—*blech*—and you barely have to dance with him because, honestly, he sucks at it. But you wouldn't be alone."

"I won't be alone anyway. Practically the whole town is going to be there."

"True, but we both know not being alone and having a date are two totally different things."

She's right. It is two different things, but still. I'll be fine. It's just one night. Like breakfast with my family and dinner with his. We will be fine spending one night apart and pretending we aren't sleeping together.

"Can you please just drop it?" I ask, returning to my spot at the stove. The sauce is fickle, and it's already starting to stick to the bottom of the pan a little bit, but I think everything will be okay. "I just really want to focus on the wedding, all right?"

"Fine," Izzy says. "Consider it dropped. But I am finding you someone to dance with at the very least."

I resist the urge to roll my eyes, especially since I know this is as close as Izzy's going to get to dropping this topic. "Fine. Whatever. But just one dance and nobody handsy."

She grins, looking entirely too pleased with our deal.

I already regret it.

CHAPTER TWENTY-ONE

Noah

"That's three."

I look up to find Ezra walking out from the back office. "What's three?"

"Weddings. We have three additional weddings booked for this place, which means we've not only recouped the renovation cost, but we've profited as well, and we haven't even had Izzy's wedding yet."

My jaw drops. I wish I could say I'm surprised, but I'm not. And it's all because of Odette.

She has worked her ass off to make this place what it is. Sure, I did most of the manual labor, but it wouldn't have become what it is without her guidance. She knew exactly what this place needed to make it a sought-after wedding venue. Now it is.

Ezra's lips pull up into a rare smile. "With this and the news that the old man is selling us the rink, this is turning out to be a damn good week."

I've tried not to focus on it too much with all the extra work I've been doing to make sure the cidery and farm are perfect for Izzy's wedding in a few days, but Stick Taps Community Iceplex is officially happening.

We've been talking about it for what feels like forever, and I can't believe it's coming to fruition. I'm even more excited about it after my trip to the rink with Odette. The way she lit up when I told her about it and her reassurance that I could do it. Her faith in me. I don't know, it shook something loose inside of me that's been building for a long, long time.

"Are you finally going to admit turning this place into a wedding destination was a good idea?" Ezra asks.

I grunt, but he's right. It was a damn good idea. We now have that extra level of security to do this. And truthfully, this whole thing hasn't been as painful as I thought it would, though I'm sure a lot of that has to do with Odette.

She actually kind of made the process . . . well, fun.

It doesn't hurt that I think *she's* fun too.

I never thought I would be in this position again, but lately I've been finding myself thinking about something I haven't in a long time—a future with someone.

More specifically, a future with *her*.

I know Odette worries about the curse and wants this to be casual and fun, but I . . . I don't think it is anymore.

Wild, considering I've spent the last several years swearing off relationships and any talk of marriage. But those things don't sound as scary as they once did, and I think that has a whole hell of a lot to do with the dark-haired beauty I can't seem to stay away from.

I like her. *A lot.* I like spending time with her and the way she makes me laugh. I like how she calls me on my crap. I like how she isn't afraid to be herself with me.

I just simply like her, and I don't want this thing between us to end.

For days I've been trying to figure out how to tell Odette how I feel about her. The last thing I want to do is stress her out more than she already is. I can tell she's still anxious that something will go wrong with the wedding, even though everything is coming together perfectly. I don't want to add to that by telling her I broke our number-one rule.

This isn't just fun for me anymore. This could be the start of something real, and I have no fucking clue how Odette feels about that.

After the wedding, I tell myself. I'll talk to her after the wedding. Give her time to come down from it all. I know she thinks I'm not going to want to see her or talk to her anymore just because she's not out at the farm every day, but that couldn't be further from the truth. At this point, I don't think I could go a day without seeing her, and fuck if that isn't a whole other bag to unpack.

"Careful," Ezra says. "You keep smiling that dopey smile like that and you're going to be the one renting out the farm next."

I take the rag I'm using to wipe down the table and throw it at him. It plops loudly against his crisp, powder-blue dress shirt. Ezra and I are pretty different in how we dress for work. He's usually in slacks and a nice shirt, but I much prefer my jeans and boots.

"Okay, one, gross." He peels it off himself, leaving behind a wet spot. His usual frown is in place as he throws it onto the table. "Second, I'm just saying. I've never seen you so damn happy. It's nice. I mean, a little weird, but nice."

"I thought you were against Odette and me being together?"

"Nope. I never said that. I just said I think you're an imbecile for hiding it from your sister. I still firmly believe that part." He gives me a pointed look. "I actually happen to think you and Odette are a great fit."

My brows shoot up. "Really?"

"Really. You complement one another nicely. She's, you know, all bubbles and sunshine, and you're . . . well, you're kind of a dick. It's a good balance."

"Careful, Ezra," I say. "That was actually almost nice of you."

"Yeah, well, shut the fuck up and get back to work."

"You forget you're not my boss?"

"No, but did you forget to lock the chicken coop?"

"Huh?"

He flicks his chin in the direction of the windows. "The coop. Did you close it?"

I look over my shoulder. "What the . . . fucking shit. Son of a bitch. Where the hell did she come from?"

Tootsie struts through the property like the free-range chicken she wishes she were.

"No clue." Ezra claps me on the back. "But you better get on that. I don't want any bad reviews for Izzy's wedding, especially not when we're booking up so fast. Gotta make a good first impression."

Ezra returns to the back office, likely to hide away and crunch more numbers on I don't even know what at this point. That is his forte, not mine.

After dropping the rag off at the counter and letting the other bartender know I'm heading outside, I push through the back doors and catch up to Tootsie.

She looks up at me like she is unsurprised to see me.

I chase her back toward the coop, where the rest of the chickens are still tucked away safely, and thank goodness for that.

"How?! How could you possibly do this to me? *Again?*"

Cluck.

"No, I don't want a *whatever*. I want to know. What's your secret? How are you doing it? How the fuck are you escaping?"

Cluck.

I grab the wire on the coop, shaking it. "I secured this thing. I know I did. There is no damn way you're getting out of here without a bit of help."

Cluck cluck.

I pinch the bridge of my nose. "I swear, Tootsie. I am one more incident away from turning you into chicken nuggets."

"What have I said about threatening the livestock?"

I turn to find a bright-eyed and bushy-tailed Odette, but not even seeing her lifts my mood. Not when Tootsie keeps escaping, and not when I slept like complete shit last night.

I even went to bed early. I had my book and a cup of tea. I did the whole slow, steady breathing thing. But none of it helped. I lay awake until 2:00 a.m., tossing and turning until my alarm finally went off just before six.

I have a distinct feeling it has to do with the fact I was missing the woman standing before me.

We've spent practically every night together as of late, and going to bed with the sheets cold beside me has never felt right since. I couldn't settle my mind. I couldn't stop thinking about what she might be doing, even though I knew she was hanging out with my sister. Something about a last sleepover before Izzy's wedding. I have no idea. All I know is that I missed Odette, and now I'm cranky because I slept like crap, and my damn chicken is still escaping.

"What are you doing here?"

She smiles, despite my grumpiness, and I can't help but to think back to when she said she liked that side of me. "Gee, Noah, it's nice to see you too."

Shit. I'm being an ass.

"I'm sorry. I'm happy to see you. I truly am. It's just . . ." I hitch my thumb over my shoulder toward the chicken coop. "Tootsie is still escaping, and the wedding is in three days."

She screws her face up. "That is a bit of a problem."

It *is* a problem. The last thing I need is to have my chicken running around and causing havoc everywhere.

I need to figure this out, and I need to figure it out *now*.

"Can I help?" she asks, and I fucking love that she wants to step in and try to fix it.

I shake my head. "No. This is my thing. I need to handle this."

I realize then there's a van in the parking lot just behind her, and a bunch of dudes are unloading what looks like instruments.

"What's going on there?" I ask, nodding toward them.

She follows my gaze. "Oh, that? The band wanted to practice in the space, to make sure they get the acoustics right or whatever. Is that okay?"

I shrug. "Yeah. Whatever. It's no big deal."

She smiles softly, then closes the gap between us, pressing up to her toes and kissing me quickly.

It's reckless, considering it's daylight, we're out in the open, and there are all kinds of people around, but fuck, I am so glad to feel her lips on mine. It's exactly what I was missing today.

I give her a look that says *What was that for?* and she knows exactly what I'm asking without me voicing it.

"Wanted to," she says simply with a lift of her shoulder. She flashes me a grin that has me a little weak in the knees, though I'd never admit that out loud. She motions toward where the band is still unloading. "I'm going to go make sure they get settled in okay. I'll come back later?"

Translation: *Do you want me to come back later?*

I nod. "Yeah, I'll see you later."

I'm rewarded with another smile.

She wiggles her fingers and saunters back over to the barn, and I watch her go every step of the way.

Which is exactly how I don't miss every single one of those fucks ogling her.

I get it. She's a gorgeous woman. But she's *my* gorgeous woman.

No, Noah. Not yours. Not really. But you want her to be.

I tape that thought shut inside a box in my mind, then get to work on the chicken coop.

It takes me a while to sort out, but in the very back corner, I find the slightest flaw in my design. I shoveled away too much dirt in one spot by a few inches and didn't tamp down the fencing tight enough. It's just enough space for Tootsie to burrow herself in and pop free.

"I got you now," I say to the chicken, then get on with fixing it.

All the while, my eyes drift back to the barn and the guys still hovering around Odette.

She laughs at something one of them says, but I can tell from here that she doesn't really find what they say funny. It's the kind of polite laugh you give an unfunny comedian at an open mic night. Just enough not to hurt her feelings.

But these chucklefucks don't realize that. They think they have her. They think she's hanging on every word of theirs. And I know this because one of them reaches out and grabs her arm, squeezing it.

He touched her. *He fucking touched her.*

I drop my tools and march over to her before I even realize what I'm doing. I slide up next to her, wrap my arm around her waist, and tug her back against me.

If Odette is surprised by it, she doesn't react. Instead, she sinks against me, like I'm a comfortable blanket and she's been searching for me on a long winter night.

"How's it going over here?" I ask, staring each one of them down, especially the one who dared to lay a hand on her.

"Holy shit," one says, staring up at me with wide eyes. "You're Noah Stevens."

"Like *the* Noah Stevens," another speaks up.

"As in the guy who scored a hat trick in game seven of the Stanley Cup Final in double overtime, giving the team a win, Noah Stevens."

They all seem completely starstruck. I think I might actually enjoy this if it weren't for the fact that these guys were just flirting with my girl.

My girl.

Fuck. There I go again, saying Odette is mine when she's not.

Still, it doesn't stop me from tightening my hold on her.

I'm jealous.

It's strange. I've never been like this before, not with Chelsea or any of my other ex-girlfriends who came before her. I was never bothered by this stuff. But seeing these guys fall all over the woman pressed against me? I don't know. It brings out a side of me I have never experienced.

One of the guys takes his hat off and thrusts it toward me. "Can you sign this? I can't believe I'm meeting you right now. I mean, I knew when we booked this gig that you owned the place, but I thought it was just like one of those celebrities owning a brand sort of deal, you know? I didn't think that you would actually be here."

I almost feel bad for my possessiveness. *Almost.*

"Guys," Odette says, holding her hands out to stop him. "While I'm sure Noah here is very flattered by your admiration, this is still his business, and he's kind of in the middle of work. *We're* kind of in the middle of work. We have a rehearsal, so let's get on with that so you can get out of here. We still have a lot to set up for the wedding, and we're burning daylight."

The guy looks a little dejected, but nods anyway, putting his cap back on his head.

Odette ushers them away and then turns toward me. She's so close I can see all the different shades of blue in her eyes, and they're absolutely gorgeous in the warm summer light.

She's grinning up at me, and all it does is pull my frown deeper.

"What." It doesn't even come out a question.

She laughs lightly. "Nothing. Nothing at all."

I narrow my eyes, not believing her. "I didn't like the way they were looking at you, okay?"

"They were just being nice, is all."

"Being nice my ass," I grumble. "I know being nice, and they were being way more than just *nice*. They were looking at you like you were a piece of meat."

"They were not. You're overreacting."

"I'm not. I promise you I'm not. I see you, Odette. I know what those curves do to a man."

"Oh?" Her fingers dance along the hem of my plain orange T-shirt. "Care to elaborate on that at all?"

She blinks up at me, and I know what she's doing. She's toying with me. She's trying to rile me up.

And fuck if it isn't working.

"Odette . . ." I warn. "I am not beyond pulling you to the back side of the barn, pressing you up against it, sinking my cock into you, and letting those assholes hear every damn moan that leaves you because of me."

She gulps. She knows from experience that I'm being completely serious. I don't know what it is about her, but I lose all sense of myself and do things I would normally never do, like fuck her outside. We could have easily been caught, but I didn't care.

Luckily for us, it was late, and there were only a few customers inside the taproom. We were completely out of sight, and the only way they could've caught us was if they came searching for us.

But even now with a full cidery and band inside the barn, I still want to whisk her away and have my way with her until she's nothing but a mess beneath me.

"All right. Fine. You win. I'll behave," she says. "But only for now."

I fully believe her.

"I'm going to head back in there, but do you think you could do a mini signing session later? The last thing I need is for these guys to continue to fan over you and totally blow their set during the wedding."

I don't want to sign anything for these assholes, but it wouldn't be for them. It would be for Odette, and I think I might do anything for her.

"Yeah," I agree. "I can do that. But only if you promise to come get me if they start being even a little bit inappropriate with you, and I'm serious. I mean a glance that lingers too long or a squeeze on your arm. Anything."

She nods, a grin curling on her lips. "I still don't think they were flirting with me, but yes, I will let you know if the boys I'm not even remotely interested in or attracted to decide to look at me too long."

"Not attracted to them, huh?"

She wrinkles her nose in genuine disgust. "Not even a little bit."

"Yeah? What exactly are you attracted to then?"

"Oh, you know. Guys with deep-brown hair and eyes that match. Cute little crinkles right at the corners." She reaches up, tracing her finger beside my eye, right over those crinkles she's talking about. "A nose that looks like it's maybe taken a high stick or two."

"Or that's been beaten up by a bathroom door," I add, circling my hands around her waist.

She giggles. "Or a bathroom door. Somebody a little rough around the edges, but in all the best ways. Somebody who has experience. Who isn't so green. Who has lived a life and maybe has a few gray hairs to prove it."

Her hand dives into my hair right at my temples where the said gray hairs lie, and I lean into her touch, pressing a kiss against the palm of her hand.

We are being so damn reckless right now, yet I can't find it in me to care.

"You know . . ." she whispers. She pushes to her tiptoes, her beautiful pink, full lips ghosting over mine, then my cheek, and right to my ear. A shiver races down my spine. "Someone old."

I drop my head back on a groan as she laughs, pulling away, leaving me missing her far too much, especially when she's just called me old yet again.

"Oh, and hey, Noah? Remember when I said that I kind of like a grumpy, growly side of you? Well, I think I like the jealous side even more."

She gives me a saucy smirk before turning and walking away, an extra sway in her hips as I watch her go.

Fuck. I swear this woman wants to be the death of me.

The wildest part? I'd let her be.

CHAPTER TWENTY-TWO

Odette

"Oh my gosh. You look gorgeous."

Izzy twirls, her dress spinning out around her calves. She giggles. "Really? You think so?"

I nod. "Yes, definitely. And if you look this incredible for your rehearsal dinner, I cannot wait to see you in your gown tomorrow."

"You've already seen me in it."

Izzy was one of those lucky brides who walked into a shop and found *The Dress* within thirty minutes. She had it picked out before she even had a venue.

"Yeah, but this is different. This is the real thing. Hair and makeup, and then walking down the aisle toward the love of your life and absolutely beautiful future."

Izzy's eyes shimmer with unshed tears. "Oh, Odette. Have I told you lately how much I love you? How lucky I am to have you as my best friend?"

"You haven't, but I'm willing to hear you out at any time."

She laughs, dabbing under her eyes to keep the tears at bay. "Oh my gosh. I can't believe I'm getting married tomorrow. *Finally*. I feel like I've been waiting for this day my entire life, you know?"

Oh, I know. Maybe even better than most. I've only been keeping a wedding wish list since I was twelve.

I regretted throwing it away the second I woke up the next morning. Sure, I had Noah in bed beside me, which was great, but not even that could have fixed the sadness that had settled into my chest.

I had finally given up. I said for years that I was done planning. That I had made peace with the fact that I was never going to get married, but still, I clung to that wish list just in case. Crumpling up that paper and throwing it away felt like I had finally closed that chapter in my life.

But the second I did, I wanted to open it back up.

I *still* want to open it back up. I've tried to start my wish list over a few times, but nothing has felt right. And how could it? I had that same one since I was a little girl. I took it with me through middle school, when we moved here to Port Harbor in high school, through college, and it was sitting with me the day that I opened my business checking account. It was there for my first wedding and even the last disastrous one we don't talk about. That piece of paper has been there with me through all of it, and now it's gone, all because I wanted to prove to myself I wasn't interested in marriage.

I was wrong. I am interested. I am *very* interested.

Seeing Izzy and how happy and excited she is to marry her best friend makes me want it even more, the curse be damned.

"You're next," Izzy singsongs, almost as if she can read my thoughts. "You're going to meet someone at this wedding. I just know it. There are plenty of single guys we went to high school with, and Craig has so many amazing friends you're going to love."

"Izzy . . ." I groan. "I thought we tabled this discussion."

"And I did. I said nothing about any of those guys being your date for the wedding. Besides, you're already kind of sort of going with Noah anyway."

"What? I am not!"

"Well, no. Not technically." She blows out a puff of air, like she's irritated with me. "But you *are* going to dance with him or else I'll cry, and you really don't want to make me cry on my wedding day, now do you?"

Of course I don't want to make her cry. What's even worse is that I *want* to dance with Noah, but I can't. I fear we'll give ourselves away instantly.

How I'm even going to make it through this dinner without doing just that is beyond me. It's getting harder and harder every day to pretend like I don't have feelings for him, and this wedding is going to be the ultimate test. I just know seeing him in a tux will completely unravel me.

And it's not just how hot I know he'll look. It's more than that. It's how I know he's going to look at his sister with nothing but love and happiness in his eyes, even though he doesn't believe in marriage anymore. It's how he'll swing his mother around the dance floor. And how he'll let the little kids of Port Harbor stand on his feet as he dances with them too. It's all the little things he'll do that will make me want to break our rules more and more.

But I can't think about that now. My sole focus needs to be on Izzy and Craig getting their happily ever after. Maybe I can think about mine later.

"All right." Izzy claps her hands together. "I'm ready. Are you?"

I nod, and we make our way from my apartment, where Izzy will be staying tonight. She and Craig might have done things a little backward, having already bought a house together, but they want to do the night before the wedding the traditional way. The rehearsal dinner is the last time they'll see each other until tomorrow's ceremony.

I drive us along the waterfront toward the diner where the rehearsal dinner is being held. Craig didn't seem too thrilled about the venue at first, but once he saw how happy it made Izzy, he didn't seem to mind so much anymore.

I'm glad because I sure could use a fat stack of pancakes right about now to get me through this evening.

"No!" Izzy lets out a cry that nearly has me running off the road and straight into the sidewalk.

"What?" I slam on the brakes. "What is it? Is it a spider?!"

"What? No. My earrings." She rifles through the small clutch in her hands. "I forgot my earrings."

"Oh? For tonight? We can just run back to my apartment." I flip on my blinker, ready to pull into a parking lot and turn around.

"The ones for tomorrow. They're from my grandmother. She wore them at her wedding, and my mother wore them at hers, and now I'm supposed to wear them to mine."

"Shit."

"I'm so sorry," she says. "Please don't hate me."

"As if I could." I wave a hand. "It's fine. I can run by in the morning and grab them. I could . . . crap."

"What?"

"I can't go in the morning. I have to be at the cidery to let the florist in."

I check the clock on my dashboard. *We're late.* I'm sure that's not a shock to anyone, especially not Noah, but if I step on the gas, we could have time to stop by Izzy's and make it to the restaurant, even if we are only a few minutes late.

"We can go now."

"What? Won't we be late?" Izzy chews on her bottom lip, ruining her lipstick, which she'll need to fix.

"It's fine. You're the bride—you're never late," I reassure her, making a U-turn, taking Harborview Boulevard toward Izzy's neighborhood.

Thankfully, Port Harbor isn't known for its traffic, and we lose only five minutes by the time I pull my car along the curb.

"You stay here," I tell her as I throw off my seat belt. "Don't want to risk getting your dress dirty. I'll run in and grab them real quick."

She sighs in relief. "You're a lifesaver."

"Jewelry box?"

"Yes. The door code is—"

I put my hand up. "Please, I know the code."

She laughs as I fling open my door. I jog up the driveway as best I can in my heels, then punch in the code—Izzy and Craig's date-iversary. I don't bother to close the door behind me, leaving it open for a quick exit, and race up the stairs toward her bedroom.

I pass photos lining the hallway, many from back in college when Izzy and Craig first started dating, and smile. All their years together have led to tomorrow. To the gorgeous mermaid dress Izzy picked out, to the vows she's been working on relentlessly, and to the life I know they're looking forward to building. I can't wait to see them finally get their happy ending.

I push into the bedroom, going straight for the jewelry box on the dresser.

I'm so focused that it takes me a minute to realize what's happening behind me. To get a good grasp on what I'm seeing in the mirror.

Then I scream.

"What the fuck?!"

There, in the middle of Izzy and Craig's bed, is Craig with a woman on top of him. Naked. Completely bare.

"Odette?!" Craig hollers as I whirl around. "What the fuck? Get the fuck out!"

He yells at me. That sleazy, slimy bastard yells at *me*. As if *I'm* the one in the wrong. As if he doesn't have his dick tucked inside some woman who is *not* his fiancée.

The fiancée he's marrying *tomorrow*.

Craig and his friend, who looks vaguely familiar, scramble to cover themselves, and while I'm grateful for it, it's too little, too late. This image is already seared into my brain.

This terrible image. This horrible deed. The one I'm going to have to tell my best friend about on the night before her wedding.

My best friend who was all smiles just ten minutes ago. The one who couldn't stop giggling when talking about her fiancé. The one who is irrevocably in love with the man before me.

This will crush her. This crushes me.

Feet pound up the stairs, and my heart plummets.

"Odette?" Izzy calls. "What is it? What happened? I heard you scream and I—"

I spring into action, rushing toward her to block her from seeing this too. This doesn't need to be scorched into her memory like it is mine. She doesn't deserve this, and Craig certainly doesn't deserve her.

"It's nothing. It's nothing, Izzy," I tell her, trying to keep her from going any closer to the door.

She pauses, brows slamming together, and I swear in that instant, she knows. She knows exactly what I'm shielding her from without ever having to see a thing.

"No," she whispers, shaking her head. "No, no, no."

She shoves past me, and this time I let her. I hate myself a little for the fact that I let her, but it's a necessary evil.

Then I hear her choked sob, and my heart breaks right along with hers.

I knew it. I knew this was going to happen. I mean, not Craig cheating on Izzy, because I thought he loved her. I thought that they were forever. They . . . they gave me hope.

Hope.

Ugh. It's such a terrible thing. An awful, rotten, no-good thing.

I can't believe I let myself buy into this. Let myself get caught up in this wedding and think for one second the curse wasn't going to come back and bite me or someone I love in the ass. I can't believe I let myself dream of a future. Let myself believe I wanted one. Or that maybe the curse was broken.

I can't believe I've let myself fall for Noah.

And I have fallen for him—*big-time*.

But this? Seeing Craig break Izzy's heart like this? I don't have hope anymore.

All I have is fucking heartache. For my best friend. For my business. And for myself.

I don't have time to think about that now. I need to be there for Izzy.

I turn around just as Craig finishes pulling up his pants.

"Craig . . ." Her voice is scratchy and laced with pain. "How . . . how could you?"

"Isabelle," he says, crossing the room toward us.

I step in front of her, blocking him from getting any closer.

"Really, Odette?" He sneers at me.

"Yes, really. You aren't going anywhere near her."

"I never liked you, you know."

"The feeling's mutual," I toss back.

But that's not true. I *did* like Craig, which makes this even harder. I thought he loved Izzy. He's never shown any signs of not being head over heels for her.

Or maybe he has, and maybe I just ignored all the signs. Maybe Izzy has ignored them too.

"How could you?" Izzy repeats to him. "And how could *you*, Tara? I was in your shop just last week buying candles."

Tara. That's right. She co-owns the candle shop with her mother.

"I-I-I'm so sorry," she says, her eyes wide with surprise. "I . . . I had no idea."

"No idea? We're getting married. *Tomorrow.*"

"Izzy, I swear. Craig said you broke up. I ran into him at the bar last week, and he told me the wedding was off. We've been texting ever since, and today he invited me over—"

"Shut up!" Craig screams at her, and she flinches at his outburst.

I feel bad for Tara. It's clear she had no idea he was a lying sack of shit. A lying sack of shit who apparently went to a bar last week when his fiancée was sleeping over at my house.

God, how could we have not seen it? He practically threw us out the door when I picked Izzy up for our slumber party.

"How long have you . . ." Izzy takes a calming breath. "How long has this been going on, Craig?"

"This is the first time."

"The first time you slept with Tara or the first time you cheated on me?"

He winces. "With Tara."

The woman in question gasps, just as shocked as we are.

"What?!" She lets out another sob, and it's the worst sound I've ever heard. The only thing holding me back from attacking this prick is that Izzy needs me much more than I need to punch him.

I reach out, grabbing her hand, letting her know I'm here for her.

"How long?" she asks. "How long have you been lying to me?"

"I . . . fuck, Iz. I don't know." He exhales heavily, eyes rimmed red with unshed tears.

He looks sad. Broken. I just wish I could tell if it's because he actually feels bad about what he did or if he's upset he got caught.

"I'm sorry. I'm so fucking sorry. But this . . . this is why I proposed, Iz. I . . . I have a problem. I *know* I have a problem. Getting married will fix that, though. Once we're husband and wife, I won't have to do this anymore. We'll be together for real."

Her face crumples. "Together for real? We're already together for real! How is this"—she holds up her hand, flashing the very ring Craig put on it—"not real?! How is *five years* together not real?"

I can't believe that's how much time she's wasted on the man who clearly doesn't love her.

That's a long time to squander, especially for something that ended in heartbreak.

Heartbreak, which is inevitably how the thing with Noah will end too. This right here has proved that. It's proved that the curse is real and that it's unafraid to touch those I love.

"I can't believe this." Izzy shakes her head. "I can't believe you'd do this to me."

"I know, baby. I know, and you have no idea how sorry I am. You have no idea how much this has been eating me alive. I just . . . I couldn't stop, you know? They were all just so tempting."

"They?" She lets out another cry. "I don't even want to know how many. Please never tell me how many."

"Baby . . ." He tries to reach for her again, and I smack his hand away.

He glowers at me, but I don't back down.

"What the fuck did you even come up here for?"

What he really means is, this is all my fault. I'm the one who got him caught and is breaking Izzy's heart.

"My earrings. She came up here to get my grandmother's earrings. I didn't want to . . ." She shudders out a breath. "I didn't want to get married without them."

Izzy turns to me, and I hold her as sobs rack her body. I hate this. I hate this so fucking much. I hate Craig too. I hate his smug face and his fancy job. I hate his gym bro lifestyle and his obnoxious friends too.

I hate that he hurt my best friend.

"Hey, Craig, you home?"

We all freeze, and Izzy stiffens in my arms. Tara's eyes grow twice their size, and she looks like she's hoping a hole would open in the floor and swallow her up.

"I used the code. I hope you don't mind. I was just coming to check on you. Izzy isn't at the rehearsal dinner yet, and neither is Odette, but that woman is late to everything." Noah chuckles lightly as his feet land on the stairs. "I just wanted to stop by and make sure everything was okay."

His steps grow closer, and I revel in the fear that inches into Craig's eyes with every single thud of the heavy boots against the floor.

I turn just in time to see him round the corner at the end of the hall.

He pauses, tipping his head to the side. "Odie? What are you doing here? I thought Izzy was staying at your place. Are you . . ."

His words die as he sees his sister curled around me.

"What happened?" he barks as he races toward us.

I don't try to stop him. I don't *want* to stop him. I want him to see this. And I want him to get his revenge on Craig.

I let Izzy fall into his arms as he stops before us, and if this were any other moment, I would smile over how gently he takes her into his arms and whispers into her ear that everything is going to be okay.

But this isn't any other moment.

"What happened?" he asks me.

I can't find the words to say it out loud. All I can do is lift my hand and point.

Noah's eyes follow my finger, landing right on Craig.

Then Tara.

And right back to Craig.

I see the second it clicks.

Then suddenly Izzy is no longer in his arms. She's back in mine as Noah stomps across the room and snatches Craig up by his throat.

I briefly think back to the time when he had that exact hand wrapped around my throat in the bar as he speared me with his cock.

This is nothing like that, yet I still find it exhilarating, especially watching Craig get what he deserves.

"What the fuck did you do to my sister?!"

"Nothing, man. Nothing. I—"

His protests die there. Not because he's out of them, but because he can't talk anymore. Noah's made sure of that as his grip tightens on his throat.

"Want to try that again?" Noah growls, and it's nothing like the growls he uses with me. It's menacing. Spit flinging off his lips.

He loosens his hold, just enough for Craig to say, "I'm sorry. I fucked up. I—"

It constricts again, Craig wheezing as the air is choked out of him.

"I'll kill you," Noah says, and it's eerie how calm his words come out.

Then he draws his fist back and punches him.

Then again. And again. And again.

The room descends back into chaos. Izzy is crying harder, and I'm yelling "stop, stop, stop" over and over. Tara is screaming because . . . well, I don't even know why.

"Noah!" I scream his name this time, and it works.

His fist stops midair, and when he looks at me, it's like I'm looking at an entirely different person.

I've never seen him like this before, and that includes all the fights I've seen him get in during his years playing hockey.

This is something different, something way more intense than that ever was, and that's saying something because those guys hit each other for fun.

No. This is a bone-deep rage.

And it only makes me love him more.

"Noah," I say, softer this time. "That's enough."

"It will never be enough," he responds, but still, he lets Craig go, and Craig falls to a bloody heap at his feet.

Noah drops down, his lips going to Craig's ear. He whispers something I can't discern, but I can only assume is a promise that his next beating will be even worse if he ever comes near Izzy again.

Noah rises to his feet, scoffing at Craig's limp body, and he drags his sister back into his arms, where her sobs grow even louder.

That's how we stand for several minutes. The room is silent, except for Izzy's cries and Craig's strangled breaths.

I glance to Tara, who is looking at Craig with her hand over her mouth, tears streaking down her face. I wonder if she feels bad for him. I don't. Not in the least.

Izzy's sobs slow, and with a flick of Noah's chin, I take her from his arms and lead her from the room.

"Izzy, wait!" Tara calls.

We turn toward her.

"I am so, so sorry," she says, tears streaking down her face. "I truly had no idea. You have to believe me."

Izzy gulps. "I do, Tara. I believe you. I just . . . I can't look at you right now. I'm sorry."

"Don't apologize to me. Ever. Not after this."

Then Tara looks at me, and I read the silent question in her eyes.

Can we talk about this later?

I nod, then let her pass, not missing how Noah stares her down with heated eyes.

He's just as pissed at her as he is at Craig, and a part of me gets it, but Tara is a victim in this too.

We slowly make our way down the hall, leaving Craig alone in the bedroom. He made this mess. He can clean it up.

"You'll be hearing from my lawyer," he manages to threaten. "You won't get away with this."

"Oh, Craigy, I am *so* fucking looking forward to that," Noah tells him.

We walk out of the house, and I steer Izzy to my car, carefully closing the door behind her. Her shoulders slump forward as she buries her head in her hands and sobs.

"Where are you taking her?" he asks, face hard as stone as he takes in his sister's weeping form.

"Back to my place."

He nods. "I'll . . . I'll go to the diner and let everyone know."

"Thank you."

"It's no big deal." *Of course* that's what he says.

He reaches out for me, and I do the hardest thing I've ever done in my life—I pull away.

His brows inch inward, then he looks down at his busted and bloody knuckles.

"Shit. Sorry about that. I . . ."

But I'm shaking my head halfway through his explanation.

"Odette?"

"I can't."

"Can't what?"

"I can't. Can't do *this*."

"What do you mean? Like right now? I know Izzy is in the car, but—"

"It's not her. It has nothing to do with Izzy. It has everything to do with me. Everything to do with . . ." Anger pulses through me. "It's the *fucking* curse. I *knew* this career was a risk. I knew that creating happily ever afters for people when I had this horrible dark thing hanging over me was hazardous, but I didn't realize that it would ever affect Izzy. I didn't realize she would get her heart broken too."

"What?" he says in disbelief. "Izzy didn't get her heart broken because of the curse. She got her heart broken because Craig is a fucking asshat. A giant slimy asshat who is lucky I left him breathing. It has nothing to do with you or the curse. You can't . . . Odette, you can't keep letting it control your life."

He doesn't get it, though. He doesn't understand what it's like to watch the people you love get hurt over and over again. My grandmother never found true love, even though she gave it hell. Now she's old and alone, and it breaks my heart to see her like that.

And my mother . . . God, my poor mother. My father walked out on us and never looked back and her second attempt failed just as spectacularly.

My aunts and cousins too.

And now Izzy . . . fuck, I never wanted this for her. Deep down I hoped that the bad luck I had with weddings was just that—bad luck. That the couples who got divorced quickly after I planned their weddings were just anomalies. That it wasn't because of my darkness.

I was wrong, and I don't understand why Noah can't see that. I don't get why he can't see that I can't keep doing this. I can't keep trying. I can't keep letting my heart get broken or getting my hopes up that *maybe* something will work out.

And I absolutely cannot love Noah Stevens, even though I do.

He's already been hurt once before, and I can't hurt him again.

He might be enough for me, but that might not be enough for the curse, and I won't let it break him too.

"Odie?" He takes a step toward me.

I shake my head, giving us back the distance he just took. "No, Noah. I can't. I'm . . . I'm done."

"You're . . . done?"

I nod, pushing my chest out. "I'm done. *We're* done." I exhale a steadying breath. "Besides, that's what we said, right? Just until the wedding. We weren't going to last longer than that anyway."

Even though I believed we could have. Even though I wanted us to.

But I can't risk it now. I might not survive the next heartbreak.

I dare a peek up at him. I've never seen him look so grumpy before, and that's saying something.

"Noah?" I hedge.

"No." He shakes his head, his hands going to his hips as he lifts it, looking anywhere but at me. "No. You're right. That's what we said. Just fun until it isn't anymore, and I guess it isn't. Whatever. Besides, I have a lot of work to do. Got the farm to take care of. The cidery. The rink. Renovating my house. I'll be too busy for lo—" He cuts himself off, rolling his lips together. "I'll be too busy."

His mouth may be saying all of this, but I swear his posture says something else. A part of me wants him to take it all back. I want him to stand here and fight for me. To fight for *us*.

But how can I ask that of him if I'm not willing to do the same myself? How could I ask him to beg me to try again if I'm too damn scared to do it?

So I don't.

Instead, I open my car door, doing my best to ignore his sweet gesture of helping hold it open even when I've just broken things off with him, and climb inside.

"See you around," he says, before closing it softly.

I turn the key and the car fires up. Izzy reaches over, lacing her fingers in mine as I pull back onto the road.

I make it past one house, then two. My eyes go to the rearview mirror, where Noah stands, watching me drive away, looking every bit like I've taken his heart with me.

And it's funny, because I left mine with him too.

CHAPTER TWENTY-THREE

Noah

My knuckles are killing me, but I wouldn't take a single one of my punches from yesterday back. Craig had it and more coming. He's lucky he can even walk after what I witnessed. It took everything I had to stop swinging on him and not go back and finish the job after the girls left.

I squeeze the glass in my hand just thinking about it. I can't believe that fuckwad. I can't believe he would hurt my sister like that. I thought he was a good guy and would make Izzy happy. I was wrong. So fucking wrong.

The cidery should be buzzing with people today to set up for the wedding, but instead it's empty. The lights are dimmed to almost nothing, and I'm sitting at the bar at nine in the morning with a pint of Glove Save in my hands.

I told myself it was just so I could rest my knuckles against the cool glass, but that's a lie. It's because I'm fucking sad.

I'm sad for Izzy, for my parents, and for them not getting to watch their daughter walk down the aisle today. I'm sad for the town that was looking forward to this, and I'm sad for Odette.

I'm also sad *because* of Odette.

It about killed me yesterday when she pulled away from me. The last time I felt that bad was when I realized I was giving up hockey for good.

But hanging up my skates pales in comparison to how I feel right now—Odette-less.

She was never truly mine in the first place, but she damn sure felt like it.

She felt like it in the nights we spent together and the soft smile she sent me when nobody else was looking. She felt like it when she whispered my name into my ear anytime I made her feel good. She felt like mine with every confession uttered into a darkened room and every shared laugh over a bad joke.

She just felt like mine, and I still want her to be.

The worst part is that I understand the complete look of dejection on her face when she pulled away from me. I know why she shut me out. Everything she had worked toward for the last ten weeks blew up in her face. It was already supposed to be her last chance. I can't imagine what that felt like for her.

But can't she see I want to be there despite all that? Can't she see I don't give a shit about some curse? That I'm not afraid of it? And that all I want is to be with her?

I should have told her that and not let her walk away. I shouldn't have agreed it was just fun or participated in her game of downplaying what was happening between us.

I should have stood up and told my truth.

But I didn't.

And so here I am.

I lift the pint of Glove Save to my lips, taking way too big of a drink for it being so early.

"I thought I might find you here."

I turn to find Izzy strolling through the doors of Stick Taps. I didn't even hear her open them, so lost in my own thoughts.

"What are you doing here?" I ask as she strides across the bar.

Her eyes are puffy, and she looks like she slept for maybe a total of forty minutes. She looks terrible, which is kind of ironic given that she was supposed to look like a princess later this afternoon.

"Morning to you, too, Bubs."

She settles on the stool next to me, laying her head on my shoulder with an exhausted sigh. I press my lips to her forehead. We're not usually the touchy-feely kind of siblings, but today it feels warranted.

"Men are awful."

I laugh, taking another drink of my cider. "I can agree with that."

"I don't just mean because of . . ." She doesn't say his name. She doesn't have to. "You're included in that statement as well."

"Me? What did I do?"

"Odette."

Just hearing her name sends a burst of need through me. Fuck, I miss her so much, and it's only been hours since I saw her last.

I don't let Izzy know about those feelings, though. It's not like it matters anymore anyway. "What do you mean?"

She pulls away, giving me a pointed look. "You know exactly what I mean, Noah."

"I truly don't," I say casually, lifting the pint back to my lips.

Izzy punches my arm.

"Hey! What the hell was that for?"

"Because *I know* something happened between you and Odette, you big ass."

I sigh. "Come on, Iz. You're imagining shit. There's nothing— Ow! Stop hitting me, dammit!"

"Then stop lying to me. I've been lied to enough over the last five years, don't you think?"

I wince. Fuck. She had to pull that card, didn't she?

"How long?" she asks.

She doesn't need to elaborate. I know exactly what she's asking— how long have we been sneaking around?

"You remember that storm that rolled through earlier this summer?"

"How could I forget? I lost power *and* all the ice cream in my freezer because *someone* doesn't allow me access to the cidery generator." She pouts momentarily, then narrows her eyes at me. "So, since then?"

I nod. "Since then."

I take another drink of my cider, letting that sink in for her.

It's too long to be hiding that from her, that's for damn sure, especially after learning that her fiancé has been hiding a whole hell of a lot from her too.

I dare a peek over at her. She's staring intently at the bar—the same one I had Odette screaming my name on top of just a week ago.

"Are you mad?" I ask.

"I mean . . . I don't know. It's gross, for one. You're my brother, and she's my best friend, which means she's like my sister. So that's a little strange, but I don't think I'm mad."

"Really?"

"Really."

Relief washes over me. Thank fuck. It was the one thing I was worried about the entire time. I didn't want Izzy to hate me for falling for her best friend. I didn't want to risk our relationship.

"How'd you know?" I ask after a few quiet moments.

She shrugs. "I don't know. I had my suspicions for a while."

"You have?"

"You two aren't as sneaky as you think you are."

Sure, we had a few moments where we slipped up, but I didn't think anybody had noticed, let alone Izzy. She was so busy with her wedding that I didn't think Odette and I were even on her radar.

Apparently I was wrong.

"I didn't catch you in the act or anything, which would've been absolutely disgusting, by the way."

"For me too."

"It was so many other little things that clued me in," she continues. "For starters, you can never seem to take your eyes off her or her you. You constantly seek the other out for silent affirmation. Then there were the excuses to be together. To work together. The fact that she was 'babysitting' your cat for you. And, of course, your beloved gray flannel hanging up next to her door."

Shit. I was wondering where that had gone.

I really thought we were doing something right by sneaking around so we weren't making a big deal of it before the wedding, but I guess it was all for no reason if Izzy and Ezra caught on so quickly.

"Which brings me to why I am here." She punches me again.

"Ow!" I rub at the spot. For someone so small, she sure hits hard. "What the hell?"

"That's what I want to know. What happened between you two yesterday? She's been quiet and distant all night, and I know it's not just because she's walking on eggshells around me because of what happened. It's more than that. So, what did you do?"

"Me? I didn't do a damn thing."

And that's kind of the problem. I *didn't* do anything. I just stood there and nodded, and I went along with whatever she said, even though everything inside me was screaming, *Tell her you love her.*

I didn't, and now it's too late.

"I did nothing," I whisper.

"Why the hell not? You know Odette. You know how she feels about the curse. You know that that woman always has one foot out the door, ready to run and blame the curse for everything. She's beating herself up for what happened yesterday when none of it was her fault at all, and it damn sure wasn't that ridiculous curse's fault either."

I agree with her on both fronts. Odette had nothing to do with Craig and Izzy's demise. The blame solely falls to Craig's shoulders. My girl shouldn't be bearing that weight at all.

"I understand why she got scared, though. I know what it's like to have your future ripped out from under you."

"Yeah, and so do I. Join the club. BYOS."

"BYOS?"

"Bring your own snacks." She rolls her eyes. "Look, Noah, I get it. I understand why you're both scared. You have issues from your relationship with Chelsea, and Odette has issues with the so-called curse. You both feel like you're doomed to fail because of your past. But you're not your past. We're in the here and now. Things change. People change. *Circumstances* change. Like, for example, someone who swore off marriage might suddenly find himself falling in love again and want just that. And maybe another someone could feel the same way. And that first someone is on the brink of letting that second someone walk out of their life for good because they're chickenshit."

"Gee, Izzy, I don't think you could possibly be more subtle than you're being," I say sarcastically.

She shrugs. "I'm just trying to be direct, which is something you two should try."

I sigh, running a hand through my hair. "I get it, okay? I should have said something to her. I shouldn't have let her walk away. Why the fuck do you think I'm drinking at nine in the morning?"

She grabs my glass of Glove Save, draining the rest of it. She wipes the back of her hand across her lips. "To be fair, drinking sounds like a great idea right now."

I have no doubt she feels that way after yesterday. I felt bad witnessing it, then having to go to the diner and explain to everyone why our bride and groom wouldn't be showing up or going through with the wedding. It was traumatic for me, and I was only the messenger.

"How are *you* the one comforting *me*? You just discovered your fiancé was cheating on you last night. What the hell are you even doing here?"

For the first time since she walked in, her facade fades. Her shoulders inch inward, and she slumps against the bar top. "I don't know. I guess I need the distraction. Or maybe . . . maybe I had my suspicions for a while."

She says that last part quietly, and it makes me want to punch the prick all over again.

"He works a lot, you know? He's always been like that, so a part of me told myself he's just dedicated to his job. Or that his clients were demanding. But I don't know. Lately, though, something just felt a little off. It's like we were in two different places. I was right. He was apparently in other women's beds, and I was . . . well, I was ready to start a future with him. Maybe even a family one day."

Her voice breaks when she says *family*, and I wrap my arm around her shoulders, hugging her close.

"I'm so sorry, Iz."

"Me too. But I guess it's better to know now than walk down the aisle and find out later. That would've been an awfully expensive mistake, and you would know."

I chuckle lightly. I *would* know. I had the same feeling that Izzy did before I married Chelsea, but I told myself it was just nerves. I said to myself that we were meant to be, and I was just making a big deal out of nothing.

I was right, though. We wanted different things. She wanted a life of glitz and glamour and parties and keeping up with the Joneses. I just wanted to play hockey and go home to my girl afterward.

Sometimes I wonder how much heartache I would have saved myself if I had listened to my heart back then, but then I guess I wouldn't be where I am now. I wouldn't have that comparison. I wouldn't know what I had with Chelsea is so vastly different from what I had with Odette.

I wouldn't know that I am hopelessly in love with the woman.

"You said earlier you weren't mad about me and Odette. Does that mean you're happy about it?"

"Uh, yes, because two people I love are in love."

"Love? You think Odette is in love with me?"

"I *know* she is. Has been since she was, what, like sixteen?" She laughs. "God, she was *so* obsessed with you back then. So much so that I had to tell her that I didn't want to hear any more about it, I couldn't stomach it. I thought maybe she grew out of it, but I guess not. She was just biding her time, apparently."

She's wrong. Odette couldn't have loved me all that time. She had so much other stuff going on in her life, like graduating from college and starting her business. She wasn't thinking about me at all.

"Stop it," Izzy says.

"Stop what?"

"That." She points at my face. "Stop thinking you're not enough."

"I wasn't . . ."

But the rest of the denial never comes.

"Look, do you remember when you came back that one offseason when we all went camping?"

"Yeah, that's what started Mom and Dad on their whole 'let's get an RV and travel the country' thing. Why?"

"Because I knew then that you and Chelsea would get divorced. Or at least I hoped you would."

"Gosh, thanks for that, Iz."

"Can you really blame me? You were unhappy as hell."

I remember that summer. I *was* unhappy. Even though I told her six times what our plans were with my family, she threw a fit when we loaded up the cars and RV. Then she proceeded to tell me I was doing everything wrong, even though out of the two of us, I was the one who had been camping before.

"I hated that for you, you know," Izzy says. "I wanted you with someone who made you laugh and made you smile and understood you. Not someone who nitpicked your every move. Chelsea was . . . fine. But it just never seemed like you were enough for her, something I'll never understand, because you're an amazing man, Noah. But I'm not just saying that because you're my big brother and I love you to death. Heck, that's why you should believe me even more. I've never lied to you about anything. Like remember that one time you wore that hideous tan suit with the hot-pink tie?"

I chuckle. "Oh, I remember. And the twenty texts you sent me while I was on the ice. Those GIFs you sent were brutal. One message was just a hundred puke emojis, and I'd know because I counted."

She looks completely unapologetic about it. "Right. I saved you from ever wearing that ugly thing again. I was the only one who was honest with you, because clearly your tailor wasn't. They took your money and ran. But that's beside the point." She waves her hand. "What I'm saying is, I would never lie to you. I would never sit here and tell you you're enough when you're not. And you are, Noah. You *are* enough. You're enough for Odette. Just because I didn't get my happily ever after doesn't mean you shouldn't get one either. Talk to her. Tell her how you feel. If she still says no, that's on her, but at least you won't live with the regret of never having tried in the first place."

She's right. I do need to talk to Odette and tell her how I feel. It might not turn out how I want it to, but then I couldn't say I didn't try.

"For what it's worth, I don't think she'll say no."

"No?"

She shakes her head. "Nah. She might be scared, but I know her. She's my best friend, after all. The one you're *sleeping with*," she says pointedly.

I shrug, probably not as sorry about it as I should be.

"So you'll talk to her?"

"I'll talk to her."

"And tell her you love her, right? I mean, you do love her, don't you?"

I chuckle lightly. "Yeah, Izzy. I love her."

She claps her hands excitedly, and fuck if that doesn't bring a tear to my eye. She just went through this awful thing yesterday, yet here she is smiling and laughing, and still believing in love.

I'm glad. I don't want her to sit around miserable like I did for years. I don't want her to swear off relationships or marriage or getting close to someone just because she's scared of getting hurt again.

Izzy is stronger than I'll ever be, and I wish I could be more like my little sister.

I clear my throat, pushing down the emotions that lodge there. "So, any big plans for the day?"

She hits me again. "Too soon, Noah. Too soon."

I grin into my glass, going to take a drink before remembering too late that it's empty.

"You know . . ." Izzy says, looking around the cidery that's half finished for the cocktail hour. Odette spent all day yesterday working on it to ensure it was perfect for today, making a few last-minute changes to the table situation. "You guys did do all this work."

She doesn't have to tell me that twice. My back is still killing me from the hours I spent working on the barn, that damn chicken coop, all the weeds I pulled, and the mowing I did. Not to mention the painting and helping Odette move stuff around in the taproom. I haven't been this tired since the end of a hockey season.

"I don't think we should waste it," she announces.

"Wait, what?"

"Yeah." She nods. "Let's not waste it. Let's have a party."

"A party?" That's the absolute last thing I thought she would suggest on today of all days. "You can't be serious."

"Oh, I am very serious. I did not cram planning a wedding into ten weeks for nothing. The whole reason I wanted to get married this year was so Mom and Dad could be there to celebrate with me, and I wouldn't have to call them back from their big RV road trip."

Is that why she rushed her wedding? I had no idea. She kept saying it was because of her anniversary, but I always thought there might be another reason. Now I know.

"Mom and Dad are still here. You guys have already done all this work, everything is paid for, and the taproom is already practically ready. We'd just need to finish the barn. A party makes sense. Besides, I'm a free woman now, and I want to celebrate that." She bumps her shoulder against mine. "What do you say, Bubs? Do you want to party?"

Honestly, no, I don't want to party. I want to find Odette and I want to tell her how I feel. But I also want to give her a little space. Maybe stepping away from this situation will give her a clearer perspective.

Or maybe that's just me being afraid again.

I huff out a breath. "Oh, what the hell? Let's party, little sister."

"Yay!" She shimmies back and forth. "We can invite everyone in town. Throw out the guest list. Anyone who wants to come can come. It might look like a wedding because I wouldn't want all your and Odette's hard work to go to waste, but it won't be. It'll be a . . . a . . ." She taps her finger on her chin. "I got it! A liberation celebration!"

I grin. A liberation celebration sounds exactly like what she needs.

But she's right. This place will still look like a wedding, and it gives me an idea.

"You know how you said I need to tell Odette how I feel?" Izzy nods. "I think I have a few ideas . . ."

CHAPTER TWENTY-FOUR

Odette

The last thing I want to do after the last twenty-four hours is party.

But here I am anyway, walking into the wedding I planned. A wedding that's not happening. A wedding that has now turned into a liberation celebration.

According to Izzy, it was all her idea. She didn't want to waste all my or her brother's hard work, and I absolutely love her for that. She just got her heart ripped to shreds yesterday, had her whole future snatched away from her, and she's worried about us.

That kind of selflessness is what started our friendship in the first place years ago, which makes what happened to her yesterday an even harder pill to swallow.

I have never been so mad at someone before. It's why I let Noah land punch after punch. I wanted to jump in and join him, but he's had a lot more practice at it than me, so I let him be.

The ride back to my apartment was brutal. I've never seen Izzy cry so hard before, not even when her grandfather on her dad's side died, and it killed me that I couldn't hold her through it.

Which is exactly what I did when I finally got her into my apartment. I sat on the couch next to her, and I just let her cry. She went through two boxes of tissues before she finally came up for air.

Then she ranted. And ranted some more. Just when I thought she was done, she kept going. I don't blame her one bit. If I were her, I would still have things to say.

I *do* have things to say. To Noah.

I'm just not sure I'm ready to face him yet, even though I miss him more than I've ever missed anyone else before.

So badly that after Izzy finally fell asleep around 2:00 a.m., I had to give my keys to Beans, who then took them right under the couch with her. I was too tempted to drive out to the farm and see Noah one last time.

My nervousness to see him is exactly why I'm walking into this party thirty minutes late.

Well, that, and I am horrible at being on time.

"Odette!" my mother calls out, making her way through the packed barn toward me.

She wraps me in her arms, hugging me tightly, but it's nearly impossible to focus on that.

"What are you wearing?" I ask when she pulls away. It's a lavender dress with puffy sleeves that went out of style nearly twenty years ago and detailing that's just as tacky, yet it looks vaguely familiar.

"Oh? This old thing? I found it in the back of my closet. This is what I wore to your aunt Collette's wedding." Ah, so that's where I remember it from. "Can you believe it still fits?"

She twirls, showing me the back. It doesn't fit. In fact, it's only zipped up halfway, but it still looks great on her.

"Why are you wearing it, though?"

"It's a party, isn't it? Figured I'd dress up for the occasion." She winks at me.

Hmm. Weird. But I suppose she's right.

I opted not to wear the maid of honor dress Izzy had picked, swapping it instead for a simple black one that hits just above my knees. It's minimalist and something I'd probably wear to a funeral instead of a party, but since I feel like that's where we're at anyway, it's fitting.

"Well, it looks great. Is Nonna here with you?"

"Yes, dear. She's right over there." She points to where she came from, and I spot my nonna sitting at a table with all my aunts surrounding her.

Each one of them is wearing something more ridiculous than the last. Krista is wearing a lavender dress similar to my mother's. Rita wears an all-white pantsuit—a veil covering most of her face. Collette has on a cream A-line dress and a big, matching floppy hat.

Then there, right in the middle, is my nonna, wearing a wedding dress. *An actual wedding dress.* One I know quite well from old photos. It's the one she wore when she married her first husband.

They look so silly and out of place, yet somehow exactly like they belong.

What in the world is going on?

"That dress sure is . . . something."

My mother giggles. "Isn't it? I remember swearing up and down as a child that I would never wear something so gaudy at my own wedding." She leans in, her hand up to her lips as she whispers, "Mine was way worse."

She's right. It was worse. I've seen the pictures of that too.

"Best friend!"

I turn just in time to catch Izzy in my arms as she launches herself at me.

She's wearing *her* wedding dress too.

This one makes a little more sense, given what this day was supposed to be, but still. I don't understand how she's not curled up on the couch with a tub of ice cream. That's precisely where I want to be after what happened with Noah, and we weren't even officially together.

"How are you?" I ask, my eyes searching hers. I haven't seen her since she left this morning. She said she was going for a walk and never came back. I called her six times before she finally picked up and let me know she was okay and told me about this party.

"Miserable." She smiles brightly, contradicting her words. "But this party is helping—my liberation celebration!"

Several people around us cheer, raising their champagne flutes into the air.

Those were supposed to be for the toast, congratulating the new bride and groom, and now here they are celebrating her singlehood.

"Come on," she says, dragging me farther into the barn I spent so long working on with Noah. "Come enjoy the fruits of your loom."

"Don't you mean labor?"

"Bah." She waves at me. "Whatever."

I wonder briefly how many drinks she's had tonight, but then I remember what she's been through and realize it doesn't matter. I couldn't blame her either way.

I wave to Lucille, Jody Ann, and all my other cousins on the way through. Peaches shakes and shimmies, a cat I'm sure is going home with someone else tonight in her arms. Brian swings Lydia around on the dance floor to a song I recognize, only there are no lyrics, and I'm just so utterly shocked by how happy everyone seems.

I'm also shocked by how amazing this place looks. I tried to contact the rental companies this morning about deliveries, but nobody returned my calls. I figured when they hadn't called back, it meant they had gotten my messages.

I wanted to drive out to the farm to make sure none of them had arrived anyway, but I couldn't bring myself to do it. I was too afraid to run into Noah.

I'm still too afraid to run into him.

But I can't focus on that now. The only thing I'm focusing on is how amazing this place looks.

The chairs and tables are set out exactly as we had planned, with tall fake candles in the center of each surrounded by flowers. Upon closer inspection, they aren't the white, soft blue, and peach arrangements of calla lilies, lisianthus, roses, and sunflowers I had ordered.

No, these are dahlias, gerbera daisies, roses, hops, and celosia in shades of autumn. While I love all those types of flowers, it's not at all what Izzy wanted.

Shit. I can't believe they messed that up so badly, and I'm actually relieved I didn't have to deal with that disaster during a real wedding.

Big round Edison bulbs surround the exposed beams, giving off soft and low romantic lighting. But for some reason someone has hung something off them. I press to my tiptoes to get a closer look, and it takes me a moment to realize what I'm looking at, because it's so poorly crafted—a paper crane.

"What the . . ."

"Come on," Izzy says, still dragging me along.

We pass the dessert station, and it's impossible not to notice that it's filled with fritters, cupcakes that look eerily similar to the cotton candy ones from For Goodness Cake, and peanut butter M&M'S instead of the delectable cream puffs, gorgeous chocolate-covered strawberries, and macarons I had ordered.

These are all things that *I* love.

In fact, there are many things around this barn that I love, from the floral arrangements to the paper cranes and even the band playing Taylor Swift's instrumental tunes.

I don't know how, but I know instantly who was responsible for this.

Noah.

I skid to a stop, and Izzy nearly bounces back to me like a rubber band.

She looks back at me, tipping her head to the side, a lazy grin on her lips. If it weren't for the fact that we're surrounded by all my favorite things, I might believe that grin is because she's clearly had one too many ciders tonight.

"Izzy . . . what's going on?"

Her grin kicks up higher. "Why, whatever do you mean, Odette?"

"Come on. Don't bullshit me. I—"

"Oh, is *that* the card you're going to play? You don't want *me* to bullshit *you*? Really?"

And in that instant, I know.

"You know," I say softly, the words nearly a whisper. She nods. "How?"

"Because you two are completely obvious, that's how. Plus, Noah confirmed it for me this morning when I went to see him."

She went to see him? I want to ask her how he looked. Are his eyes as tired as mine from a sleepless night? Is his hair a wreck like he's been running his hand through it? Or was he perfectly fine, nothing out of place?

"He looked like shit, in case you were wondering."

I exhale, though it doesn't make me feel any better. I don't want him to look like shit. I don't like that he's hurting, especially not when it's my fault.

"Are you mad?"

She giggles. "That's the same thing he asked." She pinches her fingers together. "Just a teensy bit mad, but only because you didn't tell me."

"But you said—"

"That it would be gross if you two got together? Yeah, that's because it *is* gross. But my love for both of you eclipses that. I just want you happy. That's it. End of story."

She beams at me, and a weight I didn't realize I'd been carrying lifts off my shoulders.

She wants us happy. I want that too.

"Odie."

It's one word. Two syllables. But they send a shiver right down my spine.

I close my eyes. Not because I don't want to see him, but because I'm scared to. I'm afraid that once I look at him, I'm going to regret walking away from him even more than I already do.

I'm scared that I might do the most reckless thing ever . . . and tell him how I really feel.

When I open my eyes, Izzy is still grinning at me like a fool.

She steps toward me, taking my hands in hers. "You can do this. I know it's scary, but I have a feeling it will be worth it."

She's right. It is scary. So damn scary that my knees are shaking, and I think I'm about a minute away from bolting.

But more than that, I want to turn around.

I want to see Noah.

So, with a steadying breath, I do.

He's handsome. No, he's *beyond* handsome.

I've seen him in a lot of suits over the years thanks to hockey, but he's never looked this good before.

He's trimmed the scruff that usually lines his face, and though his beautiful brown eyes are tired, they're also full of hope.

Dammit if that doesn't spark some in me too.

"Hey, darlin'." His voice is as smooth as a pint of cider on a cold winter night.

"Noah," I respond.

He steps into me, but it's not with the same confidence he had before. It's a little stuttered and unsure, and I know it has to do with me pulling away from him last night. He's afraid I'm going to run again.

I want to.

But I also want to stay.

"What is all this?" I ask quietly, acutely aware that we have an audience.

It feels like the whole town is packed into this barn, and all eyes are on us. Even the music stopped. Lydia and Brian stare at us with that same hope I see in their son's eyes. My nonna, mother, and aunts all look on from their table.

Given the Chambers family history, I expected to see trepidation, but there is none. In fact, I don't think I've ever seen any of them look more confident than they do at this moment.

I'm not sure if that terrifies or encourages me.

I look back at Noah, who is watching me closely.

"This is your party."

"My party? But this is supposed to be the liberation celebration."

"It is," he says. "But it's not just to celebrate Izzy getting rid of that ass clown. It's to celebrate *everyone's* liberation."

I glance at my family. Is that why they're wearing their old wedding attire? Are they celebrating their liberation too? Is it from . . .

"The curse."

"Yes," Noah says, reading my mind. "They're here to finally put that wretched Chambers curse behind them. And I think it's time you finally face it too."

"Face it? What do you mean?"

He reaches into his pocket and pulls out a piece of paper I have stared at since I was twelve.

It's wrinkled, so he handles it with care as he unfolds and flattens it out.

My wedding wish list.

It's the same one I rolled into a ball and tossed aside. The one that I swore I was done with. The one I thought was lost forever.

He kept it.

I had no idea he went back to the living room and dug the paper out from under the couch, where I'm sure Beans inevitably took it. I never would have thought Noah picked it up and kept it.

"Noah . . ." I say his name because I can't *not* say it.

He drags his hand through his hair, and I don't miss the way it shakes.

He's nervous. I've never seen Noah nervous before, not even when facing down Detroit to win the Stanley Cup.

"Look, I know you say you don't believe in marriage," Noah says, "and I'm not here to try to trick you into that. That's not what this is about. This is about giving you everything you ever dreamed of. I won't lie to you—when you crumpled up this piece of paper and gave it to the cats like a toy, a tiny part of me was relieved. I was glad that we were on the same page. I didn't want marriage, and you, a damn wedding planner, didn't want it either. But I couldn't help but feel this heavy weight that settled into my gut as I watched you throw it away. It was like you were tossing away all your hopes and dreams, and I couldn't stand it. And I really couldn't stand the fact that it was all because of the curse."

His lips pull down into a frown.

"I know you think it's real, and I can understand why," he continues, then gestures toward my family. "I mean, they've had it rough as hell. Nobody denies that. But I think a part of you has hidden behind that for years. You've blamed your failures on that. You've closed yourself off so much because you're afraid of what it *could* take from you that you've forgotten how to live. And I . . ." He rolls his tongue over his lips. "I'd like you to give it a try with me."

He wants to try with me? Does that mean . . .

"Noah . . . what are you saying?"

"I'm saying I love you, Odette. I know that goes against what you wanted this to be, but I can't help the way I feel. I've tried. Trust me. I was as big a skeptic as you. But it's because of *you* that I believe again. I believe in love and a future. In forever, even, especially if it's with the right person. I believe in *us*, and that's a whole hell of a lot stronger than any curse because you're *my* right person, and I want you to be my future too."

This was not what I expected when I walked into this barn tonight. I figured I'd drink, dance, and spend the evening consoling Izzy. I had no idea I'd be walking into a love confession.

I wait for my heart to thunder in my chest or my palms to sweat. For my breaths to grow quicker and quicker. Or for that flight response to kick in.

None of that happens, though, and I know it's because I love him too.

"Noah, I—"

"Wait," he says. "Before you say anything or turn me down, just please know that even if you don't feel the same way, it's okay. I'll wait. I'll wait until you're ready and until you believe me, no matter how long that might be. I'll spend every day proving to you I'm not going anywhere and that I'm not letting any idea of a curse chase me away. I'm going to love you no matter what, and I'm going to be here."

My lips twitch. "Can I talk now?"

He nods, swallowing roughly and dropping his attention to the floor.

I step closer to him until the tips of our shoes are touching, then slide my hand over his face and tilt his chin up until I can see his brown eyes.

He's nervous again, and I have such an urge to kiss him, but I don't.

First, I have to tell him how I feel.

"I'm glad you're going to be there, because I plan to be there too. Right along with you, fighting these doubts every step of the way. Because I love you, Noah. I'm. . . *ugh*, I'm so damn in love with you I can hardly breathe sometimes."

His breath stutters as if to drive my point home. "You do?"

"I do. I really, really do. Does it scare me? Yes, immensely. But I'm okay with that. I'm okay with being scared if it means being scared with you."

He drops his forehead to mine, sighing. "Thank fuck."

Then he kisses me.

Noah Stevens kisses me in front of everyone.

His hand cradles the back of my head, holding me to him, not caring at all that we're giving the whole town quite the show as his tongue traces along the seam of my lips.

He just keeps kissing me, and I let him.

Our kiss slows after some time—way past appropriate—and I can't help but giggle.

"What?" he asks, lips still ghosting against mine, almost like he can't help it.

"Happy."

It's all I say because it's all I *can* say. It's true. It's real.

I am happy and can't remember the last time I truly was, not like this.

I pull away, looking around the barn.

"Noah, this party . . . it's incredible. You made my wedding wish list."

"I had a bit of help. Nearly the whole town chipped in. And don't worry—we donated the old flowers and found something to do with the food. Let's just say we're all going to be eating a whole lot of cream puffs, strawberries, and macarons."

He truly thought of everything. "I can't believe you did this. Thank you."

"It's no big deal."

I grin. It *is* a big deal. It's always a big deal, but he does it anyway.

And it only makes me love him more.

"You're amazing, you know that?"

"Oh, darlin'," he says, grabbing my waist and tugging me closer. "I'm nothing compared to you, and I plan to spend the rest of my days telling you so." He rubs his nose against mine. "I love you, Odette Chambers."

"And I love you too."

The curse tickles the back of my mind, but I push it away. I'm done letting it run my life. I want to live. I want to be happy like I am now. I want late nights of watching cheesy TV shows. I want Pork and Beans to have parents who adore them. I want skating lessons, to drink cider, and to help keep this farm in line. I want Tootsie waking me up at dawn.

And I want it all with Noah Stevens.

EPILOGUE

Noah

"Wheels, wheels, wheels!"

The young skaters pick up the pace, rushing down the ice toward the net, and I grin.

Fuck, I love this. The second I strapped my skates on for our first training session at Stick Taps Community Iceplex six months ago, I knew I had made the right decision. The year Ezra and I spent trying to sort out layouts, choose paint colors, hire employees, and everything else that came with building the rink was all worth it.

The cidery is thriving, the farm booked for weddings for the next two years. Ezra was quite pleased by that, which was a bit weird to witness. Then again, he's been a little more chipper lately, and I'm not quite sure what to make of it yet.

"You're doing great, Carlson!" I call to the goalie who has just let a goal in. I skate over to him, stopping short of where he's sitting on his knees, head bent. "Just need to get your glove up a bit higher." I grab it, lifting it to where it needs to be. "There. Just like that."

"Thanks, Coach," he says, then drops into his stretches.

I skate back to center ice. This is the six-to-eight group, so the kids look comically small next to me as they wait for me to drop the puck.

I let it fall, and each player scrambles to get possession. And by that, I mean they fall face-first on the ice.

It's hilarious, but I love how fiercely they're fighting.

I watch their play as they run all around the rink. We do this over and over until we call it a game.

Carlson skates up to me. "Thanks for the advice on my glove. I think we won because of that."

"You won because of you. Not me." I tap his helmet. "I'll see you next practice, kid."

He waves at me, then skates off to the dressing room to change out of his gear.

I pick up the discarded pucks and grab the nets, moving them over to the side to make way for the free skate we're holding later this afternoon.

That's when I see her.

A smile forms on my lips instantly, and I skate over to the boards, stopping before her.

"Odie."

She giggles. "Noah."

I lean over, giving her a quick kiss because I don't feel like hearing a round of "ewws" from the kids still straggling behind.

"What are you doing here? Not that I'm not happy to see you. I just thought you were coming by later."

"I was going to, but my nonna wanted to watch." She points to the stands where her grandmother sits, smiling as she watches us. She has a blanket wrapped around her lap, a puffy jacket, mittens, and a warm hat covering her ears.

I wave to her. "She's still watching too much hockey, isn't she?"

"She's the Seattle Serpents' biggest fan. Ken got her hooked on it big-time."

Odette's mother and Ken have been dating since the wedding-turned-liberation-celebration. Apparently Ken's a big hockey fan, and now Odette's grandmother and mother attend games in Seattle. It's been fun to watch them fall in love with the sport.

Almost as fun as it's been to watch Elaine find her happiness.

I'm not saying that the curse is broken for everyone, but I think the Chambers women have finally realized that their lives don't need to be dictated by something that may or may not be real.

I know Odette has.

"You look *very* hot out here, by the way."

"Really? I'm kind of cold."

"I'm flirting with you, Noah. Certainly you're not so old that you can't tell when a hot, younger woman is hitting on you."

I narrow my eyes at her. "What'd I say about calling me old?"

"That you secretly love it just like I love those gray hairs that multiply daily." She runs a finger over said locks.

She's lucky we're in public. I have half a mind to bend her over my knee and spank her for that.

Instead, I press my lips to her, kissing her hard, not caring about the kids still lingering.

She's breathless when I pull away, and I can't help but grin down at her.

"What was that for?"

I shrug. "Wanted to."

She smiles. "I love you, you know."

"Oh, I know, *fiancée*."

It happened last month. We were lying in bed in the middle of our latest binge show, and I looked at her and knew.

So I reached into my bedside table, pulled out the ring I'd been keeping in there for months, and asked her.

There were a lot of tears and a little apprehension—that old fear of the curse rearing its head—but she accepted. One thing we instantly agreed on? We will not be cramming planning our wedding into ten weeks. We're taking our time. When we know it's right, we'll know.

We did, however, start our own wedding wish list.

The only thing on mine? *Marry the woman of my dreams.*

I don't care about all the other details. That's Odette's thing. I just want to marry her.

I think back to a year and a half ago when I was dead set against ever getting married again. Now look at me, absolutely in love with this girl and looking more forward to the day when she walks down the aisle toward me than anything else.

Funny how things change like that.

"I'd better get back over to my nonna. I don't want to leave her unsupervised for too long. You know how that old bat can be."

I chuckle lightly, then press my lips against hers once more.

"You can't keep kissing me like that in public, Noah," she says once we part, our breaths still mingling as I rest my forehead against hers.

"I'll do as I please, Odie."

She doesn't argue with me about it. Instead, she gives me one last peck before sauntering away.

I watch her go, eyes locked on her. My eyes will always be locked on her.

Because while I might have been against forevers once upon a time, I'm not anymore.

I found mine, and I'm never letting her go.

Odette

"That boy is so in love with you."

I smile as I settle back next to my nonna. "Guess it's a good thing I'm so in love with him, too, huh?"

She shakes her head with a slight grin. "Never thought I'd see the day." She bumps her shoulder against mine. "It was you, you know."

"What was me?"

"Breaking the Chambers curse. It's why your mother is so happy with Ken. Why Collette found love with Dale and why your aunt Rita is married now. You did it with true love's kiss."

"Nonna . . ." I laugh at her. "I did no such thing. We weren't cursed. Just a little unlucky, remember?"

"Bah." She waves me off. "You're our savior, Odette. I don't care what you might think, but you fixed us all."

She's wrong. I didn't fix us. *We* fixed ourselves.

Doubts still creep into my mind. I still worry about the future and what-ifs. I still fear that every wedding I plan will be my last, even if my business is now booming to the point that I have to turn couples away quite often. Even though Izzy's wedding never happened, the liberation celebration was such a hit, and the brides loved the story so much, they still wanted to book with me. My first wedding after that was perfect from beginning to end. Not a single issue. It brought in more vendors and more clientele, to the point that I'm not even sure when I'll have time to plan my own wedding.

I glance down at the ring on my finger with a grin.

Noah proposing was a huge surprise. I was terrified at first. What if I become *too* happy? Would the curse rear its head and knock me back down a peg?

I didn't know, and I still don't know, but one thing I never worry about? Noah's love. I know without a doubt that it's the purest, realest, and most unwavering thing I've ever experienced.

I've never been happier than in the last year and a half. I had no idea that my heart belonged on the farm with him and Tootsie, who is still somehow escaping her coop, or with Larry and her attitude. I had no idea it was there with Pork and Beans, who are so inseparable it's not even funny. I didn't realize it lay with the cidery or late nights working on making this iceplex what it is today.

I had no idea it belonged to Noah.

I hoped it would someday, but I thought that was just a childish dream.

I was wrong, and I've never been so glad to be proved as such.

Now that I have him, I'm not letting him go. He's not going anywhere, and neither am I. If the curse wants to try to tear us apart, we'll face it.

Together.

ACKNOWLEDGMENTS

Hockey is one of my greatest loves. Romance is another. Combining the two always feels like coming home. I've previously written about only active hockey players, so writing about a retired one was fun. It was nice to see what their life might look like after they've left the game. Noah's life? Well, I think it turned out pretty damn good, especially with Odette by his side. These two tried to fight it, but they failed, and I'm glad they did. They're perfect together and deserve their happily ever after.

As usual, this book wouldn't be possible without a few people . . .

Henry, my very own happily ever after. The way you let me slip into these fictional worlds and disappear from real life for months at a time . . . it's commendable. I know I don't make it easy, which makes your support all the more meaningful. I love you.

My wonderful editing team at Montlake. I bet if you lined up ten authors and asked them who enjoyed doing edits, there's a good chance all would flee because *nobody* enjoys doing edits. But you almost make me do? I don't understand your witchcraft, but I'm grateful for it anyway. Thank you for helping make this book what it is.

Aimee, Kimberly, and the rest of the team at Park, Fine & Brower. You're all incredible, and I couldn't do this without you.

Nina, Kim, and my VPR team . . . I can't express enough how much I love you. You've changed my life. I owe you so much.

My incredible readers . . . thank you for following along on my author journey. Can you believe we've been on this ride for ten years? It feels like just yesterday I was writing the acknowledgments for my first book, which I didn't think anyone would read. Look at me now, huh? It's wild! Thanks for sticking it out with me.

And finally . . . me. This book wouldn't be possible without me. I know, I know. *Duh.* But I mean it wouldn't be possible if I hadn't pushed through and kept going. Sometimes life tries to knock you down. Sometimes your health tries to stop you. And sometimes . . . sometimes it's your brain that says you're not good enough. So, to the version of me reading this in the future who has inevitably forgotten I even wrote this, I am so proud of you. You're a badass. Keep fucking going.

ABOUT THE AUTHOR

Photo © 2019 Perrywinkle Photography

Teagan Hunter writes steamy romantic comedies with lots of sarcasm and a side of heart. She loves pizza, hockey, and romance novels, though not in that order. When not writing, you can find her watching entirely too many hours of *Supernatural*, *One Tree Hill*, or *New Girl*. She's mildly obsessed with Halloween and prefers cooler weather. She married her high school sweetheart, and they currently live in the Pacific Northwest. For more, visit www.teaganhunterwrites.com.